The *Shifting Sands*

by
Layne West

Bloomington, IN

authorHOUSE

Milton Keynes, UK

AuthorHouse™
1663 Liberty Drive, Suite 200
Bloomington, IN 47403
www.authorhouse.com
Phone: 1-800-839-8640

AuthorHouse™ UK Ltd.
500 Avebury Boulevard
Central Milton Keynes, MK9 2BE
www.authorhouse.co.uk
Phone: 08001974150

First published by AuthorHouse 10/16/2006

ISBN: 1-4259-3528-1 (sc)

Printed in the United States of America
Bloomington, Indiana

This book is printed on acid-free paper.

Synopsis

In ancient days of myths and magic, long before the great river rose to be the sea, there existed an elite civilization. These people were the rudimentary forefathers of the Egyptian and Greek cultures. The unfolding episodes of, "The Shifting Sands" depicts this ancient civilization's daily dramas that dealt with life, death, love and war.

This was a time when a handful of hideous monsters still roamed the earth. One calculating female monster took no greater pleasure than preying on these people while they were sexually engaged, attempting to fulfill their reproductive doctrine.

To keep their society from being extinct, procreation was vital and ceremonial. In order to successfully propagate strict guidelines were mandated by the scriptures of their ancestors. Any deviation from these scriptures would set off a chain of dire circumstances, which would plague new generations to come.

True virile men were scarce, due to the monster that preyed on a select few who were not neutered by the King before his death. Beautiful craving, sex starved women competed from all walks of life, seeking out these men to aid them instinctively, by siring their offspring.

The beautiful young middle aged Queen of Patrious has not only become recently widowed, she as well has remained barren prior to the King's death. This has affected her so, that her mental state has become confused and frail. An elderly Oracle who visits her kingdom predicts that the Queen will soon lose her mind. Furthermore her rein will turn into dust, to be spread by the winds, unless she successfully mates with the brave and chiseled adversarial warrior who has slain her husband, the King, in hand to hand combat.

This is an awkward and complex situation, but adding to her dilemma, the Queen's comely and mischievous counterpart warrior sister has her eyes set on the same man. Female alter egos clash creating countless insurmountable feminine inner conflicts.

However, before any serious reproduction can be achieved, the Queen must rid her Kingdom of a deadly Harpy monster. This monster, who the people have named "Vampressa," is the evil villain that has devoured the genitals of all of the Queen's remaining warriors. She uses their reproductive seed fluids to fertilize her eggs that incubate high in a hidden dormant volcano nest.

Read on and open your ear to a legacy of love, war and the determined survival of an ancient race. All, in the days of their lives that were intermingled amidst the desert's mirages that appear and then fade in, "The Shifting Sands."

About the Author

By: Victor Perillo
Former agent of Gary Coleman.
Current Film Producer and Screen-Writer.

Your author, Layne West, brilliantly transports us to a mystical methodical land upon reading the first page of this story. Then, without hesitation we are led into this world created by Layne that reeks of phantasmagoria, fantasy and eroticism. It is only through the colorful and descriptive writing of West, that we become so accepting of the principle characters and their plight. After the first page is turned we never look back to question, "Where are we?" We have been swept away on a magic carpet ride by the author to a land where women are the epitome of sexual dominance.

Aaron, our hero warrior can battle beasts of beasts, but cannot be superior to the comely and sexually radiant Queen. It would be any mans erotic dream to be scolded and dictated to by this powerful woman cat. If dominatrix empowerment be your whim, then the "Shifting Sands" will satisfy all of your desires.

"Fight the battle, stay true to your Queen and return the victor, then you shall be rewarded" say's the Queen as she massages the bulge in Aaron's leathers. With metaphoric poetry interwoven into every scene like a powerful aphrodisiac, West does not once tire us throughout this entire sensuous saga.

As one reads Layne West's writings their sensuality becomes instantly recharged. That the belief that men are the dominant stronger sex no longer is so. Sigmund Freud would endorse this book on the basis that,

"Sex controls and dictates our every move." That the leading character represents the masculinity within all men and the beautiful, seductive and often chameleon-like Queen represents all women. "The Shifting Sands" dramatizes just how powerful the eternal woman cat's dominant influence can be on mortal man.

In conclusion of Layne West's colorful and sexually uninhibited writings, you will be resolved that this story does not linger in the world of "XXX, Cheap Sex." There is too much poetry and human value contained within this literary piece.

If you explore West's crisp on site visions throughout this book you will feel as if you could touch or speak to any of the characters at any time you wish. While reading, you will instinctively feel the hot breath of every predatory monster that looms around or over any given sandstone and dune on the back of your neck.

Discovering there really is no other place like it, one hesitates to put the book down, only to return to their daily routine.

"The Shifting Sands," is in a category all of its own and well it should be, as this story is a welcomed departure from the typical romance novel.

VIC PERILLO

Prelude

CUTTING THROUGH THE NIGHT'S DARKNESS LIKE A RADIANT CANDLE, GLOWS A LARGE OIL LANTEREN THAT ILLUMINATES THE FACE OF AN ATTRACTIVE MIDDLE-AGED WOMAN WHO HOLDS THE LAMP.

SHE MOVES THE LAMP SLOWLY FROM SIDE-TO-SIDE AS WITH THE OTHER HAND, SHE TIPS HER SAFARI HAT BACK. CAUTIOUSLY, THE WOMAN LEANS FORWARD AND TOUCHES THE LINES OF ANCIENT HIEROGLYPHIICS SHE HAS JUST DISCOVERED. METHODICALLY HER FINGERTIPS TRACE THEM AND AS THE LIGHT FLICKERS ACROSS THE LARGE STONE BLOCKS, AN INTENSITY OF INTEREST CROSSES HER FACE. SHE SPEAKS IN A PRECISE, BARELY AUDIBLE WHISPER AS SHE INTERPRETS LINE AFTER LINE OF THE SMALL HAND-CARVED DRAWINGS AS FOLLOWS....

Chapter One

The sun beats hot upon the sand as occasional swirls of dry, desert breezes twist jagged sand crystals into my back. It has been six moons and four suns since I was captured, and sentenced to this hell of hard labor. Guards, and masters watch our every move as we break rock under their command, for the recently-widowed young Queen's palace now under her review.

Every day at noon-time a covered chariot brings her through this open mine. I see the result of our labors rise on the distant horizon, between wisping respites of sand and mirages yet, I am not allowed to look at her as she passes without retribution, but I feel her eyes intense upon me. I know she sees.

The first day, head bowed as I toiled, she commanded her chariot to stop, before me and felt her eyes hot on my loins and chest. Then aloud, sternly she demanded, "Sentry, who is this one?" I dare not even peek for two helmeted guards stand intimate to me; one with whips, the other with a bladed chain.

A pain seethes within me, for I have been lonely, since the end of battle, for the sight of a maiden and her soft touch. It was there, regretfully, that I was cut from my dove. Now willingly, I visit visions of the young Queen as slight and beautiful from the accounts of my loyal soldiers, while we were under siege. One day I must see her. Soon I must prove this vision and the legends of her magical, long, golden-brown hair and slender stance. What is it in the distance I now hear? The sounds of hooves, of galloping stallions, the creaking wheels and squeaking leathers of her steeds? Yes, it is to be!

Through the rising dust from the sandstone valley, I glimpse a wink of the flared nostrils of her jet-black steeds and the covered chariot. From the side I see her silhouette in silks.

"Down, maggot!" Shouts the guard with a razor sharp whip across my back. I bow and swing to crush more rock at my feet. For now I shall concede. Abruptly the chariot stops nine paces from my side. I'm certain a twitching glance from the corner of my eye shall go unseen.

Instead, I listen as the horses flutter and stomp, as they are held tight at a halt. There is a long silence as the powders of sand settle. "My lady," a master and sentry acknowledge in unison. I hear the carriage door open with a squeak, then, a small footstep touches the earth.

Within immediate moments, the aroma of sweet flowers envelopes my sphere. The fragrance becomes stronger as I hear her approach to me. Head bowed, perspiration dripping, I continue my labor. So close now, I see her princess feet and lower satins creating their shroud in the quiet right before me. What shall I do? Her beautiful aromas mix with the stench of the guards at my side. Their whips and chains dangle, plain to see.

Sweat burns one eye, then the other so the silks draped from her thighs, I barely see. But I can't be impaired, for she may address me.

The silence continues, as I know she looks at me. All that can be heard is hammers and toil. I hear her whisper, but is it directed to me? No! I cannot take this any longer; I must stand tall and see. Wiping sweat from my eye, I rise to the stance of a marble statue to the sky, my eyes lock with hers.

She is beyond lovely to see and the legend of her splendor is true. I stand tall and broad, yet inside I melt away as does the dampness on stone as the sun rises. "Slash!" A whip lashes across my chest and brow. Bladed chains slash my abdomen and thighs. Once again, "Down, Maggot!" They continue but I do not yield, my eyes still locked with hers, drinking in her beauty as an aphrodisiac to the pain. Unwillingly I fall to my knees, yet her eyes remain silent, still locked with mine. A whip wraps my neck from behind and my back painfully meets the sharp, crushed rock. My blood trickles into the sand and as the sky goes gray, faintly I hear, "Stop! Bring him to me."

When I again awaken, I do not know. My limbs are chained about me and my neck is collared to the masonry. I am in a dungeon of sorts, free from debris and with fresh straw. I hang in pain, wondering if I shall see her again, when suddenly I hear clanking of armor as four guards arrive. A huge reaper in a black robe and hood strides through the stone, cavern-like hall and confronts me. As he places a hood over my head, I feel the worst; surely I am about to die.

With the shout of a command, all five salute and depart in military fashion. They march away amidst the stone wall's and torch flames. The hood over my head is old and smells of dried blood, the fabric is cracked and worn. By twisting my neck I can clearly see through the threads. It is empty in the torch-lit corridor and now only silence is at my side.

Small mice begin to approach, then retreat as I hear footsteps approach. These are different, lighter, softer. I hear giggling and young laughter as two women in white wraps near, the smell of sweet flowers now overcomes that of this damp cell.

One carries an urn and the other, a flat bowl and soft white cloths. They stop abruptly before me and stare me up and down, as if in awe. Of what is to come, I am unsure. "Continue as instructed," a soft, stern voice orders. I look from them, struggling to keep a line of sight through the threads and see it is she, the Queen. Her beauty is refined and shapely, her presence formidable. She approaches me with overwhelming fragrances and takes the cloth from the girls, dips it in the bowl now half-filled and gently swabs my wounds. "Return to your chamber," she firmly commands and they scurry off as the mice did before them.

Her deep blue eyes become gentle and focus on my chest and stomach, not my individual wounds as she works. I see the scarlet water as she draws the cloth from the bowl. She is very pretty and her face shows concern. Laying the cloth down, she ponders my hood and concentrates her view as through the fabric and into the area of my eyes. But surely she cannot see.

With lightning speed, she whips the hood from my head, tosses it to the stone floor and directs her wide, anticipating eyes at mine. In a fleeing instant she relaxes, turns and rewraps her face with her silks, once more just beneath her eyes. Now facing me again, her hands and arms rise high and the Royal maiden's rings and jewels shimmer in the torches light. She removes a silk ribbon of ruby red from her loin and presses it to my lips, then to my brow. Finally, she places the ribbon around my neck and gently asserts. "Return this to me." After inflicting a penetrating glance, she slowly turns and walks from the chamber. I cannot speak as I note the outline of her naked body beneath her satins in the dim light. I hear her shout sternly, "Guards Cut Him Down…"

*   *   *

I awake as the early morn's sun warms my eyelids. I open one eye, but the other, dried blood still has shut. Nothing has changed. Was it just a dream? No, all is still the same, somewhat. She continues to be absent. The golden straw still abounds, however I seem to be free. All aromas are now comforting and I feel rested, as my emotions are temporarily void.

With more interest now as I awaken, the other eyelid breaks and I clearly see the small mice have returned in a circular fashion, gossiping amongst themselves and almost smiling at me with their small pink lips. I rise to my feet and they scurry off, looking over their shoulders as if in defeat. I now view my environment.

The barred door is now ajar into a corridor of the suns light. I'm drawn to it, as the breeze coming through it is fresh, warm and inviting. I sniff the distant sea breeze as I move through the corridor to a courtyard.

I see green grass on its floor with a small, babbling stream equally dividing it. Robust stone walls, surround the emerald mat, topped by four towers with tall dark openings that flank the corners. Is this also to fade, as did the visions of this place from the mines where I toiled?

As I turn my head, from the corner of my eye I see a sweeping red figure that adds contrast to the south turret's tall, dark window. It is she? Please, to the Gods above, let her stay. She looks down upon me unwavering. Is she vixen or angel? What is the true soul of this red beauty above me?

I kneel to bathe in the cool, fresh waters of the stream, splashing my face with both hands. The crystal clear fluid runs down me as I continue to cleanse my body from yesterday's sun and where she swabbed my wounds. I look up once again, realizing she remains, her eyes fixed on me. I then stand and pretend to pay her no mind.

I walk about the yard, as the only sound is that of the castle's colors gently flapping in the light breeze. I wonder if she still sees me and turn my head quickly, to focus on the tower's opening. It seems as if the sands from an hourglass have long drained past, but her silhouette still stands and her eyes are focused upon me.

She raises her arm and points to me as her satin attire ruffles in the breeze, then slowly lowers her arm alongside her thigh. Her finger still points, downward to the base of the tower. My eyes follow her lead willingly, drifting past the stone to an area to which she points. There I view a large, wooden door, its clasp free and dangling. Is this an invitation? Quickly I look up for a response and see her finger still pointed downward, her stance and eyes unchanged.

I slowly walk across the courtyard toward the door, staring up at her as I do and I enter the shadow of the tower, cast by the morning's light. Now looking nearly directly upward, I see her soft figure when the breeze is just right. Pebbles fall from the opening where she stands and the sand that accompanies them drifts into my eyes. I close them briefly, to shield them. In less than the second it took me, she is gone from the opening.

My heart sinks as I feel as though I've been made love to and cast aside. But wait, the huge wood door is opening, from which slowly emerges a small, shaman-like man in brown robes. A long gold cross and chain hang from his neck onto his garments. He smiles, yet says nothing. He raises his arm and open hand, motions me to ascend the flight of winding steps within the circular structure.

I nod to him and enter. He is old, with rosy cheeks and thin white hair. He warns me in a creaky voice, "She awaits you. But be cautious, you are very late."

"I know not time throughout my odyssey and ordeal," I reply as I stand frozen at the bottom of this towering stone. What is to be? I look upward into a faint glow of cool blue.

Behind me I hear a creaking sound, then a loud thud as the room turns dark. I look back and the door has slammed shut. No handle or inside clasp do I feel. Resigned that I cannot escape or know if I even want to, I turn to the stairs and am drawn upward.

Slowly I climb. Is this a ruse? I ponder. Inside me, I feel it's a cruel possibility. I feel certain I'm half-way to the top by revisiting visions of the structure's exterior. I pass a small window opening to the outside and my thought is confirmed. I glance back once again; in time to see a small dove land on the sill and cock her head at me with one black eye, close enough to see a small glossy reflection of my face within her eye. Then, as if perturbed, she flies off in a dash.

The bouquet of the Queen's rich perfume now envelops me beyond control and lifts me farther upward. My eyes break the crest of the floor at the top step, but I see nothing of her, only the grandeur of a circular room. I see the opening where she stood moments before and pass to it to cross the stone floor festooned with colored silks and satins hanging tethered about, many shrouding a large, canopy bed strewn with shimmering jewels and fluffy silk coverings. Yet, I find her not, even though I am certain I now stand at her very spot.

It is a long way up from the courtyard floor. The stream where I bathed now appears but a length of thick-twisted, dark-blue yarn. As I look outward to affix my stance, I feel an intense body warmth close to my bare back. Afraid for a second I'm to be thrust out, I calm after her familiar fragrance is upon me.

"Do not turn," she commands, as she places her hands atop my hips. She is so close, the warmth of her breasts feels as if they are gently touching my back. Softly, but sternly, she continues. "What you see are the horizons of my kingdom. Although many surround me in my court, there are times that I am lonely and have no one dear. Absorb within me your fears, ills and joy, but remember it is unwise to discard that which took root in fertile fragments of the heart. Mingle throughout my land and people as if you are my General of Arms. Find peace with your thoughts. I will know when the time comes for your return to me.

Now go! Bring me back your message of our intimate future on the sixth day that the sun rises in the eastern sky."

She removes her hands and steps back; I turn slowly as I'm shown my return path to the spiral steps from which I gained entry. Wanting to look at her, yet, I feel I should not, so I take the first step down and pause. I know she is behind me as I still feel her warmth. I cannot leave like this. I turn firmly to her, even though I now stand lower with our brows even. She remains unfazed, as I am overwhelmed with her mesmerizing pools of blue. A chip of eternity tumbles to the ground in slow motion as I slowly kiss her soft lips through her veil. She remains unchanged.

Suddenly I hear a man behind me cough, as if to clear his throat. As I glance to him I see it is the elderly robed man.

The clergyman notes, "Your visit is over for now. The door below has been reopened for your departure. Fresh clothes and a weapon have been placed in the adjacent tower room for you." He then moves upward past me into the Queens quarters, takes her by the hand and they disappear into the satins that adorn the space. As I descend the stairwell, I hear them softly speaking but am unable to make out their exchange.

*   *   *

"My lady, is this the one?" questions the old man.

"Father, what do you ask?" the Queen replies.

He continues; head down, but his eyes looking up into hers. "Is this warrior slave the one who will sire the first royal child?"

Without responding, she crosses to the stone window, looks out at the panorama. Finally she replies firmly. "Our reign of royalty must live on. As it is now, it cannot. He is wise, broad, chiseled in strength and a brave warrior. We shall see, Father, we shall see."

*   *   *

Having traversed the Queens' village for five suns, this day's sun is at its set. I must give her my answer soon. Other than elderly men and women, I've seen few children, yet many maidens of widespread ages. However, I see no male counterparts to these women. At mid-sun on my last day here, the older women, who seemed wise, told me that many men were lost to war or the plague on the battlegrounds and more were lost to horrific Khamsin sandstorms upon their attempted return from battle. They also ask me to return to their tent at dusk, while the moon is full silver.

Atop another tower of the Queen's courtyard are my quarters, dry and clean opposite the Queen's opulent suite. Clothing of hides and sandals of heavy leather, as well as a large sharp broadsword were left for my use. A young serf keeps my water vases fresh and oil in my lamps. For food I am treated well among the Queen's court.

As the sun of this day sets, I contemplate my visit to the large tent where I'm told the wise women reside. I am told they are only of the night and that I am to arrive when the full moon turns silver.

Awaiting that time, I cross to my window balcony and view the sunset to time my departure into the dunes at the edge of the village. There I shall find those women and seek their knowledge. As I stand here looking across the way, I see the Queen's lamps remain unlit. The sun setting behind my tower casts a broad, shaft-like shadow far unto the courtyard below.

Within a second of my initial viewing, fragments of the tower's pointed clay roof fall past my face and into the dark shade. I hear heavy clawing and scratching above me, as if something or someone large and unbalanced, is grasping to keep from falling, or possibly attempting to take roost.

As I continue to observe the shadows in the yard, my momentary calm turns to horror. I see another shadow atop the roof of my abode, the monster "Harpy" which has found me once again. This loathsome, voracious creature of evil, bearing the head and trunk of a woman and the tail, wings and talons of a condor, has come to fill its gullet with varied prey. Chameleon-like, she transforms her face from stunning beauty to a blood curdling fright. She lures men and fellow beast alike to their deaths, like the sirens on the rocks at sea. People have given her the name, "Vampressa".

So, my old nemesis has followed me to this place where I was to start anew. A deafening screech echoes from above as more tile falls past my space to the earth below. I see the shadowy outline of the beast as she springs from the towers roof. Then, slowly she flaps her broad, deep violet wings off into the orange red, setting sun.

If the villagers are to be spared, I must go quickly, the place is in danger. I'm certain they must close their shutters and hide this night. But, I must go to the tent of the women, even before the moon goes silver to warn them of this impending horror.

I travel from the edge of the village, crossing over the first dune and looking down into the shallow valley between the mounds of sand, I see the flickering glow of the wise women's lamps from inside the canvas walls. Looking over my shoulder, my eyes strain to see if the beast is near, for surely the tent's light can attract the monster. For now, I see no harm in sight.

Approaching closer, I hear music of sorts. Jingling and resonance much like flutes fill a melody of low notes. Incense burns somewhere as its fragrance wafts through the air to tickle the senses of my nose and shadowy outlines of women dancing almost seductively are projected through the tent's cloth walls and transparent silk openings.

What am I to surmise, for this reads differently from what I was told? This setting is by far the opposite from yesterday's visit, at mid-sun with the older women. Nevertheless, I must warn them of the danger that lurks and then gain their wisdom of peace for my return to the Queen.

I hesitate to proceed, in that the moon is not yet silver, but then I envision Vampressa slitting their tent with her dagger-like talons and devouring all within.

If I am to be the Queen's General, I must enter now to warn them of the continued impending danger and then possess their knowledge. With that clear to me, I throw the entry-netting curtain to the side. I proceed through the large sand tent's main foyer opening hall.

My eyes behold a luxurious sight. Candles and lamps are lit about. Beautiful, scantily-clad women dance in a circle intertwined with the flickering lights. Faint veils and scarves cover little of their naked bodies. Then all goes silent as flutes and jangling notes from the hoops and jewelry on the six women stop. They stand still, looking my way. Five with long dark hair and deep brown eyes smile at me and I'm tempted to lust. The sixth one has golden blond hair and she comes across quite stern, however pleasant to the eye. This woman of beauty carries a large serpent coiled around her torso, neck and breasts and appears unhappy at my arrival. Is it that the moon is not yet full? Is this the source of her displeasure? As she approaches, the snake hisses as its slit tongue flaps between its needle sharp fangs.

"Why are you here" she demands angrily, her nostrils flaring.

"I am here to speak to the wise women led by Samanda," I reply.

"What business do you have with Samanda?" she asks, now so close we nearly touch and before I'm able to respond, she grasps the snakes' head in her hand and forces it between my thighs. I am petrified and stand as if I were stone.

Although her hand still holds the serpent's head at my loins, she stands straight and looks up to me again. Now eye-to-eye, she huffs, "What business do you have with Samanda?"

In a quivering voice I reply, "The Queen asked me to tour her village and learn her people's ways. She has asked me to be her General-of-Arms and I must give her my reply at tomorrow's dawn."

The beautiful spitfire of a woman screams shrieks of hideous laughter and the others resume dancing and chanting. Silver and gold rings jangle louder. The flute music resumes more intensely than before.

All this is accompanied by pounding gold and silver hoops ringed with small bells upon their bodies. Fearful, I dare not move, for the serpent's head is near the center of my thighs and beads of sweat trickle from my every pore.

Clad only with the serpent, the woman bends slowly in front of me, while at the same moment she raises the viper's head to her mouth. Her eyes still strain upward, locked with mine.

She places the snake's head into her mouth. The bells, flutes and jangles grow louder and louder. Her cheeks indent as she sucks the breath from the serpent as the noisy array of bells and hoops heighten. I am aghast at what I view, but do not so much as twitch a portion of my flesh.

In a sudden climax of the music's heightened wail, the snake goes lifeless and uncoils, falling from her now totally naked body. It lands on the floor, its pale, yellow belly up. I am in disbelief and there is a dead silence all around. She stands upright slowly and then presses her sweaty, naked body firmly against mine.

Cautiously, I lower my eyes, confirming her position. I see as well as feel her warm breasts molded into my chest. With a demonic grin, she senses I am far too frightened to be adequately aroused, so quickly, before I can think to separate she raises both arms, places her palms on each side of my throat, then curls her fingers toward her, digging all ten long, pointed nails deep into the back of my neck. Unable to break free from her, she pulls my head and face downward, close to her lips. Now she opens her mouth and hisses softly like a serpent, then covers my lips with her own.

I try desperately to keep my lips shut tight as the pain from her nails imbedded in my neck, becomes excruciating and I cannot break free to breathe. Cracking my lips so slightly to try and take in some of her air, she forces her tongue into my mouth, then captures mine between her teeth.

I become faint and top heavy as she leaps up on me wrapping both legs around my waist and digging the heels of her glass slippers into my lower back. I struggle to stay upright as she voraciously sucks the breath from within my lungs. I succumb, falling backward to the floor with her atop me, like a panther devouring its prey. I pass out.

I rise upward to the bright light of the Sun God, Aurouras. He has his ovens stoked to a flaming orange rage to smelt his golden ore. The heat is near unbearable. Suddenly I'm cast downward through a dark-blue sky filled with his cauldrons of bright molten gold. The cauldrons tip slightly and their contents trickle into the sea below. The molten white gold splashes into the water, creating clouds of steam as it coats the bodies of mermaids playfully swimming about. Much to their distress, it is hot and as it is cooled by the chilly seawater the gold solidifies around them, cementing their movement. They squirm violently for a few moments, flapping their tail fins. Then, they become lifeless and descend one-by-one into the murky abyss below.

"Their Queen mother, the Aqua Goddess, "Serpentina," glides about the depths in anguish and distress unable to rescue her daughters. Ouch! I now feel the hot, molten gold dripping on me..."

I awake to see the woman dripping hot wax on my chest from a candle she holds above my stomach. She ceases when she sees I awake, then leans down to my face and announces, "You are early, my new Master General. I am the one you came to see. I am Samanda."

The music, dancing women and flutes resume from where they halted. All six women giggle and laugh as I sit up, horribly dazed.

I jump back, landing on my buttocks as the snake, now revived, crawls across my leg and exits under the tent's wall. Samanda dons an amber body veil and returns to me, hand extended to help me to my feet. She says, "Arise and walk with me to the room where we lounge." After what I've just been through, I follow her command without indecision. As we enter her chamber of delight, I am overwhelmed with its sweet aromas and plush decorations. It is like the room atop the Queen's tower. Samanda asks that I sit on a large, soft feather mat that covers much of the floor. Still somewhat weak on my feet, I willingly accept her offer.

Remembering now, why I came here, I begin my dialogue to warn her of the danger that lurks above in the night sky, but Samanda stops me. "We are well aware of the loathsome female monster you describe. It is she who desecrated the reproductive chain of our people. We are also aware of her presence near the village this night and have given her a maiden as a sacrifice so that you can safely be with us in this room this evening."

I try to understand the words that come from Samanda, but become troubled. She continues, "You were told not to visit us until the moon grew silver for a reason and that is why I was so upset when you appeared before the agreed time we made with the monster. Vampressa was in this very chamber when you first entered our tent and so I had no choice but to make it appear I killed you. If I had not, she surely would have ripped you limb-to-limb on the very ground where you stood."

I am now slowly understanding Samanda's words, but I wonder if through her violent acts upon me, she truly saved my life moments before?

"We will talk more of the Harpy monster later. For now her danger is at safe distance and we have an equally important matter at hand."

"What would that matter be?" I asked and as if ignoring me, Samanda moves behind a silk curtain briefly and returns with a leopard skin carafe.

She kneels beside me, gives me a passionate wet kiss, and apologizes, "I'm sorry for my actions upon your arrival. Please accept my explanation and share our wine." I've not refreshed my palate with fermented juices since my days on the battlefront, so this offer comes with warm welcome.

The wine tastes unusual, very strong, yet pleasingly cool to the taste. Samanda takes the carafe from me and places it to her lips. I now see her differently than before, equally as attractive as the other five women, yet somehow different, as if wiser. She also bears a slight resemblance to the Queen in looks and mannerisms.

After she takes a long swallow from the jug, the ruby red wine drips slightly from the corners of her lips and we both laugh. She places the wine to my lips, filling my mouth as I tilt my head back, then leans me against a high stack of satin pillows and again fills my mouth with the wine. We both laugh again.

I am quickly attaining a very relaxed state, contrary to my many months of hard labor in the mines and nearly six days of confusion since my release. I have also been attempting to affix some scope to my future in this new land. Samanda says, "Relax my new General of Arms, I'm sure you will serve the Queen well as time passes and you deal with the trials and tests set before you over the weeks to come.

For a moment, I want you to close your eyes as I speak. I will share with you a portion of the wisdom you seek." I am truly at ease now and Samanda's voice is soft and reassuring. She continues as I rest my eyelids. "Now we must get to the reason you have been summoned here this night. I want you to listen with your heart to what I speak. Layla awaits to enter my chambers. She is without child and our kingdom will not flourish without fertile loins. She is at time with the moon, ripe for conception. You must be tested before you can accept stature among our people."

"Please stop," I say as I open my eyes and sit forward. Samanda interrupts, "No, I will not stop. Now listen to me carefully. Layla is healthy and without disease, her time is now."

It seems I find myself in yet another quandary. I explain to Samanda that I have a woman who waits for my return, that I desire to bring her to this land after I achieve status.

She responds, "This woman, your dove of sorts, as you say. How do you know she is still alive after so much of your village has been ravaged by war? I think not, sir. Certainly she is dead. Here, drink more wine and think about what I say." I refuse the wine and continue to convey my feelings. Samanda appears to understand my plea and gently pushes me back into the pillows. She tells me to take ease and forgive her for being unkind with her thoughts.

Now, she says, "Rest more, you have had a long journey. Tomorrow awaits you and your return to the Queen's tower. Finish the wine before you rest. I will burn incense by your side to bring you sweet aromas to further ease your mind."

I know she is correct, that my path has been long and soon the new sun will light the horizon. I heed her advice, drifting in and out of sleep as the pleasant smoke romances my nostrils.

I dream of peaceful places with green meadows lined with bountiful fig trees. From out of the trees and onto the meadow, my love strides. Her hair, a beautiful auburn, sweeps over her left shoulder. She approaches me, lays me back onto the grass, kisses my stomach and chest, then moves her mouth upward to my lips. I lay helpless, not wanting this to end. She caringly caresses me and slowly slides her hands down my waist to my inner thighs where she excites me so that I willingly allow her to remove my leather wrap from around my hips. Now she undresses and is completely naked on top of me with her soft full breasts touching my lips. I put my hands on her upper arms as she guides my manhood into her. Leaning back she places her weight upon me while lamenting our love making coo's.

Suddenly I hear something amiss. A wretched screech and the sound of heavy movement of air and erratic wind flow. I open my eyes and in shock, find a beautiful, black-haired maiden in my lady's place. We are locked together and to the point of excitement that makes it impossible to withdraw from this act.

The screeching is so loud that my ears ring. On my back with the maiden riding up and down on me, it's obvious her excitement has turned her deaf. But I'm looking straight up at the canvas ceiling which I see waffle from the wind force outside, when suddenly two, huge, webbed feet with fang-like talons tear downward through the tent's canvas and penetrate the black-haired maiden's torso.

I lock hands with hers tightly as she is in utter shock and horror. Gazing up at the beast, I squeeze my fingers tightly into the maiden's who now screams from pain, her blood oozing down onto me. The monster, knowing my strong will from past experience, releases her fangs and leaves the maiden for dead as her wet, red body collapses down lifeless on top of me. Samanda and the other women rush to our aid from the far chamber and attempt to doctor Layla's injuries.

I quickly stand to do what I can to help, but realize I am far too faint to remain upright and fall to my knees and back into my dream. But the meadow is now gone, as are the fig trees. There is no grass and my dove is nowhere about. I become cold and pass into a deep, dark void of sleep. I feel I'm locked into this state as many suns rise and set, when I hear a familiar voice say, "Sir Warrior, it's time you rise." I awake to see the kindly old man and look around. I am in my tower suite.

What has occurred? I know it wasn't a dream for I can still smell Layla's blood and hear her cries of horror.

"Excuse me, sir warrior, it's time you awake, for the Queen awaits you." the man urges.

Chapter Two

The sixth day has now come. Even though my mind and body are in severe disarray from the twisted circumstances since my arrival here, I now stand at the base of the Queen's tower, undaunted.

I stride up the spiral stairs to her quarters, past the small window from whence I earlier spotted the dove looking at me. The dove is not here this day. Could Samanda's words be pure when she spoke of my first love's demise? Is this a message from the Gods?Once again I reach the level of her bountiful fragrance and the vision of her image lifts me closer to her chamber. As I break the crest of the top landing, I survey the plush room about me, then seek her out. I view the silhouette of a woman behind silk curtains dipping perfumed oils from a vial and applying it to her legs and feet.

"Come to me beyond the veil of my room and stand to my attention," her voice commands. I cross the stone floor and slowly pull back the curtain, immediately making eye contact with her. She continues, "Come to me and stand before me so I may view your stature after so many days." Obliging her, I take a few short steps beyond the open curtain. "Come closer, so I may whiff the aura of your being after so many days." Now standing so close that my knees are a needle's length from hers, once again I obey her command, as she remains seated. "Stand tall and look straight forward, Sir Warrior, then recite your findings to me since we last spoke in this very room." I hesitate with unease as I feel her eyes focused on my cloth wrap. Then she volleys out "Speak… to… me… now!"

"I have, for the past six suns toured your kingdom and have had many conversations and interactions with your people. Although I am not certain of your Majesty's will for me, I pledge to be a loyal servant to your Royal Sovereignty. I am deeply troubled at what I have found on many fronts. However, I wish only to serve you and bring you great pleasure in this land."

The Queen challenges, "I see. Does that mean you will only answer me with truthful statements when I ask questions of you about my people and their land?"

"With the greatest of honor for you and for our people to unite as one, I could do nothing other."

"So, let me query further. I wish you to tell me of your findings of Samanda when you visited her tent."

I know I must be truthful and am not sure how to answer this encompassing question. Quickly I recall that evening and am not entirely positive of its conclusion. "Your Majesty, there is much to recall of my meeting with her. In my duties, it must be clear that I am direct with you. Can you state further, please?"

"Sir Warrior, last night when you visited Samanda's tent, did you encounter several beautiful, nearly-naked women dancing about you?"

"That I did, your Majesty."

The Queen continues, "Did you, as well, encounter the Harpy monster, Vampressa, upon this same visit, Sir Warrior?"

"That I did too, your Majesty."

"Warrior, in that we have not witnessed her presence here for some time, it would seem Vampressa has followed you to my village. I am undecided on how to go farther under these circumstances. However I do have two possible solutions. The first is very bad for you, yet not all that beneficial to me. The second is bad for Vampressa and possibly still bad for you, but good for the fertile women of my land."

"I know not of what you speak, your majesty."

She snaps to me, "Close your lips as I speak and you shall learn my situation. You alone attract the Harpy monster, because you are virile and capable of multiple acts of procreation. You have brought about a duplicated occurrence that has killed off the strongest of my warriors on the battlefield. It happens when they are caught in situations of lust while taking peace between battles in the moon's glow.

"Vampressa has devastated my ranks in the field, not sand storms and disease as you thought. Let me ask you, Sir Warrior, did you too lust on the evening you visited the tent of Samanda and her women?"

Cautiously I reply, "Yes, your Majesty. I unwillingly fell into a period of lust that seemed to exceed my control. Somehow I felt I was engaged with my own mate left behind during the battle in which your ranks captured me."

"You must listen closely to me," the Queen continues, "I too, am without children and my agony heightens now that the King was slain in the battle wherein you were captured. So it may be that you owe me services far beyond those of Master General. Only the passing of three full moons will assure me. Therefore, when you leave my chambers this day, you are to return to your abode, where you will ponder this meeting with me. You will speak to no one and be given only water to consume for three suns. On the dawn of the fourth sun, Samanda will appear to you with my further direction. If you are to truly be my General of Arms, you will obey her commands without question. If you err, even once, I will see that you are staked out for Vampressa to dine upon. Now leave and return to your tower."

I turn and bow my head as I walk for the spiral stairwell. Taking one step down with much remorse, I smell her upon me as she states "Stop and turn to me." I obey this order and turn to see her beautiful veiled face as it glides to me. Without expression through her veil she places her lips to mine and holds them there. I cannot help but bring my palms to her narrow waistline, but she pushes them away, removes her lips and says, "Good luck and may the Gods be with you." She saunters back behind the silks as I turn and descend the spiral steps to impose sentence upon myself for the next three suns.

When I reach my room at the far tower's top, I cross to see if I have adequate supplies of water. All seems in order as I find a small quantity of dried dates as well as two casks of fresh water. I look up from where I stand and see out my window that another female figure has joined the Queen in her tower.

Conflicting images in her window opening appear peculiar to me. The Queen is certain as she passes the opening, then disappears. The other woman passes in a plush robe and it is she, of whom I am uncertain. Now both fade away into the rapture of her space. It is not for me to dwell on, although I do ponder what my eyes have just retrieved. I lie back on my bunk and seek to achieve a rested mind and body, while I await my orders to be delivered by Samanda on the dawn of the fourth day.

*   *   *

After the warrior left the Queen's quarters, the reflection of a beautiful woman appeared to the Queen in a full-length oval mirror with ornate gold trimmings around its edges, behind transparent silk curtains. Her reflection appears in a long, dark, burgundy robe. The Queen approaches the mirror and pulls back its crepe shrouding. The woman is Samanda, who, as the Queen knows, has been there during the conversation between the Queen and the warrior slave.

Samanda speaks. "So, my sister, why so stern with whom you secretly are falling in love with? Can it be that even though you asked me to test his sexuality and person, that you are now becoming jealous of such acts with myself and Layla?"

"Do not create a comedy of my feelings in something of which you can only speculate, my sister."

Samanda pushes her. "I assure you that this warrior you currently possess as a slave can bring you great pleasure in many ways. He stands tall and broad with great strength. It took a large quantity of the morphine aphrodisiac cocktail and much sweet scented opium smoke to bring him down to where we could act on him against his will. Believe me, my sister; we viewed his long, slow, yet gentle, love-making caresses. We as well, became stirred as we viewed him and Layla intertwined for a period beyond the sand that passes through the hourglass. I would desire another opportunity, with your permission, to…"

"Stop my sister! Go no further with your description of the act. It is unkind to me, as I have remained faithful to the King, even after a full season of his death has passed. My desire is not to share your lustful visions, but to procure a strong and healthy mate to assume his duties to me as a woman and Queen of our nation."

The Queen pauses a moment, attempting to compose her thoughts. She calmly continues, "Tell me of Layla's injuries. You must also inform me of what went amiss in the arrangement you had with the monster, Vampressa."

Samanda's face no longer bears a pleasant smile as she reports, "Your warrior slave came upon our tent too early, due to a fear he had for our safety when he spotted the monster earlier that evening perched atop his tower." The Queen shivers with the thought of the Harpy monster roosting on her very fortress. "Vampressa was in our lounge, behind a curtain upon his arrival. We made much noise and danced about to try and distract her, but to no avail. She still peered through our curtains at him. If he'd paused a short time longer, she would have been off to the location where we placed the virgin for her. I knew not what to do, so I approached the warrior and although overwhelmed with his stance, saw no other thing to do but mount him and suck the air from his lungs until he succumbed.

"The monster smiled, as if impressed with this deed of mine and swooped off into the distance. We thought all was safe for the moment so I poured hot candle wax on his stomach to revive him and prepare him to mate with Layla as you had instructed."

The Queen interrupts Samanda, "What went wrong? And speak to me of Layla's condition, please."

Samanda acknowledges the Queen's concern and continues, "I believe Vampressa discovered that she had been tricked. You see, the mother of the maiden offered conceded that her daughter, while still a virgin, was older and with fever. She told us her daughter had been doctored for a long period with potions and ceremony and that she would not be of this world to witness the third sunrise. She believed her daughters sacrifice could save our men at battle if put to the proper terms with the monster. I'm sorry I failed you, my sister.

"As to your concerns of Layla, I can only tell you that she was slashed severely. Her pretty face will be no longer. Her breasts, back and upper arms were gashed as if she were nude on the battlefront without armor or weapon. If not for the strength of your warrior slave and his locking of his hands with hers, she would have surely been plucked off him, flown away by the monster and devoured. Layla will recover slowly and we will attend to her needs as required."

The Queen quizzes Samanda further, "Tell me more of her state. Were there punctures to her below her ribs and back; injuries that may alter her ability to carry a child full term, if, in fact she did conceive during this traumatic attack and horrific event?"

Samanda replies, "We can only call upon time to gain that answer. However from what we witnessed, she surely will be with child and has no injury below the last rib."

The Queen turns, walks to her window, stares outward and proclaims, "It is imperative that we must now set our course to avenge this brutality. We can no longer wait for the few remaining men on the battlefields to defend us and conquer other lands, so, plot your strategy and concur it with the warrior slave. It is now up to the two of you. There remains no other hope. All will be lost if you do not succeed. I will become a withered shrew before my time, crumbling into dust along with the demoralized people of our kingdom.

"Let him rest for three suns without drugs or trickery, so he can regain his thoughts accurately. Take him food on the rise of the fourth sun and tell him of his mission with you in the hours to come. Then he may also adequately examine this task. Now depart Samanda and keep in mind that I desire no more contact of your flesh with that of my slave."

Samanda responds cordially, "Thank you my sister. I shall send you messengers as the new horizons brighten. I will not fail you on this mission."

The Queen interrupts, "Tell the warrior I request that he alone bring me Vampressa's bloody, dead carcass upon your return. Go now!"

Samanda exits down the long spiral staircase and crosses the courtyard. Looking up at Aaron's tower window, she reluctantly strides through the elegant stronghold's large open iron gate.

She pauses momentarily then mounts her black stallion and rides off, thinking, "I know my sister has been long without companionship and so I wonder if her thoughts can be in disarray. Surely an enemy slave cannot become a Queen's counterpart. General-of-Arms? I question. Hmmm... the slave would be far more fit socially for a woman of my stature. My sister has frequently harvested beyond the seeds she has sown. But I must banish these evil thoughts from my mind. This man, Aaron, seems to have placed a deep-rooted spell on me of some kind, which I will not let come between my sister and me. We must work united to save our kingdom, create a strong race and rid this land of the evil Harpy monster. I will seek council from my Father and the elder women, then relay our plan to the warrior slave."

*   *   *

The sun has risen on the fourth day. Samanda arrives, pulls up to the base of the warrior's tower by covered chariot and hops to the ground. She leans back into the carriage, removing a woven basket containing food and ale. She passes through the lower tower and ascends the staircase. Upon reaching the top stair, she sees the warrior asleep on his bed. She quietly crosses to his side where he lies naked. Her dark thoughts reoccur.

"Why cannot this brick of a man be mine to hold, serve me and make love to me", she thinks as she watches him inhale and exhale during his sleep. She relives the event of just a few nights ago when she and the other women brought the warrior's comatose body to his quarters after he passed out from the drugs and Harpy attack. She recalls how they all swabbed his body of Layla's dried blood. Now she becomes aroused, forgetting her sisterly promise and begins caressing the warrior's mid-section with sweet oil dabbed on her palms from a small leather flask. Aaron stirs and awakens abruptly from her touch.

"Forgive me, my future General-of-Arms," Samanda quickly airs, "I brought you cooked meat and freshly cut fruits. I only touched your stomach to measure your sure pain of hunger for the last three days with no food to eat."

The warrior is startled. Realizing he is without clothing, he quickly fetches bed cloths from his side and covers his loins. "Samanda, you have come as the Queen stated. I thank the Gods above that my last days here in this land have not been a dream gone horribly wrong."

"Not to worry, my soon-to-be General of Arms. Here let me hold your head to me and awake in your own time," Samanda says, as she stands by the bedside where the warrior sits.

Samanda, not unlike the Queen, has been long without companionship and her will to oblige her sister's wishes is quickly fading. She now turns the warrior's head firmly with both of her hands and attempts to move his face to an area of her body well below her jeweled navel. She contorts her thighs and sighs uncontrollably. The warrior bites into the center of her scanty undergarment and Samanda no longer feels a need to grasp his head. She continues agonizing so loudly, it can be heard in the courtyard. She drops her hands to his shoulders and lifts her hips, locking his head and face deep between her thighs. The warrior, unable to help himself places both hands on Samanda's buttocks and squeezes them tightly, pulling her passion patch deeper onto his face.

"Stop! Please stop tempting me, we must go no farther, Samanda! This cannot be the Queen's reason for you to come to me," the warrior laments in torment and pushes her away from him.

Regaining her wits, Samanda counters, "You are correct sir, please forgive me?" Samanda slowly calms down from heavy breathing, "You are correct, my Master General. I was ordered to come to you to speak of war. As you must know by now, the Queen and I are of the same blood.

We spoke after you departed her quarters, four suns ago. She asked me to come here and discuss creating a new army for her kingdom's defense against the monster, Vampressa. As well, she chooses to meld our city of Patrious with your village of Nemmin, so that we may all propagate together and live in peace and harmony."

The warrior, contemplating his options, replies, "What will become of me, Samanda? You have shared your secret of your blood, but I fear I have a secret far more complex. A moment so private that it may very well cost me my head by your sister's hand."

Samanda tries to be reassuring, "My sister knows many things as do I, Sir warrior. It might be you are taxing yourself when you need not. Tell me of what it is that you speak so guardedly?"

The warrior continues. "First, neither you nor your sister, know my name. If you did you would surely understand my dilemma.

"I was trained to be a brutal warrior and it has only been since my capture that I have become tamed. The beatings and hard labor in your mines broke much of my instinct to kill. The soft moments you and your sister have provided me are not of my past. I have now become accustomed to these precious moments and wish them not to end."

Samanda interrupts boastfully, "You are the warrior, Aaron. You killed the Queen's husband, our King, during a fierce fight on the battlefield. You rammed your sword deep into his gut and twisted it. He died quickly, as you were trained to do to your enemies. Now may we get to the urgency of war with Vampressa and the adversarial out-lying villages, my Master General, Sir Aaron?"

Aaron thinks, "I cannot believe these women have known all along of my victory over the King, moments before my capture. How can the thought of making me one with their kingdom be from the heart?" He asks, "Miss Samanda, may I have further conversation with you before we speak of new conflicts?"

"Yes, but I must depart soon. Be quick with your words."

Aaron asks, "How can a woman as regal as the Queen, not only forgive me for my combat actions slaying her mate, welcome me to her breast?"

Samanda moves slowly toward Aaron. "No one has said you were forgiven, Sir Aaron. That can come only after you have proven your wisdom to be far beyond your virility and stature. When we return from our conquests, you must drop the dead, bloody body of Vampressa at the Queen's feet. Upon fulfillment of that deed, she will smile on you and look into your eyes. Then you will be greatly rewarded and invited to lie with her as her mate.

"Now I must go. You have been advised of our mission. It must not fail. Use the days ahead to sort out your strategy. Upon my return, we will leave our village and begin to build our flanks," Samanda pauses as if she knows she must depart but is hesitant.

"And if by error we fail?" Aaron questions.

Samanda crosses to the stairwell, turns sternly to Aaron, smiles, "Then you will be mine alone, Sir Aaron, mine to do with whatever I choose. And I promise I won't waste you for Vampressa to dine upon." She then wisps herself down the staircase, giggling like a young girl.

"What an array of outcomes there can be with the circumstances at hand. Surely on such a mission there will be an opportunity for my escape. But where? How? We will see!"

"I may be able to reunite with my love from seasons past. Can this be what the Queen spoke of when she said, 'Absorb within me your fears, ills and joy, but remember it is unwise to discard that which took root in the fertile fragments of the heart.' The woman is quite wise.

"My decision will be to aid the Queen and her people. Surely she will then allow me to return with my maiden as we achieve happiness and live without the hardships of constant war. I must also convince Samanda to gain release of my fellow prisoners from the mines, so that I may be flanked by them. I will assist her in recruiting her flank, yet ponder the source of her warriors. I draw no answer. She is a very capable woman and her idea exists, I am certain. We will resolve this upon her return. Above all the cunning Harpy must die and the people of my home town must be freed from the oppression that has been subjected upon them from our barbaric warring neighbors!"

*   *   *

Samanda exits the tower. In the courtyard, the old man in the brown robe approaches her. He says, "Samanda, my child, we are prepared for you in the Chapel conference hall as you requested." He takes her by the hand and they cross the yard to another large, wooden door. He pulls it open and they enter into a cavern-like room with a long, wooden table at its center. Several older women, dressed in clergy-like robes and wimples, are seated along its sides. Some of them are the same women whom Aaron met at Samanda's tent. The old man seats Samanda at his side on the far end of the table. They place their hands on the table and settle in, all heads turn toward them.

Samanda begins, "Mistresses of the Divine Order. I'm certain that our Father has explained my coming. Things are no longer as they were in our youth. Our King, now deceased has left a legacy certain to be our demise. His policy of neutering all our males unsuitable to fight as warriors has drawn us a dark future. We are all knowledgeable of his actions, as some of your own sons suffered that fate. It seems his idea to retain only the fittest as breeding stock has left many women barren, who would be otherwise with child."

An older woman interrupts. "Pardon my interruption Miss Samanda. Possibly, you are too young to remember the scores of women who were raped and fell to sodomy while our brave warriors were at battle. The infidel men came out of the dunes upon the departure of the warriors. I myself still bear scars from two of those acts upon my person. I understand our dilemma. Our King, from time-to-time disgraced himself enough, so let us not add this issue to his legacy."

Samanda resumes her dialogue. "Forgive my disrespect, Grand Mistress. I am only concerned for our race and culture. I, too, desire to bear offspring and not many seasons will pass before my time in that light will dim. Not only are there few resources available for procreation, Vampressa has returned. She has been preying on the warriors of whom we speak for many moons. Scores of our soldiers have been decapitated after she buries their bodies in the sand, to suffer for days in the hot sun. Upon returning she plucks off their heads like a raven strutting about a freshly blooming garden. Moreover her greatest pleasure is devouring both mates during intercourse, at the precise moment of climax.

"As she ages, she has become ghoul-like in her obsession to destroy the reproductive chain of mankind. One of our own, Layla, was recently viciously sliced about the face and breasts by the Harpy as she had intercourse with Aaron. She was fortunate that he possessed great strength and was able to defend her from the monster.

"We have confirmed reports that there is great unrest in the outlying village of Genipsus, which borders the town of Nemmin, where our new Master General of Arms was captured more than one full season ago. This, once General of the enemy, has willingly converted to our ways and will prove to be a courageous warrior. He is also dedicated to the Queen."

The old man interrupts Samanda and addresses the council. "Mistresses of the Divine Order, Samanda was asked by the Queen to seek our knowledge. There is no question of the dire circumstance at hand, that left unchecked, will mean our people and nation will be lost into the shifting sands of time. I ask you to pause this council and discuss what you have been told as I take Samanda into my chamber that is reserved for ceremony preparations. We will return when one of you knocks on my door with a solution for Samanda to carry out. Samanda, my child, please come with me."

The old man takes Samanda by the hand and they enter to his room. Sitting at a small table, full of parchment writings, he looks over his shoulder to reassure himself that the door is secured before he speaks softly to Samanda. "Samanda, as the ladies crossed the courtyard to enter the Grand Hall today, there was an obvious commotion noted from the open window where the Queen's warrior prisoner is kept. Some of the women who are familiar with this man asked if we were providing him with prostitutes to influence his transformation. The occurrence was very difficult for me to explain and it was my good fortune that a noisy flock of waterfowl passed above and the women rushed for shelter to avoid their droppings. I hope your indiscretion does not affect any decision they may provide. The other matter is your counterpart, the Queen. I'm certain you are aware that she is grooming this fine specimen of a man for herself. It would be of grave circumstance should she find…" A knock comes from the door and the man closes abruptly with, "We must return now. Be very cautious with your words."

Samanda rises, her face flushed as she realizes the man, as well as some of the older women, heard her cries of ecstasy with Aaron. Composing herself as if nothing undue had happened, she swiftly resumes her position at the head of the long table. The old man seats himself as well. "Such a short conference, my ladies, would indicate there was little indecision," he offers.

The forewoman speaks, "You are accurate, Father. For we did not attain our age and wisdom upon the rise of this morning's sun. We were quite aware of that which Samanda addressed even before our arrival on this day. Our thinking is aligned with that of the Queen. We, therefore, have this instruction for Samanda. Listen to this man your sister chooses to mould into her own. We trust she has a fruitful vision, beyond our comprehension. Obey his commands on the field. We are well aware of his fierce warrior status from stories brought to us by travelers across the land. We are of great contentment of his conversion and thus must continue to harness his abilities to our advantage. Let him select his own flanks wherever he may find them.

"As for you, Samanda, you are to be at his side with your troops. We have sent word to an old ally of ours who we seldom call upon because of her own crusades against darkness. Her name is 'Kaybra,' a tall, staunch, warrior woman who keeps her flock well-protected on a delta island. You will find her at the end of the next two suns. Follow the river until you reach the sea, where she and her troops will await you. You will then merge with her and besiege your joint forces to make war upon Vampressa and defeat the village of Genipsus to end its conflict with Nemmin.

"One final matter, Samanda. As I stated, we did not gain our wisdom with the rise of this morning's sun. Aaron is your commander; you are not his. There will be one among your ranks who will have a personal eye on the horizon. This covert individual shall be known only to this Order and to the Father. Should you return unsuccessful, or bearing a child from Aaron's loins, you will be cast into a cell for public display. Now, gather your wits and depart! There shall be no further delay!"

Samanda is unruffled. She stands, purses her lips and bows before the women. She exits the hall quickly and crosses the courtyard to her chariot, where she pauses to glare at Aaron's window and inflicts her patented nostril flare in its direction. She then proceeds to untie her horses' tethers and drives from the courtyard. As she passes under the Queen's tower, she envisions her sister standing at her window. Staring upward coldly, she smirks at the empty window, waves briefly and lays her whip to the horses' backs.

Moments later Samanda arrives at her tent, enters, disrobes and summons the other women to surround her. As they gather, she entreats them, "Dusk is upon us, so light the torches and lamps, gather your instruments and bring me my viper. In the morning's dawn I must depart on a long journey of war. We may never be together again. Hand me the adder and let us begin the ceremony."

Samanda takes the snake and wraps it around her waist as a belt. She holds the serpent's tail and mid-body firm to the small of her back with one hand as the snake's head dangles down behind her. She then spreads her legs, bends over and with her other hand pulls the remaining length of the constrictor, headfirst up between her legs and holds it tightly to her body, between her navel and breasts. "Ladies, please begin the ceremony," she orders, as the snake hisses.

The music and circular dance around Samanda begins as on the night of Aaron's arrival. The same incense wafts its way though the tent and once again the sounds of the bells attached to golden hoops drummed on their bodies heighten the rhythm.

This time, oboe-like tones accompany the frenzy of noise and dance as the snake becomes excited and begins to constrict around Samanda's waistline and upward between her legs. The noise of the music becomes louder and louder as the viper constricts deeper into Samanda's flesh. She squeezes her eyes tight and grasping the constrictor's head and neck firmly to her body, with a crisis like expression on her face, she falls onto her back. Her breasts heave and bounce as she falls to the sandy floor and her rib cage protrudes as the reptile is now wrapped tighter than before. The reptile emits a heavy, mucus-like slime as Samanda opens her eyes and rolls them far back into her head so only the whites are seen. She moans as her body writhes in rapture, then opens her mouth wide and begins hissing as she firmly yanks the snake's head toward her mouth.

She is too weak to accomplish the ritual in its entirety and starts to shake. She opens her palm, releasing her grasp on the snake and the music stops instantly. The other women stand quietly in a circle around her and the only thing heard is the soft oboe-like horn in the background. The oboe's music is soothing to the viper and it slowly uncoils from around her body. The women now disperse, tend to the flickering lamps and candles around them, gently extinguishing them. One large oil lamp remains lit by Samanda's side. In the dim light Samanda begins shallow breathing after lying comatose from the time she released the constrictor's head. Two of her attendant's take the snake from around her and return it to its basket. The oboe stops and all is silent. One woman kneels alongside Samanda, kisses her on the lips softly and airs, "Farewell, Warrior Princess. Return to us with peaceful tidings." She then extinguishes the last lamp and the tent goes dark.

Chapter Three

Aaron's night has been one of contemplation. He's still partially asleep when the old man enters his room and approaches his bed. Aaron sits up and his visitor explains that Samanda awaits his arrival in the Grand Hall now, as the sun is just beginning to rise. The old man departs.

Aaron dons his loin wrap and sandals, then crosses the room to retrieve his broadsword. He stands straight and stretches, looking out his window down to the large, wooden door that opens into the Grand hall across the courtyard. He looks up to his left and sees the Queen standing in her turret's window, her eyes fixed on him. She crosses her hands in front of her body, just below the tie on her robe, pauses and slowly turns, then walks into her room. Aaron searches his mind since her burgundy robe looks familiar. Rearranging his thoughts Aaron inhales the fresh morning air, then descends the spiral stairway.

As he walks off the small cobblestone footbridge over the stream that splits the courtyard, he sees the door to the Grand Hall is open slightly. He turns for one last glance up at the Queen's window before entering the Hall, but she is no longer there.

Aaron enters the large room and sees Samanda standing by the long tableside viewing numerous maps and charts strewn about its top, her back is turned to him. It appears she has not heard him enter as she is intensely rifling through the documents. In an area farther down the table, he sights a crossbow, arrows and several small hand weapons; including bladed chains and sharpened metal discs. Next to them sits a man's leather military outfit cut at the waistline, with laced boots to match. Samanda now feels his presence, turns to acknowledge him with a pleasant, "Good morning, Sir Aaron."

Samanda is in her own military outfit with boots laced to just below her knee, a short leather skirt cut at her upper thigh with several short, leather paddles woven in around it. Her bare midsection is wrapped with a wide, black belt bearing a large, gold buckle with a coiled serpent engraved at its center. Behind the buckle is a sharp bone-handled combat knife. Her breasts are harnessed tightly upward in a revealing leather top. Her ravishing golden blonde hair hangs long to her shoulder. Her belt is drawn so snugly that her figure approaches an hourglass-like form. Aaron is electrified by her new appearance, as this outfit emphasizes Samanda's femininity as well as her muscle tone.

"Good morning," Aaron replies.

Samanda struts authoritatively around the end of the large table and confides, "It is the wish of the wise women and the Queen that you lead the crusade against the evil that lurks across the land. I will be at your command, but first you must be advised of their further wishes from which there will be no variation.

"We are to journey south, two days along the river and merge with a fellow warrior woman called Kaybra. Kaybra is very much with the knowledge of Vampressa and her blood curdling kind. She, it seems, has readily restored her village from a similar fate they suffered some time ago. Kaybra's ranks will cover us from the south as we move northward to the battlegrounds and the place where Vampressa feeds and nests.

"We've had no reports from messengers for many suns, so we know not the condition of our warriors battling your old village of Nemmin and its neighbor, Genipsus. It will be up to you to recruit your flank to arrive from the north upon them as we press upward from the south. As you are well aware, with this application of successful warfare, the grand gorge will be to their backs and so they will be forced to a peaceful existence or be driven to their deaths over the cliffs into the Valley of the Damned, that lie at the bottom of the gorge."

Aaron interrupts Samanda, "My warrior princess, it seems you have much of the situation in hand. Why is it they placed me in your command?"

"You are in command, Sir Aaron, because we have no troops to enter the battlefield from the north. Moreover, you are known as a worthy adversary atop your steed. I am merely explaining the logistics. It will be your decision how we apply strategies as each new morning unveils the sun. Should our mission fail, it will not be the fault of myself or Kaybra, with you as our leader. We are in your hands. I'm certain the Queen knows exactly what she wants."

Aaron is slightly confused and wonders if he will really have Samanda's complete cooperation. He surmises she has taken on a bit of a disdainful attitude, but attempts to quell the conversation. "I will need an Order signed by the Queen to release my men from the mines. They will be loyal to me and can flank the northern region of which you spoke. Their spirits were broken long before the Queen summoned me to her side. They will gladly obey me to gain their release and be once again under my command," Aaron closes, watching to see Samanda's reaction.

Samanda smiles broadly at Aaron, now knowing she has his full attention, she swaggers close to him and snickers. "Consider the order signed. Now come with me to the table's edge so that I may fit you with your uniform of war. Surely, such a brave man as you would not go into battle in sandals and a loin cloth."

Aaron takes her hand and moves with her to the area at the table where moments ago he spotted the uniform. She looks into his eyes and with her hands, undoes his loincloth, which drops to the floor. Never losing contact with his eyes, she reaches behind her with one hand and lifts the new leather battle apron up off of the table. She then reaches it around his waist and places it on him, pulling its clasp tightly just below his navel. It is so tight that Aaron is in discomfort, so she forces her fingers behind the clasp and tugs the leather wrap upward, "There, it's just right, a perfect fit. You can put on the rest without my assistance. I will go get your Order from the Queen and ask her to send it by messenger to the mine before you arrive. Your commissioned steed is strong and white, tied outside the entry gate. Load him with the weapons you see on the table. Soon you will command your men into formation and send them on their way.

"The elder women wish you to accompany me to meet Kaybra and we must obey them. I will meet you at the edge of the village, where the chariots are kept. There we will be provided with supplies to make it the entire distance."

Aaron interrupts, "Samanda, I have never engaged in battle this way. Are you certain of what you speak?"

"Positive," she snaps back. Then, with her hips swaying, she pompously exits the corridor in the direction of the Queen's tower.

Aaron is surprised at Samanda's attitude, then suddenly realizes how unkempt he appears, standing there in the middle of the Grand Hall with only a warrior's apron and flimsy sandals. He quickly dresses himself and gathers the weapons from the table as directed.

*   *   *

Samanda is now meeting with her sister in her tower suite. There appears to be unrest between the two. Samanda asks, "Do you think it wise, my sister, to allow this former prisoner slave to release his men from the mines?"

Looking into the large oval mirror, the Queen wisely replies, "Do you think it is in good faith for you, my sister, to continue to lust after this man? Sometimes I hear and see things of which you are not apparently aware. What was the cause of the woman's moans across the way coming from Aaron's tower before your meeting with council during yesterday's morning sun?"

Samanda retorts, "Oh, my sister, where are your thoughts? As I reached the top step of his abode my sandal strap snapped off and I slipped down the stone stair, scraping my shin on the rock. It hurt badly for some time so I shrieked while in extended pain. That is what you must have heard."

The Queen, looking at Samanda's legs in the mirror, responds back, "Unusual that such a painful injury would have left little indication of such a damaging mishap! But now, I will give you my final command relative to my property. Keep your WHORISH hands off him! If you continue with these temptations, he will be able to make no decision other than to join himself to your loins. You have already been warned once as a temptress. Thus if this goes farther, your naked body will be tied by ropes to bars of a cage, filled with hungry lions in full public view!

"Now you, not a messenger, will take my written order immediately to the prison mines before Aaron's arrival there. He may then rank his men. Remember, Samanda, although this man is a great warrior, he will remain a mortal until I receive his seeds through our scripture's official Reproductive Ceremony. Now go!"

Samanda appears to be truly shaken by her sister's statements. Upon receiving this last reprimand, her reflection in the mirror disappears. Then she quietly turns and descends the tower, walks across the courtyard to her charger where she sees Aaron in his new uniform loading weapons onto his horse. She pays no attention to him, mounts her horse, crops him on the neck and rides off toward the prison mines.

Aaron returns to the Grand Hall to study the maps and charts that cover the large wooden table. A great deal of time passes and much consideration is spent on his strategy. He then rolls the pertinent documents up, secures them with a string tie and places them under one arm. When he turns to exit, he is taken aback when he sees the Queen enter the room. He greets her with a bow and, "My lady."

The Queen is dressed in the same wispy, scarlet silk outfit she wore when she swabbed the warrior's wounds in his cell. Her veil is in place and she looks at him approvingly. Much of her shapely legs show through her gown as she looks at Aaron. Then she strides around him methodically, closing in as she does so. She approaches intimately and begins to pet his breast armor. Broad shouldered, he towers over her petite figure. Aaron remains cautiously silent.

Faint tears begin to seep from the Queen's eyes. Her highness' loyal subject puts his fingers close together under her chin and lifts her face to see her eyes. She closes them as he leans to her. Aaron parts her hair and kisses her on the forehead. The Queen reopens her eyes and with her tears dripping, asks, "The red lace I gave to you when you last saw me like this. Will you ever return it to me as I asked, Sir Aaron?"

Standing like a great General, he replies, "I shall return it to you, my lady, but only after I banish the scourge that exists on the outer regions of your kingdom."

"And will you be loyal to your Queen in her absence, my warrior?" She asks.

"I will, my lady, with only the purest of thoughts for you."

She whispers back, "Then, will you hold me close one last time before you depart?"

Aaron places his arms around the royal maiden, gently pulls her to him and with his hand, cradles her head to his lower chest.

She continues to sob, then slowly regains control of herself. Pulling her head from his chest, she notices his tanned skin is wet from her tears. A smile can faintly be seen through her veil as she attempts to wipe her tears off Aaron with her fingertips. She giggles softly, like a young girl and then states hopefully, "At least we will be rid of Vampressa for eternity when you return."

Aaron nods his head, "Yes, we will, my lady."

The Queen continues in her hopeful little girl voice, as she now looks up deep into the warrior's eyes, "And at least we will once again have peace in our kingdom and raise our offspring. Correct, my General of Arms?"

Aaron, taken off guard with the implications of her last words, inadvertently drops the scrolls from under his arm. But he recovers his thoughts quickly and Commander-like, staring straight forward, he reassures her, "Correct, my lady."

Her majesty continues once again, in little girl-like fashion and says, "Here, let me pick those up for you. It's too far for a warrior of your stature to bend."

The Queen slowly goes down on one knee in front of him to retrieve the documents. Aaron, standing at attention, glances down as she does. He is surprised when he glimpses the woman's now uncovered breasts, which have dropped out of her low cut silks due to her stooped position. She makes no attempt to return them behind the fabric, but is jiggling about, attempting to reach the rolled documents. Aaron quickly lifts his head, returns to a military stance and stands patiently for a few moments. It seems to him as if the Queen has been on her knees far longer than needed to pick up a neatly tied scroll.

Feeling somewhat flustered, he ponders what the Queen is doing for such a period. Stealing a glance downward he sees the Royal maiden staring directly at the bulge in the center of his tight leather loin wrap. He then crosses his hands casually down in front of him over the wrap. As he does so, the Queen clasps one of his hands and tugs on it. She uses this new hold to raise herself back up to her feet. Her Highness then takes Aaron's other hand, pulls it to her, opens it flat and places the scrolls into his palm. Aaron, with a sense of relief, exhales a shallow breath.

The Queen begins to gently massage the bulge in Aaron's leathers with one hand. "Remain true to your Queen. Return a victor and you will be rewarded by three ceremonies beyond your imagination. The first will represent your victory, with you as the head of our warriors. The second will reflect your lion's heart to indulge and comfort our people. The third and final ceremony will thrust us together on my altar into a timeless destiny of immortality. It will be solely for you and me." The Queen realizes Aaron is now trying to find words to say, but places her index finger to his lips, "Be silent, my General of Arms. Take my unexpected visit to the fertile fragments of your heart and return safely to me. Farewell."

Aaron stands quietly, helpless with his thoughts as he watches the Queen's slight, revealing body gently saunter away into the shadows of the Grand Hall's exit corridor.

*   *   *

Much later, Aaron rides his fresh steed to the location of the chariots, immediately after freeing his men from the prison mines. This is where he was instructed to meet Miss Samanda.

She acknowledges his arrival and asks as he dismounts, "Tell me of your instruction to your men, Sir Aaron. Were they strong enough to mount the horses I provided?" Samanda is very cocky, which displeases Aaron greatly.

Aaron replies, "Samanda, ease your temperament when speaking of my men. They have been mining the Queen's stone for over a full season and have been often beaten by your sexually frustrated, eunuch guards for their own hideous pleasure, as well as being starved for their additional amusement. Remember, I bore witness to those acts and suffered in a similar manner on several occasions. If we, as you say, are to be cohorts, let us treat each other with equal respect."

Samanda realizes she has misspoken, but seeks no forgiveness. She hops onto the bare back of her horse, digs her boots into his gut. As they gallop off, she shouts back to Aaron, "The Harpy monster will not slay herself, Sir Warrior. Let us move on!"

Samanda and Aaron ride into the sandy dunes toward the river. Aaron's horse, while sturdy, labors to catch up with Samanda, due to his load of weaponry.

As they ride, Samanda stays a full length in front of Aaron for a disturbing reason. She also realizes that she must tone her mouth down in order to carry out her seductive plot. The alluring princess warrior maps out a provocative course in her mind of which the first step is to make certain Aaron has full view of her shapely bare bottom rising up and down as she rides. "My sister shall never know of the warrior and I, if done properly," she chuckles to herself. Her thoughts continue, "Of one thing I am certain, Kaybra must be the snitch, who will report on any of my actions to seduce Aaron. Therefore I must conquer him before we reach her camp. I shall combine the water's edge, fire and darkness to accomplish what I deeply desire."

The couple has ridden the entire afternoon and into early evening. Just as Samanda orchestrated, Aaron is beginning to weaken after being subjected to her shapely backside for many hours. He tries desperately to cleanse his thoughts with other, foreign topics. But then at one point, those arousing thoughts drift to the woman that he loves, the one he left behind upon his capture, now over a year ago. He revisits a time when they, too, rode together in a time of peace and happiness. Yet the more his thoughts indulge that occasion, the more focused he becomes on Samanda's body. Suddenly his horse misses a step and regains his balance. Aaron has to think quickly after almost being thrown and realizes he must break his former train of thought. He shakes his head profusely and then spurs his steed alongside Samanda's charger.

Both horses are now eased down to a slower pace. Aaron speaks to Samanda, "Samanda, please slow to a canter so we may speak." The horses slow to a fast walk. "The sun is half set and we must make camp for the night. The air is becoming cool and I know of a small wooded area ahead where we can have wood for a fire to warm us through the night."

Well aware that her fast pace and sexual antics are beginning to take their toll on Aaron, Samanda asserts, "I, too, know of a small wooded area, Sir Aaron, mere moments beyond the place of which you speak. If you will follow my lead, I'm sure you will find my location will place us in a better position for tomorrow's journey south. It is on the bank of the river we are using for our guide to Kaybra's camp. As well, I will need the river to bathe in before my first meeting with this legend of a woman."

Aaron reluctantly agrees to Samanda's lead. They trot toward her described location.

They arrive at the river's edge and dismount as darkness now descends upon them. Samanda and Aaron gather deadwood from the small forest and place it on a large pile. Aaron strikes flint to some dried leaves he has placed onto the pile and soon it is ablaze. With the fire crackling in front of them, they sit on a large rock, partially submerged on the shoreline. Samanda has taken rations from a sack on her horse and offers to share them with Aaron. He thanks her and begins to eat.

Aaron is curious of Samanda's sister the Queen, so he asks, "Samanda, does your sister have a name by which she is addressed among her peers?"

Samanda answers, "My sister's name is only to be used by those peers. If I was to tell you what it is and it slipped from your lips, it can cause grave circumstance. If I were you, I would be unconcerned at this point in time. When we return as victors, you will learn far more than just her name in your preparation for the third ceremony."

Unable to understand the meaning of her words, Aaron continues, "Then tell me of her past so I may ponder my future under her reign."

Samanda remains silent for a period, secretly wishing Aaron would ask questions about herself. But then she decides to confide in him and reveals some intriguing information as received by Aaron. He listens intently as she begins, "I guess as our new General of Arms, you will learn that of which I am about to state much sooner than later. My sister and I are great granddaughters of the Goddess Aphrodite, although this is not how she attained the Royal Throne. Her husband, the King, purchased her from our parents at a young age. She was more mature in shape than I at that time and if it were not for that, he likely would have purchased me in her place.

"Our father, also a brave warrior, fought many distant battles at the King's side. When my sister and I were of an age that we started to develop into women, our father was gravely wounded saving the King's life. The King brought him back home to be with us to die. It was then he laid his eyes upon my sister, who he had last seen as a small child. He promised my father on his deathbed that he would make his daughter the Queen and paid our parents much in gold and jewels for her hand.

"After the King took my sister from our abode, he placed her in his harem. Shortly thereafter our father died and our mother was greatly disappointed in his arrangement for my sister. She went to the Divine Order of the wise women of that day to protest and the King was then forced by the Order to fulfill his promise to our father or face disgrace of Royalty.

"Due to the King constantly imbibing, he became frustrated sexually and so there was never a reproductive ceremony.

"As time passed he became angry due to these frustrations and regularly beat my sister. He often locked her in her tower, ignoring her for days with no food or attention. Finally, he was asked by the elder warriors not to accompany them to battle with such an angry disposition. However, he was a mighty and capable fighter, even after forty-one seasons of his life had passed when you slew him, Sir Aaron. You should feel extremely fortunate to sit with me on this rock this day."

Aaron is astonished by this information and shows empathy for the two women's situations by placing his arm around Samanda and patting her shoulder. By now it is very dark and much time has passed.

Aaron rises and goes off to gather more wood to keep the fire stoked for the remainder of the evening. While he is gone Samanda removes her military garb and wraps a blanket around her naked body.

Aaron returns from the darkness and places the load of wood on the fire. The flames rise high, illuminating the sandy beach and the large rock on which Samanda leans with her blanket around her. She is sobbing, with elbows down at her side and holding her forehead with both sets of her fingers outstretched. Aaron, concerned approaches, he asks, "Samanda, what is wrong?"

Holding back her apparent grief, she begins, "You know that on the day after joining Kaybra, both of us may die, either by Vampressa's claws or by spears and arrows fired at us from the warring villages. We may have only one more day together as we know each other now. Before I die I must know why you won't love me."

Samanda pushes herself away from the rock and in the fluttering firelight stands before Aaron, looks into his eyes and then drops her blanket.

Aaron, fighting arousal all day long from his view of Samada's nude bottom bouncing out from under her leather skirt, becomes even weaker by the moment with each of Samanda's sobs. Her continued sobbing shrugs, causes her tears to drip off of her naked breasts at the nipple. For several long moments he stands inches from her admiring her beautiful, bare skin and full bosom. Beginning to lose control, he lowers his eyes to her golden triangle. It brings a flashback to his lovemaking act with Layla. Reliving the event with her atop him Aaron closes his eyes tightly, to fight his instincts and then agonizes as he imagines Layla's genuine pleasure-filled moans. Then, in an instant the image vanishes and he envisions Vampressa's razor-sharp talons pierce the canvas tent. He reopens his eyes in shock and screams, "NO!"

Samanda misunderstands his reaction to her modeled naked stance and now begins to legitimately cry real tears. Aaron sees her reaction and feels even worse for Samanda, who takes his outburst as his continued rejection of her. He bends over, picks her blanket up and shakes the sand from it. He then gently wraps it around her, embraces her with a surrounding gentle hug and applies a traditional kiss to her forehead. Soon, Samanda calms down as Aaron picks her up in his arms and carries her to a warm spot by the fire's edge. As he lays her down, he reaches for his blanket, rolls it up and places it under her head. He whispers, "Sleep well, Warrior Princess, for tomorrow's sun will soon rise."

Samanda, basking in what falls short of her original intentions, thinks to herself, "Yes, it will, Sir Aaron. Yes, it will." She falls fast asleep by the warm fireside as Aaron pats her hair.

*   *   *

Aaron awakes in the rays of the new sun to find Samanda's bedroll empty beside him. He looks around to gain some kind of fix on this new day, then hears Samanda scream from the direction of the woods. He jumps up and runs across the beach to her side. She is quivering horrified, pointing to the muddy ground beneath a large tree where she stands. Aaron asks, "What is it, Samanda?" Samanda, points to the ground and replies, "Look! Can you not see?"

Aaron looks where she points and observes a very-large, webbed footprint in the soft mud. "Look! Look up at this tree," Samanda exclaims. Aaron turns, looks above him and sees a huge broken branch dangling from the tree. Its bark is scratched and peeled off near the fracture in the bough.

Realizing the likelihood of what they suspect, the two face each other. They both turn their heads as one to the spot where they had been sleeping, only a short distance from the webbed imprint. Samanda grabs Aaron and clings tightly to him, reiterating, "Master General, as I said, we could be easily killed at any time. We must live each day to its utmost."

Aaron, a brave warrior, is unfazed by her comment. He takes her arms from around him and gazes across the sky as he approaches his horse. There he removes a crossbow from the harness, draws it back, cocks it and places an arrow in its slot. He walks guardedly back to Samanda, takes her hand and then returns her to the extinguished fire.

He says, "We must begin our journey today under a cloud. Please prepare the horses for our ride while I cover you." Aaron continues to scan the sky and perimeters of the small palm forest with his crossbow ready as Samanda loads the gear. They mount their horses and ride slowly along the riverbank in the direction of Kaybra's encampment.

After awhile, they pass between two tall sandstone formations. Anticipating an ambush, Aaron speeds ahead to secure the gateway. Samanda looks to the tops of the rock formations as she rides cautiously between them. After she passes Aaron's post, he joins her side. They are now beginning to become easier with their thoughts. They believe that if Vampressa was about, she would have surely attacked when they passed through such a vulnerable area as this last rock formation.

The mid-afternoon sun is now at its full height and beats its sweltering rays upon them. Conversation between them is sparse. Samanda plans her strategy for the remainder of the day, she is well aware that she has only until dawn before they merge with Kaybra's troop. Aaron rides at her side, constantly investigating the sandstone skyline with falcon-like eyes.

Samanda breaks the silence and blurts out, "The Gods cast drastic heat upon us this day!" She pauses until Aaron looks her way. Then with one hand, tugs the leather lace tie in her top that binds her breasts snugly together. Aaron looks to her just in time to witness her bulges separate as the lace now loosely crisscrosses her bosom. Samanda quips, "I'm hot!" and the scantily-clad comely female warrior whacks her horse across the neck with her crop and away they go, galloping far in front of Aaron. Aaron, concerned that she is getting too far ahead, should he need to protect her, signals his stallion to catch up with Samanda's.

As he gains on her, he sees her leather halter-top has dropped to her waist and becomes irritated that she risks her safety to taunt him. He rides faster to catch up, to scold her action.

Samanda looks over her shoulder and sees Aaron gaining. She immediately urges her horse to run faster, putting more distance between them.

Aaron sees Samanda, now quite far ahead, is approaching a similar sandstone formation, to that which they passed sometime ago. He becomes more concerned for her safety and kicks his steed hard in the ribs. Gaining only slightly, he sees her pass between the sandstone pillars and calls out,

"Samanda, wait!" He quickly returns his eyes to the sky and rearms the crossbow.

As he reaches the point where he last saw Samanda. Aaron slows to a canter as he passes between the pillars and looks around for her. Although he can see far into the distance, she is nowhere. He stops and yells out, "Samanda!" Becoming more worried as he looks about the clump of rock, once again he yells out her name, once again he receives only the forsaken echo of his voice coming back to him from the rocks. Contemplating the possibility that Vampressa may have seized Samanda and her horse in the brief time she was out of his view, Aaron feels remorse that he did not handle Samanda's prior advances upon him in a different manner.

All is quiet and the only sounds that can be heard are the caws of three ravens hopping from rock-to-rock and curiously peering at Aaron. He becomes sadder as he realizes he must possess some feeling for the woman. He starts walking his horse slowly, in an ever-widening circle trying to regain his female comrades trail in the rocky, sandy, ground of this area. Once more, now approaching desperation, he yells out, "Samanda, are you there!" The solo return of his echo once again haunts him and Aaron feels quite alone.

In silence, bewildered and saddened, Aaron rides like a somber defeated warrior in the direction of Kaybra's camp. As he emerges from the rock formation he hears a faint feminine moan and the muffled snort of another horse somewhere nearby. He dismounts and leads his horse toward two large, nearly identical boulders. There, in an opening between them, he sights the tail of Samanda's horse swishing about. Her horse is blocking any further sightline between the rocks.

Aaron approaches the animal and coaxes him away from between the rocks. There he discovers Samanda, still half clad, wedged upright tightly where the two boulders meet. She seems unconscious but bears no marks of injury about her body. Aaron is very relieved to have found Samanda. He goes to her, pulls her from the rock's wedge and caresses her bare back as he hugs her to him. "My love, are you injured? Please speak, I beg you. Please speak to me, Samanda."

Samanda's eyes have been closed all along, but now with her chin resting on Aaron's shoulder during their embrace, they pop open and gleam, as if in victory. She speaks, "Please hold me tighter, my General, my back is in great pain and your strength gives me relief." As Aaron tightens his embrace, she wiggles her sweaty, upper body against his. The crafty princess sighs as if this self-prescribed remedy is curing her pain and Aaron becomes mentally blinded as he rejoices over his partner's recovery.

He asks, "How did this come to pass that you ended up in the crotch of this huge boulder, my love?"

"I was attempting to play a game with you to raise our spirits, when a serpent spooked Windra, my horse, and he threw me into these rocks."

Samanda continues to contort her breasts and groin area of her body against Aaron, but he is unsure how to respond without once again rejecting Samanda. He continues to hold her tight as if to contain her movement, but finds himself becoming sexually aroused. Samanda feels his erection growing through his war apron and begins to smile. Not wanting this interaction to cease, she increases her seductive movements and coos, "I love you as well, Sir Aaron. I know you have loved me all along. It is just that you have had far too much to think about these last days. This is why it has taken you this long to speak those words to me." Aaron quickly recalls calling her "My love," and is now feeling the discomfort from his arousal fighting for space under his tightly wrapped leather apron. In an attempt to calm himself he tries to push Samanda away gently, but she is having nothing to do with his actions. With her arms around him firmly, she begins digging her long, sharp, painted fingernails deeper into Aaron's back as he struggles to escape her grasp.

Caught up in a sexually stimulating quandary, Aaron's strategy is to finally yield to Samanda's desires. He begins kissing her madly about her face, lips and breasts. The more intense Aaron becomes, the more Samanda relaxes. With her now sexually dazed, Aaron is able to gently move her body from his and cautiously places her inches away from him to regain his composure.

Samanda begins to cry. Angrily gritting her teeth, she begins pounding Aaron's chest, then pushes her bared breasts up with her hands as far as possible, yelling at Aaron, "Why will you not take these to be your own? Are you without a soul?" Then she throws her arms forward to resume striking Aaron.

Samanda takes one final swing at Aaron with her closed fist to his midsection before he can recapture the wild woman into his arms. She continues to cry and fight him uncontrollably. Aaron hugs her and wipes the tears from her cheeks.

Aaron has figured out that the horse and rock incident was an elaborate ruse by Samanda to capture his attention. However, he continues to feel sad about her and her sister's situation and feels he must identify his emotions for this woman and reveal them. He continues to caress her and rock her from side-to-side to calm her. As she quiets down, Aaron speaks softly, "Samanda, it is true, I do possess a love for you that I have not yet identified. Please give me time to sort my thoughts."

Samanda stops sobbing and looks up to Aaron, "So you are certain you have a love for me, Sir Aaron?"

Aaron, looking down into Samanda's face, is once again reminded of her unique similarity to her sister and replies, "Yes, of that I am certain, my love."

Samanda continues, "Can you make love to me tonight on the beach by the fire with that love you have for me, Sir Aaron?"

Aaron feels he is in a situation of déjà vu similar to the one with the Queen just before his departure. He replies, "Let us talk by the fire tonight Samanda and learn our individual needs for a healthy heart. When we can conclude those issues beyond any doubt, I desire to make passionate love to you."

Samanda is suddenly without pain. She smiles broadly at Aaron, pulls up and secures her top, skips to her horse, mounts him and says, "Please, Sir Aaron, let us depart so we may make camp by the river's edge and be rested for our meeting with Kaybra at daybreak."

Aaron knows he may have just made a huge mistake by confiding to Samanda his uncertain passions for her. However, he could find no other way of quelling her distraught emotions. The forgiving General-of-Arms felt the unfortunate woman needed some resolve so she would become refocused on the larger task at hand: war and destruction of the Harpy monster.

*   *   *

The two warriors have ridden all day toward their destination as the sun fades. They have had playful conversations about simple things and serious talks of war strategies. They crest a large sand dune in the early darkness and looking into the distance, spot the torch-lights from Kaybra's encampment. Her camp is a beehive of activity as they can faintly see and hear her people moving about across the water on a large, flat triangular island.

Aaron and Samanda smile at each other with relief, as they know the first leg of their journey will be complete at sunrise. They steer their horses carefully down the dune to a sheltered wooded valley at the riverside to make camp. Descending the sandy mound they smell game cooking, the aroma wafting across the river from Kaybra's delta village.

This smoke that drifts across the river to them from her fires makes them hungry, so they assemble dead branches and limbs, piling them high for their own fire. Samanda insists the fire is built near the water's edge and made much larger than the night before. Aaron is puzzled, but holds back his questions. He lights the fire just as he did the night before.

Aaron kills a large sand rabbit with his crossbow while gathering wood and Samanda skins and secures its carcass to a wooden spit she fabricates.She rotates it over a corner of the embers as Aaron sits in the fire's light, studying his scrolls to determine his troop's position. He knows the weather has been good and so calculates his men should be one day's ride toward the northern outskirts of the warring villages of Nemmin and Genipsus. He again rolls up the documents and returns them to their pouch, then walks to where Samanda is serving the cooked meat and sits on the blanket by her side.

She asks, "Will your portion of such a small animal be enough to cure your hunger, Sir Aaron?"

He replies, "Yes, my lady. I have been sustained on far fewer rations than this in the past. Thank you."

The couple has had two days of rugged travel in blistering heat concluded by chilly nights. Aaron appears drawn and looks forward to a relaxed evening. Samanda, however, is not and has extracurricular plans. Theirs is a pristine setting this night with the moon peeking from time-to-time in and out from behind the fluffy arid desert clouds.

Both appear captivated by their surroundings, for the terrain in this place is quite beautiful with the sea glimmering where the river meets it in the occasional moonlight. Kaybra's island, located at the river's mouth, casts a glow like the embers in their fire unto the waters. It is soothing to both Aaron and Samanda as they sit in the dessert quiet listening to the peaceful lapping sounds of the river on the golden beach. Their fire crackles and pops in the background.

Aaron lies back on the blanket, gazing up at the heavens, pondering the battles in the days before him. Samanda stares at this chiseled structure of a man, lying beside her and becomes fixed on the fire's reflection in his eyes and across his sun-soaked skin. Erotic visions begin within her. She scoots closer to him, perches herself up, squatting back on both knees and asks softly, "How do you love me, Sir Aaron?" Aaron remains silent. She continues, "Tell me how you love me, Sir Aaron. When you were concerned of my absence and injury today, you promised you would tell Samanda of your heart on this night."

Aaron is torn. He knows he must respond to maintain his honor, yet he cannot deny he is still in love with his dove from Nemmin. He is also very attracted to the Queen. Samanda's resemblance to her sister confounds Aaron's response further. He stalls again while he collects his thoughts.

Samanda remains calm, certain she can somehow force a phrase from Aaron that can condone her sensuous acts on him. She has prepared an oily skin potion before their departure from Patrious two days before and draws the vial from between her harnessed bosom where she planted it earlier. She pours it into the palm of her right hand and very slowly leans above Aaron and smears the substance beneath his rib cage and around his navel. As she applies the lotion, she once again loosens the drawstring to her top, which as she rubs both palms slowly across his abdomen, reveals the tips of her breasts. Samanda insists impetuously, "Tell me you love me!"

As she becomes impatient for a response, she curls her fingers and scrapes her razor sharp nails through the oil she has just applied. Aaron responds immediately with, "OUCH! Sorry, Samanda! I was thinking of tomorrow's conquests and I do have a love of you, but it is still difficult to determine. As you know your sister is poising me to fulfill a desire of hers that I am not entirely privy to. The Queen is a beautiful woman, not unlike you. Both of you, in fact by your actions, have awakened a part of me that was rendered dormant through many years of my strict training."

Samanda interrupts him, "You can love both of us, Sir Aaron. That is an accepted practice in our culture, especially if she proves barren. It would then be left to me to conceive the Royal child from your loins." She pauses and gently resumes rubbing his stomach.

For a short moment, her statement appears to Aaron as a possibility. Trying to sort out the truth, he again recalls Layla being forced onto him.

His mind is spinning and feeling Samanda's affects on him, he blurts out, "What of my dove, Samanda! What of her feelings?"

Samanda snaps back, "I told you, she is dead! You must move on as a brave warrior and put her in the past. Tell me, did your dove appear to you in the Queen's tower window upon your second visit Sir Warrior?" Samanda stops quickly because she knows she should not know about this occurrence.

Aaron is now even more befuddled. He misses the fact that there is no way Samanda can know of the absence of the white dove on his second visit to the Queen's tower. Actually believing the woman he really loves is likely to be dead, Aaron becomes sad. "Please, leave me with my thoughts Samanda. You know I care deeply for you, but with that information of which you speak, I need a period of silence."

Samanda replies, "I understand, Master General." She stands up at Aaron's side as he lies on his back and begins to slowly and seductively disrobe. Aaron is in agony with his thoughts, but Samanda continues her attempts to excite him. She drops her leather clothing down on top of his oily abdomen and his stomach muscles flinch when her skirt and top hit him. Samanda, standing tall and naked spreads her legs and straddles his body.

In the flickering firelight, she sucks in her glimmering, jeweled navel and heaves her breasts out, then looks down at him. "You will make love to me, Sir Aaron, before the new day's sun will rise." With the fire flickering soft light on her shapely body, Aaron is mesmerized gazing up at her sexual delights. "I am stepping into the river now to bathe for you, Master."

Not uncommon of Samanda, she once again has accomplished her goal. Aaron has only had sex one time in over a year, with Layla. He relives the encounter in his mind and begins breathing heavily as he observes Samanda's nude body splashing around playfully in the fireside's moonlit river.

Samanda does not realize she is not only exciting Aaron, but has drawn the attention of a large, black, river crocodile resting in the reeds nearby.

From Kaybra's camp, soft musical tones, jingles and women chanting in low, melodic voices float across the water. Suddenly, drumbeats begin and the music increases in tempo, further antagonizing the reptile.

Samanda seizes upon this musical extravaganza and begins to flail about in the water. A little less than waist deep in the shimmering ripples she starts belly dancing while inflicting ecstatic twitches throughout her limbs to maintain Aaron's unwavering attention on her.

The crocodile is as moved by her gyrations as is Aaron. The reptile slowly whips his eel-like tail, propelling him toward Samanda.

Aaron spots a small wake in the water with two illuminated marbles at its center heading in Samanda's direction. The water is very dark with many glimmering reflections afloat and his attention is taken from the subtle wake when Samanda calls out, "Help me, Master, I cannot stay afloat!" To Aaron, due to the shallow mud pocketed shoreline, Samanda appears to once again feign self-inflicted tragedy. Although he is completely aroused by Samanda, only within a few short leaps from him, he remains only at the end of his blanket, watching her antics intently to make sure there is no real danger.

In an instant, Samanda's facial expression turns to utter horror, her eyes bulge and she screams in terror, "OUCH… OH…OUCH… PLEASE… PLEASE HELP ME!" Aaron is now certain that something is drastically wrong. He leaps to his feet immediately and just as he does, the croc lunges up through the water, flopping and twisting about with Samanda's body clenched between his jaws. The slimy black reptile twists and splashes her flopping legs and arms about the water's surface.

In an instant, Aaron tears his war apron off, grabs Samanda's combat knife from her discarded garments and attacks the croc. The huge reptile releases Samanda, then lunges at Aaron as Samanda wails in the background.

The water swirls and boils as Aaron wrestles ferociously with the snapping, aquatic beast. Seizing a split-second opportunity, he jabs the knife through the crock's eye, into his brain and twists the blade with a flick of his wrist. Instantly, the reptile floats belly up to the water's surface.

Samanda is crying and crawling though the shallow water on her hands and knees toward the shore. Aaron, drenched and bloodied from combat, picks her up, takes a few short steps and collapses with Samanda in his arms into the slippery mud. They both lie face down in the slippery, clay putty. Their bodies still in the water from the waistline down, panting deeply from exhaustion both Samanda and Aaron's stomachs pat the waterline and mud as they inhale and exhale. Aaron catches his breath first and carefully rolls Samanda over onto her back. Samanda is covered with a coat of wet yellow clay from her chin to her waist and is laboring hard to breathe.

Aaron, somewhat exhausted, strains to rise to his knees, slips his arm beneath her body and arches her upward. With water still dripping from his long curly locks, he leans down over Samanda, covers her lips with his and begins blowing into her open mouth. He continues to pump air into her lungs until he hears her softly moan. He stops briefly, lifts his head up, and then looks down to see if her eyes have opened as he watches her face intently. Shortly thereafter, her eyes open wide and she smiles at him. "Samanda, are you injured badly?" he asks.

She whispers back, "No, my hero. I am only shaken. Come to me." Samanda reaches her arms up around Aaron's neck, pulls him back down to her wet, muddy, naked body. They lie there, he on top of her, breathing as one as the water laps onto the shoreline around their loins. They close their eyes and rest in this position for some time.

Samanda awakes, places her hand below the water's edge and proceeds to fondle Aaron. Feeling her caress, Aaron opens his eyes and raises himself a few inches above the determined women. Wet mud from Samanda's breasts have created a mirror imprint on his chest. He straddles Samanda and looking down on her realizes he is quickly becoming helpless to her hand motions on his manhood. "Please, Samanda, stop." Aaron pleads.

"But you are my hero. I am only trying to be obedient by washing the mud from your sheath," she replies, smiling.

From Aaron's vantage point, he sees that the yellow clay that coats the front of Samanda's torso is drying. It begins to crack apart slightly and then goes back together again as she takes shallow breaths in and out. The water laps up and across her pierced navel jewelry as the scheming woman lies on her back underneath Aaron. The tips of her breasts have become firm in the cool, night air.

Aaron, becoming uncontrollably aroused, looks toward the nearby fire, closes his eyes tightly, and clenches his jaw, thinking, "How shall I proceed with this sensuous maiden's enticement? Her firm hand on my swollen shaft gives me such painful pleasure that I cannot reason properly. If I perform this act, what will I report to the Queen and how can I face my dove if she is unharmed upon my return?" He opens his eyes and pleads, "Please? Please, Samanda, you must release me!"

Aaron's appeal falls on deaf ears as Samanda firms her grasp upon him. Aaron struggles to pull back and slips deeper into the clay, but Samanda refuses to release her grip as he tries to stand. She shoots back at him, "Master, you are delirious from the crock's bites. I am now waxed and in position to receive your seed. Please do not fail me at this moment?"

Aaron has returned to a crouch and has his feet under him, but when he tries to stand, they slip into a deep mud pocket and his feet and legs sink down into it. He is stuck to his knees in the mire. Samanda, still hanging on is pleased. Knowing Aaron is now very vulnerable, she takes her free hand, cups the water in it and splashes it onto his mud-covered loins. It quickly becomes obvious to her that this excites Aaron even further and so she jiggles her clenched hand. The other is cupped with water.

Aaron, now on the verge of relenting, is totally prone. He tries one last plea, "Samanda, please no. Stop your actions…" Samanda, however is relentless in her pursuit of his body and strokes Aaron faster and harder. She pulls on him to aid her to her knees in the mud in front of him.

Her actions are occasionally painful and the thought of striking Samanda briefly crosses Aaron's mind. But having never struck a woman in his life, he counters by attempting to push her body back by forcing her shoulders from him.

Unable to move his legs, Aaron is hopelessly trapped. The muddy wet commotion of the situation does little to diminish the sexual excitement between them. Every time he grabs for Samanda's wet shoulders she easily wiggles and slips away. Aaron briefly gives up the struggle, becoming exhausted he places his hands on his hips and then closes his eyes. Samanda, unfazed, continues splashing water onto him and she grips him so tightly that, the tendons in her forearm flex. He groans with discomfort as she does this, attempting another strategy, Aaron appears to totally succumb to Samanda's designs. However, his heavy breathing in anticipation of her next move gives him away.

Samanda stops stroking Aaron, who in a continued attempt to discourage her, chooses not to open his eyes and look downward. She raises her free hand between his thighs. Smiling up to him, she firmly closes her hand around what she knows she would find there. Aaron's plan is foiled and he is throbbing with ecstatic anticipation over Samanda's next maneuver. She casually says, "Master, forgive me, but I must take advantage of this rare occurrence. It is written that once I receive your seeds, you will have no choice but to love me for eternity. Now stay still and I will give you as great a pleasure as you will give me."

Aaron, trembles with Samanda's last statement. She opens both squeezed hands, releasing him. Now Aaron opens his eyes and looks down at Samanda. She locks her eyes upward to his, places both of her hands on top of his, pushes them firmly to his side, opens her mouth wide and moves in on him. He cries out, "No! Samanda, No!" But Samanda is a strong woman and by the time Aaron frees his hands from hers, it is too late. She has replaced her first grip with her serpent, sucking lips, far down on Aaron. Both of her cheeks hollow deeply as her lips tug on his manly stalk. Mightily trying to hang on to his values he screams, "Stop, please, please, no more! Please stop!!!"

Samanda takes no direction from Aaron, so he reaches down with both of his large calloused hands and cups Samanda's petite head between them. He attempts to force her head back, but she struggles to stay onboard by reaching around his backside and clamping her fingers into his buttock. Aaron, endures this new inflicted pain, curls his fingers tightly into Samanda's hair and scalp and once again attempts to pull her mouth off him. As he does so, Samanda gently bites down for an instant, warning him not to try that again. She is going nowhere. Her action brings his excitement to an even higher level and he groans aloud, "Oh. Oh," acknowledging her threat is well understood.

Aaron, over-indulged now between the heights of pleasure and pain, realizes he is Samanda's helpless captive and throws his head back, moaning loudly in anguish and delirium, as he gazes into the moonlit sky. He is instantly mortified as he clearly sees Vampressa circling high above them like a vulture. Terrified of the obvious he screams out, "Samanda, you must stop! Vampressa is circling above."

Samanda is so completely indulged, she quickly convinces herself his statement must be a ruse to get her to stop, so she bites down on him hard this time and rapidly shakes her head back and forth, like a spoiled little girl indicating, No! No! No!

Already warned once not to try and withdraw, due to his second offence, her last bite was not a playful one. Aaron excitedly and painfully bewails, "OW...OW...OW!" He grips his hands back onto Samanda's shoulders, bows his head and closes his eyes again to accept his fate. Samanda continues to work on Aaron. Sensing he is about to fire his seeds into her mouth he slides his hands to her neck and squeezes uncontrollably as he groans to a climax.

Aaron exhales, sighs and drops his arms to his sides. Samanda continues to suck on him as if certain there is more to come. Aaron, completely defeated whispers, "Stop Samanda, please? Stop."

Suddenly Aaron feels something cold pressed across his bare abdomen. He opens his eyes to see a broadsword's flat side pressed up against him just above Samanda's lips. The blade's edge faces down and Samanda's eyes are still closed. He screams, "Samanda open your eyes!" She finally does and peers upon the huge sword's blade. She sees her nose and lips reflecting back to her from its glimmer. Samanda quickly cocks her eyes up and to the left as Aaron turns his head in the same direction. They see Kaybra towering over both of them grasping the sword's handle.

Kaybra scolds Samanda, "Remove your mouth from this man's appendage or you shall possess it permanently." Samanda, looking to Kaybra, slowly withdraws her ruby red wet lips from him.

Aaron, shaking, announces, "Thank you, Kaybra. May the Gods above praise you for your action."

Kaybra flings her sword onto a dry area of the beach. She, a head taller than Aaron, steps behind him, bends down, places her arms under his and pulls him up and out of the mud. This sight makes Aaron look as if he were a mere boy. She takes two steps toward the fire and sets him down on the blanket, kneels, and then wraps the blanket around him like a shawl. Samanda has meanwhile scampered from the waters edge, gathered her clothing and dresses in the shadow of a nearby boulder.

Kaybra is impressive, lanky and well-proportioned with long, straight, black hair down to the center of her back. Her skin is a deep tan color and she wears a white leather outfit and white headband that accentuates her dark skin. It greatly resembles Samanda's uniform in style except for her top. While it is just as revealing as Samanda's it has thick aquatic-like reflective scales woven throughout it. When she walks, the scales make a jangling sound. She is an attractive younger middle-aged woman.

Kaybra moves halfway between Aaron and Samanda, puts her hands on her hips as if in disgust. She looks back and forth at each of them and states, "The next time I go hunting for Harpy monsters, I'm sure I'll know where to find two pieces of live bait for my traps. Have the two of you not experienced enough terror from Vampressa that you carry on this way?"

Aaron is miffed for he feels none of this would have happened if it were not for Samanda's sexual aggressions. He casts a sullen look across to Samanda. She cowers, glances at the ground and slinks behind the large rock. Aaron turns back to Kaybra. "When you spoke of using Samanda and me for live bait, you stated 'Monsters.' Forgive me for my thought, but are you telling us there are more monsters out there besides Vampressa?"

Kaybra replies, "There have been many changes in that breed of monster since your youth when you and your father battled them. We will speak more of this matter upon tomorrow's dawn. For now, you and Samanda must harness your horses and come with me to my village of tents. There you will be able to bathe and rest in safety. Please be prompt, so that we may cross the river in the remaining moonlight."

Samanda and Aaron, still partially soiled from their muddy sexual escapade, follow Kaybra's command. They follow her along the river a short distance where she finds a shallow watery path across the shimmering currents to her island.

As they ride, Aaron wonders how Kaybra knows about him and his father.

Chapter Four

As day breaks across Kaybra's sandy delta encampment, there is much hustle and bustle throughout the village. Aaron awakes from all the disquiet in the small, round, top tent provided to him by Kaybra the night before. He has slept well and is adequately rested. He dresses in full uniform and exits the tent's canvas opening to relocate an area he and Samanda were shown the previous evening for the morning feast.

This is truly a village of tents. Some are very small, others, carnival-like. The smoke from small campfires burns throughout this nomadic looking village. Odors come mostly from food cooking. Small wind-chimes tinkle in the background from the faint sea breezes as Aaron strides his way between the poles, ropes and stakes supporting dwellings. Murmurs are heard from the village's people who mill about.

Aaron becomes uncertain of his path from the night before and worries he may have lost his way. Then he spots Samanda in front of him, passing on a main artery of foot travel. Samanda is in route from the tent assigned to her the night before by Kaybra. Aaron signals her with a whistle and they join pace to locate the camps breakfast area.

As they walk, Samanda asks, "How did you rest last evening, Sir Aaron?"

"Quite nicely, thank you. I see your wounds from the large reptile are superficial. Do they cause you any pain, my dear?"

Samanda replies, "I am in a little distress, but I must speak to you about last evening."

"Go on." Replies Aaron.

Samanda speaks further, "I am dedicated to you for saving my life from now until my last day, Master. You should be concerned of your scars from the beast, not mine. Now I love you in far too many ways to tell you. Your every desire will be my command. You are a sturdy man and possess the heart of a true King. Forgive me for my acts upon your person in the moonlight. Some day you will understand and when that day comes, you will have no question of your love for me."

Aaron is impressed by Samanda's beautiful radiance and finds it difficult to spurn her advances from last evening and replies, "You are forgiven, Samanda, but we must wait until that day you speak of before we go further with our bond. Please try to understand."

By now, they have reached Kaybra's huge round table of bounty. Kaybra defines its head by merely being seated at it. There are sixteen seats surrounding the table and all but two are occupied by Kaybra's fellow warriors, who are both men and women. The two empty seats are one at her left and right. In the center of the table is a smorgasbord of aromatic cooked and fresh morning foods.

Kaybra signals her guests to be seated in the two empty seats. Upon their being seated, all join hands, close their eyes and tilt their heads back to face the sky. Kaybra chants aloud unto the heavens. "Let the Gods be with our forces in our coming battles. Let the shifting sands of time bury our foes as the hourglass of time drains. Instill within us, your ancestor's hieroglyphs of death, judgment and eternity. May the great God, Anubis, accurately weigh the hearts of all of those who fall."

All members at the table release their hands, lower their heads and talk amongst themselves, peeking occasionally at Samanda and Aaron. Kaybra barks out, "Be still with your thoughts, my warriors! My old friend, the Queen of Patrious, seeks the feat that lies before us. Seated by my side are her chosen warriors, Samanda and the great warrior, Aaron, of whose conquests we are all familiar.

"The villages of Genipsus and Nemmin to our north continue to make war between themselves. Should this conflict spill beyond the battling factions, the peaceful existence of our own land will be threatened.

"Messengers tell us that many, if not all of the Queen's men have been killed or ravaged of their reproductive organs. That this hideous atrocity has been accomplished by a Harpy known as Vampressa. She feeds on them to fertilize a large nest of her own eggs, hidden somewhere in the desert.

"The situation is of dire consequence to the continuation of the Queen's race. Should the monster's nest hatch, we as well may become Harpy victims, as did our ancestors generations ago.

"Now, dine. Upon completion of your meal, cross the river to the east and move your troops north to the western outskirts of Genipsus. Make camp and await our arrival. We must align with the warrior, Aaron's, forces, who will converge on Genipsus from the northwest.

"Aaron will lead Samanda and myself. We will detour the usual routes, taking a shortcut by way of the Valley of the Phantom Pyramids, which will ultimately place us in the middle of both of our forces. With Aaron's lead, our combined forces will converge upon Genipsus. With this strategy, their troops will be trapped by our flanks between the Gorge of the Damned and the rapids of the river.

"No warrior, male or female, is to fight the monster, Vampressa, except for Aaron. If he alone does not slay the monster, he will be identified as a coward by the Queen of Patrious and their union will be incomplete.

"You have been given your instructions. Gather your rations, weapons and supplies. Now feast and depart."

The warriors gobble down their food with little discussion and depart as Kaybra has instructed.

Samanda, Kaybra and Aaron remain seated and have been in a complex discussion regarding the lineage of Harpies; Vampressa in particular. Due to many generations of her forefather's writings on the subject, Kaybra has become an expert of sorts on the different Harpy breeds.

She explains to Aaron that because he as a young warrior and his father scourged Vampressa from their village years ago, it has angered her. The Harpy now feels she has a score to settle with him. Kaybra continues, explaining that he would be a trophy for Vampressa if she could extract his seeds and use them to fertilize her eggs. The result would be an army of his offspring under her command. Kaybra tells him of the ability of some Harpies to transform their feathery bodies to appear as objects and animals they are not. She admits, she has no personal knowledge of Vampressa individually, but cautions him with what she had read in her ancestors ancient scriptures.

Samanda, although concerned with Kaybra's topic of conversation, focuses the bulk of her attention on Aaron.

Aaron asks Kaybra how she is so familiar with the Queen. Samanda and Kaybra look at each other and smile. Samanda shakes her head slightly, signaling "No" to Kaybra. Aaron, perplexed with Kaybra's silence, asks her to define her earlier statement of a union between him and the Queen. Once again, the two women turn to each other and hold back a giggle. Kaybra, smiles, "Remain loyal to the Queen, Sir Aaron, and you will find out in due time.

"As of now, our horses have been harnessed and prepared for our journey. Would it be your command that we depart for the Valley of the Phantom Pyramids at this time, Sir Aaron?"

Aaron says nothing, but rises from the table, gives the girls a solemn glance and places the palm of his hand outward, saying, "To the tent stables, my ladies." The girls get up and Kaybra, who towers over the other two, swaggers off, hips swaying in her tight, white leather battle skirt. She heads to where their horses are tethered with Samanda and Aaron behind, looking like two youths following their mother.

Departing from Kaybra's camp, the hooves of the warriors' magnificent steeds splash into the river from the sandy shoreline. They ride three abreast, through a shallow area of the river's wandering flow, around the island. They reach the east side of the river and signaling their chargers in unison, break into a gallop, riding northward along the river.

They reach a point where Aaron points across to the west side of the river. Samanda and Kaybra turn their heads to see what it is he motions them to look at. They see remnants of the large burned out campfire, where Samanda forced her sexual advances on Aaron the night before. It still smolders, emitting thin strings of smoke high into the sky. Aaron makes a face at Samanda and rolls his eyes back into his head. Samanda ignores Aaron's antics, refocuses on the trail and abruptly signals her horse to resume its pace.

Sometime later, all three slow their horses to a walk and continue at this pace until mid-day. As they walk they have extensive conversations reaffirming Aaron's battle plan and timing. Aaron has calculated, barring any mishaps, his troops should arrive at their post by dawn of the second sun.

He also begins to question Kaybra's influence on him to take the route through the Valley of the Phantom Pyramids. Kaybra, understanding his concern, recites from her ancestor's scriptures, "You must trust my decision, Sir Aaron. It is written that the Valley of the Phantom Pyramids holds a multitude of mystic knowledge, for it is here that spirits dwell as far back as the beginning of mankind. It is also true that many are possessed and evil. However, a like number of them are just and fair-minded. As the sun sets each day, they engage each other in gladiator fashion to see which side will prevail, giving the victor the undisputed right to rule the following day.

"We pray that when we arrive, the just and fair-minded spirits are victorious and rule that day. One of my couriers has placed rations and a tent near the area where we must make our camp tonight.

"Tomorrow we will enter the Valley and seek information as to the whereabouts of the Harpy nest. Hope is much of what we have left, Sir Aaron, for if the eggs hatch, our nations will surely fall."

Aaron concedes to Kaybra's knowledge and influence. Samanda appears worried as she affectionately glances at Aaron. Then once again, they spur their steeds as one and gallop away from the river northeastward over the sands.

As they approach the horizon, they spot the large clump of bound goods, left by Kaybra's courier. Upon reaching the spot, they dismount and tie the reins of the three chargers together. They stand obediently as the their riders fetch prepared water portions from the supply bundle to quench the their thirst.

Evening is soon upon them and they set up their small tent. Kaybra asks Samanda to not burn the small amount of brush and timber she has gathered, explaining her concern that the flames might attract attention to them. The tent is of a heavy material and camouflaged to match the surrounding sands.

Kaybra enters the small, tent and motions Aaron and Samanda to come join her. Once inside, Kaybra lights a miniature oil lamp and the three sit around it in a triangular fashion. They dine on dates, nuts, and wine from a large, goat hide flask.

After a brief conversation, Kaybra announces she is going to retire. Aaron and Samanda look around, questioning the available space inside the tent. But Kaybra insists they all stay inside for safety and to maintain the comfortable temperature from their body heat. Aaron and Samanda proceed to roll out their blankets.

Kaybra prepares her bedroll and without a second thought, unlaces her top, unsnaps a ruby clasp between her breasts and pulls the top off. She then wiggles out of her war skirt and tosses both to the side. Remaining seated on her blanket, she bends forward with arms outstretched, unlaces and removes her boots.

Samanda notes Kaybra's uninhibited demeanor. Not to be outdone, she follows her lead and does the same. Aaron, somewhat startled, forces himself not to react. He reasons it must be a nightly procedure for Kaybra. While bent forward undoing her boots, both Samanda and Aaron, in such a confined space, are forced to notice the huge size of Kaybra's shapely breasts. Kaybra might be a large woman, but certainly not unattractive.

Kaybra, upon removal of her footwear, sits upright and looks down at her bosom, crisscrossed with impressions of lines from her tightly-laced top. Using both hands she gives each breast a slow, deep massage. When finished with that procedure, Kaybra grasps each one, and jiggles them upward briefly, as if to fluff them up. She then lies flat on her back and falls fast asleep. Once again, not to be outdone, Samanda does the same, mimicking Kaybra.

Aaron, sitting between two totally naked women, stares at them in disbelief as the oil lamp flickers its dim light across the naked women's bodies.

He is intrigued by something he noticed during Kaybra's self-massage, so he leans over Kaybra's uncovered bosom to confirm what he thought he saw. Her massive breasts are now flattened slightly across her chest, which makes it clear to see that they are badly scarred in several places. The proud flesh looks the result of long-healed punctures and slashes. Her nipples are large and dark, the areola nearly white, in sharp contrast to her deep bronze skin at her tan line.

Aaron thinks, "What type of injuries has this lavish structure of a woman suffered?"

As if reading Aaron's mind, Kaybra opens one eye and whispers, "I will tell you tomorrow. Now go to sleep."

Samanda has also awakened and jealously reaches to Aaron, pulls him by the hair from above Kaybra's chest and onto his bedroll. After she has him settled at her side, she stretches over Aaron's head in the cozy proximity of which the three lie and blows out the oil lamp. All goes dark.

Aaron, tired and distraught, falls asleep quickly and immediately finds himself in an obscure dream world where his thoughts whirl him down, through a spinning vortex as he is deposited amid a raging battle. He lies in a fetal position, helpless, with the hooves of clashing warriors' horses thrashing about him, each barely missing him. He hears a female voice call out, "Lie still, Sir Aaron and I will save you!" He raises his head, slightly up through the dusty horses' bellies and combating warriors to see Kaybra valiantly dividing her opponents as she urges her mount to where he lies.

She comes closer, while deflecting many arrows and swords from her by using her arm shields. She finally reaches a spot near where he lies and as Aaron looks on, choking in the dust, an arrow skewers itself through both her breasts and Kaybra throws her head back in shock. A chucked spear now smashes far into her rib cage and her face shows excruciating pain as she pulls at the spear to remove it. As she tugs at the spear, a flurry of arrows strike her, most penetrating her chest. Her white outfit is drenched in blood as she falls to the ground, her body tumbling over and over, up to Aaron. He looks at her in tears as she tries to speak to him, but only scarlet fluids come from between her lips. She closes her eyes and her body goes limp.

Aaron is jolted awake from his nightmare in a cold sweat, languishing in disillusion. He flints the oil lamp aglow and checks both women. They are both safe and rest peacefully. Unable to return to sleep, he quietly exits the tent and stands, staring up at the stars. He wipes his face, head between his hands, questioning the limits of his own strength and mental endurance.

A short time passes and he feels a tap on his shoulder. Startled, he turns abruptly and finds Kaybra standing there, her long, black hair pulled down covering her nakedness. She speaks, "You have come through much turmoil since the last full moon and your prior labors in the mine, Sir Aaron." Kaybra pulls Aaron against her naked body. She cuddles him and places his head between her breasts and rubs his back. She continues her attempt to soothe him as she invites him, "Come back into the tent and lie down with your women warriors. We are a unit that shall not fail each other. Now, come. Dawn will soon be upon us."

Aaron takes her hand and lets Kaybra lead him back to bed.

The millions of stars that shimmer throughout the night sky creates an eerie shadow onto the desert floor, cast from Vampressa, as once again she circles her prey from high above.

*   *   *

The three warriors have broken down their bivouac and have their horses harnessed. Aaron has divided and secured most of the supplies among the steeds. Should they return that way, he buries the remaining lot in the sand topped by a stone marker.

Like three crusaders against evil, they mount up and gallop off toward the sunrise. By high noon, they begin to see what they believe are the images of the Phantom Pyramids in the far distance. They ride toward them, but the distant images grow no larger. They drive their chargers harder, but once again the pyramids are no closer. Aaron throws his hand up and halts the charge. They stop to confer about this strange situation they have encountered.

Looking around as they speak, they notice monumental pyramids to their immediate rear, in the direction from which they just rode. In disbelief, they turn back to the direction they were heading and find an identical sight. Kaybra says, "This is the place. Quick, follow my lead!"

Kaybra gallops between the endless rows of pyramids and with their mounts snorting, Samanda and Aaron follow her in an identical pace. From time to time, Kaybra cuts her charger to the left, then to the right, dodging around the pyramids for no apparent reason. The other two mimic her every maneuver. Suddenly they emerge into a large, square opening surrounded by rows and rows of pyramids situated in repeated frame-like formations out and around the clearing. They halt their steeds and are in awe as they gaze around them at the pointed maze of structures extending into the skies.

All around them goes deathly silent and the horses begin to snort and twitch nervously. The wind slowly picks up, blowing between the structures' bases into the center square. Strangely it blows inward from all directions, gaining velocity and hurling tumbleweeds and walls of sand through the aisles between the pyramids.

The three riders urge their steeds beside one of the huge pyramid foundation blocks closest to them. They grab their bedrolls from behind them and wrap their bodies to shroud themselves, in an attempt to thwart the fierce sandblasting onslaught. The wind reaches fierce proportions as it circles the center square, turning itself into a raging cyclone with its enormous, dark-brown, funnel cloud forming before them.

Just as mysteriously as the storm manifested itself, it begins to subside. The immense, swirling cloud becomes faint and settles to the ground. As the dust fades, a tremendous structure appears in its place. It is a coliseum of great proportion, circular in structure, much like the winds that formed it. It is magnificent in appearance, towering well over half the height of the pyramids that surround it, with scores of flags anchored around its roof, flapping in the breeze. Each colorful flag depicts a mythological creature. The bright colored flags carry insignias of wealth and good of mankind. The deep violet, black and grey flags bear coiled asps, skulls and demonic representations on them.

Aaron, Samanda and Kaybra stand at its base in awe. They hear the voices of thousands of people roaring outward from within its interior. Sometimes the voices cheer with praise and applaud; other times they boo and hiss with displeasure. The three secure their horses and cautiously enter the stadium through its regal arched entryway. They find scores of spectators seated around the perimeter of the structure in curved bleachers that rake upward from the center ring. They're screaming and yelling at four gladiators going at each other with whips, bladed chains and metal-spurred balls they swing about.

The trio seems to go unnoticed during this fracas of bloody entertainment. Kaybra tells the other two, "It is written that they cannot see us, for they are of another dimension in time." The three walk about, staring at the spectators, people of every age and gender, who all appear to be from another era. Eventually, they find an empty row of seats high, in an upper mezzanine and the three sit, just as the crowd stands and roars. They cheer with approval as the final gladiator is slain by his opponent. The victor turns and bows to a large, unoccupied golden throne high up, in a royal grandstand directly opposite from them. The helmeted swordsman exits the ring and enters into a dark, shadowy arched opening that tunnels down under the rows of the stands.

Darkness begins to set in, creating a crescent shaped shadow that arches across the interior of the stadium. The shadow, cast from the structure's massive circular wall, steadily creeps to the other side like an eyelid slowly closing. The golden hue cast upon the desert fades to darkness as the sun falls below the horizon disappearing behind the framed grid of pyramids to the west.

A nervous murmur is heard from the spectators, as if the arrival of darkness has somehow tantalized the crowd. The arena is now pitch black and curiously dead silent, as if great anticipation has numbed everyone's tongue.

Dozens of white, glowing orbs, one by one emerge from the sandy, blood-drenched center ring, looking like large, round bubbles escaping from pools of hot lava. Then, they float upward, to the top of the stadium walls where they hover, side-by-side, like one huge bracelet. High in the air, they create a radiant cylinder of ghostly, white light that beams downward, on the center ring.

The mass of spectators "Oohh and Aah," at the sight of this radiant spectacle. The last orb floats up drifting toward Samanda and gently touches her extended palm briefly before it rises and completes the ring of light. Once again the crowd goes silent, although a few viewers try to shush the others to bring complete quiet to the air. Everyone waits with great anticipation.

Soon, their patience pays off. The curtain of darkness at the right of the ring is broken and a soft murmur echoes through the arena. The curtain unveils six, sparkling-white armored skeletons, who proceed into the cylinder of light from the black. They act as pallbearers, carrying a large, carved, golden sarcophagus into the center of the ring, which they set on the sand. They bow to the vault and return into the darkness from which they came. Upon their exit, six other armored skeleton pallbearers enter from the left. This squad of six, are dark grey and break the darkness placing their polished, silver sarcophagus beside the one of gold. Then, just as the other six, they bow to their coffin and exit in the same fashion as did the white pallbearers before them.

The two sarcophagi are of contrasting designs. One glimmers gold in the white eerie light, its top carved with pastoral settings of fruit trees growing from monetary tokens. The trees are plentiful and have songbirds in their boughs, chirping notes that float on the air. The sides are completely covered with carved heads of wise, owl-like fowl.

The other sarcophagus glows pewter grey into the light. Like a map going in every direction, it has shiny black carvings of demons and snakes twisted together surrounding its exterior.

As if pressure was building up inside, thin ribbons of deep purple smoke oozes from between the lid and the box. The heavy vapor flows down the side of the coffin and increases until thick billows of dark purple and ruby fumes drain out of the ominous container to the floor of the ring, carpeting the entire circle. The choking smoke begins to billow upward into the cylinder of light. Like wine, poured into the bottom of a straight, clear glass vase, its level rises.

Both coffins are now nearly covered, when suddenly the horrendous sounds of wailing voices are heard, like those of tortured men and women screaming. The shrieks come from deep within the silver and black vault. Remnants of sulfur smelling smoke, permeates the air of the circular structure as the spectators are frozen to their seats. Not a sound is heard from them. Moments after the agonizing voices begin, naked men and women appear, splashing around amid the thick smoke, engaged in an intense, sadistic orgy. The participants curse and scream at each other as they engage in the lewd sexual folly. There are so many naked bodies squirming tightly together and flailing around, that some spill over the edges into the darkness. Those meeting this fate scream out tortuous, descending calls, as if they were plummeting off a cliff to their death on the jagged rocks below.

A loud, demonic growl overcomes their cries of pain and the lid of the pewter sarcophagus blows off, spinning high into the air. It tumbles end-over-end until it stops ascending and then falls downward into the center of the arena, splashing back into the violet pool of damned souls. A suction begins inside the coffin and the growling roars are accompanied by demonic cackles as the pool of smoke mixed with the members of the wailing orgy are pulled back into the box. As it is drawn back into the sarcophagus, the red solution resembles spilled wine, filled with flagellating maggots being sucked into a straw.

The golden sarcophagus remains in its place, unscathed in the wake of this gruesome event. The center of the ring is now as it was and all voices, smoke and noises have faded away.

Aaron, Samanda and Kaybra are drawn to the edge of their bench and join hands. They cannot take their eyes off of the lit cylinder. Kaybra whispers to her companions, "According to the writings of my ancestors, there is much yet to come."

With those words just out of Kaybra's mouth, the lid to the golden sarcophagus slides slowly to one side by two large, golden hands that place the lid at the edge of the box and then it tips onto the ground. The golden hands return into the sarcophagus.

A giant pharaoh slowly emerges from the box. He is an awesome golden color from his headdress to his sandals. He squeezes out of his ornate casket, and stands tall. Several times larger than either sarcophagus, he towers over his opponent's smoldering coffin and dons a huge, golden mask with a smile permanently jeweled onto it. In his right hand he clutches a sharp, pointed weapon in the shape of a huge phallus. It is the length of his leg, from hip to toe. Edged on both sides, the blade twinkles along its razor-sharp edges. He sticks the point of his weapon into the ground beside him, rests his hand on its hilt and tilts his head down, staring into the open pewter sarcophagus at his feet.

More horrific roars come from inside the box and two puffs of violet smoke blast out at his knees, accompanied by loud, hideous cackles. Immediately following the cackling, suddenly a flock of chicken-sized Harpies whiz out of the box and attack the pharaoh's neck and facemask. They bite and scratch his eyes and throat and the pharaoh lets loose his sword, needing both hands to pick his attackers from his face.

Knowing the Pharaoh is now distracted, his adversary leaps from his pewter vault. He is a monster part lion from the center of his back to his forehead with the face and jaws of a crocodile and hindquarters of a hippopotamus. In a targeted lizard-like leap, he attacks the pharaoh about his upper thighs and groin. The pharaoh desperately tries to rid himself of the Harpy onslaught.

The golden giant groans from pain as the monster's gator-jaws crunch together between his legs as he collects the Harpies by their legs and viciously shakes them. Their feathers fly about in the air like a down pillow that's split. The golden giant, now with his smiling his face, beats them into bloody submission across the head and eyes of the attacking monster. Their carcasses are plucked and dismembered. Tossing the carcasses aside, the pharaoh swoops down to retrieve his saber and when he does so, the monster releases him and retreats like a cornered animal. The two spar round and round in the circle, tossing and wrestling for hours, each grappling for a position of dominance.

Aaron is entranced by the conflict before him, while Samanda has noticed a young girl seated with her elders a few rows in front of the trio. The girl has been constantly squirming back and forth, viewing the action and then her elders, but mainly Aaron, Samanda and Kaybra. Several times Samanda and Kaybra have noticed that she gestures to her elders, pointing at the three warriors who are seated directly behind them. The elders appease the young girl by turning and looking in their direction, but they obviously do not see what she sees, so they hand motion to the child as if she is crazy.

The battle has raged for several hours and the first rays of the new dawn are quickly approaching.

The next time their young admirer looks their way, Samanda and Kaybra beckon the young girl to come to them. She cautiously looks to her elders and then crawls the two rows up to Aaron and the girls. Although Aaron pays little attention to her, Samanda and Kaybra immediately gain a rapport with the girl by letting her handle some of their glittery jewelry.

After talking with the girl they learn she has overheard her parents speak of the giant Harpy's attacks, as well as her notorious hidden nest of eggs. The women coax the girl into asking her elders specifically about the nest's location. Kaybra pulls an emerald pin from her headband and offers it in exchange for this information. The girl smiles with glee, scampers back down to her elders and whispers in their ears. At first, they shush her and point toward the confrontation in the arena, but as she persists, they relent to keep her from distracting them from the action before them. The youth hops back up to the two women to convey what she has learned and consummate the jewelry proposition.

By now, the many hours of battle are showing wear on the pharaoh and the triple dispositions of the monster. Unyielding, the pharaoh quickly raises his phallus-shaped weapon high in the air with the blade pointed down. The monster, also weakening, makes a wrong move and the golden pharaoh jabs his weapon of fertility through the beast's rib cage and out the other side. The beast flops around like a gaffed fish, then collapses, with blood gushing from the massive wound. Even in death one of his reptile eye-lids still twitches.

The giant pharaoh bends down and grasping both ends of his long weapon, picks it up with the monster's lifeless body dangling from the blade. Standing up straight, he raises it above his head and offers it to the crowd as he pivots around. The crowd screams and cheers, showering him with loud applause for his victory.

The pharaoh walks to the pewter vault, which continues to smolder, then lays his weapon on it, crossways, over the rectangular opening. The beast's head and rump hang downward into the opening of the vault, as if it were on a spit over a fire as the golden pharaoh walks calmly back to his own portable tomb, slowly steps inside, scrunches down and magically fits his body flat inside.

Just as the first twinkle of sun touches the flags atop the arena, the two teams of skeletons race to the center ring. The pharaoh's six skeletons wait impatiently for the monster's six skeleton pallbearers to un-skewer the remains of their beast. They agonizingly try to get the dead animal into its coffin without getting blood on themselves, when finally, one skeleton from the Pharaoh's team marches to where the others work and jerks the sword from the hideous villain's carcass. The monster's body falls into the box. He then returns the sword to the Pharaoh's tomb and places it inside the coffin with him.

Both teams of skeletons secure the lids of their containers, pick them up and march off into the shadows.

Samanda, Aaron and Kaybra stand to seek the exit from the arena, but realize no one else stands beside them. The spectators remain seated, talking between themselves enthusiastically about the battle between the titans. As they walk down the ramp, past the young girl with her elders, it is obvious the elders still cannot see them, but the young girl smiles and waves vigorously with Kaybra's emerald pin clenched tightly in her other hand.

The three descend the raked tiers of seats and find the grand, arched opening through which they entered. They exit the stadium and find their horses waiting at the base of the pyramid. Someone or something has mysteriously watered and fed them. Samanda and Aaron look at each other in disbelief. Kaybra states, "Such a benevolent act would have never come to pass if the Pharaoh would have perished in today's conflict." As if to thank the Pharaoh, they all turn to face the stadium, when they do this, to their astonishment it has now vanished. The only thing that remains is the dusty desert floor square surrounded by the huge pyramids.

Samanda points to a small shinny object a few yards before them, it twinkles as it reflects the early morning sun. It lies directly below where they were seated moments ago when the stadium still stood. Kaybra walks to the object, bends over and picks it up. Holding it between her fingers and blowing the dust off of it, she immediately recognizes it as her emerald pin that the young girl so happily cherished.

A tear comes to Kaybra's eye. Closing both eyes and squeezing the pin, she tilts her head back remembering the cute child, when she has a vision. The vision is of the youth urging Kaybra to be on her way before disaster ensues. The ground begins to tremble and Kaybra's eyes pop open to find the pyramids are beginning to rumble and shake from the tremor. The young girl's voice cries out in Kaybra's head, "You must depart, the Harpy eggs will begin to hatch on the eve of the second sun!"

Kaybra runs back past Samanda and Aaron, mounts her steed and yells out, "We must go! The Harpy nest is likely hatching fledglings as we speak."

Samanda and Aaron quickly mount, kick their chargers and disappear off into the maze of pyramids. Once again they follow each of Kaybra's equestrian maneuvers and when they exit the last alley coming out into the open desert from the quaking pyramids, they rein in their steeds to a halt. With horses jittery, the three warriors turn nervously to glance back and find it as earlier, all the pointed tombs appear far off on the horizon.

Aaron is now tiring, as is Samanda, who addresses Kaybra, "My dear warrior sister, I understand the urgency of finding the Harpy nest, but is there someway we can gain a short period of rest? We are all badly drained, both mentally and physically from the ordeal in the coliseum. In this state, I'm uncertain of our effectiveness."

Kaybra places her hand atop her brow like a visor and looks to find the location of the sun, then looks in the direction to which they were directed by the young girl.

Somewhat uneasy, she replies, "Your point is well taken, Samanda. I will only be able to lead us to the approximate location of the harpy nest. From that point on, Aaron must lead us to the southern edge of Nemmin. We will rest for a short period at an oasis not far off our path, which I visited many seasons ago. It is very beautiful, but we must not let ourselves be tempted to linger there." So they trot off in the direction Kaybra indicates, in search of the oasis.

The three are famished and their rations are running low. After two more hours of riding, they spot a grove of palm trees. It is a welcome sight.

The grove is filled with a plethora of fruit and nut trees and in the center of the trees, a cool, blue pool of clear water. Aaron and Samanda quickly dismount, race to the pool, kneel and splash water on their faces. Kaybra, however is more guarded. She dismounts slowly, looks in all directions and finally approaches the rippling water.

Samanda and Aaron quench their thirst and then lean back on their knees. Looking about this pleasant spot, Samanda sighs, "This is certainly a lovely place to pause, so I see why you say one might be tempted to dally here, my sister." Samanda, wasting no time to find some enjoyment, stands up beside Aaron and strips off her uniform, then tosses it at his side. She turns her head, smiling to encourage him to join her and plunges into the water, splashing Aaron. He turns to Kaybra, acting moderately embarrassed and shrugs his shoulders.

Kaybra says, "Let her refresh herself for awhile, Sir Aaron. We need to discuss strategy. Let us go back by the palms. You will still be able to see her from there." The two walk away from the shore a short distance and seat themselves under a growth of palm trees. Aaron glances at Samanda in the water; who is still playfully splashing about.

When he turns to Kaybra, he notices she's fidgeting with her top, as if to rearrange it for comfort. As she does this, she accidentally exposes some of the scars Aaron saw two nights ago upon her breasts. His eyes are focused on her large bosom as Kaybra looks up and immediately knows what Aaron is wondering.

Kaybra shakes her long, black hair down over the back of her shoulders with her hands, then tidies her headband and heaves her chest out toward Aaron. Aaron's facial expression goes blank.

Kaybra grins and cups both breasts with her hands and gives them a small jostle. She says, "I suppose I did tell you I would explain what you ponder. You see the metal scales on my top are for a purpose. It is because of my size and great strength that I have intimidated many male warriors in my day. In seeking vengeance, during battle, they are drawn to these."

She jostles them again, a little more vigorously this time and continues; "My breasts have been punctured by arrows and slashed by swords during combat. It appears that warring men receive great sadistic pleasure from doing so. Upon such an injury, I grab them while in pain. As I suffer, I have heard men boast to their comrades during battle, 'That will give the mother dog something to remember!'

"My top is of three layers of leather. The metal scales protrude from the center layer of leather to which they are securely fastened and proven very effective against these perverted attacks to my body." Kaybra reaches for the ruby clasp between her white, leather cups. Staring into Aaron's eyes, Kaybra suggests, "If you would like, I could expose them and define the origin of each scar?"

Aaron quickly replies, "No. No, that is not for me to concern myself. But I am sorry to hear of such ruthless acts upon your person in battle."

Neither one has noticed that Samanda has returned from her dip and stands close to them. She is dripping wet and completely nude, except for the clothes she holds in front of her. She quips, "So, have we figured a new strategy for war that deals with the magic ruby that secures your cups and leather lace, Miss Kaybra?"

Kaybra fires back, "Samanda, Aaron has expressed concern for me during battle, so I have explained to him the reason for my breast armor and how effective it is."

Samanda wads her leather garments into a large ball and throws them in Aaron's face. She then turns her shapely, body around, wiggles her bare behind and heads back to the pool. Aaron uncovers his head in time to see Samanda splash into the water and turns to Kaybra, "Let's discuss the location of my men."

Aaron and Kaybra discuss the dispositions of their troops in the field and agree that the time for both armies to converge on Genipsus is soon approaching. However, they estimate they have a little time to spare, to eat and rest since both are certain their field commanders will bivouac until they arrive. The real urgency now, lies in finding Vampressa's nest before her eggs hatch.

Kaybra ends the discussion by describing her understanding of the location of the Harpy nest. They stand, look around and find Samanda has retrieved her blanket from her horse and is fast asleep under a palm tree. The two agree they have some time to do the same, so they walk to where Samanda lies and join her in the shade.

*   *   *

Only a few short hours have elapsed when the trio awakens rested and hungry. They gather berries, nuts and fruits for their journey. Their water bags are replenished and secured to their harnesses as they depart the oasis. Samanda and Aaron lag behind Kaybra by two horse lengths.

Aaron pleads, "Samanda, please do not be upset with me. Kaybra is a very open woman, not unlike you, I did not want to pay her disinterest when she told me of her injuries."

Samanda replies, "I only hope you pay similar mind to my injuries, should I receive them. But for now, I only desire that you remember the location of this oasis, so that just you and I may return here someday in the future for our special occasion without Kaybra."

They snap their horse up alongside Kaybra's steed. Aaron rides between the women.

As they slow to a walk, Aaron asks Kaybra questions about her culture's ancient scriptures. He is also eager to learn what the young girl, back at the Valley of the Phantom Pyramids, spoke of to her and Samanda while he was preoccupied with the event there.

Kaybra responds, "Our scripture speaks of the daily battle at the arena. It says that the Valley of the Phantom Pyramids is in the area that we traversed, but rarely found intentionally. It is also written that should one find himself suddenly surrounded by the giant pyramids, it is imperative he rides with fury between the stone aisles. With luck, the horseman will find the center square the monuments envelope. If one dallies, however, they will be swept up in the mammoth circling cloud we witnessed and dispersed into eternity. The battle in the arena happens every night and has, since the beginning of the existence of the Gods.

"The golden Pharaoh is not always the victor and the outcome of the conflict dictates the nature of the following day. We must pray that the Pharaoh continues to slay the beast during our battle campaign. Any night the monster is the victor, despair prospers on the following day. The circumstances and victor of this daily conflict will likely seal our fate.

"The spectators are well familiar with all the beasts released when the monster is victorious and Vampressa is one of the monster's favorite colleagues in terror. The young girl and her family have witnessed from what direction Vampressa arrives on the days the monster wins the conflict. They are no strangers to her devastation. The information she shared dictates the path we take.

"Soon we should come upon a massive mound of caked sandstone looking much like the top of a dormant volcano. At its base will be a rock-formed opening where an ancient troglodyte resides. He is fat and round, about the same size of the hole in which he lives. He is a troll of sorts and rolls on his belly to get around. When he is excited or angered, the odor he emits from his cave is overwhelmingly putrid. He is Vampressa's alarm system. As she forages about our kingdoms, her nest is left unprotected. So, if the troll spots intruders, or any danger is near, he urinates and excretes a horrible-smelling body gas. He then rolls his grossly fat, pudgy body around rapidly, forcing the odor out of the cave's opening for her keen scent to receive. Vampressa can be far, far away from her nest and still smell the troll's stench in the air. She has been known to flap her broad wingspan and return in moments, hence devouring the trespassers to her lair."

Samanda harks out, "Look in the distance." The three recognize the volcanic image on the horizon before them. With brush and vines intertwined into its base, it rises from the desert floor through this jungle-like patch of trees.They embark upon it with caution.

As they walk their horses around the perimeter of the tangled foliage, Aaron finds a path into its dark green hue. When he motions the girls of his find, they ride to his side and Kaybra scrutinizes the emerald corridor opening. She whispers, "Wait, listen." All becomes still. Even the horses have locked their legs and stopped swishing their tails. No sounds come from within the jungle, not even birds singing, animals chattering, or breezes. Only silence.

Kaybra comments that not only does she find this peculiar, that additionally these circumstances are absent from any of her readings. Then Samanda exhorts them, "Listen, my comrades and you will hear the faint noise of what sounds like a waterfall." The other two agree and they all disappear into the vines and broad leaves in the direction of the sound.

The jungle is hot and humid, the air is thick and steam rises from below. Their bodies are soon drenched with perspiration. Every so often there is a slight break in the green ceiling above them where they peer upward to see glimpses of the volcano's crest. The soggy path soon begins to swerve left and sharply upward. They proceed cautiously and reach a point on the trail where they emerge upward above the jungle's sweltering foliage. Aaron holds his palm up to halt the two women behind him.

The trio scans the top of the steaming jungle in awe, for from their vantage point, they can see far across the treetops into the desert, with the volcano before them. The waterfall they heard gushes from an oblong hole in the slope, with a large rock in its center. The stone equally divides the flow and splits the water into two flues, like a serpent's tongue. Below the falls, between the two streams, they spot a cave. The round opening itself is not very large, but it's ornamented with garish, evil-looking, carved faces on boulders that collar its opening.

The three look at each other, realizing this must be the home of the troglodyte. They also agree it will be wise to tether the horses here and that the noise of the falls will shroud any noise they may make. Aaron, Samanda and Kaybra arm themselves with a large cache of weapons and then ascend the slope. They carry ropes and spikes as well.

They are in a tight formation for safety and to communicate effectively amid the increasing roar of the falls. Like insects traveling upward between the streams, they come to a landing in lower proximity of the cave's opening.

Judging from the size of the opening, Kaybra guesses she must be the same approximate height of the troll and explains a daring plan to the others, "The troll is a man and I am certain he is of my size, in height. I will lure him to a place at the end of his cave with a seductive dance. Aaron, take Samanda above his cave opening to the rock lodged in the waterfall directly above. The first tier of pools, into which the water falls, is not far below this point. So, after you dislodge the rock, it will fall directly downward, closing the entry hole to his cave. That feat will either kill him or trap him permanently inside the cave."

Aaron objects, "What if the boulder misses its mark and tumbles to where you stand?"

As if in anticipation of this question, Kaybra replies, "To avoid such injury, I'll dive off that wide ledge in front of the cave into the pool below. Then we will regroup and continue upward to the Harpy nest."

Samanda and Aaron look at Kaybra as if she's lost her mind, but Kaybra commands, "Now go! There is no other remedy at hand, and the hour glass drains swiftly." Kaybra proceeds to scale up the sandstone rock toward the troll's cave. Samanda and Aaron, with weapons and tools tethered to them, scurry upward in the direction Kaybra ordered.

Kaybra reaches a point, mere inches below the troll's ledge and pauses there until she can see her comrades are near their destination. She breathes shallowly, as she sniffs traces of the troll's foul odor. She removes her clothing and drapes her white uniform over a tree branch growing from a crack in the stone near her.

She looks at Aaron and Samanda and sees them grappling with their ropes and tools to secure them to the boulder that splits the water flow. When they are secure, they signal Kaybra, who nods back up to them in acknowledgement.

Kaybra stands erect, wearing only her knee high, white leather boots. She raises her arms over her head, places her fingers over the ledge above her and pulls herself up and over the ledge.

On top of the ledge in front of the troll's cave, she stands up slowly from a squat and advances to the mouth of the cave. As she does so, she realizes the ledge upon which she stands, is coated with a heavy, yellow slime, its smell repulsive, she ignores the odor and begins to dance seductively while chanting an enticing melody.

The stench becomes stronger and a putrid puff of air emerges from the cave. The large naked beauty looks into the dark hole and sees two white orbs staring out at her. She escalates her act into a frolicking belly dance around the ledge, which entices the obese troll to the cave opening to look Kaybra up and down. He is a perfect fit in this opening.

He grins, grunts and sputters in an unintelligible dialect. Convinced her plan is working, Kaybra wiggles and gyrates even more intensely as the grimy ball of a creature rolls out farther and fondles himself rapidly. Kaybra throws her arms upward to Aaron and Samanda signaling them to release the boulder. The two struggle desperately to dislodge the rock with ropes and a pry, but with every attempt they make, the big stone only rocks slightly back and forth. Samanda and Aaron desperately work around in the noisy gushing stream as the troll rolls closer to Kaybra, making a slurping sound as he revolves closer to her over the goo.

He rolls inches from her and winds up head down. Kaybra looks down at his ghastly face, which is viewing her naked body from the bottom up. Although extremely nervous, she does not waver. She throws her arms and head up once again as part of her act, to study her comrades' progress and sees that the boulder is teetering back and forth out of the hole as they work.

She smiles with relief, but when she again looks down to quickly analyze her situation, a look of despair crosses her face. The troll, now close to her and upside down looking up across her nude body, has also seen what she has. His face turns mean and he begins urinating profusely on himself. He also emits gas that propels him back toward his cave's opening.

Kaybra snaps her head upward just in the knick of time as the boulder careens down right before her. Fortunately, her calculations were accurate and it crashes to the ledge lodging itself in the cave opening.

She falls to her knees in relief, knowing the troll is either dead or hopelessly trapped behind the rock. There is however, something Kaybra did not calculate. The water's flow is no longer divided and sheaves of the newly-formed waterfall cascade straight down onto the fallen rock in its new position. It ricochets off it to where Kaybra kneels and its force smashes Kaybra's large, shapely body down onto the ledge. The current beats her about as she flips about, struggling to hang on. The slime on the ledge affords her little hope for a handhold and her body is forced across the gooey stone landing. Within an instant she is flushed over the edge by the torrential deflection of the newly created single rapid.

Samanda and Aaron witness Kaybra's dilemma and quickly rappel down the side of the slope to her aid. They see Kaybra has survived the fall off the ledge, landing in the tiered pool below. Now she splashes out from under the thundering falls as it gushes into the small tarn.

Samanda and Aaron run to the edge of the pool and Aaron spots a pack of stinging eels squiggling directly toward Kaybra. He calls out to her and points to the swarm of eels as she swims for shore, but the roar of the falls muffles his exclamations and Kaybra is so busy paddling toward them she cannot hear. In an instant, the water around Kaybra's body swirls into a rolling boil, as the eels attack her. They swarm around her, latching onto her flesh from every direction and whipping their tales. She screams in anguish from this unexpected onslaught.

Aaron jumps into the pool with Samanda close behind him and they frantically swim to Kaybra and pull the eels off her body. Kaybra moans in pain as her two comrades finally slide her onto the sandstone shore. She rolls around, screaming, as if she were on fire. Dozens of the silver-green flapping creatures still dangle from her sun browned nude body.

Aaron and Samanda cut and pull at the aquatic pests until Kaybra is freed from the last one as Aaron snaps it in half with his knife. Samanda fetches Kaybra's white war garments now floating at the waters edge. She and Aaron sit beside and comfort Kaybra as she lies on her back, still gasping for breath.

Gradually, Kaybra comes out from her shock and takes Samanda and Aaron's hand with hers and smiling upward, gives them each a wink. They return the smile, clutching her hands in theirs in victory.

Now reunited, the two pull Kaybra to her feet even though she is still short of breath and pocked with red rings from the eel attack. Samanda wrings out Kaybra's clothes and helps her dress.

In an attempt to be polite, Aaron turns his head and feigns preoccupation with some pebbles on the shore with his foot as Kaybra gingerly fastens her garments. She has a painful expression on her face, for her white leathers burn the places on her body that come in contact with the eel bites.

Now composed, the three ascend the slope and pause halfway up, beside where the waterfall pounds on the rock at the mouth of the troll's cave. They nod to each other, agreeing that the boulder they dislodged earlier is tightly wedged into the cave opening. Not only that, but now the once divided waterfall beats directly down on top of it. Noting the cave's plugged opening drips with water from around the rock, they conclude it is very likely the ugly troll has drowned. The trio smile at each other, as if victorious in yet, another battle.

Soon thereafter Samanda, Kaybra and Aaron reach a place on the slope that is a very short distance from its summit. They pause and scan the sky in all directions for any presence of Vampressa. As they hug the slope, they each note the warmth of the mound in this area and assume that the heat must be from the sleeping molten lava below the mound's crust. Kaybra exclaims, "What an excellent climate to incubate fertile Harpy eggs." They continue to crawl upward.

The heads of the three adventurers break the summit's crest as one and their expressions are in awe at what they view. The flat floor of the volcano is merely two or three feet below them and encompasses an area similar to the larger pond in the oasis where they rested earlier that day. Moreover, the entire area is covered to its perimeters with large, ostrich-sized eggs packed together as if protruding from the openings in a huge honeycomb.

Slight whiffs of steam spew up around them. The three turn their heads to each other in astonishment.

As they stare at this sight, Samanda whispers, "Duck." The others spot what she sees and hug the ground, watching Vampressa, who has just swooped in from the far side of the volcano and hadn't spotted the trapped troll's, water-drenched cave. The three witness the Harpy spread her large wings and gently land in her huge nest. She struts about, jostling her eggs around with her webbed feet and cocking her head as she eyes one egg after another.

She picks up one egg that appears slightly different from most of the others and cradles it up to her with her with her webbed hands. She expectorates a thick yellow colored milky substance onto the egg and before it can run off of the egg, she rubs the substance around it. Soon the egg begins to glow, as do several others in the mammoth nest. Placing the egg back carefully where it was, the Harpy cackles and screeches hideously, then shakes her head up and down and laughs as though she just accomplished some dastardly deed. Vampressa immediately leaps upward, flaps her wings and flies off into the identical direction from which she arrived.

Kaybra, guardedly whispers, "Vampressa just performed a fertilization ceremony on that egg and through the ritual, all of the eggs possessing the strange glow have also been inseminated. They must be destroyed. As soon as Vampressa's speck in the distance disappears, we must act."

After a few short moments of waiting, the three leap into the nest where the eggs incubate. They are equipped with weapons and tools and immediately begin stabbing and crushing the glowing eggs.

Many eggs contain nearly full-formed embryos of infant Harpies. Some are so close to hatching that they make faint, shrill tones similar to Vampressa's hideous screech. The others seep a gooey, green yolk upon being smashed. Kaybra, Samanda and Aaron work their way across the plateau, like fierce warriors engaged in battle. After a long period, they have stabbed, crushed and destroyed the majority of the eggs. A few unfertilized eggs remain when Aaron calls a halt. "Samanda, Kaybra, look to the horizon, it's Vampressa there in the distance. This should not be the place or circumstance where I do battle with her. I have another plan which will not place the two of you in danger. Hurry, let us descend back down to the jungle where we can find a place to hide."

It does not take the girls long to heed Aaron's warning. The three race for the edge of the shallow flat nest, but Kaybra pauses when she sees two last unfertilized eggs that haven't been destroyed. She is torn with indecision, but in a split second she veers off toward those eggs. Aaron motions to Samanda, pointing to Kaybra. They then look back to the horizon and see Vampressa's image is quickly growing larger. The two reach Kaybra and begin pulling and tugging at her to get her to safety, but she calls out, "No. Please, let me destroy the two final eggs. The one on the right is beginning to glow!"

Aaron and Samanda both scream at her, "Kaybra there's no time, now come!"

Kaybra is undaunted by the couple's plea, but by using their combined strength, Samanda and Aaron force Kaybra to the area on top of the summit from which they arrived. They bound over the edge and rappel downward, alongside the waterfall, reaching the point where their quest of destruction began. Dashing from the base of the mound toward the horses, they discard their tools and ropes as they run.

Aaron wastes little time with the steeds. He unfetters them and leads them quickly down the curved trail at a trot. Samanda and Kaybra take their horses' reins from him and they soon enter the dark-green shadows of the jungle. Huffing and puffing, they pause briefly to mount and ride deeper into the thick foliage.

Atop the volcano, Vampressa has landed, and is uncontrollably furious with what she finds. The beast flutters and swoops around insanely, her motions like a waterfowl skipping across the surface of a pond to gain altitude. She races madly about the crater, her talons skimming the tops of her destroyed eggs. Her screeches of anger can easily be heard echoing into the thick matted jungle foliage below.

Aaron motions to halt. He asks, "Will the monster pick up our scent from within the jungle, Miss Kaybra?"

Kaybra has a puzzled look on her face but replies, "I'm uncertain, but I do know she is far less efficient when her prey is not out in the open. We must remain deep within this forest, where we are too shrouded by the trees and vines for her to find us this night. So, we must bed down under the broad leaves for our safety until daybreak. If we rest and sharpen our weapons, Vampressa will be helpless to vent her anger upon us in tomorrow's bright sunlight."

As the sun sets, Vampressa takes an aerial tour of the dormant volcano and its surroundings. When she finds the troll's cave is permanently sealed, she becomes even more outraged. Once again, she screeches and eyes the top of the boscage below her. She flies over it and as she swoops lower, she spots the ropes and tools the trio discarded during their hurried retreat. They leave a trail into the underbrush.

Samanda points upward to a small opening in the palm ceiling and as Aaron and Kaybra look up, they see Vampressa glide past the opening. The three hurriedly leave the thin glade and head deeper into the jungle. After a short ride, they view the end of the path that leads into the desert. The sun is now set and their position has become very dark.

The steamy, green mat below the palms now begins to cool in the night air and it creates a sense of relief among the trio. That relief soon turns to caution as they look upward, listening in the quiet, they hear the all too familiar sound of swirling air movement above the trees from Vampressa's wings.

They remain frozen in their stance and each silently prays that none of the horses coughs or snorts. Shortly, the sound disappears into the distance.

Aaron advises Kaybra and Samanda, "I will be a sentry while you two rest. Tie your horses to this bough next to mine, for in moments we will be unable to see no farther than an arm's length. We must also bed down in such a fashion that we all touch each other. Now take my hands and let us find an area to lie down."

Samanda and Kaybra follow Aaron's suggestion and tie their horses to the same branch as Aaron. Taking his hand, they find a soft, clear spot under a huge broad leaf tree that dwarfs them by its size as it acts like an awning over them. A light rain begins and seeps through the jungle's ceiling. The raindrops pitter-pat onto the top of the huge leaf and trickle off its edges onto the ground. The two women become mesmerized by these placid sounds and drift off as Aaron sits tightly between them with his sword in hand, gazing out into the darkness

As Kaybra sleeps, she has an erotic dream, which involves Aaron as her lover. In her dream Aaron is very aggressive and passionately tries to make love to her, while in turn she is unwillingly resisting his every action. Aaron is starting to make Kaybra hot, when she pushes him away and questions, "Aaron what of the Queen? Samanda and I are forbidden from becoming sexually involved with you. It is I, that was appointed to watch over Samanda and then report to the Queen of any sexual transgressions she may impose on you. As much as my heart aches to feel your skin intermingled with mine, I must not yield to your advances."

Aaron embraces Kaybra once again, "Kaybra, I have been infatuated with you since the evening by the river when you coaxed Samanda to remove her lips from my manhood. I must have you and make love to you like no other man is capable. Please speak to Samanda, she has the ability to communicate with the Queen from afar by inducing a trance-like state upon herself. With all that you will sacrifice in the battles that lie ahead, surely she will allow you to receive the pleasures I offer as a token of appreciation."

Kaybra has a flashback of the evening by the river that Aaron speaks of and remembers vividly the length and girth of his masculinity. Hot with passion, she embraces Aaron as he hastily strips her from her clothing, spreads her legs and mounts her. Aaron, now above Kaybra is sweating profusely as time-after-time he pounds his erection deep between her legs.

Kaybra, while basking in the sensual pleasure Aaron provides, feels drops of Aaron's perspiration dripping down on her breast and face. Strangely the drips are cool and increase in number beyond what would be considered usual. Within moments Kaybra now chilled and drenched awakes from the dream.

Still very much sexually aroused she looks around in the darkness to find that the rainy drizzle has increased to a downpour. Aaron with both women huddled close to him, places fallen broad leaves over them to shield them from the cool pelting raindrops.

Grabbing Aaron by the wrist, Kaybra can't help herself, but then after a long silent stare into his eyes, she refrains from going farther, "Thank you, Sir Aaron, for shielding me from the rain that woke me."

With water dripping from his locks, Aaron looks to Kaybra somewhat puzzled that she firmly grasps his wrist, "You are welcome Miss Kaybra, but it was a minor deed." Aaron looks at Kaybra's hand around his wrist and then gazes slowly back into her eyes, as if cautiously questioning her prolonged grasp and then Kaybra's fingers slowly open as she removes her hand and uses it to help Aaron arrange the leaves. She pulls one of the larger leaves over her head and lies back down. Aaron sits between the sleeping women holding a similar leaf over his head and resumes his lookout post.

Chapter Five

As the sun rises the next day, the three warriors exit the evergreen tunnel into the arid desert sands. They ride slowly, scanning the skies in every direction, with their personal weapon in one hand. To Aaron and Samanda's surprise, Kaybra has chosen a large, white, leather whip for her personal weapon of the day and rides with it coiled around her upper arm and shoulder. Its handle is readily accessible to Kaybra as it dangles in the front of her left breast. Aaron asks, "With such a device, I would think a warrior of your stature could inflict much injury in many directions. Tell us of the notches carved in your weapon's handle."

Kaybra responds, "The notches, Aaron, represent the number of combatants I have slain with this tool of both offence and defense."

Aaron is amazed, there are so many notches on Kaybra's whip handle he cannot count them from his vantage point. Samanda interrupts, changing the conversation, "Kaybra, is there any way of telling if the Golden Pharaoh was again victorious as we slept last night?"

Kaybra replies, "Only the outcome of this day will afford us that answer."

Samanda looks worried as they ride.

Kaybra asks Aaron, "You mentioned a plan last night atop the Harpy nest to slay Vampressa. Is it a secret or will you tell us its detail?"

Aaron thinks a moment, then explains his strategy to the women. "I must locate my dove when we reach Nemmin." Each woman does a double take upon this disclosure. He goes on, "My dove's name is Uma. She and I will trick Vampressa to her death on the night of the next silver moon.

We will make love on the top of a large dune that I will show you as we near my old village. I shall bury my sword at my side in the shallow sand and just as Vampressa swoops down to plant her talons into Uma, I will raise my sword and jab it through the Harpy's heart."

Kaybra is startled by the idea and queries him further, "What of Uma, should you miss Vampressa on the first lunge?"

"I will not miss, Kaybra. I will not miss!" Aaron emphasizes.

Samanda is truly miffed with his proposal and sternly puts him down "I told you the woman you call Uma is dead, Aaron! What of us? You told me you have a love for me!"

Now Kaybra is confused and Samanda is upset. Aaron announces, "We have now reached the region with which I am familiar. As agreed and mandated by the Queen, both of you are now under my command." With that, Aaron spurs his charger and gallops ahead, heading northward in the direction of Nemmin. Samanda's face registers contempt for Aaron as she watches him ride off.

Kaybra turns to Samanda. "How can you be certain Aaron's woman is dead?"

Samanda turns to Kaybra with a blank face. "Because I was the one who killed her." Samanda then kicks her horse and gallops off to catch Aaron.

Kaybra shrugs her shoulders, as she is even more confused now. She watches Samanda ride off and sighs, "What have the Gods done to this woman?" then, spurs her steed to catch up with the others.

Aaron knows his troops should arrive at their destination, north of Genipsus, on this day. However, he feels pressed for time, so he orders the three to ride hard through the day, so they take only two short respites to relieve the horses from the heat. As late afternoon approaches, Aaron sees familiar landmarks that reassure him of his course.

Samanda is tiring from the overall action of the past few days and pleads to Aaron, "Sir Aaron, please, let us take time for ourselves. I am becoming badly chafed from such a hard drive."

Certain of their location Aaron accedes to her wishes and the warriors halt their drive, dismount and walk their lathered horses to a large group of sandstone boulders.

They find a cool shadow on the east side of the rock formation and sit. At first there is an uncomfortable sullen silence as the trio briefly glance to one and then the other. Kaybra sits with her legs bent up in front of her, then leans forward. Resting her forearms on top of her knees, she looks back and forth between the other two, pondering who will speak first. She is uncertain of her own thoughts and so reserves any comment at this time. Samanda and Aaron sit in similar positions with Samanda rubbing oil onto the inside of her thighs.

Finally, Aaron breaks the silence. "When I was a young man, my father and I visited these stones on many occasions and at this very location we plotted against Vampressa. At that time, we had no idea her nest was just one long day's ride south of here. When I grew older and after my father passed, I used to recall our conferences here." Samanda fixes her eyes onto Aaron as she continues to soothe her burns.

Kaybra asks, "How did it end, Aaron? That is, your battle against Vampressa."

Aaron goes on, "The Harpy was much younger then as well. Her appetite at that time was mostly for our stock and we would stand guard in the fields at night, shooting flaming arrows at the monster. Often we could not see her, but as she flapped her wings, the sound they made, as you already know, was unmistakable. We aimed at the proximity of this sound.

Most of the time our arrows merely discouraged her from returning to our homestead, since there were plenty of other unguarded pastures she could prey upon. On one occasion, my father shot the lead flaming arrow to light the sky and as it flew upward into the darkness, it illuminated Vampressa's body as she hovered over one of our young oxen. I then fired my flaming arrow and it went into her lower leg. She screeched in pain, her cries resembling those she made upon discovery of her shattered nest. My father and I cheered as Vampressa hissed at us and flew off. The flaming arrow not only punctured her leg, but the small blaze created a stench from her burning feathers."

For the last few moments Kaybra has been watching a large tarantula creeping closer and closer to Aaron's spread feet. She is so interested in Aaron's speech though, she doesn't warn him.

Aaron still in dialogue, continues, "Ever since that night, Vampressa has tracked me off and on over the years. While I was in my village of Nemmin during the war with Patrious and Genipsus, we had no idea that the beast was feasting on our opponents in the moonlight. If we knew that, we very well may have praised her."

During his spiel, Aaron has leaned back, placing his palms on the sand beside him. He stiffens his arms to support himself and tips his knees outward. Kaybra, engrossed with Aaron's story, has momentarily forgotten about the huge spider. It now crawls on the sand, just below Aaron's knees.

Samanda finishes her oil rub and looks up to Aaron, spotting the gaudy insect, but is speechless as she sees it is about to disappear under Aaron's gaping war apron. She holds one hand over her open mouth and points frantically at the huge spider, then nudges Kaybra sitting beside her. Samanda, not wanting to disturb Aaron's story telling, wiggles her finger toward his crotch.

Aaron wants to exhibit his prominence as a leader and has become quite the authority figure by holding the women's attention. He sits chin up, casting his eyes over the ladies' heads, as if he were a prophet of his day.

Samanda breaks Kaybra's trance and in an instant, Kaybra uncoils a length of the tip of her white whip from around her shoulder. She aims for the tarantula and flicks her forearm and wrist. The whip cracks out a loud "SNAP" and the tarantula's body is split in half.

Aaron is instantly mortified as he just viewed the tip of Kaybra's whip nearly emasculate him. Unaware of his very precarious circumstance, he leaps to his feet in shock; hops around, cupping both hands over the front of his apron.

Samanda and Kaybra hold their hands over their mouths, trying desperately to hold back laughter. Aaron is both dazed and incensed with the women's behavior and glares down at them. By now, the two women can no longer restrain themselves and burst out laughing. Making a feeble attempt to stop chuckling, Samanda points to the two halves of the recently deceased tarantula. Aaron looks down to the large spider's split carcass and immediately gets the whole picture. The girls explode with boisterous laughter realizing their General-of-Arms pulpit-like stature has been instantly diminished.

Aaron realizes Kaybra's action saved him from a devastating bite. He quips down at the two giggling women, "I am pleased that I have provided such an entertaining moment for both of you. When you regain your senses, it would be wise for us to mount and ride for the southern outskirts of Nemmin." Samanda and Kaybra are laughing and rolling about, holding their sides.

Totally humiliated, Aaron strides to his horse. The women wipe tears of laughter from their eyes and stand, looking at each other, still giggling as they stumble across the sand to follow Aaron, now quite humbled. He smirks to Kaybra and Samanda, "North to Nemmin, ladies" and jerks his horse's head and they gallop off.

The trio has again driven their steeds hard from the rock formation to the southern outskirts of Nemmin. Darkness is nearly upon them when Aaron raises his hand, halting them.

They have just crested a broad mound of sand and to the north in the distance they faintly see fires burning in Aaron's home village of Nemmin. Only Aaron knows the dune they are on is the one he spoke of earlier, the mound where he plans to bring his longtime mate, Uma, and set his trap for Vampressa on the next full moon.

Aaron points to a hollow at the north base of the dune, a concave basin-like area in the sand that will conceal them from any view across the horizon and be an ideal spot to set camp for the night. He signals the other two to follow and they descend into the spacious sandy pocket.

As they enter the gentle crater, they find it littered with wood and Aaron asks the women to help gather wood for a fire. Kaybra warns it may not be a wise decision after their bout with Vampressa the night before. But Aaron looks about the darkening sky and reminds Kaybra that Vampressa has never attacked a man or woman without at least the partial light of a silver moon. Kaybra reluctantly agrees and assists him and Samanda to gather the firewood.

Later, the fire crackles into the midnight sky. The three have dined and rest quietly by the fire on their blankets. Samanda lies on her back next to Aaron and stares into the sky. She pines, "Today was relatively uneventful and so I would think the Golden Pharaoh was victorious in last nights battle with the beast." Little does Samanda know how deadly wrong she is.

Aaron and Samanda tilt their heads in Kaybra's direction. They see she has finished her usual bedtime ritual and is fast asleep. Her blanket covers all her body, except her head, where in Kaybra's long, dark hair is pulled back over her shoulders. Samanda strokes Aaron's cheek with the back of her fingers as he lies inches away from her. She gazes over his broad chest as he closes his eyes and nods off. Samanda whispers softly in his ear, "Someday you will be mine alone, Sir Aaron. You will make passionate love to me at the snap of my fingers. You will be all mine." Samanda slowly closes her eyes and joins the others as they sleep tightly by the flickering fire.

Aaron is gradually awakened by a soft, enchanting female voice. The voice is very monotone, but yet, somehow melodic and soothing. Like a soft tune, it floats through the air to him from afar, "Aaron…Aaron…I knew you would return to me…Please, wake up Aaron, and come to me…Please come, Aaron…Come to me…Come to…Come…" One by one, Aaron's eyelids slowly crack open. He thinks that possibly the voice has been manifested by a virtual dream.

He lays there still listening with both eyes wide open as the voice continues. "I missed you so much while you were away, my love. Please rise and come to me? " Aaron lifts his head and sees that both Samanda and Kaybra are still fast asleep. The tender voice continues, "Yes, Aaron, that's it, rise. Rise, Aaron, Rise."

Aaron quietly gets up, so as not to disturb the sleeping women. He sits up and then kneels. Again, he hears, "Rise all the way now and come to me, Aaron. Be still, my love, do not wake your friends. I'm over here. Stand and come to me, come to where I wait for you and make love to me as you once did…"

Aaron eyes the flickering shadows that border the darkness and is astonished to see the faint outline of a woman embedded within the distant amber hue the fire casts. He stands to his full height and stares at her, but she is too far away to identify. Yet Aaron is familiar with her voice, so he takes one step toward the figure, when it whispers a little louder, "Wait Aaron, pause and bring your blanket with you. Bring it for us to lie upon and make love…" Aaron is becoming somewhat hypnotized by the woman's voice. He looks at his sleeping partners, then crouches down to pick the blanket up.

"That's it, Aaron, that's it. Now come to me." The voice continues and Aaron draws closer to the figure that stands about halfway up the mound that the three warriors descended a few hours before. As he nears it, he can't believe his eyes; the tantalizing figure of a woman is Aaron's very own, Uma.

She wears a chic pastel gown. The transparent body veil hugs her every curve and the mere sight of Uma after so long, immediately arouses Aaron. He is so astounded by her radiance that momentarily he is helplessly frozen in his tracks.

Uma invites Aaron closer to her, reaching out her arm with her fingertips down. She entices Aaron to come even closer with, "Take my hand, my true warrior...Take my hand and lead me to the top of the mound...Join my loins there and make love to me under the stars as I caress your body." Aaron's longing for Uma continues to grow with her every plea.

The mesmerized warrior smiles and runs toward her outstretched hand, heady with tears of joy. He approaches the spot where she stands as she quickly and playfully turns and trots farther up the mound toward its top. As she does so, she pulls her flimsy garment up around her waist to further tease Aaron. Her bare bottom and hips wag back and forth as she climbs, now but a few short feet in front of him.

When she reaches the top of the mound, she turns to Aaron and reaches out both arms, inviting him to her. Aaron grabs her and hugs her closely, rocking her back and forth in his arms.

He turns their embraced bodies so that he can look over her shoulder, down the hill, where the glowing fire ring below appears much smaller, but its orange hue still glows up the side of the sandy mound.

Aaron recalls Uma's tiger-like lovemaking tactics as she pushes herself slightly away from him. Then, she clenches her silky lapels and rips the flimsy gown from her body and heaves her bared bosom against Aaron's chest.

Aaron is madly in love with Uma and having missed her for two long years, decides to forgo any conversation and fulfill her immediate desires. He is so insanely aroused, that he shakes as he spreads the blanket atop the dune. As he stands, Uma, too, quakes with lust and Aaron gladly allows her to rip his loin garment from around his waist. He holds Uma's head in his hands as she drops to her knees and fondles him with her lips and fingertips. Aaron throbs with pleasure with every lick and touch she places on him.

Aaron stops her, "Wait! Please, Uma, let us become one once again." He gently pushes her down onto the blanket. Uma is twitching with anticipation as Aaron is now above her. She spreads her legs to gladly accommodate Aaron's manly wand as Aaron takes one fleeting glance at the fire that glows below the hillside. He looks once again into Uma's eyes, finds his mark and pounds her with passionate love.

The two figures are as intertwined as a braided rope. With their love reconnected, they roll and toss atop the blanket. Suddenly, Uma displays an aggressive act; with her arms and legs wrapped around Aaron, she squeezes him tighter and tighter, raking her nails across his muscular back, digging them deeper and deeper into his skin with every pass. His arousal initially heightens with these acts and he closes his eyes tightly. His face grimaces in painful pleasure as she increases crushing him within her lanky clutches. Aaron chokes out, "Easy, Uma," but to no avail. Her appendages continue to constrict his sweaty tanned body, tighter and tighter, as he begins to groan in discomfort. The woman's breasts swell, becoming hard and pointed. She presses them firmly into Aaron's chest as she constricts him even tighter. Aaron is on the verge of climaxing, but is in so much pain that he is bound in a state of euphoric limbo. Using her nails like talons, she begins to puncture the flesh on Aaron's back. Aaron panics and pleads, "Uma, enough…Uuummma, stop!!! Oh Uuummma!"

Aaron reopens his eyes and goes into shock at the sight of Uma; she is not Uma at all. Aaron screams out the name, "VAMPRESSA! VAMPRESSA!"

The monster cackles as she hops around the top of the dune, flailing about and clutching Aaron as if he were a child's toy doll. She holds Aaron's head close to her mouth as she scolds him, "Is this the night you are going to slay me?" She laughs hideously, "I tell you, you will not live to be a hero, for I am Vampressa and I shall live into eternity, soon, I will extract your packet of reproductive seeds, then, Sir Hero, I will leave you here in the sand, bleeding to death. But I'll make certain you live long enough to watch me fly off to make certain my last two eggs are both fertile!! Ha, ha, ha!!"

Aaron is convinced he's done for, but makes one last desperate attempt to free himself. He pushes Vampressa's shoulders away from him and attempts to head-butt her. She hops around the top of the dune, cradling Aaron within her folded wings where they are face to face. Again Aaron pushes her head and shoulders away to attempt yet another head-butt. He strains much harder this time, gains a significant distance away and mustering all his might, he closes his eyes, waits a moment and bashes his head into her forehead again.

But Aaron's struggle merely angers Vampressa even more and she slams him down on his back, places one webbed foot over his neck and the other atop of his legs. Standing over him, she cocks her eye down at Aaron's genitals as Aaron, squirming to free himself, is turning blue from the lack of oxygen and cannot speak.

Vampressa throws her head up into the night sky and cries out one last nasty screech before she completes her deed. In that instant, Aaron is staring up at Vampressa's horrid face. Aaron is fading and his thoughts confused. He sees what he thinks is a long, white snake that has emerged from the darkness and coiled itself around Vampressa's long, feathery neck.

Vampressa's eyes bulge as the white serpent squeezes her throat. She frantically pulls at it with her webbed digits and is now the one gasping for air. Her newfound dilemma forces her to step off Aaron who soon sees it's not a snake around Vampressa's neck, but the long, braided end of Kaybra's white whip.

Aaron looks on as Kaybra tugs on the handle of her whip, flipping Vampressa backwards, onto her rear. Vampressa kicks her webbed feet back and forth, like a helpless baby duck on its back as she struggles to upright her now totally-reclaimed bird body. At the same time, Samanda is jabbing the Harpy with her spear.

Aaron rolls to one side, propping himself onto an elbow, exhausted as he watches the tussle between the women and Vampressa.

The tip suddenly breaks off Kaybra's whip, which gives the monster a reprieve. When Kaybra tugs on the whip's handle again, it unravels from around Vampressa's neck and the Harpy thrashes about, trying to regain her balance as Samanda keeps her at bay by continuing to poke her with the spear. Vampressa flutters and hops around in the loose sand, hissing and screeching at her attackers as Kaybra uses the remaining length of her whip to begin flogging Vampressa. Feathers fly all about the air during this beating.

Vampressa continues to hiss and sneer as she retreats backward across the dune, but Kaybra and Samanda are relentless in their attack. Vampressa flaps a backstroke with each retreating step she takes and is able to gradually lift off.

The evil Harpy's feet dangle slightly above Samanda and Kaybra's heads as she gains altitude. In one last-ditch attempt, Kaybra snaps her whip out, which encircles the monster's leg as Samanda heaves her spear at the Harpy. Vampressa grabs the spear in midair before it can harm her, then turns the spear, against Kaybra. Kaybra's whip uncoils from around Vampressa's foot as she loses her balance and falls to the ground.

Aaron, trying to regain his breath, rolls onto his back to hear Vampressa cackle as she ascends, "I will return for you, my beauties. One day I'll feed on your guts in the silver moon's glow until you beg me for mercy."

The feathery monster is far above them by now and scolds the women with a hiss and cackle, repeating her threat to them over and over, for she knows she is out of reach of what is left of Kaybra's whip. But Vampressa jeers down one last menacing caw, "Ha, ha, ha," as she hovers above Aaron and the two women who call out to Aaron, "Look out!" as the monster curls her feathery arm back and pitches Samanda's spear at Aaron, as he lies motionless. Luckily her spear merely nicks the inside of Aaron's right upper thigh as it comes to rest between his legs. He jerks his head and shoulders upward, screaming, "Vampressa, one day I will thrust this spear through your evil heart!"

Small, grey feathers float downward through the darkness, which look like flakes of volcanic ash. Vampressa disappears into the night sky, her annoying cackles becoming less audible as she gains distance from the trio.

The girls rush to Aaron, who sits up and moans, his hands wrapped around his thigh. Kaybra picks Aaron up, places him gently over her shoulder and the three naked warriors descend the mound into the fading fire's light.

*   *   *

The two women have been doctoring Aaron's wounds throughout the night and into the early morning hours. The wounds are serious, but not life-threatening. They have made bandages from spare undergarments and wrapped them around Aaron's right leg, chest and back. The women have also fashioned a tent from remnants of other cloths and extra blankets. Aaron lies quietly, shaded from the sun, with both Samanda and Kaybra by his side.

Aaron speaks, "I will be rested soon and then I must proceed to Nemmin." But Kaybra and Samanda are not quite as convinced as Aaron. Samanda shakes her head from side-to-side disapprovingly.

Kaybra suggests, "I think it would be a healthy thought for our commander to at least replenish the sleep he lost last evening."

Aaron finally concedes to her notion, lays his head down and immediately dozes off. A comfortable breeze blows beneath the makeshift tent and the two women converse as Aaron restores his body and mind with much needed rest.

Speaking softly so as not to awaken Aaron, Samanda tells Kaybra, "I am puzzled by Aaron's actions last night. Why would he do battle with Vampressa while we sleep?"

Kaybra does not tell Samanda that she awoke shortly after Aaron's departure from their bedrolls. At first she, not unlike Aaron, thought Uma had truly come down to Aaron from the hill and chose to let the two reunite. That is, until she heard Aaron scream out the Harpy's name atop the dune.

Obviously Samanda did not witness the image of Uma, so, Kaybra covers for Aaron and replies, "Aaron is a noble warrior, Samanda, but his expertise is not in slaying monsters. His expertise is in the strategies of war and hand-to-hand combat. I believe that last night Vampressa tricked Aaron somehow. Trust my words, when we reach the battlefield, all will be convinced of what I speak."

The women continue to tend to Aaron as they whisper on between themselves about different topics. Kaybra leads the discussion, directing it to a point where she plans on asking Samanda more questions about Uma. But just then, Aaron awakens and the two women go silent.

Aaron says, "It seems your advice to me, ladies, was fruitful. I feel well restored and have little pain from my injuries. Now, help me to my feet, for I must go to Nemmin."

Samanda says, "And what of us, Aaron, do you expect Kaybra and I should be idle while our injured commander leads the front?"

"Not at all, Samanda, but I know the people of my hometown. If the two of you rode in with me, it would cause them alarm. Not knowing the reprieve that we bring to the village, they might attack us. There is no need to place the two of you in danger unnecessarily. Our journey is far from over, so I will enter town in a hooded robe and mingle with my old neighbors. I will tell them of our plan to assist them in the battle against Genipsus. The warriors I left behind are likely engaged in the northern battle line, so I will enter the town from the south, inconspicuously.

"It is my order that you two rendezvous with Kaybra's troops stationed to the southwest of Nemmin. After once again securing the trust of my people, I will join my troops with yours to the northwest. We will drive straight south where our two flanks will converge and I will order this new, united army to charge east. It is then that we shall crush Genipsus. However if they do not yield by surrender, we will drive them off the cliffs, into the Gorge of the Damned.

"If you are expeditious with your ride, you should unite with Kaybra's troops well before darkness is upon you. But remember to arm yourself toward the sky while on your journey."

Kaybra nods acceptingly. Samanda is reluctant and states, "If you do not come to us by the third sun, we will charge without you, so do not dally with any of the women in Nemmin."

By now, Aaron has everything pretty much together for his trip into Nemmin. He mounts his horse, smiles down at Samanda, salutes Kaybra and rides up and out of the sandy hollow in the direction of Nemmin. The two women stand at attention as Aaron disappears over the edge of the shallow pocket, then losing sight of their comrade they begin to break down what is left of their camp.

Following a light ride, Aaron soon comes upon Nemmin, where he spots an old farmer on an ox-drawn cart piled high with straw entering town. Two large goats are tethered behind this cart and Aaron slips his steed close in between them. As Aaron enters the streets of Nemmin, he draws little attention from the few people he sees as he peeks out from his hooded robe and from side-to-side occasionally catches a glimpse of an old acquaintance.

Aaron intends to make his first stop his old home before his capture and sees it on the next block of small, stone buildings. It is all he can do to maintain his casual pace behind the wagon.

As the wagon passes his home, Aaron cautiously guides his horse off to the tie post near the front door. Slowly he dismounts, ties his horse and approaches the door, nervous with anticipation.

His fist quivers as he knocks on the door. Several moments pass and no one answers. He tries again, knocking a little harder. This time the door slowly creaks open and Aaron expects to see Uma's pretty face. But as the door opens, she is not there. He removes his hood and sees a small, old woman, Uma's mother.

The woman immediately recognizes Aaron and embraces him. She says, "My son, I was certain you were lost or worse, perhaps tortured to death in the prison mines."

Aaron gently caresses the old woman, reassuring her of his condition and finally finds the courage to ask of Uma's whereabouts. There is a long silence as the woman lowers her head and begins to weep. She covers her mouth with the her fingertips and whispers, "Gone."

Aaron replies impatiently, "Gone?"

The woman continues in a low feeble tone of voice, "Yes, she was killed shortly after your capture."

Aaron angrily demands to know how his love was killed and her mother continues. "Within a short time after your capture, the Petrious warriors converged upon our town. Many of our women were beaten and raped, but Uma was furious with the enemy's assault tactics and ran into the streets with one of your swords. As she slashed away at the men, a woman warrior rode through the carnage, screaming out to the male warriors, "Stop, you dogs, leave these women alone or I shall order your heads for the Queen." The men obeyed the woman warrior's directive immediately.

"There was much commotion in the streets. Uma was so upset as she swung her blade back and forth at the men and did not hear the woman warrior's command. As the woman drew closer on horseback, Uma lashed out and sliced her across the right calf. The lady warrior's response was immediate. She flinched with pain and reflexively jerked around and rammed her weapon through Uma's throat. Uma grasped her neck and fell to the ground, bleeding and gasping for air.

"The woman warrior sat atop her horse in disbelief at her own deed. She again screamed at the male warriors to disburse as all grew silent as Uma lay there in her own blood, her eyes wide open, gazing upward at the horsewoman.

"The horseback woman jumped off her steed and cradled Uma's lifeless body. As I witnessed the entire clash between the two she sobbed and begged my forgiveness. The warrior woman then pulled a small, scarlet kerchief from her bosom wrap and placed it over Uma's open eyes.

"She looked up to me and said, 'Please forgive me for this tragedy of war. Somehow, someday I will repay you.' The horsewoman wiped a tear from her eye and threw her weapon down beside Uma. Then she rode off, following in her fleeing male warriors' hoof prints."

Aaron experiences a great deal of emotional pain hearing this account of Uma's death. He tries to stay strong for Uma's mother and asks the frail, old woman, "The sword the woman warrior left at Uma's side, do you possess it to this day?" Uma's mother turns and walks to another room of the small abode, shortly returning with the sword. Using the weapon as a cane, she renters the room.

Aaron takes the weapon from her and examines it from end to end. The handle has a twisted, golden shank with an oval insignia jeweled into it. The insignia depicts a coiled snake and Aaron drops his arms and genuflects onto one knee. He drives the point into the floor, clasps his hands over the handle and sets his brow against his crossed hands. Aaron silently weeps inside.

Finally, he looks up at the old woman and says, "Mother, you know of my love for your daughter, so please take me to where she is buried and leave me there alone. When you return, gather the village fathers to this home so that I may speak with them after I visit Uma."

*   *   *

Kaybra and Samanda have been riding toward Kaybra's camp for some time and have talked about many things as they ride. Kaybra's curiosity compels her to once again inquire of Samanda's knowledge of Uma and at first Samanda avoids the topic. But Kaybra is politely persistent with her inquiries, so finally, Samanda relinquishes the information Kaybra seeks.

She begins, "Two seasons ago, the battles between Genipsus and Nemmin became a threat to our kingdom of Patrious. There was much dissention within renegade troops coming from Genipsus and much of the turmoil spilled over into our outlying colonies of farmers. Frequently, the renegades would attack transports coming into Patrious by way of our usual trade routes. Although the King of Patrious was a warrior throughout his life, he had become dull and overindulged himself with wine and other spirits, so when messengers brought him the news of the conflict between the two villages to our east, he ordered their annihilation. That gave him cause and self-worthiness.

"If it were not for those conflicts that endangered our trade routes and colonies, we would have had little concern. Nevertheless, the order was given. I fought on the battlefield the day Aaron slew the King. It was a raging conflict and there were many casualties on all sides. However, our warriors far outnumbered those of either Genipsus or Nemmin, which caused mass confusion on all fronts.

"Once the King was killed, great rage erupted and the army of Genipsus aided us in the capture of Aaron and his men. Once they were taken, the warriors of Genipsus turned on the King's ranks. Then, to make the situation worse, renegade troops from both factions sought revenge against the people of Nemmin.

"By the time I reached Nemmin, there was chaos throughout the streets. Soldiers from both sides were out of control. Many women were being raped and killed as their children watched. Old men and women were being beaten and dismembered. I tried to bring an end to the pillaging by raising my sword and ordering the offenders to stop in the name of the Queen. Just as I did, my right leg was slashed and without a thought, I turned to the attacker and thrust my blade into the offender's throat. It was Uma.

"I felt horrid, for I had perpetuated what I tried to quell. I looked down into her eyes as she clutched her neck. She was barefoot and wore a peasant's gown. The streets became silent and one-by-one the soldiers left the village. I dismounted and tried to assist Uma, but it was much too late. I took a red scarf from my top and placed it over her open eyes. Then, I threw my weapon down and begged the forgiveness of an old woman who stood by her side."

Kaybra can tell Samanda is distraught with the event and tries to console her. "Samanda, it was an error of war. Try not to dwell on your actions from that time." But Samanda remains silent as the two women continue their journey.

*   *   *

Aaron has returned to his residence after visiting Uma's grave. Many older men are gathered, greet him pleasantly and welcome his return.

Aaron listens intently to the men about the status of their war with Genipsus and learns the troops that remain to defend Nemmin are minimal.

Moreover, the Harpy attacks on the Queen's men have also taken their toll and security is near a breach. Also, he learns that all was calm before the Harpy attacks on the Patrious warriors and the Queen's troops had managed to bring order to the warring villages. The overwhelming opinion among the men though, indicates the warriors of Genipsus have made a pact with Vampressa.

One of the town fathers tells a story he heard from herders passing through Nemmin. The herdsmen witnessed a small group of younger and middle-aged women coming from Genipsus late one evening. The women entered the Patrious encampment and disrobed, they danced about, taunting the men and eventually enticed them one-by-one into sexual intercourse with them. They would lure the Patrious warriors into the shadows of the moonlight and position the men on the top of them.

One herder then told of a large, condor-like bird that would swoop down and pluck the men off the women's spread out bodies and the women would giggle after each man was seized upward by the giant bird. Then they would slip back into camp and lure another victim into the shadows.

After hearing this, it doesn't take Aaron long to surmise the situation at hand. With the Queen's men all but gone and the balance of them recently deserted, the danger from Genipsus has returned, full scale.

Aaron then reveals his strategy and tells the men about Kaybra's troops stationed a short distance west of Genipsus and his troop of freed prisoner warriors located just north of Kaybra's encampment.

Aaron asks that a messenger be sent immediately to warn Nemmin's remaining warriors who patrol their defense line north of town. He is concerned that they may be overcome in the drive eastward from his and Kaybra's troops. Thus he asks the old men to tell their field commander to hold his line strong as Aaron's united army fights eastward into Genipsus.

The men acknowledge closure of the meeting by touching hands. Then they nod to Aaron and depart in single file. Aaron hugs Uma's mother and though the dwelling is Aaron's home, he asks permission to spend the night. The old woman smiles and leads Aaron to his accommodations. Once in his room, Aaron redresses the wounds he received earlier from Vampressa and retires for the night.

*   *   *

Kaybra and Samanda have been settled into Kaybra's camp for a while.

Samanda asks, "When shall we calculate Aaron's arrival with his troops from the north?"

Kaybra ponders momentarily and replies, "If all is in order, Aaron should join us on the second sunrise. He will likely order our merging troops to rest for a time and then synchronize their advance upon Genipsus."

The two women enter their tent, remove their clothing and settle in. Kaybra begins her nightly ritual of massaging the strap marks left from her heavy warrior-type bra and her methodic hand motions compel Samanda to lace her fingers into Kaybra's. Kaybra pauses, raises her head and looks into Samanda's eyes.

Samanda says, "You have already assisted us so much in our cause, let me soothe you this evening." Kaybra is slightly surprised by Samanda's approach, but her curiosity surrenders to her desire to assist.

Samanda softly asserts, "Lie back my sister-in-justice and let me care for you." Kaybra slowly lies down on her blanket. As she flattens out on her back, Samanda straddles her hips, then leans forward and begins kneading Kaybra's shapely breasts with her fingers and hands. Kaybra allows herself to be indulged as she finds great comfort in this treatment.

With Samanda atop her, Kaybra pulls her long black hair up over her head, spreads it out above her like a fan onto the blanket with both hands and begins to sigh in a comforting tone.

Samanda reaches over and retrieves her personal vial of body oil. She rubs a generous amount between her palms and begins massaging Kaybra's midsection. She carefully rubs the oil into her bronze skin as Kaybra releases her tension and begins to softly moan as Samanda continues her gentle rubbing.

Samanda again retrieves the oil from where she placed it moments before and tips a few drops around Kaybra's navel jewelry and with her finger pushes the small pool of oil in a circular fashion around Kaybra's navel.

Kaybra pulls Samanda down on top of her and Samanda places her head between Kaybra's breasts as if they were offered as a pillow for her. Kaybra rolls her own head to one side of the blanket as she reaches over for the lamp.

Samanda whispers, "My sister, I am worried. What will the days ahead bring?"

Kaybra blows out the lamp and in the darkness whispers, "I can only tell you that as leaders of this land, the three of us shall find we have a date with destiny. Now, rest well tonight, my sister." They fall asleep.

*   *   *

Aaron is ready to depart Nemmin as dawn breaks, knowing he has to drive northwest for a large portion of the day.

Most people of his village have been informed of his earlier arrival and now gather to bid him farewell and good luck. He gently kisses Uma's mother on her forehead and mounts up, kicks his charger and salutes his people as he gallops out of town.

*   *   *

At Kaybra's camp, the two women have finished their morning meal in company with Kaybra's two field Generals. The Generals told Samanda and Kaybra of a grotesque site they encountered, not far from camp. All agree that the area should be investigated.

The Generals are a man and a woman, Kaybra's most trusted confidants and the four ride a short distance south, along the trail over which the troop arrived. The Generals leave the beaten path and ride over a dune as Kaybra and Samanda follow.

Suddenly, all four come to a halt on the far side of the mound. They gaze across the vast sandy desert floor below unbelievingly. It is littered with remnants of the Queen's original Royal Army. Bones, skulls, rib cages and other rotting body parts are scattered over the large area, intermingled with tarnished weapons and shields. Some carcasses are also those of horses. The four estimate that this scene of carnage must contain the majority of the Queen's troops sent to Nemmin and Genipsus.

The breeze picks up and the odor of death it carries, forces all back to the top of the mound. The male General reaches into his saddlebag and pulls out numerous objects of women's clothing. He hands them to Kaybra, who then passes them to Samanda.

He explains that these flimsy, female garments were found clutched between the bony fingers of the victims lying in the drifting sands below them.

Kaybra orders her Generals back to their troop to insure order, then motions Samanda to join her as she rides down the mound toward this place of death. The women shield their noses from the gusts of wind that increase from time-to-time as they walk their horses throughout the remains. It quickly becomes apparent that all of the soldiers have had their pelvic bones either crushed or removed. The women warriors look to each other as if cautiously dumbfounded and then return to Kaybra's encampment.

Upon their arrival back at camp, Kaybra meets with her Generals and Commanders throughout the day, with Samanda at her side.

*　　*　　*

Aaron nears the prearranged station of his troops and can see Kaybra's tents and fires on the distant horizon to the west as he proceeds northward. As he reaches a position north of Samanda and Kaybra, his horse stumbles on something protruding from the sand. He dismounts to investigate, kneels and dusts the sand away from the object.

He jerks back upon seeing what he has unearthed, a bony stem of an adult male's neck vertebra. Shaken, he looks around and views scores of the vertebra stems sticking out of the drifting sands around him.

He reasons that the tales of Vampressa's skullduggery are true and in anger over his own encounter with the beast, Aaron scans the skies, certain Vampressa, looms about, somewhere. Now with more determination than ever, he hops aboard his mount and snaps him off in the direction of the prearranged meeting place with his troops.

*　　*　　*

Meanwhile, Kaybra and Samanda have wound down their conferences. It is now late afternoon and they discuss Aaron's perceived location. Kaybra once again assures Samanda that all is on course.

*　　*　　*

Aaron arrives where he is to rendezvous with his men and is disgruntled to find they have not arrived yet or worse, that he possibly misdirected them. His anxiety eases when he sees horsemen approach him from the far-distant western horizon. Aaron dismounts and throws together a makeshift campsite for the night. He impatiently awaits the men's arrival as he listens to their horses' hooves thunder toward him.

Aaron's field Commander, Demitrious, is the first to arrive at his side and salutes him as the rest of the troop filters in. The man is out of breath as he dismounts. He explains to Aaron that they have been plagued with problems since their departure from the prison mines of Patrious.

He continues about encountering high waters where he was to cross the river. He further states that on two separate days they were besieged by giant locusts and sandstorms.

Aaron's temper softens upon learning of their difficulties. He is after all, pleased that the troop did in fact make the trek from Patrious intact. He wanted to forge southward to join up with Kaybra's army upon his troop's arrival but realizes his men and horses need some well-deserved rest. So he orders his warriors to prepare an encampment for the night.

The men prepare to assemble a large fire from a nearby stand of dead trees, but Aaron stops them and orders the men to make one small fire per ten men so as not to draw attention to their location. They obey his command without question.

As nightfall sets in, the men gather in groups around their respective campfires. Aaron has called his most prominent comrades to sit at his fireside and discuss his battle plans into the early evening dusk

*   *   *

Samanda and Kaybra figure that Aaron will probably meet up with them the following morning and decide to make it an early evening. They prepare only a very small fire. Both reflect on the possible outcome of the following day's battle. Then, suddenly Kaybra changes the topic. "Samanda, are you certain of your love for Aaron? It wouldn't be proper to lead the man on just because you feel guilty for killing Uma."

Samanda smiles replying, "There's no question in my mind of my love for Aaron. I am convinced that he, single-handedly will slay Vampressa and some day we will be wed."

Kaybra asks, "My devoted comrade, but what of your sister, the Queen and her altered ego? Her dominant personality will ultimately possess this one-of-a-kind specimen of a man."

Samanda stops her speech abruptly, wipes the smile from her face and gives Kaybra a retributive glance. Once again, Kaybra is puzzled and tries to quiz Samanda further. But Samanda is unpleasantly uncooperative and insists they promptly find their bedrolls.

Kaybra reluctantly follows Samanda into their tent. Shortly thereafter, Samanda's arm reaches out of the tent's entry opening and pulls its flap snugly shut. A heated argument comes from inside as the two women's quibbling voices continue into the night.

*   *   *

Aaron has also gotten his camp bedded down and can hear his men rustle about throughout the darkened grounds in anticipation of the following day's conflict. He concludes his meeting with a short briefing session around his fire, where he shares with them his conversations with the elders from their hometown of Nemmin.

It is not very late, but most of the men are already snoring away. They have fallen asleep quickly due to their exhausting misfortunes of their journey to this juncture.

As Aaron lies next to his nine comrades, he stares off into space at the thousands of tiny stars scattered in the darkness above. He is confident that he has brought successful closure to this day.

He tries to relax, but his rest is interrupted by muffled girlish giggles he hears coming from somewhere off into the nearby darkness. Aaron looks to his two field Commanders near him and they silently nod to him, affirming that they, too, hear the faint laughter. Aaron nods back and all ten men around the fire snap their eyelids shut as if fast asleep.

A soft pitter-pat of footsteps comes near them and each of Aaron's warriors slightly crack their eyelids open. They find a bevy of beautiful, naked women standing over them, fondling their thighs and abdomens with their fingers and palms. They softly sigh and breathe deeply as they wax themselves with their fingertips while the men still pretend they are sleeping soundly.

The women begin to pout and appear frustrated that their siren-like attempts to engage the men in sexual acts are ignored. They increase their gestures and moan louder, imitating multiple orgasms. Now becoming more frustrated that their fruitless seductive gestures, are still drawing no attention from the men, one woman motions to the others to go down on the sleeping warriors.

As the first woman slips her hand up under Aaron's war apron, he yells out, "Capture the nymphs! Tie them up! Restrain them with your ropes!"

An intense tussle ensues and the nymphs scream obscenities at the men as they kick and bite them to avoid capture. They scratch at Aaron and his associate's eyes as they curse at the men. The scuffle sounds like men wrangling with a pack of wild bobcats. The nymphs kick and punch at the warriors' groins. But soon, the men overcome the women and bind them with ropes and leather ties.

After this physical bout with the scorned naiads, the naked women stand bound together panting like a cluster of captured wild animals. Their hair is straggled about their heads, necks and faces.

The leader of the women squirms and contorts her limbs to try and get free and when she realizes it's hopeless, she spits in Aaron's face. The other nymphs join her, spitting at the other men and cursing them profusely.

Aaron orders, "Bind the lot of them onto the stand of dead trees. We shall deliver them to Samanda and Kaybra when we merge our troops in tomorrow's early morning sun."

Aaron goes to his weapons stash and retrieves his crossbow. He is furious at the nymphs for conspiring with Vampressa, so he loads a sharp, especially-deadly-looking arrow into the nock of the bow and stares contemptuously into the eyes of the leader as he slowly approaches her. He cocks the crossbow in front of her. It clicks, now ready to fire. The nymphs, still trying to catch their breath as they tug at their restraints, become suddenly silent and stand still as their eyes stare at the razor sharp point of the arrow.

Aaron reaches the curvaceous, bound woman, who leads the feline pack. She is a wildly looking beautiful woman, but that has not swayed Aaron's obsessive anger at her. He takes two steps to her and raises his crossbow. Fighting back her personal fear, the nymph's haughty leader begins to breathe more heavily than before and with a scowl, the dark Queen of the whores locks her unusual eyes upward, deep into Aaron's as if daring him to harm her.

Aaron's men, uncertain of what is about to happen, are frozen in silence as they peer on.

Aaron places the point of the arrow just below the woman's sternum. As the point pricks her skin, she twitches and reflexes, pulling her stomach in as far as she can to avoid further injury.

Although now forced to breathe delicate, shallow breaths to take in much needed air, her facial expression remains fearless. The arrow's point pricks her each time she nervously exhales. A slight trickle of blood runs from the open wound.

She and Aaron continue to stare at each other, both faces emitting contempt for the other. Finally, Aaron breaks the silence, "I have never killed any of a deadly group of sluts before this evening, but should anyone in your group try to escape, it will be my pleasure to make you my first." Uncertain if the women will heed his warning, Aaron hands his crossbow over to his field commander and orders him to gag the prisoners so they do not further disturb his soldiers during the night, then alternate guards to watch the scorned wild women until daybreak.

The men peel their eyes from what they have just viewed and promptly obey Aaron's orders. Aaron and the remaining men return to their bedrolls, as in chain-gang like fashion, his guards march the tied, and naked women to the dead trees where they restrain and gag them until daybreak.

But Aaron is still upset with the actions of the nymphs and so he plots their demise as he and his comrades fall asleep.

*   *   *

Having retired early the night before, Aaron's troop is up and have a head start on the new day. The camp has long been broken down and the warriors are mounted with their supplies in place.

The captured women are now partially-clad in their skimpy silks that were located in the early morning sun and Aaron orders his second group of ten men to place the nymphs on the horses' backs, directly behind each man of the first group that he leads. The order is followed and each woman is promptly secured to the backside of Aaron's horsemen. Aaron orders that their leader with the unusual piercing blue-grey eyes be placed behind him on his horse.

The sirens with arms around the men's waists, have their hands and wrists bound together tightly in front of the men's stomachs.

Aaron raises his right arm, motions his seventy-some horsemen to follow him in official formation as the troop canters southward, toward Kaybra's camp.

*   *   *

In anticipation of Aaron's early arrival, Kaybra and Samanda have been awake for some time. Kaybra orders her troop of over one-hundred-eighty warriors to prepare for battle, for it is not a long distance between Aaron and Kaybra's camps.

*   *   *

The leader of the nymphs, bound behind Aaron, attempts to engage him in conversation. She stretches, placing her chin up on his shoulder. "My women are hungry, and we haven't eaten for days. Can you provide food for us at some point, Master General?"

Aaron turns his head slightly and replies, "Did you feed the warriors before you had Vampressa pluck them from your engaged loins? I'm sure many of them had not eaten for days as well."

The woman remains silent for a long period after her request for food, then finally speaks again, "Would you care to know my name, Master General?"

Aaron replies, "To me, you shall only be known as a common slut."

She sees she is getting nowhere quickly in her attempt to soften Aaron's tough stance, so lacking finesse, the maniacal woman tries squeezing her long pointed nails into his gut, while simultaneously biting at his back.

She makes little progress in either attempt and so defeated, the woman screams out, "I am not just a slut! I am Queen of the sluts of Genipsus. I am called Dilyla! Some day soon I will feed your naked carcass to Vampressa and when I am done with you, you will never forget Dilyla until the day you die!!!"

Aaron is bemused by Dilyla's scolding, and continues to trod along as she twists and squirms around behind him. Dilyla continues on as they ride, "I will get you, master warrior. I will get you..."

*   *   *

Aaron's troop now becomes visible to Samanda and Kaybra as they approach from the northern horizon. At first the two women applaud and cheer upon this sighting of Aaron and his flank. Samanda has been drawn to Aaron for some time and longs for his return. But, the women's delight quickly turns to dismay as his warriors near, for they have spotted the long-legged, rough-looking beauties tied firmly to Aaron and his accompanying front line of horsemen.

When Aaron enters Kaybra's camp, both Samanda and Kaybra place their hands to their hips and cast jealous frowns in his direction.

Samanda's expression turns into a pronounced scowl as she watches Dilyla, wiggle and tug her forearms into Aaron's gut.

Aaron's front line has now come to a halt, before his two female comrades. His second row of horsemen stops behind the first. They all dismount and approach Aaron, to unbind Dilyla's arms.

Kaybra is confused, but Samanda is hot with fury. Dilyla's bare feet no more than touch the ground when Samanda pounces on her like a panther. She pins Dilyla on her back and starts slugging her alongside her head, but Dilyla fights back like a trapped animal, kicking and scratching at Samanda.

Aaron leaps off his horse and pulls Samanda to her feet. Dilyla's face is bleeding from Samanda's attack. Aaron's men lift Dilyla from the sand and rebind her and the rest of the nymphs together, just as they were the night before.

Aaron leads Samanda and Kaybra a short distance away and explains in great detail his encounters of the past day. Kaybra nods affirmatively, understanding the situation, but Samanda is a little more reluctant. However she has definitely calmed down.

Knowing that a small portion of Kaybra's encampment will remain stationary when the others go to battle, Aaron convinces Kaybra of his plan and asks her to first give the whores some food and drink. Kaybra agrees and after the women have eaten, he asks they be imprisoned. Kaybra again agrees, to have her remaining people confine the nymphs until their troops return back to the encampment from battle.

Samanda, still not entirely pleased with the idea, says, "Do you wish to practice sex with the sluts upon your return, Commander? I am certain that would be ill-fated preparation for you to join the Queen's royal loins."

Aaron takes Samanda by the arm and leads her away from Kaybra. They walk away a short distance and Aaron reassures Samanda that all is well between them. Samanda gradually discontinues her curt glances and finally gives him a huge welcome back embrace as she kisses him on his lips.

By the time the two of them return to Kaybra, she has already introduced herself to Aaron's leaders. The men look up to her in awe of her size and beauty and so it becomes obvious that a powerful allegiance has just been formed between the two forces.

Kaybra assures Aaron that the nymphs have been led off to a confined area of the camp and that they will be secure until the trio returns from battle.

Smiling, Aaron moves to the top of a small mound in the center of the encampment that was created by Kaybra's people for use as a podium of sorts. Now the scores of men and women warriors fix their eyes on Aaron as they hush each other and become silent as he rotates his stance around delivering his speech to them from the top of the mound.

Aaron raises his broadsword high over his head with both hands and shouts, "Assemble your troops and prepare to charge toward Genipsus. The time for war has come!"

Chapter Six

All troops are now under Aaron's command forging their way eastward toward Genipsus. In approximately a half-day's ride, they encounter the first line of Genipsus' defense. Their adversaries, while well-armed, are almost barbaric in appearance. They number around one-hundred-and-fifty. Approximately half have mounts. But they are no contest for Aaron's combined force of well over two hundred and twenty troops. They lose nearly two-thirds of their number during this first battle and the remaining horseman quickly retreat to Genipsus. There are only minor casualties on Aaron's side.

With Kaybra to his left and Samanda to his right, Aaron leads his flanks in pursuit of the fleeing enemy, but the barbarian's horses are fresher than Aaron's cavalry and open the distance from their pursuers. Soon they disappear into a tall, narrow, rock entrance of a large sandstone canyon in the distance.

Aaron now realizes he must rest his steeds or lose effectiveness in any future pursuit, so he calls out to halt his forces. His loyal followers immediately obey and stop in place.

Aaron then pulls his horse out in front of his war party and raises his sword high into the air as he turns the steed to face his troops. He commands, "Field Generals forward."

It takes little time for the dozen Field Generals to disperse from the military mass and come to Aaron's side. Not to be left out, Samanda and Kaybra look to each other, and then trot forward and merge into the group.

Aaron commands his Generals to bivouac their men for the evening and to give special care to the horses. He also orders the Generals to meet him at his campfire after they are settled in and to bring with them a scout and armed guard. The Generals disperse, but Samanda and Kaybra remain by his side.

Kaybra asks, "What is your plan, Sir Aaron?" Aaron explains, "The canyon into which our enemy entered, according to my charts, is a dry tributary that leads to the Gorge of the Damned. I believe the initial clash we have just concluded is a ruse to trick us into following the barbarians into an ambush.

"The soldiers from Nemmin have had to endure a hard drive since their departure and more research is needed into the writings on the charts. After the meeting with the Generals and their aides, I will explain further."

The three dismount and set up camp for the evening. Samanda has difficulty locating wood for the evening fire, but Aaron tells her not to be concerned because a large fire would only draw attention to their camp. Kaybra tends to the horses as Aaron studies his maps.

As darkness sets in, Aaron's Field Generals arrive with their designated aides. They sit, with legs crossed, around a very small fire that Samanda has scratched together.

Aaron rises. With the flickering firelight slightly illuminating everyone's face, he states, "We are at war, my friends, with a very cunning adversary, so be prepared to encounter unusual tactics from those we pursue. I order each one of the chosen guards to dutifully watch the perimeters of our camp through this night.

"In addition, I ask each one of you who has been picked as a scout, to listen carefully to my words as I show you my charts."

Aaron is convinced a trap lies ahead in the canyon, so he orders the scouts to sneak off into the darkness and survey the top of the cliffs that tower over the canyon. The Master General tells them to be quick and upon their return to awaken him with their information if he is asleep. Stealth-like, the scouts slip off into the darkness afoot.

Aaron orders his Field Generals to be prepared to mount their platoons much before daybreak. The generals then return to their individual camps to spread the word.

Kaybra and Samanda are both tired from their ride and the skirmish. Kaybra fetches her bedroll and after a shortened version of her bedtime ritual is soon asleep.

Samanda, although equally exhausted as Kaybra, has, as usual, other plans. She places her bedding directly beside Aaron's, sits on her bedroll and then looks at him. She pats her hand on his blanket, suggesting him to lie down beside her.

Aaron is as tired as the others and so he accepts Samanda's suggestive gesture. Aaron then disrobes as he kneels, removes his armor and lies on his side facing Samanda. Instantly Samanda snuggles her naked body tightly against Aaron's.

Aaron knows the seriousness of the next day's possible outcome, but after the precarious situation that was created by delivering the nymphs to Kaybra's camp, he is reluctant to shun Samanda's advances. He whispers in her ear, "Go to sleep, Samanda, we must assemble our troops before sunrise." Samanda places her face directly in front of Aaron's, looks at the suntan wrinkles on his forehead and runs her fingers through his hair. Aaron's eyes slowly close as he drifts off. Samanda's fingers come to stop as she joins Aaron in slumber.

The campfire has died out. It is now an hourglass of time before daybreak. Samanda opens her eyes to find that Aaron is absent from her side and so she feels around in the darkness for him without success. His bedroll is gone as well. Slight panic overcomes her as she gropes around on all fours trying to locate Kaybra, but Samanda discovers she is missing as well.

In the quiet, Samanda listens intently. She hears the movement of horses through the darkness, mixed with a murmur of voices. As Samanda dresses and gathers her battle attire, Aaron and Kaybra ride up to her. They have Samanda's steed tethered behind them, ready to ride. Samanda quickly dons her garments and takes her horse's lead rope.

Aaron speaks softly, "Samanda, mount, we must assemble into battle formation." Samanda listens to this directive attentively.

Darkness is still upon them, but Aaron seems to have no problem locating his direction. The three walk their horses a short distance and Aaron whispers, "Halt abreast and stand in formation." As he says that, Samanda hears the directive repeated into the early morning darkness to both, her left and right. Each time it is repeated, it is heard farther away to each side of her. Finally, after Aaron's directive has reached the end of his two lines of warriors, the new sun's rays break the horizon.

Aaron is between Kaybra and Samanda. To his right is a column of one-hundred-twenty mounted warriors, each abreast of the next. To Aaron's left is an equal amount of mounted warriors in an identical formation.

The sun crests the top of the canyon's walls and immediately a troop of barbarians on horseback charges out of the canyon towards Aaron's line.

Aaron's cavalry stand like stone statues across the sands as the Genipsus warriors are fast approaching. Still Aaron's line remains locked in formation.

Well aware that an onslaught from the barbarian's charging platoon will soon be upon them, Samanda and Kaybra give each other nervous glances, but Aaron, like the rest of his multitude, looks forward without expression.

Just as the cries of the enemy reach an un-nerving level, the barbarians pull their horses to an abrupt halt a short distance in front of Aaron's line.

The barbarians become quiet as though confused by Aaron's tactics. One points to Kaybra. Her size and beauty clearly stand out by comparison to her comrades. That puzzles the enemy even more.

Aaron's unflinching face-off intimidates the warriors from Genipsus. They begin arguing amongst themselves and while they carry on their dispute, Aaron gradually raises his arm. When his extended palm reaches full height, one-hundred-twenty crossbows are drawn upward to his right and the same number to his left. Then Aaron closes his fingers into a fist and jerks his arm down. The crossbows are fired at the Genipsusans.

Arrows plunge into the backs and ribs of the opposition. They scream and call out in pain, then fall off of their horses into the sand.

Aaron now raises his sword and yells out, "Reload and charge!!!"

Aaron is in the lead. His flanks form a "V" formation as he gallops forward. Samanda and Kaybra are only slightly off his side.

The remaining barbarians realize they've been taken off-guard as they turn and race toward the canyon opening. They are now less in number than before and Aaron's army quickly shortens the distance between them as they enter the canyon's narrow passageway.

Although Aaron is right on his enemies' heels, he halts at the mouth of the canyon, with five warriors on either side of him. The remaining right flank turns upward toward the canyon's southern ridge as his left flank gallops to the top wall of the canyon on the north side.

Meanwhile, Aaron's lead party remains in place as they watch their fellow warriors above them crest the tops of the weather carved valley and disappear onto the sandstone shelves.

Aaron orders his platoon to dismount and arm. They scatter across the narrow canyon opening, each warrior possessing a stash of arrows for their crossbows and other weapons. All remain silent as they crouch with their weapons pointed into the canyon's entrance.

The party gives each other a quick glance when they hear the enemy returning from inside the gorge. The screams from the barbarians increase in volume as they are accompanied by the sound of galloping hooves.

Suddenly, the remaining members of the original attack group of barbarians flee from the canyon, right into the laps of Aaron's unit. The ground thunders and occasionally thuds as they near.

The timed thuds shaking the earth exceed the impact normally created and felt by pounding horse hooves. With the increasing vibration of each growing thud becoming louder than horse's hooves, the members of Aaron's troop look puzzled.

But then, Aaron commands, "Fire on the barbarians!" as the majority of the enemy troop is looking over their shoulders back into the canyon. Due to their distraction from what ever it is that pursues them, they are an easy mark for Aaron's squad.

The front running enemy horsemen are easily felled as Aaron, Samanda, Kaybra and their squadron fire their crossbows, creating a pile of dead bodies almost plugging the way into the canyon. A few of the dead men's horses disentangle themselves from the carnage and race off in all directions.

All once again becomes quiet, except for the moans of the dying enemy. Yet, the ground still quakes as the ominous pounding sound draws nearer. Rocks tumble from the canyon walls as the vibration convulses the sandy canyon floor.

Aaron notices one enemy warrior is still alive, trapped under his dead horse. He is far back in the canyon opening, looking back into the canyon from a vantage point not available to Aaron or his comrades. The man's face is distorted by horror as he screams into the direction he views. He squirms in panic and tries to free himself from under his bleeding, lifeless horse. Then, without warning, the tremors stop as the disabled warrior continues to shriek and wriggle around trying to free himself.

The mouths of Aaron's brigade drop in awe after seeing what continues to horrify the enemy horsemen. Suddenly, the head of a huge, monstrous, fanged lizard has appeared at the end of the entryway into the canyon. This reptile's head easily dwarfs the size of Kaybra's battle steed.

The giant lizard turns its fanged head and peers outward down the canyon's opening corridor at Aaron's group. Its forked tongue slithers in and out as it views the troop from directly above the trapped barbarian.

At that moment the barbarian breaks free and takes a few, fumbling steps over his fellow warriors' dead bodies toward Aaron. Aaron lifts his crossbow and aims at the man, who freezes as he momentarily stares at Aaron, then back up to the lizard's head, poised above him.

Now, the lizard spots the man's movement on the ground below him and redirects its focus from Aaron's stunned comrades to the petrified barbarian.

In the wink of an eye, the reptile snaps up the screaming enemy warrior with its fanged mouth, throws its head back and gobbles him down like a waterfowl would a squirming frog. The monster's throat bulges, outlining the barbarian's body as it swallows him into its gullet.

The monster gulps for the final time, then redirects its attention to Aaron's platoon crouched at the opening of the canyon.

The group, as does the monster, realizes there is a significant distance between their two positions, so the giant lizard slowly turns its body and tries to posture itself advantageously by coming around the corner from inside the canyon. As it does, its full body mass is plain to see. Not only is the beast immense, its slimy, dark green skin is torn and pocked with what appears to be old and new wounds. Blood oozes from some and the odor of rotted flesh permeates the air emitted from the canyon opening.

With a raised hand, Aaron directs his followers not to move. He then slowly crawls, combat style, to where Samanda and Kaybra are crouched.

The three whisper between themselves trying to analyze the impending danger before them. They all agree that the size of the creature will likely not allow it to pass through the very narrow strait half-way into the sandstone entry corridor. Meanwhile, the accompanying warriors remain locked in their positions, their eyes open wide in the direction of the beast as it methodically approaches.

Aaron continues to speak softly to the women, "It seems the barbarian's plan was to draw our army into the canyon and then exit, leaving us to deal with this monster. Though barbaric in appearance they are a clever lot, so we must be very cautious about any move we make at this point. It can also be that we are currently amid another ruse. Therefore we must not flee, but allow this situation to set its own course for a short period." Samanda and Kaybra are deeply concerned with Aaron's irrevocable determination, but nonetheless give him an affirmative nod.

The lizard has now positioned its body full length headfirst into the narrow canyon entry. Its slimy, wide, green-and-yellow belly squishes down and flattens bodies of deceased enemies as it crawls forward. It continues to creep along approaching the narrow spot of which Aaron indicated to the women.

Samanda whispers, "Sir Aaron, I think we should flee this location while we still have the opportunity. Surely you must agree."

Aaron ponders Samanda's statement briefly as he scans the immediate area, then states, "Be still, Samanda, if the beast's slides its slimy, vile body through the opening, he will surely be upon us in one leap. You must have faith in the instructions I gave our troops now positioned atop the North and South walls of the canyon."

The fanged monster has now wedged itself into the narrow strait of the canyon's entryway. As surmised, it is a tight fit for the ugly beast, but not tight enough. The reptile lunges forward and with each lunge, inches of its slippery, slime-covered belly slides farther through the sandstone narrow.

Samanda grabs Aaron's forearm and squeezes it tightly with every determined advance the lizard makes. Kaybra, frozen in her tracks, looks on with eyes equally as wide as the rest of the troop.

The beast grunts and snorts as it claws itself forward on the ground, but another sound spills outward, past the reptile. This sound comes from the canyon's upper weather etched ridges, the sound is of swords clanging against each other in battle.

The scouts Aaron sent out the night before had discovered well in advance the tactics the barbarians from Genipsus use in combat. Thus Aaron's wisdom has positively reset the course of this individual battle.

The noises coming from the battle on the upper edge of the canyon soon turn from the sounds of clashing sabers and horses snorting, to the agonizing cries of the barbarians as they are driven into the gorge.

Hearing the commotion, the huge reptile, instinctively twists its head and neck up and back around to its rear. Straining its squinty, diamond-shaped lizard eyes, it views the screaming Genipsus barbarians as they plunge downward into the rocky canyon floor.

The accumulation of all of these fresh bloodied bodies splattering onto the rocky canyon floor appears to interest him far more than the slim crop of Aaron's small band before him.

Now more of the enemy warriors begin to fall from the opposite canyon ridge and that is too much for the monster to ignore. He tries to wiggle his plump midsection backward.

As the Queen's newly recruited, army of warriors continue to succeed with their drive, Aaron and the women silently cheer their comrades on.

Finally, the beast manages to squirm backward into the high straight walled valley and in doing so, he abruptly does a turnabout and pounces on the largest pile of dying barbarians. They cry out in disbelief at what is happening to them, for they are too crippled and maimed from their fall to even try to escape. The reptile munches and rips away at their bodies, occasionally raising his head and swallowing two or three screaming Genipsain warriors at a time.

Aaron orders his war party to mount, but stay in place until he returns. Aaron spurs his steed into the narrow opening of the valley as Samanda and Kaybra, in unison, yell out, "No Aaron, no!" But Aaron pays them no mind as he drives his horse through the carnage to a point, dangerously close behind the lizard's switching tail. He looks up to the top edge of the canyon wall to his right. There, he spots his field commander atop his steed and raises his sword, motioning to the man to continue onward toward Genipsus.

The beast turns his head as he chomps on his new find of fresh meat and stares at Aaron briefly. Then, with his jaws dripping with bloody drool, he contentedly turns back to his feast of raw barbarians.

Aaron then sees his other field commander sitting victorious on his horse atop the north canyon ridge wall. He motions an identical command to him, to also continue his assault. The General nods to him knowingly and directs his men to forge on to Genipsus.

Aaron smiles, realizing that he has averted an ambush of his entire army by not pursuing the barbarians into the canyon. Moreover, he is pleased his army has killed scores of the enemy that he believes represents the majority of his opposition's horsemen in the field.

Aaron's attention is then directed back to the feasting beast as it turns its head around again and eyes him up and down. This time, the giant lizard lets out a loud prehistoric-like roar while wagging its forked tongue at him.

Aaron immediately turns his horse toward the exit from the gorge and races back to where Samanda, Kaybra and the others await him. He smiles to them and calls out, "Onward to Genipsus!" The victorious group gallops up the south slope of the canyon to catch up with their advancing army.

Once they reach the height that overlooks the basin, they pause momentarily to look downward and view the now distance-dwarfed lizard as he continues to fill his gullet on their enemies' bodies. The group cringes at the sight, shake their heads and continue on, following Aaron as he charges off toward the location he has ordered the rendezvous.

After a short, hard drive, they merge with both flanks not far beyond the canyon's eastern end.

Upon his arrival Aaron motions his two hundred troops to gather around him. After they surround him, he directs, "We must ride until the Sun sets on our backs. There we will find a large stand of palm and date trees at the outskirts of Genipsus. It is there we will camp for the night. We will conceal ourselves deep within this remote stand of trees in order to remain undetected until daybreak. If we are expeditious with this advance, word of our victory in the canyon will not have yet reached the village of Genipsus. There, I will again meet with my field commanders and plot the escalation of this conflict upon the enemies' village at tomorrow's dawn."

The horseback warriors split slightly, leaving a cramped path for Aaron, Samanda, and Kaybra to leave their midst and take the lead. After they exit the crowd, Aaron orders the advance and the entire army thunders off over the distant sand dunes in the direction of Genipsus.

As the Sun sinks in the western sky, Aaron's calculation of distance and time has once again proven to be impeccable and after a long ride, his invading army arrives at the long grove of trees.

His field commanders note where Aaron, Samanda and Kaybra enter the forest of broad leaves in order to assure the location of their later meeting with Aaron. But now they must set up their own camps and soon the rest of the army finds its place alongside the tree line that demarcates the dark green foliage. From a distance they look like ants disappearing into a cluster of tall grass.

After all have secured their campsites, a half-moon eventually levitates itself upward into the night sky and Samanda has gone to great lengths to find a cozy, soft area of fallen palm leaves that lie below a tight clump of trees. She insists that the three should bed down for the night there.

After tending to the horses, Aaron returns to the site Samanda and Kaybra have anxiously prepared for their stay. While he was away, the two women spoke at length of their personal feelings for Aaron and about his brave, cunning and effective battle strategies. They look at him with deep admiration as he sits upon the bed of soft fallen palm leaves.

In the moonlight, the Master General now awaits his field commanders as he contemplates his next move against his foes. Samanda and Kaybra approach their comrade and sit on either side of him.

Soon, Aaron's commanders approach the spot where the three sit. As the men appear, they pull back the surrounding low hanging leaves in curtain-like fashion. Aaron welcomes them in and butts fists with them, acknowledging today's victory. He invites them to sit with him and the two women.

All listen intently to Aaron, "Our victory today was a success because of the joint cooperation of all involved. It is my honor to lead such an army of capable, brave men and women warriors, from Kaybra's delta island and my own village of Nemmin. At daybreak, we shall encounter one last challenge before we may return to our families. Up to this point, our casualties have been light and I can only pray to the Gods for an additional, final victory tomorrow." Aaron stretches both his arms out and adds, "Join hands in this circle we make and let this unit be one with the Gods. A short ride to the east in the early morning's light will put us up against the last brigade of barbarian warriors that defend Genipsus.

"Not unlike our troops, they will be men and women alike, heavily armed with bows, arrows and a variety of hand weapons. He who cowers first shall fall by the side into a pool of their own blood. And the women warriors of Genipsus are some of the fiercest fighters in the land, so have no mercy upon them." Aaron directs his words specifically in the direction of Kaybra and Samanda.

"Once again we will ride quietly in the shadow of the rising sun. I will utter no command aloud. As I raise my saber to the sky, wait for the first light it reflects, from the dawn's ray. Then when you see its glint, advance in a quiet canter toward the enemy line. Now go and advise your troops of this tactic I have devised, then let them rest until it is time."

Aaron's commanders slowly rise, turn, and walk back into the tree-shrouded moonlight.

Samanda and Kaybra are once again taken by the authority Aaron has seized upon and by his brave actions on this day. They both rub Aaron across his back and shoulders as if to reward him for his courageous demeanor.

Aaron basks in the women's gestures as he lies on his back on the soft bed of leaves. Samanda has had a long day as well. She lies down next to Aaron and places her open hand on top of his lower stomach. She yawns and soon appears to be immersed in a fast deep sleep.

Kaybra, on the other hand, is not so fatigued. She perches herself up squarely on her knees, where Aaron can clearly view her in the moon's blue grey glow. She scoots her legs slightly, so her knees touch Aaron's side and he opens his eyes a squint to find Kaybra looking at him seductively. Curious of Kaybra's intent, Aaron now opens his eyes wide and looks up at her as she places her fingers of both hands to the center of her chest on the ruby clasp that secures her leather cups together. The large captivating female continues her seductive smile downward unto Aaron and then pops the ruby snap apart. The garment recoils from her bosom and lands on the ground behind her. Her large breasts have burst from their white leather harness and spread slightly apart.

Aaron's body flinches from Kaybra's never-before-seen provocative moves. When he does this, Samanda, still very much asleep, removes her hand from Aaron's abdomen and rolls over away from him.

Kaybra's smile widens as she begins her nightly breast massaging ritual. But it is different on this night. She places both hands under one breast at a time and pulls it up toward her face as far as she can stretch it. The white underside soaks up the moon's blue-grey hue.

She now turns her eyes from Aaron's and with a painful expression on her face looks down at her contorted breast as she tugs it upward. Then suddenly she throws her hands outward and lets it drop back down, where it bounces and jiggles momentarily. Kaybra moans softly and does the same to her other breast.

Aaron senses he is becoming rapidly aroused by her movements and whispers, "Kaybra, please stop what you are doing. You will wake Samanda."

She drops the other breast, moans a little louder and then says, "No she will not awaken. Earlier, when you tended to the horses, I gave her a mild sleeping powder so she could sleep well through the night. After all she needs her rest for tomorrow's battle."

Aaron is shocked by her statement as he considers the longhaired, bronzed beauty's possible intentions.

Kaybra continues to tug upward on her breasts, moaning louder each time she squeezes them, occasionally glancing at Samanda to be sure she still snores away.

After taking a quick view of Samanda himself, Aaron concedes that Kaybra has likely drugged the woman.

Kaybra is a strong-willed woman, one third larger than Aaron in stature and he becomes slightly concerned for his safety should he upset the formidable, self-stimulated giantess.

Kaybra drops her right breast down and then shakes her shoulders back and forth sighing as her huge bosom jostles rapidly from side-to-side. She then reaches a hand to Aaron's loin leathers and shoves her long fingers down inside the top of his wrap. With one harsh swift jerk she rips it completely off him and it is now revealed that Kaybra's taunting seduction has been productive.

Aaron's manhood is steadily becoming more erect and excited. He chooses not to react, but just lie still.

Kaybra slowly lifts her fingers up to her white leather headband and unties it. When she does, her long, black hair falls down over her naked back and bare shoulders. Extending her arms and hands behind her head and using her fingers, she takes wide strands of her long straight jet-black hair and places them over her chest, creating a fibril veil of sorts. The pale un-tanned tips of her breasts peek through the long dark strands of her hair with her contrasting dark nipples at their center.

Kaybra then holds one end of the headband high over Aaron's upper thighs. The tie strands dangle down, tickling Aaron's upper inner thigh area as she swishes it back and forth. She continues to move the strands up and down his inner legs as if toying with a playful kitten, then slowly lowers the headband in a circular twirling manner, wrapping it gently around Aaron's fully erect appendage. She turns her face to Aaron and gives him a cocky grin to imply that he should submit to her every desire, or else. Next, she tugs at the end of the headband, pulling it snugly around the base of Aaron's masculinity.

Aaron is unsure of Kaybra's next move and although in a state of mild panic, he is very much aroused by her deeds upon his person. He fears any wrong move might upset Kaybra, causing her to tighten the leather headband around him, not unlike what he's already seen her do with her deadly white whip.

Kaybra firms the coiled headband slightly tighter, then stands and removes her war skirt feverishly. She tosses it aside unto the dried broadleaves. The determined woman then straddles Aaron, who remains motionless on his back. Staring at him, Kaybra slowly goes down once again to her knees, her tummy rubbing against his erection.

She leans forward, going nose-to-nose with her male comrade and with her elbows firmly on the ground, forearms extended, she closes her hands over Aaron's cheeks. He struggles and shakes his head in an unwilling manner.

But Kaybra begins kissing Aaron wildly, forcing her tongue into his mouth. Her large breasts are now flattened and slide across his perspiring, muscular broad chest as she moves on him.

Aaron can no longer resist. He finally succumbs to Kaybra's advances and responds by kissing her, running his fingers deep into Kaybra's thick hair and pulling her head to him. They both are quickly reaching ecstatic heights.

Kaybra, her lips still locked with Aaron's, slides her left hand below her jeweled navel, loosens the headband and grasps Aaron's throbbing shaft firmly. She forcibly places it into her hottest spot, then leans back, and undulates back and forth atop Aaron as though she were a well-experienced woman of the night. Aaron moans both in pain and pleasure as Kaybra rhythmically pummels him with repeated, hard thrusts.

Aaron tries to gather his wits through the ecstasy of the moment, but Kaybra leans forward again and braces herself with her hands on the ground beside Aaron's head. As she does this her breasts sway about, intermittently they slightly tickle and touch Aaron's nose and lips. She shrugs her shoulders, which causes the gyrations of her breasts to intensify, a motion that taunts the muscle-bound warrior madly.

Kaybra's strength renders him helpless and he is now completely overcome by her sensual assault. He captures her breasts as they sway back and forth, in his mouth. He licks and sucks on her stiff nipples as they pass by, but whenever Aaron successfully captures one of Kaybra's teats in his mouth, she teases him by pulling back and popping it out of his mouth as she sighs.

Then she relents, forcing her bosom farther into his face ululating, "Harder Aaron! Please suck me harder!" Aaron pauses momentarily and shakes his head at what he is doing. He fears he will lose his seeds deep into Kaybra's loins if he does not withdraw immediately and so he attempts to push Kaybra off of him and to one side. But with each of his attempts, Kaybra forces herself down yet harder on Aaron. She begins to groan, louder, "Oh, ah, ah," as her naked body trembles and quakes. She grabs her breasts, in her hands, forces them upward and throws her head back. Continuing to cry out and quiver, she drops them and outstretches her ringed fingers stiffly upward into the night sky as she savors her pleasure. Sparks fly from her fingertips like lightening and zap upward into the night sky.

Aaron's resolve is weakened by Kaybra's cries even more when her beautiful bosom plunges downward and bounces about.

To Aaron it is like in slow motion as he watches Kaybra's breasts jostle and jiggle around before coming to a complete rest.

Conceding he is all but done, he places his sun-darkened hands around Kaybra's imposing pale un-tanned buttocks and claw like, squeezes his callused fingers, clinching them further into her shapely soft skin.

Even though Kaybra continues to grind away, he pulls her down tighter and when he does, the colossal woman shrieks, "Oh, ah, ah, ah" and Aaron's groans of pleasure unite with hers.

Aaron is definitely Kaybra's captive, beyond the point of no return and on the verge of ejaculating. His excited state-of-mind peaks higher when he views the seductive women's dancing, jeweled navel. Then casting his guilt aside, Aaron tightens his grasp on Kaybra's buttocks and mightily thrusts his loin upward until he feels he can go no deeper. In ecstasy he hurls repeated injections of his semen deep into the mysteries of the dark warrior woman's hot, sweaty, quivering body.

Afterward in shallow stages, Kaybra calms down, recovering to a paced deep breathing. She gasps out, "Do you have any idea of how long I have waited for a moment such as this. Oh my God! Thank you, Gods above, thank you!"

She again leans forward and kisses Aaron on the lips, saying, "You have elevated my strength for tomorrow's battle. Thank you, my brave warrior comrade. I shall never forget this moment and this act will remain our secret if you wish."

Aaron is completely exhausted, for Kaybra is a heavy woman and still sits atop of him, smiling and continuing to gently rock back and forth. She glances back down to Aaron and sees he's uncomfortable and agonizes, "Forgive me, Sir Aaron, for my thoughtlessness." She gracefully lifts herself off of him and crawls inches away, then turns on to her side. Smiling broadly she covers herself with several large leaves and closes her eyes.

Aaron's thoughts are turbulent about what has just happened. He wonders if he has impregnated Kaybra with this act. He looks to her as she continues to smile, obviously fast asleep. Still dripping wet with passionate juices and their combined sweat, the sexually ravaged warrior is shaken and quickly reaches over to retrieve his leather wrap.

Just as he finishes securing it around his waist and lies back, Samanda awakens slightly, quite groggy. With heavy eyelids, she snuggles up to Aaron, places her arm around his mid-section and drifts back to sleep.

Expressionless, Aaron stares upward at the moon that disappears and then reappears between the gently swaying treetops.

Since the battle at dawn is near, Aaron knows he must void his thoughts and emotions for now. By the position of the stars and half moon, he understands there is ample time for a good night's rest. He prays for answers in his dreams, then the very exhausted man joins his comrades in sleep.

*   *   *

Early the next morning, there are clanking sounds coming from the equipment of Aaron's army, which is assembling throughout the forest. The sounds wake him and he fears he has overslept, but realizes the dark, orange hue of pre-dawn provides the faint glow.

Aaron is surprised to find that Samanda and Kaybra are completely prepared to move, even having the three horses harnessed and ready to ride. Kaybra is very energetic and acts a trifle giddy as she carries on with getting things tidy.

Aaron has slept well and is feeling vigorous. He ignores the emotions that exist from the night before and cautiously approaches Samanda. She is doing some final harness preparation on her horse just a few steps away. Try as he may, he cannot deny that he feels like he may be falling in love with her.

He smiles slightly as he notices her having difficulty with a buckle on her steed's harness. "May I assist you, my dear?" Samanda, unconcerned replies, "I have readied many a steed in my day and I'm certain this one shall prove no different than the others."

Aaron's response is, "Alright, I shall prepare to ride as well."

Aaron feels he should be guilt ridden, even though he has never expressed his feelings to Samanda. He shakes it off and turns away from her toward his horse when Samanda blurts out, "Aaron, did you sleep well last night?"

Aaron is puzzled by her question but decides to answer her as a matter of fact. He turns back to her spontaneously with "Yes, yes I did sleep quite well, my lady. Thank you for your concern." He turns around and takes two short steps back toward his horse when Samanda queries him again, "No nightmares, my Commander General?"

Aaron stops, looks over his shoulder to where Samanda still fights the stubborn buckle on the harness. When he does, Samanda's horse, Windra, turns its head to Aaron, flares its nostrils and gives him a wide-eyed look as if to say, "You had better stick with the truth with this one, Commander-of-Arms."

Aaron now truly wonders whether or not Samanda actually is aware of the sexual act between him and Kaybra the night before. He stops again, but does not want to see the expression on Samanda's horse this time. Looking toward his own steed a few steps before him, he nervously speaks aloud, "No, no nightmares, Samanda. How about yourself? How did you rest throughout the night?"

Aaron mounts his horse. Feeling a little shaken by Samanda's stern demeanor, he sits nervously. As he jostles around to gain his stature atop his charger, he looks in Samanda's direction. She has now miraculously conquered the problematic buckle, mounted Windra and is right alongside of him.

She looks straight at Aaron for the first time on this day and answers, "I slept very well, Master, but had a peculiar erotic dream. I will speak to you about it another time. Are we ready now to merge with our troops, Master General?"

Aaron glances pensively to Kaybra who has caught the exchange between him and Samanda from the corner of her eye. She sits on top of her horse, looking into the foliage innocently.

Aaron kicks his steed and the three warriors gallop through the palms and underbrush to merge with their army awaiting them on the Genipsus side of the tropical forest.

As they emerge from the tree line into the desert, it is plain to see his entire army has been assembled and awaits his arrival.

Then as the sun's first beam shines over the eastern horizon, Aaron pauses briefly, then raises his sword high over his head. Upon the first direct reflection of the dawn, the broad sword twinkles with a bright orange flash.

Having received their cue, in unison both north and south flanks proceed eastward in a quiet stealth like canter.

As Genipsus appears before them, a mere short, hard charge ahead, one hundred more warriors from Aaron's hometown of Nemmin appear and flank them on the south. This creates a large, L-shaped line of attack, with dual flanks that close on Genipsus from the south as well as from the west.

Although difficult to determine from this distance, it appears the barbarian line of defense surrounding Genipsus remains unaware of Aaron's approach.

Just as the sun rises slightly higher in the sky, Aaron knows he must give the command to advance before its bright morning rays become blinding to his warriors, so he yells out, "CHARGE!"

His command echoes down the lines of warriors and the now nearly three hundred horseback warriors break into a full gallop. The siege upon Genipsus has begun.

*   *   *

Back at the canyon of the fanged lizard, Vampressa has alit on the top of its southern edge after extensive aerial surveillance high above Kaybra's stationary encampment that awaits her return from battle. The Harpy was once again enraged upon learning that her craven partners, the wild nymph women, were being held prisoners to await Aaron and Kaybra's return for their judgment.

Vampressa is further angered discovering that the giant reptile has devoured over one hundred Genipsus warriors. She is intensely aware that her evil counterparts are falling by the wayside like helpless flies.

She launches herself off the bluff and attempts to attack the lizard from the air, diving time-after-time with her talons extended, to no avail. Each time she does that, the lizard leaps into the air at her and hisses defiantly. Vampressa is capable of many evil things, but she is little threat to this huge prehistoric, monster.

She sees that the life forms at the bottom of the canyon are now no more than mutilated carcasses. Defeated, Vampressa sets herself down on the top of the bluff and cocks her best eye downward.

She is bitterly flustered as she mentally calculates her losses since Aaron, Kaybra, and Samanda teamed up to thwart her evil efforts. First she was betrayed by Samanda the night Aaron impregnated Layla in the large harem tent. Next, her eggs in the volcano nest were smashed to near oblivion and she still has no idea of the fate of her troll who is sealed tightly in his cave. Vampressa's thoughts then switch to Kaybra flogging her with her whip and Samanda chucking her spear at her when she transformed herself into Uma's image to trick Aaron. She seethes her body up and down with anger, too, as she revisits the vision of being only a split second away from seizing Aaron's reproductive organs in her hooked bill.

Now, Vampressa finds her nymphs have been imprisoned by Kaybra's people and to make matters worse, her barbarian associates are being felled with the aid of the large warrior woman's delta island troops. That is far more than Vampressa's dark, murky heart can fathom, so the Harpy insists to herself that this disruption of her dominant evil lifestyle can no longer be tolerated and as she schemes, she leaps upward, bellowing out a loud, vengeful screech.

In the snap of a finger the dastardly monster has soared out of sight into the turbulent air currents high above.

* * *

Just outside of the mud huts of Genipsus, the clash between Aaron's army and the barbarians has been in a full rage for a significant time. The early afternoon sun shines down upon the battle.

On his initial charge, Aaron had ordered every other horseman to halt, so they could load their dual arrowed crossbows. The remaining horsemen then charged ten lengths ahead and fired their crossbows at the Genipsans.

Then his warriors who had now re-loaded their weapons charged ten lengths in front of those who just fired and once in position, fired their bolts.

Many injuries were inflicted upon the enemy by this ingenious maneuver, bringing great screams of pain and agony from the enemy.

Aaron's stealth canter caught the enemy unprepared as they stumbled around half-asleep this early morning.

His attack was continued until Aaron's army had woven itself deep within the Genipsan flanks. Now the battle turns into vicious hand-to-hand combat.

Aaron, Kaybra, and Samanda lead the onslaught side-by-side and all three are well equipped with weaponry. Kaybra cracks and snaps her whip, twisting it around the necks of the enemy. She, single-handedly, has already felled twenty-five men with it. It now drips with her opponent's blood and swatches of their flesh.

Samanda, close to Aaron's right, has wasted nine, large, Genipsan barbarians with her crossbow at close range. She is now arrowless and tosses it aside as she pulls out her personally engraved sword. She slashes away at the enemy as her horse rears, giving her a more lethal advantage angle.

Aaron, too, has left a swath of death with his blade. The combined casualties are numerous. As he slashes away at the stubborn foe, his sword continues to clang with victory.

Aaron takes a split-second to glance at the two women at his side. As he looks to his left, he now understands something Kaybra explained to him days ago. Her oversized white leather cups are covered with cuts and punctures. At this moment a speeding arrow enters her right breast and Aaron winces, but Kaybra looks toward him and grins as she pulls the projectile out of her padded armor, snaps it in half in her fist, tosses it aside and then continues to mutilate the enemy with her whip.

Turning to his right, he sees a group of Genipsan female warriors have surrounded Samanda, all armed with spiked balls on chains. They twirl them up in circular fashion, then release them at her. She dodges the first projectile as it whizzes by her head, but it clips Aaron's right temple as it sails past him.

Samanda slashes at the burly women with all her might, inflicting mostly gut and chest wounds onto them. Aaron is momentarily dazed and helpless to assist as he wipes blood from his forehead.

Samanda has slain all but one of the women. This one is smaller, thinner, but feisty. She moves between Aaron's and Samanda's horses, weaponless, but only Aaron can see this since her back is to Samanda. Aaron, though a fierce warrior, still is a fair fighter. The angry ruthless woman bites and scratches at his leg as she attacks him while he's atop his steed. Instead of felling the woman with his weapon, he shoves her away with his boot and his attacker stumbles backward, spinning around toward Samanda.

Samanda's adrenaline is pumping. As the young woman gains her balance, she comes face-to-face with Samanda who reflexively thrusts the point of her sword downward, deep into the woman's throat. Samanda's victim falls to her knees, gasping for air and as she goes down, her neck slides off the end of Samanda's sword, which now drips with the female barbarian's blood. The tattered warrior lady lies dead in the sand on her back with her hands clutched around her throat.

Even though the battle continues to rage around them, a quiet engulfs Aaron and Samanda, as if time has stopped. Samanda's eyes slowly rise from the bloodied woman, as Aaron, too, solemnly lifts his eyes upward from the dead woman.

Both Aaron and Samanda have had a momentary flashback of Aaron's lady, Uma, on the fateful day that Samanda slew her in the very same manner.

Aaron wonders if Samanda is aware that he has learned of Uma's true fate and Samanda's thoughts likewise waffle in the deafening silence of the moment. She surmises that Aaron could have possibly learned she was the one who killed his woman.

The eyes of the two comrades slowly rise from the dead woman and are now face-to-face locked on each other without expression, as though a hypnotic trance has overcome them. The battle that rages on at elbows length around them seems like it is on the outside of a clear bubble muted in silence.

Samanda's fingers slowly loosen from around the hilt of her long, pointed sword and it falls to the sand.

Then suddenly, from behind, Aaron is knocked off his horse by two large male barbarians. In a flash the spell between him and Samanda is broken and the thundering sounds of battle instantly resume. Aaron wrestles with the thugs, but they are quickly gaining the upper hand. Aaron reaches for his knife, but the larger barbarian stomps on his wrist until he releases it.

The burly enemy picks up the knife and is about to pounce down on Aaron, blade end first, but Samanda cries out, "NO!" Without a weapon, the agile female warrior leaps off her horse and onto the back of Aaron's attacker. She rides him piggyback, kicking her heels into his sides and squeezing her forearms around his neck.

The big man is shocked that a woman so much smaller than he can put up such a scrap.

He looks down and sees his partner has Aaron under control as the two wrestle in the sand. Now he wants a look at the clawing lioness on his back and with Aaron's knife still in his hand, he bends forward sharply. Samanda flies off onto the ground over the barbarian's head and lands on her back in front of him and when she hits the ground, her top's laces become untied making her leather bra slide down, below her breasts.

The grimy, wooly-haired man smiles down at her, grunting, "Ah, hah." He bends down to Samanda and grabs her by her forearm, then jerks her up to her feet.

He pulls Samanda to him and begins to fondle her bare breasts. Samanda does not thwart his efforts but chooses to coyly comply with his lusty desires. She pretends to enjoy the barbarian's hands upon her and with a lustful look up to him, states, "I will kiss you and reveal more of my beautiful, naked body if you leave us unharmed." She then begins to loosen her skirt as if to drop it down.

The barbarian pulls her to him and rubs her bare bosom against his hairy chest and Samanda pretends to be enjoying his gestures. She looks up to him and smiles, puckering her lips and closing her eyes.

The mangy warrior bends his head down, touching his lips to hers. Samanda goads him further by sticking her tongue into his mouth. When she withdraws it, he wants more and holds her firmly to him as he parts her lips by forcing his tongue between them.

Samanda begins sucking his tongue seductively, deeper and deeper into her throat as he slurps and grunts.

He is so taken by Samanda's action, that he drops Aaron's knife.

Now Samanda really puts the pressure on. She's totally captivated this dangerous adversary and has him under her control as she jumps up on him, wrapping her legs around his waist. He so totally engrossed with his perversion, that the smelly bully grabs his hands around her buttocks and squeezes it firmly to him.

Samanda continues to accommodate his long tongue in her mouth as she places her palms on each side of his neck and the Genipsan warrior grunts with pleasure. As Samanda milks his lingua with her face, she slowly turns her razor sharp nails into the back of his neck, but he is too enthralled to recognize the pain she is inflicting onto him. Initially it seems to arouse him further. Samanda then places her thumbs under his bearded chin, just above his Adam's apple and shoves her pointed thumbnails up into his throat.

The barbarian finally senses something's not right with this situation. He opens his eyes to find the cat woman's wide crystal blue eyes staring daggers right into his. Immediately, Samanda bites down hard on his tongue with all of her strength and the smelly thug now realizes Samanda has duped him. But, try as he may, he cannot shake her off as she clings to his upper torso like an octopus.

Samanda pushes her nails still deeper into his neck and trachea region as she bites and sucks harder and harder. The huge oaf groans in severe pain as he stumbles around, trying to rid himself of Samanda's restrictive hold. He squirms to free himself as he stomps about, grunting like a cave man.

In desperation he clamps his huge hands around Samanda's head, puts his thumbs into her eyes and pushes on them as he tries to peel her clamped teeth off of his tongue.

Alerted to this attempt, Samanda bites down once again, harder than the last time, and punctures her thumbnails deep into the barbarian's airway. Blood oozes from around her thumbs as he moans out aloud. Her teeth have clamped down so hard that she has bitten off a third of his tongue.

When his tongue snaps off, she flies off him, landing on her back on the ground. The barbarian goes down to his knees in front of her, trying to plug the holes in his throat by cupping both hands around the wounds.

Blood gushes from his mouth as he gasps and gurgles for air. He tries to stand again but stumbles around and falls onto his side, then rolls about, moaning and groaning in shock and pain.

Samanda leaps to her feet and spits the end of the thug's tongue out of her mouth as if it were a plug of bad chew. It lands in the sand before his very eyes as he convulses in agony, his head in a pool of his own blood.

Samanda quickly retrieves her sword, which she dropped only a few feet away just before this ordeal. She raises its hilt high before her with its sharp end pointed down and thrusts it into the barbarian's rib cage. His body goes limp.

Samanda twirls back to Aaron like a wonder woman. She finds, Aaron now has the upper hand in his fight with the other barbarian. Samanda looks about the battlefield and finds the brutal battle has wound down. As if she were preparing to face another front, she pulls her top back up in place and refastens it.

Fatalities from both sides litter the sands like dead tree stumps after a raging firestorm in the forest. However most of the casualties are their opponents.

Aaron takes one final slug at his relentless contender, which snaps his head back far enough to break his neck. The last remaining, Genipsain warrior falls over backward at Samanda's feet and lands face to face with his partner. The bloody stub of a tongue lies on the sand between the two corpses.

Aaron and Samanda stand side-by-side as Samanda wipes her victim's blood from her chin with the back of her hand. With swords drawn the two warriors scan the carnage.

Their fellow soldiers ride about the battlefield searching for any Genipsan survivors, finding none.

Aaron and Samanda turn to each other and in unison state, "Where's Kaybra?"

They quickly mount their horses and snap them around as Aaron commands, "Assemble your army to attention and approach!" His men race to Aaron and Samanda, surrounding them in a large crowded circle.

Aaron orders that the Nemmins gather their dead and return to their hometown to the south. He adds, "Now is the time for peace and thanks to Kaybra's force, we have achieved that goal. Now, return to your families with pride of your accomplishment this day."

The Nemmins disperse and depart the area just as Kaybra thunders toward the group. She is in a full gallop, speeding out of one of the streets that run between the mud and stone shacks of Genipsus.

She has an arrow stuck in her right upper shoulder and screams out, "Ride for your lives," as the ground trembles and shifts, the dried mud and stone buildings of Genipsus begin to crack apart.

As she races alongside of her alarmed comrades, she shouts, "You must hurry. Retreat to the west, while we are still able to escape."

Everyone's horse is panicked by the shaking ground and it is nearly impossible for their riders to hold them in place.

Kaybra pauses briefly beside Aaron and Samanda. Ignoring the arrow in her shoulder, she warns, "We must ride swiftly. The entire eastern edge of Genipsus is breaking up and falling into the depths of the Gorge of the Damned."

Just then, the ground beneath them drops measurably and close to the east of them, the dwellings of Genipsus crumble and slide into the gorge.

All of the troops heed Kaybra's warning as Aaron shouts, "Retreat to the green palm forest from which we arrived!"

The warriors immediately head off in no particular formation toward the broad-leafed wooded area where they bivouacked the preceding night. Genipsus is now collapsing into the Gorge of the Damned so rapidly that they are now literally driving their horses up a steep dune the shifting sands have created.

The huge "V" shaped piece of the village that has broken off, has created a large spout from which the sand now pours into the dusty abyss. The buildings of Genipsus continue to plummet into the bottomless depths of the gorge.

Aaron rides between Samanda and Kaybra, who he can see from the corner of his eyes as they all lunge upward. The desert floor now slants sharply downward directly behind their horses' hoofs. There is no time to think or do anything but drive their chargers harder. It is as if the golden granular floor were being poured into a huge crevice.

Once again Samanda cannot resist her curiosity, which defeats her wisdom. She slows her pace slightly, turns and looks back, but is unable to see any trace of Genipsus behind her. She becomes even more frightened when she sees their entire army is valiantly charging upward atop a whirlpool of shifting sand.

As she follows the troop up the dune, a new peril appears in the guise of Vampressa, who swoops down at Samanda, nearly knocking her off her horse.

Samanda loses even more ground as the shifting sands flush her farther behind the others. As she slowly descends, she sees that many of her comrades have already vanished behind her. Still others cling to large rocks, which protrude through the surface of the draining slanted ground.

Vampressa now cackles with sadistic glee at what she is seeing. She flaps her heavy wings and with a sinister sneer pumps herself up high into the air currents to prepare for another dive. This time Vampressa sets her sights on Kaybra whose horse is struggling in the knee-deep quick upward. The arrow protruding from her shoulder waves back and forth as her trusty steed lunges forward to gain distance.

So, Vampressa navigates a broad loop high above, and dives for Kaybra, her legs and talons extended like a hawk about to snatch up a rabbit.

Miraculously, Kaybra is able to dodge Vampressa's talons by quickly leaning to her left as she flies past.But the vengeful Harpy has pushed the arrow deeper into Kaybra's shoulder on her pass and Kaybra grimaces as her blood trickles out from around the arrow as Vampressa continues to hiss and screech gleefully, flapping her heavy fowl body upward once again.

Aaron sees a massive flat shelf of sandstone ahead, which is tumbling end over end down the draining incline in their direction. It skips along, flying up into the air and smashing back down. With each bounce, it rolls faster toward the three warriors.

Vampressa eyes their inevitable doom from above and flies off, giving them all up for dead. The Harpy monster contemplates her next revenge filled accomplishment on the checklist of her morose obsessions. The one she finds most intriguing is to return to Kaybra's encampment and create even more havoc. Her feathery mass becomes a small dot as it vanishes over the western horizon.

Chapter Seven

The approaching mammoth sandstone plate is so enormous that it casts a wide gray shadow over Aaron, Samanda and Kaybra as it flips end over end just before them. Finally one edge of the mass hits the sliding sand a mere two horse's lengths in front of Aaron. He hears Samanda and Kaybra shrieking at the sight and this is the first time he realizes the two women are some distance behind. He reins back and turns his horse to go to their assistance.

The shadow of the sandstone turns the area around them into near darkness as it plummets toward them with its top edge about to soar downward.

Aaron knocks Kaybra off her horse as he leaps from his steed to hers, his arm around her neck. He tries to pull her to safety as the two slide down the glissading sand avalanche. They grab Samanda whose horse is now stuck chest deep in the granular mire. They pull her close and huddle together on their stomachs as they slide headfirst downward toward the draining spout. As they move, they hear and feel a tremendous thud, instantly followed by the return of sunlight, for the huge chunk of flat sandstone has flipped over them, leaving all three unharmed.

Moments later, the large, flat rock has flipped over and over to a point where it abruptly stops. It has lodged itself across the "V" shaped spout in the upper lip of the gorge from which the earth drains. The sand begins to back up behind it like water rising behind a dam.

Aaron, Samanda and Kaybra lie on the incline astonished by what they just witnessed. Aaron turns his head to Samanda and asks of her condition. She is very much out of breath, but assures him she's alright.

He then turns to Kaybra, on his other side. She lies face down with the arrow still sticking out of her shoulder and doesn't appear to be breathing.

Aaron immediately straddles her back and is on his knees over the top of her. He wraps his hands around the shank of the arrow's shaft and jerks it out.

He quickly enlists Samanda's assistance and together they roll Kaybra over onto her back. Aaron begins to make frantic attempts to revive the woman.

He then places the heels of his hands onto her abdomen just above her jeweled navel and kneads her stomach in and out. But this doesn't elicit any response from the still beauty.

Feverishly, he places his lips over hers and blows into her mouth, raising his head and taking a deep breath repeating the process.

Samanda excitedly cries out, "Keep it up, Aaron, she's beginning to move her finger tips. It's working, Aaron. It's working, give her more air." Aaron blows into Kaybra's lungs with heightened vigor.

Aaron pauses, lifts his head up slightly and looks at Kaybra's face for some kind of response. Slowly, her long dark eyelashes split apart and her gorgeous, amber-brown eyes peer upward into Aaron's face. His face nearly touches hers.

Kaybra lifts her arms and places her hands at the back of Aaron's head, threads her fingers into his long, dark, curly hair and pulls his head down. She guides his lips to hers, tilts her head slightly, grasps his head firmly and gives him a long, wet, tongue tickling, passionate kiss.

Samanda, who moments before, was worriedly concerned about Kaybra's wellbeing, is displeased with her comrade's repeated adoration of Aaron.

Aaron manages to pull back from Kaybra's face a short distance. She still grips his head, smiles at him and says, "Thank you for pulling the arrow out, my brave warrior."

Samanda now wonders if Kaybra was actually unconscious throughout this last ordeal. She barks out, "Cease your rewarding actions upon Aaron, my sister warrior. We must assess our damages."

Aaron has a flashback of the love making session he and Kaybra had the night before as he pulls her hands from his hair and stands up. Inside Kaybra hopes she has given Aaron a little reminder of what she has to offer him, but replies to Samanda, "Forgive me, my sister. When Vampressa drove the arrow deeper into my shoulder, it caused me excruciating pain. I went limp with relief when it was removed. Honestly, I meant nothing other than to reward Aaron for his kind deed."

Samanda now dismisses the incident, jumps to her feet and brushes the sand off her.

Kaybra props herself up and twists her head around, trying to view her wound.

The three look around and find most of their army has survived the tremors and sand-slide.

One-by-one scores of Aaron's troops emerge from their shallow, would-be graves, coughing and choking they dust themselves off.

Aaron orders aloud, "Fall into formation at the top of the slide!"

Shortly, all but the handful of those who were lost, gather on the ridge atop of the slope. As they look down to where Genipsus once stood, they see the sandstone mass wedged tightly into the broken out opening that originally caused the catastrophe.

Aaron looks toward the western horizon, placing his hand over his brow as visor from the early setting sun. He faintly sees the stand of trees in the distance where they camped just before the battle.

He looks at Samanda and then to Kaybra. He sees Samanda has her horse alongside Kaybra's and is using a piece of tattered linen to doctor Kaybra's wound. He waits until Samanda has the linen fastened and then shouts, "Return to the forest!" All gallop off into the western sunset.

Upon their arrival at the palms, Aaron orders his troops to halt and his commanders to approach. After they have assembled he tells them, "We will rest here for the last time on this night. Meet with your soldiers to assess your losses. I will confer with the Queen upon my return to Patrious and ask a reward for each of your brave deeds. You who Samanda and I recruited from the rock mines, may return to Nemmin as free men or go back to Patrious to begin a new way of life, for in either place there are many qualified, beautiful, widowed and single women residing there who wish to propagate and perpetuate their legacy of being a fine brave kingdom."

Aaron affectionately gazes at Samanda, then continues, "Today's conflict will be tomorrow's victory to our future generations. We will reach a point in tomorrow's travel where I will break off to the north and ride with Samanda. Those of you who wish to settle in Patrious will ride with Samanda and ensure she arrives home safely.

"After I am certain Samanda has been escorted across the river safely, I will ride back south to Kaybra's encampment to bid them farewell.

"After they depart I will stay behind until I slay the Harpy, Vampressa. Now be gone with you into the nightfall of this victorious evening and we will meet again midmorning before our departure."

The horseback warriors slowly drift into the green foliage and Samanda enters the broad leaves ahead of Aaron and Kaybra. She calls out, "C'mon follow me. I see the place where we bedded down last night."

Everyone is exhausted, so Kaybra and Aaron gratefully oblige Samanda's wish. Shortly they come unto the same cozy spot where they rested the preceding evening.

Aaron leads their horses to a clearing to tether them in such a manner that they may drink and graze throughout the night.

The moon promises to be a little brighter on this night since it is only a few days away from becoming full.

Samanda and Kaybra talk extensively as they rest awaiting Aaron's return. They have summarized their esteemed accomplishments of the day, when peculiarly both women instinctively realize what the next topic of conversation will be. There is a long, uneasy silence between the two female icons, until Kaybra cautiously breaks the respite, "Samanda?"

Samanda replies, "What is it, my sister warrior?"

Kaybra continues softly but inquisitively, "Do you think the Queen will mind if I once again have a sexual encounter with Aaron? Just one last time before my people and I depart the region?"

Samanda rolls her eyes upward as she replies "I told you, after much contemplation, that in exchange for your sacrifices in assisting the Queen in this war, she could only concede that sacrifice the one time. Furthermore, I don't know if I can bear the sounds of your sighs and pounding flesh upon him again."

Kaybra continues, "Please give it deep thought, my sister of battle. It had been too long since I experienced such carnal pleasure and it is difficult to remove last evening's engagement with this stud from my thoughts. I am a big woman, so even in my own village many men are afraid to approach me. Those that do are few and far between. Moreover no man of any of my rare sexual encounters ever matched up to the length and girth of the instrument Aaron possesses."

Samanda replies impetuously, "Stop, Kaybra!"

Yet Kaybra continues anyway, "Please commune my question to the Queen, my loving sister. My people have made great sacrifices to assist her in this forthright cause and several of their lives have been lost through my directions. There are children in my village who will no longer have fathers and there are women now without men who will long for similar male companionship, so please, Samanda, look inward for your answer. This entire cause is about propagation so our bloodlines may continue for generations to come.

My cooperation has certainly given the Queen a reproductive opportunity that she otherwise would never possess. Surely one last encounter with Aaron would ensure my impregnation. What better gift could the Queen offer such a devoted ally, as me?"

Samanda is noticeably uncomfortable as she visions Kaybra's request taking place. She is mulling it around, negatively, when Kaybra whines, "Ouch!" She winces, grabs her wounded shoulder with her uninjured hand and shoots Samanda a droopy-eyed look of self-pity.

Samanda surrenders, "Okay one last time Kaybra! After all, this man is technically a slave, which means he's the property of my kingdom. But, I do not wish to be present at the second encounter of your combined flesh that you enjoy imposing upon Aaron. I ask that you wait until I leave with my new recruits for Patrious before you seduce him."

Kaybra smiles broadly as she hugs Samanda, saying, "Oh, thank you, my sister. Tell the Queen not to concern herself with Aaron's requests for rewards for my people. Fulfilling my desires will both stimulate and soothe my loins. His acts of sexual engagement with me will replenish my feminine desires for some time to come."

Moments after the women have concluded their agreement, Aaron separates the broad green leaves that shroud Samanda's cozy pocket from the moonlight. He kneels onto the soft pad of leaves and rolls to his side, physically depleted from the unwieldy events of the day.

Aaron falls fast asleep with Kaybra perched up on her knees, smiling down at him admiringly as Samanda's face radiates with displeasure.

Soon, the lofty moon sinks into the darkness casting a silver hue over the trio's battle soiled bodies and faces as they sleep.

*   *   *

Samanda and Kaybra both awake early the following morning and have found a bubbling spring near the horses from which they fetch water to hand-bathe themselves.

After they cleanse their bodies, they wash Aaron as he sleeps. Kaybra and Samanda, now very attached to Aaron, are pleased to refresh him with their soothing motions upon his body.

The spring water is cool and awakens Aaron. He opens one eye slightly and sees the two women doting over him with their wet cloths and smiles. Then he closes his eye and drifts back to sleep.

Samanda hums a soft lullaby as she and Kaybra wring out their cloths, re-dampen them and continue dabbing at Aaron's grime and scratches.

Kaybra wipes Aaron's feet and he sighs with contentment in his-half sleep. As she works the cloth up his legs, she has difficulty keeping her eyes off his war apron. She has flashbacks of the two having intercourse two nights before.

Unable to help herself, using her fingertips, Kaybra pushes the cloth she uses high up Aaron's inner thigh and under his war leathers. This action accompanied by her stare at the center of Aaron's bulging war apron becomes quite obvious to Samanda. Samanda stops humming abruptly and berates Kaybra, "Can't you wait until I depart? I will be gone by nightfall!" Kaybra snaps her eyes away from Aaron and quickly withdraws the cloth from inside Aaron's upper leg.

She apologizes to Samanda, "I'm so sorry, my sister, please forgive me."

During the commotion Aaron comes fully awake, sits up and wipes his hands across his face as he shakes his head. He says, "Good morning, ladies. Thank you for the comforting hand bath."

The three face each other in a small circle. They nibble on dates and nuts as they review the conflict of the day before. Much of the conversation evolves around the tremors and the sand slide and they acknowledge that they are very lucky to have survived.

Finally, the conversation turns to their departure. Samanda asks Kaybra if her wound is abated enough for her to prepare the horses for their ride this day. Kaybra nods affirmatively, as if this deed would not be a problem for her and departs from the leafy pad to ready the trio's mounts.

Samanda looks deeply into Aaron's eyes with a cold vapid expression and says, "I must speak with you before we part and this is the only time we will be completely alone to talk before I must return to Patrious."

Aaron senses what Samanda has to say is serious and that he may be in trouble with her as he recalls that she queried him earlier the preceding day about her erotic dream.

Now he has a momentary flashback of Kaybra riding his loins in the palm shrouded moonlight. He looks into Samanda's eyes and nervously replies, "Yes, my lady."

Samanda resumes, "I was not asleep two evenings ago when you administered carnal pleasure deep into Kaybra's loins." Aaron gulps aloud. His facial expression goes long and straight. Samanda is not fazed by his reaction and continues in a matter-of-fact tone, "You must perform the act upon Kaybra one more time before she departs for her home." Now Aaron's jaw drops in amazement at what he hears. Speechless, he is unable to assemble any words.

Samanda has not stopped talking. She adds, "You are quite a specimen and it is nearly impossible for a woman of Kaybra's size to be satisfied sexually by most mortal men. From what I orally encountered from you at the river's edge, I suggest you take proper time to titillate her before penetration with your full length.

"None of my girls will be available to properly prepare the two of you for the union of your flesh with hers, so you must not forget of what I speak.

"I doubt that Kaybra will ever have a similar encounter in her lifetime, so do not prematurely climax. Make the act last and give her this one final gift from the Queen of Patrious for her devotion to our cause, for without Kaybra's assistance, our race would surely become extinct."

Aaron has never seen Samanda like this and stares at her in awe. Bewildered, he mutters, "How can the Queen give me this directive when she is so far away?"

Samanda replies, "At this point in your life, you do not yet understand, but I know my sister far better than anyone else. Now, fulfill both her and Kaybra's wishes, but wait until after I depart. If you do not follow the

Queen's directive, you may stay in the desert and keep Vampressa good company until the end of your days."

Aaron is in continued disbelief as he attempts to stand. Samanda has stood up at the end of her speech and reaches down to assist her confused comrade to his feet.

Kaybra returns and announces, "The horses are ready to ride." Aaron sizes up Kaybra's full-figured stature from head to toe, while he is in a state of beleaguered anticipation of what he has been ordered to do.

Kaybra smiles coyly, "Come along, Master General, Samanda must be on her way home to Patrious."

Attempting to rid himself of shock from his conversation with Samanda and regain his authoritative demeanor, Aaron strides behind the two women in the direction of the horses. Once there, they mount and ride through the preassembled warriors.

As they ride among the troops, Aaron repeats a command, "Follow in formation to where we will split our flanks!"

Obeying that order, the warriors gallop off with Aaron, Samanda and Kaybra in the lead.

By the time the sun reaches the noon sky, the warriors are at the place where they must split up.

Aaron commands all to halt and speaks to his audience of soldiers, "It is here that we must part ways. My comrades from the Queen's stone mines will ride north with me and to where the river is shallow and safe for crossing. Samanda will accompany us to the ford and it is there that I must bid her farewell until my return to Patrious with Vampressa's lifeless carcass.

"Kaybra and her people shall return to their encampment to the south. When I am assured that Samanda and my men have crossed the river without incident, I will ride south for one final meeting with Kaybra, after which we will bid each other farewell for the last time."

Kaybra gleams with excited anticipation as she envisions Aaron fulfilling her sexual desires at this final meeting.

Aaron concludes, "Our distances are not far apart, so with favorable circumstances, I should join Kaybra before today's dusk and tomorrow she and I shall decide the fate of the wild nymphs imprisoned at your camp. Let your thoughts be with the Gods above and disperse in peace."

When Aaron finishes, the army splits and about one third of the warriors follow Samanda and Aaron to their river destination to the north.

Kaybra leads the balance of the troop southwest. After a short ride they will reach the camp that they left behind earlier.

*   *   *

Aaron and Samanda casually ride side-by-side leading their people to the river crossing.

Little has been spoken between the two to this point, for Aaron harbors mixed emotions about his last conversation with Samanda and is reluctant to visit any topic.

The accomplished warrior looks at Samanda as they ride. Her face is devoid of expression and his feelings for her are becoming more defined. He knows he is falling helplessly in love with her, but also knows he is betrothed to the Queen as publicly decreed by her specific order.

Aaron admires not only Samanda's body, but her strong convictions as well. His eyes wander to her shapely, tanned thigh that dangles from her short leather skirt. His eyes follow her leg downward toward her calf.

Slightly above the top of Samanda's high-laced boot, Aaron spots a scar on her leg that looks like a healed slash wound. He stares at the lengthy thin scar and wonders of the wound? Was that injury inflicted upon Samanda by his dove, Uma, on the day of her demise? He has fond memories of Uma. While filled with sorrow, he understands very well how her death came about. He wants to forgive Samanda, but doesn't know how to broach the subject.

He is about to steal a glance at Samanda's comely profile when she turns to him, very somber. A single tear rolls down her cheek as she laments, "I am so sorry, Sir Aaron, I am sorry. I did not want to slay your Uma."

Slight tears now dampen the corners of Aaron's eyes. He answers, "The deed was a product of war, my love. It is forgiven." He gives Samanda an understanding, but sad smile.

Nothing more is said as they ride on and soon see their destination in the distance.

Samanda's soul feels a little lighter now that her secret has been revealed. She was also pleasantly surprised when Aaron addressed her as, "My love."

When the troop arrives at the riverbank, Aaron insists he escort Samanda to the far side while the others wait in place for his return.

The two plunge their steeds into the water as always, side-by-side and soon gallop onto the sand beach of the distant side. They dismount promptly and come together at a spot on the far side of their horses where it is difficult for Aaron's men to view them from across the river.

They embrace with their heads on each other's shoulder and Aaron asks softly, "What of the Queen, my love? How will she deal with us upon my return?"

Samanda replies, "That is not for me to say, but I must question you. Are you now certain of your love for me, Sir Aaron?"

Holding Samanda even tighter, Aaron replies, "Yes, Samanda. I knew the night you swam in the river outside Kaybra's village and I saved you from the crocodile. But at that time I could not forsake Uma. She was my life and now I do not want to marry the Queen upon my return to Patrious. I want to marry you."

" Aaron, someday you will understand that with your last statement you have passed every test of time sentenced upon you to this point. Do not falter at this juncture. The Queen shall have her way. That is why our scripture was written as it was. You are her personal property and that is the way it is. Now, return to Kaybra and give her one final act of sexual pleasure, for I owe her a great deal. Our kingdom's debt to her goes far beyond a monetary solution. To successfully complete your last and final test you must drag the evil Harpy monster's dead body into the courtyard and I promise you from the bottom of my heart that the Queen will make you a very devoted wife. So go now, so that Kaybra does not worry about you."

Samanda gently pushes Aaron away. Aaron tries to kiss her goodbye, but Samanda turns her head away and stares at the trail that leads back to Patrious. Aaron places his hands on Samanda's arms, but she pulls away, forcing them to slide down her arms to her hands. Aaron holds on to the tips of her fingers, but slowly releases them. Upon their release his newfound love's palms drop to her side.

Aaron mounts his proud, valiant steed and charges back across the river. Halfway across, he pulls his horse to an abrupt halt and turns the animal sideway in the current so he can capture one last glimpse of Samanda.

She stands at the water's edge, stone-faced, looking at Aaron. Her tears now trickle from her eyes, leaving thin, glimmering, wet-streaks down her cheeks. She brings her fingers to her lips, kisses them, then places her palm in front of her mouth and blows the kiss over the waters to Aaron.

Aaron turns his horse toward the other bank where his men wait and proceeds to splash across the river to them. Upon arrival he halts and salutes them as his trusty horse shakes the water off his lathered hide. Aaron points his sword to the opposite shore and commands, "Assist the warrior princess home."

Aaron gallops to the top of a nearby sandstone bluff, stops for moment and looks down across the river. Even though he has an inspiring, panoramic view of the entire land, his eyes focus only on his troops who cross the river valley far below. Aaron watches as they climb upon the far bank and escort Samanda off between the bluffs in the direction of Patrious.

When the last horseman of his detail has disappeared into the rocky path, he turns to the south, in anticipation of yet another quest. He and his steed stand like a bronze monument on a pedestal as Aaron envisions Vampressa hovering high above, screeching her menacing caws. But, he has no idea of the impending tragedy looming before him. Unfortunately, the Golden Pharaoh will not be victorious in the Valley Of The Phantom Pyramids in the evening to follow.

*   *   *

Meanwhile back at Kaybra's base camp, the people who remained there, cheer when they spot Kaybra and the rest of her delta island troop approaching from the far distant horizon...

*   *   *

At mid-afternoon, Aaron realizes that if he is to keep his date with Kaybra, he must get underway and so he spurs his charger and off they bound southward in the direction of Kaybra's awaiting open arms... and legs.

Aaron has traveled half the distance when he sees a colorful, white and light blue cabana-like tent in the distance to the east. He thinks he also hears faint cries coming from it that sound as if they are from a young girl in distress. He reins in his horse and places his hand to his ear to try and decipher the sound, but hears nothing. He looks to the sun to get an idea of the time of day and decides that if he does not dally, he should be able to remain on schedule and still be able to check out the frail voice coming from the tent.

As he nears the single-poled tent, he stops again to listen just as a desert breeze picks up. The warm desert wind blows to him as he views tents flapping bright white and pale blue broad striped fabrics. He cautiously approaches and halts only a short distance from the tent. Once again he listens, hears nothing.

Aaron surmises that this colorful single-poled tent has likely been abandoned by nomadic herders because its torn in many places and the wind blows through it.

Aaron assumes the sound he has heard was simply the wind passing through the holes in the tent, creating a sound similar to a reed. He turns again towards Kaybra's direction and goes only a few steps when he distinctly hears a young girl whimper out with a sob, "Please help me. Will anyone ever save me? Please help…"

*   *   *

By now Kaybra has been back among her people for a brief time and given them a full report on the last days of the Genipsan war effort. Everyone is fascinated by what they hear and very proud of Kaybra and the combined armies effort.

A small, elderly woman who helped maintain the camp sheepishly approaches Kaybra and says, "All is not well, my great mistress of war. On the last evening of your absence, we were attacked by Vampressa, who swooped and ripped through our cloth village while scolding us. She leapt from tent to tent until she found the one where her nymphs were tied together and wailed, 'I'll teach you a thing or two. I'll conjure up an evil spell and cast it upon you for imprisoning the finest crop of sluts I have harvested over the years.' She tore at the nymph's tent and then untied them. As she flew away, the wild women scampered off into the night."

Kaybra is stunned hearing this report. She understands that the camp was defenseless against the vicious Harpy, so although upset, she's not angry with her people. Kaybra turns to the north, and is ready to ride, knowing that Aaron is likely underway to meet up with her. She is exceptionally concerned and her loins ache for his return.

The elderly woman taps Kaybra on the arm. Kaybra looks down into her withered old face, "There is one more thing, Miss Kaybra. The first tent Vampressa ravaged was your tent. She eyed everything you left behind, like a curious raven. She then plucked up your cherished golden javelin, cocked her horrid eye to it and read your name aloud from its engraved monogram."

Kaybra is unfazed by the woman's words and continues to pine for Aaron as she stares off to the northern horizon of wind-whispering sand dunes…

*   *   *

Aaron, after hearing the girl's pleas for help, cannot restrain himself. He pulls left on his reins and trots toward the blue and white tent. Unaware of Vampressa's most recent deed, his brilliant war strategies escape him and his actions now defy logic. He ignores caution, for this situation can evolve into a clever trap, with him as the intended mark.

Aaron dismounts a few steps away from the tent and circles it. The breeze picks up and the noise from the flapping canvas grows louder as it twists about in the wind. He peeks in through the gaping slits, but sees nothing. He has no way of knowing that the Queen of the sluts, Dilyla and two of her most trusted assistants, Fon and Nicklett, nearly have him in their snare.

Aaron finds the opening to the tent and unsheathes his sword using it to draw back the entryway fabric. He still finds nothing and sees no one inside.

Dilyla, Fon and Nicklett lie in the sand floor inside. They have dug their naked bodies into the sand and covered themselves with the desert's powdery crystals. Fon is a small woman but her large breasts cannot be effectively camouflaged with the sand. Other than Fon's bosom, the only things that remain uncovered are the women's eyes and noses.

Aaron enters the opening cautiously and at first glance finds nothing askew. Only the inside of a raggedy abandoned tent. He takes a few steps across the sand floor to the middle, beside its large wooden support pole and slowly scans the interior, his back against the pole.

He steps around it in circular fashion with his sword at the ready, still the only sounds heard are of the warm winds as they drift through the torn slats of the tent.

Now Aaron tilts his head back to look upward toward the top of the pole. The instant his sightline reaches the point where the pole props up the canvas, Aaron realizes he's been outwitted. A large, gnarly drag net, which had been suspended outward from around the top of the single support pole, has been triggered and drops down, completely covering Aaron. Its weight brings him to his knees.

Once he is covered the nymphs emerge from their temporary graves and spring into action. They pounce on Aaron as he struggles under the netting. Dilyla reaches into the weighted webbing and snatches Aaron's sword away from him.

Nicklett is a rotund woman of great strength. She has a leather strap that she threads into the snare and wraps around Aaron's neck. She pulls it tightly and Aaron gasps for air. Meanwhile Dilyla struggles to seize Aaron's hand knife.

Fon has a leather device similar to Nicklett's. She and Dilayla use it to finally bind Aaron's hands together. The women are very proficient with their attack and have Aaron rendered completely helpless within moments. As he squirms and fights to free himself, the women begin to cautiously remove their web from him.

Now Dilyla wears only a very short black leather skirt and her blue-grey eyes remain slightly crossed. She is an attractive woman and this condition actually adds to her allure. She possesses a rugged, but refined look, with her painted face and long, dark hair hanging down over her proud bare breasts.

The lanky, dark Queen walks up to Aaron and kicks him hard in the gut. He groans in pain, for Dilyla had sharpened her painted toenails and Aaron bleeds slightly from her attack.

Dilyla speaks to her associates, "Well, well, well. Look here is the big brave and capable Master Warrior at my feet." Aaron looks at her with contempt as he lies on his side fighting the straps that bind him. Dilyla bellows, "Hang him on the pole girls!"

This is not the first time the sluts have used this tent or this tactic. To perfect their craft they have attached a hook to the pole, about one quarter of the way up and soon they have the strap around Aaron's wrists looped over the hook. His muscular arms are stretched over his head and his narrow hips hang down from his broad shoulders as his feet barely touch the ground.

Fon scurries behind her victim and with another strap, binds Aaron's ankles together behind the pole. Now his abdomen is drawn inward while his rib cage protrudes outward. Aaron's breathing becomes labored. Not unlike the circumstance Aaron had Dilyla in upon her capture, now it is he that must pull his stomach in as far as he can to obtain a single shallow breath. His leather war apron is loosened due to his predicament and hangs precariously from his waistline.

Dilyla, who has been pacing around in front of Aaron, like the general in command of this operation, now speaks, "As fond as you are of tying up helpless, starving peasant women, I thought you would enjoy this treatment very much."

She moves to where she earlier stuck Aaron's sword into the sand, pulls it out, then returns to the pole where Aaron is strung up.

All is very quiet now and on this arid early evening, the beginning of nightfall has caused the dessert winds to calm.

Fon and Nicklett remain silent as their leader approaches Aaron with the huge knife.

Dilyla places the tip of Aaron's sword to his skin just below his sternum bone and reminds him of an identical situation in which he inflicted the same treatment upon her. Every time he is forced to exhale the point of the sword pricks his abdomen.

As his blood trickles into and around his navel, the dark, cross-eyed woman laughs, "Ha, ha, ha. I could ram this blade through your gullet at this very moment. But no! I shall do as I told you I would when we were on your horse. You shall die a long, painful death. I want you to remember Dilyla's face as you watch your genitals being severed from your loin."

As if intent on getting right to business, Dilayla slides the sword up under Aaron's wrap at his hip and with a quick flick of her wrist the sharp blade slices through the belt and the garment falls to the ground. Dilyla stares admiringly at Aaron's bared penis and smiles. With her crossed - eyes fixed upon it, she comments, "It is no wonder that your large woman,

Kaybra, keeps you so close by her side. It appears a certainty that you can easily fulfill her deepest and most passionate desires."

Dilyla lifts Aaron's sword upward and straightens her arm out, locks her elbow, then aims the sword's point uncomfortably close to his genitals. Aaron strains his chin downward to view the circumstances before him as Dilyla, while holding her head in place, rolls her pupils upward to meet those of the trembling warrior. A nervous sweat breaks from Aaron's face as Dilyla states, "But for now I've been told that my friend, Vampressa, has some very deep desires of her own for you and from what I view, I agree that you can easily fulfill her needs as well."

Aaron is frantically trying to think of something, anything to codify Dilyla. Contrary to his normal gentleman-like demeanor he offers, "Dilyla, upon my return to Kaybra's camp, I was going to provide you with rations and set you and your women free. You are a dark, but very beautiful woman and I planned to secretly ask you to make love to me. Now that my Uma is dead, I have no life left in Nemmin and I recently found out that the wicked Queen of Patrious wants me for her own personal sex slave. I have been recently trained in the art of giving a fine woman like you, great sensual pleasures. I would begin copulation by laying you down gently. Then I would remove your black leather skirt with my teeth. If you cut me down, I will oblige by letting your two comely assistants prepare me for you."

Dilyla actually seems to contemplate Aaron's offer for a moment. Her crossed eyes drop back to his groin. Once again she smiles, this time with a devious smirk. Dilyla begins to fantasize about the sexual act with which Aaron has tweaked her imagination. She sways her hips to and fro slightly, as she momentarily imagines Aaron upon her and that the copulation is actually taking place. Then something instantly snaps in her mind. Dilyla turns to Nicklett and Fon, jambs the sword into the sand close to Aaron's feet. Aaron's entire body shudders.

She orders, "Castrate him, I have an appointment with Vampressa who I will not betray. But before you remove his sac, take adequate time to arouse him. You must be certain that you draw all his seeds into it from deep within. Cup it with your hand, when it is firm and full, sever it and place it in this small box. If he is able to resist your lustful temptations to arouse him, force him to ingest the potion. Now carry out our ritual. I must help Vampressa find Kaybra and by dawn, we will leave the cadavers of our two lovers side-by-side for the vultures to pluck maggots from, in the scorching sun."

Dilayla runs her index finger across a thick blotch of blood dripping from Aaron's sculpted stomach. She brings her finger to her lips, places it into her mouth and smiles evilly up at Aaron.

As he looks upon her, Dilyla slowly pulls her finger from her lips. She has sucked Aaron's blood clean from it. Then, still gazing up to him with a radiant angry expression on her face, she gulps a theatrical swallow and exits abruptly.

After Dilyla's departure, Aaron looks around for the two remaining nymphs. He sees them to his left, patiently awaiting their Queen's departure. With a tenacious imposing stride, Fon and Nicklett approach Aaron with their strategy to systematically excite his libido.

Nicklett loosens the strap around Aaron's neck so he can now look down at Fon's seductive suggestions. She acts as if she has just discovered her disproportionately large breasts for the first time and because of her raw beauty and petite stance, she is tantalizing to Aaron. He closes his eyes tightly and tries to think of things unrelated to his situation.

Aaron forces himself to remember how he played with a small dog he found when a young boy. Then his thoughts turn to the times he and his father defended their stock from Vampressa's nightly attacks. Aaron becomes angry and silently prays to the Gods for his freedom.

Nicklett realizes what Aaron is attempting to accomplish, struts up to him and slugs him in the gut with all of her might. Aaron groans as his body winces from the blow and his wound inflicted by Dilyla opens wider. But, Aaron's eyes are still shut tight.

Nicklett becomes infuriated with Aaron's strength of will and repeatedly backhands him about the face, when Fon speaks out, "Stop, Nicklett, let me try this."

Fon places her hands at the side of each of her breasts and pushes her palms together, making her bosom squish together and protrude outward even more. Her nipples are now pointed and firm as she steps close to Aaron and rubs them softly on his genitals. She speaks in a soft, excited, provocative manner, telling Aaron how strong he is and how his soft penis on her tips is exciting her. Her enchanting tone turns into orgasmic sighs. But, with his eyes tightly shut and his jaw clinched, Aaron still manages to prevent an erection.

Nicklett sees Fon is making little headway with her technique. She sprinkles a yellow powder on a damp area at the center of a length of rolled linen, walks up behind Aaron and cinches his neck back to the pole. Nicklett then places the rolled linen around in front of Aaron's face. She brings the twisted ends of the cloth back past his ears and ties them together behind his head. As the rag tightens, the powdered spot on the fabric is forced into Aaron's mouth.

He struggles to fight Nicklett's advance, but to no avail. Soon the substance on the cloth is absorbed by his saliva and his fight for air merely helps ingest the potion.

Fon stresses to Nicklett that she must use some care as to not suffocate the warrior. That if he were to perish before their deed was accomplished, both Vampressa and Dilyla would be horribly upset with them.

Aaron hears Fon. Nicklett immediately removes the gag and loosens the strap around Aaron's neck. Aaron flops his head forward lifelessly in an attempt to feign his death.

The girls are vexed as they view Aaron's motionless, limp body hanging before them. Nicklett exclaims, "The potion has never killed any man before."

Fon scolds, "But you did not have to punch him in the belly so hard, Nicklett!" Aaron listens to the two women argue somewhat relieved.

Fon steps to Aaron, stares at his penis and places her small hand around his drooping appendage. Even in its impotent state, she is amazed at its size as she gently lifts it.

Nicklett is convinced she has likely strangled Aaron with the strap and is well aware of Dilyla and Vampressa's imminent wrath. She panics and urges Fon to castrate Aaron immediately. She pleads, "Sever his scrotum now, before Dilyla returns. He would have bled to death by now anyway if we had been more efficient."

Aaron barely cracks his eyes open with Nicklett's last statement. He sees Fon's dainty hand wrapped around his shaft. Within moments it begins to swell. The potion has kicked in. Aaron is fraught with despair in that he has absolutely no control over the blood pumping into his column of flesh.

Fon realizes what is happening and becomes excited. Nicklett sees as well, she entreats Fon, "Work it rapidly with your hand!"

Aaron knows he is foiled and his demise is near. Knowing the fabrication of his own death has failed, he raises his head and surrenders his pride to the two vamps, "Please, I will give you anything if you cut me down. Please release me?"

Neither nymph pays attention to him. Fon works him faster and harder than before, her nipples once again are firm. Aaron notices they are oddly located slightly above the tips of her breasts and point upward, like eyes focused on his erection. As Fon works on him they jiggle about slightly and the prolonged repetition of this sight arouses the warrior further.

Aaron sighs and moans, an unwilling victim to Fon's evil intended and stimulating seduction. As he feels his inner loins begin to percolate, he knows his fate is not far off.

Fon cups her free hand around Aaron's scrotum just as she was instructed and squeezes firmly, telling Nicklett, "It's still too soon. They need to plump up more."

By now the silver moon has traded places with the day's hot sun and the tent absorbs the glowing orbs silver beam. The inside of the tent is illuminated with a bright, blue-gray hue as moonbeams shine through the tears in its cloth walls.

*   *   *

Dilyla and Vampressa have met up. Their frantic search for Kaybra has been underway for some time. Aided by the moonlight Vampressa, conducted extensive surveillance over Kaybra's encampment and Dilyla, dressed in a peasant garb disguise, snuck unnoticed into Kaybra's camp and checked every tent. They find her nowhere.

The two reprobates fall back into the dessert halfway between Kaybra's site and the tent where Aaron is about to lose his manhood. Vampressa glides down onto the sand where Dilyla awaits her. She breaks her landing on her extended webbed feet, as she plops down to earth.

They argue about Kaybra's whereabouts. The frustrations of these two evildoers increases, further heating up their dispute and Dilyla becomes disenchanted with Vampressa's fierce temper, so she plunks herself down in the sand and curses Vampressa under her breath.

Vampressa's keen hearing picks up her words and she sneers at Dilyla, "Return to the tent and check on the sluts. I have only two eggs left in my nest and only one is fertile. Bring me Aaron's seeds in the box I gave you and if you continue to pout, I will slay you with this spear I stole from Kaybra's tent." Vampressa has been flying around all night with Kaybra's golden javelin clenched between her talons. It has a large "K" engraved on each side of its pointed end and its blade is razor sharp. This was a trophy, given Kaybra years ago for her bravery assisting another endangered village.

Dilyla is confident of Nicklett and Fon's abilities, so she chooses to sit in the sand and curse aloud at Vampressa. As she lifts off, Dilyla spits in the Harpy's direction.

*　　*　　*

Back in the tent, things have not improved for Aaron. Nicklett is becoming impatient with Fon. She urges her, "Fon, place your lips around the end of his shaft and I will place the sword blade at the base of his sac. If our timing is off, at least he will spew his semen into your mouth. It cannot be effectively gathered from the sand floor. Hold it there until you can spit the seeds into the box with his sac."

Aaron is trembling. His head hangs down as he helplessly views Fon's aggressive attempts to get him to ejaculate. He is crazed with fear, yet extremely sexually excited and his penis totally erect.

Fon heeds Nicklett's advice, but her mouth is so small that she struggles to open wide enough to accommodate Aaron's girth. Finally she succeeds in wrapping her thin pink lips around Aaron's shank and her cheeks hollow every time she sucks and pulls back on it. Bending over and placing one hand on his hip, she is in such a position that her large breasts sway back and forth under her ribs as she works.

Nicklett grabs Aaron's sword from the sand and positions herself in front of Fon, next to Aaron. Carefully, the veteran harlot places its sharp edge flat under the base of Aaron's shaft, the blade's sharp edge nearly touching his scrotum.

Aaron pleads, "No! Please no. Someone help!" He feels his delivery building, coming closer and closer with every tug Fon's wet lips make. In his final seconds, Aaron growls like a cornered wolf through his gritted teeth.

Fon has obviously assisted in castrations many times. Knowing Aaron's time is near, she squeezes her eyes shut tightly, for she has no desire to view the impending blood spatter and gore from such close proximity.

Nicklett can also tell the time is near. To insure the utmost of sperm production, she places her hand on the back of Fon's head and gives her sister's head an abrupt shove, forcing her mouth farther onto Aaron. Fon gags and froths, but still keeps her mouth in place. She knows this is her second-to-last cue from her fellow seductress.

Just as Aaron shouts out with what surely will be his last cry, Nicklett's fingers loosen from around the hilt of the sword and she drops the weapon as she falls over backward, the huge sword at her side.

Nicklett has an arrow embedded deep into her bulging abdomen. With her mouth wide open, the woman is in silent shock as she raises her head to view the embedded projectile.

Fighting to learn what is going on, Aaron looks down at her, wondering if he is next, but when he looks up to see from where the arrow came, he sees Kaybra in full white regalia, towering before him at the opening of the tent. She has already reloaded and has precise aim at Fon's bosom as it sways back and forth under her.

Nicklett is not dead, but remains speechless. She has become overwhelmed by the sight of her wound and stares wide-eyed up at Aaron as if she acknowledges the injury is fatal. Nicklett rolls over onto her side as she helplessly watches her blood seep into the sand.

Because of Aaron's moaning and Nicklett's silence, Fon still has her eyes closed tight. She feverishly slides her mouth up and down on Aaron. She is waiting for either the feeling of Aaron's warm blood dripping on her bared chest as he cries out in pain or the hot spurts of his semen squirting into her mouth.

Kaybra squeezes the trigger and her arrow flies into Fon's bosom. The dart enters the side of her right breast and goes through her left as well. The arrow's head now rests inches outside the punctured flesh of Fon's left breast.

Fon's eyelids explode open from the unidentified piercing pain. At this point she has no idea of the severity of her injury. Kaybra's arrow is lodged in Fon's breasts, directly behind her perky tips.

Looking down at her, Aaron has viewed the entire incident. Fon's eyes roll upward and back into her head. Her thin, tight wet lips slowly slide off Aaron's throbbing shaft. Fon rises from her knees and once standing, slowly drops her chin down tight to her chest, for a full view of her skewered bosom, dripping blood from four places. She flails her arms outward as she screams in agony and angry disbelief at what has just happened to her beautiful bust line.

Then the shapely siren has discovered the cause of her intense pain. With palms extended and her back hunched over, she looks at Aaron as if to say, "How could you do this to me?" and collapses to the ground. Squirming around in the sand, Fon shrieks and reels with pain. She makes several frustrating uneasy attempts to pull the arrow out, but is unsuccessful. The grains of sand stick to her wet, scarlet breasts. Soon her wails subside into soft moans.

Vampressa has backtracked and is now hovering high in the moonlit sky when she spots Kaybra's mighty image standing in the tent's opening. The Harpy seethes in anger at the sight of Kaybra, with the back of her white leather skirt and wide back strap of her leather bra reflecting the moon's light. Vampressa grasps Kaybra's golden ceremonial spear tightly in her dangling webbed feet, points it forward and soars sharply downward toward her objective.

Meanwhile, Kaybra stands proud in the tattered opening. For a moment she is in a quelled state of mind as the warrior woman knows that she has just saved Aaron's life and exhales with relief. She takes advantage of what she believes is a peril free respite to stare at Aaron's excited erection and smiles at it wantonly.

Kaybra's desire for Aaron escalates with enthusiasm and fond anticipation of her upcoming rendezvous with him. With what she sees before her, Kaybra reminisces about her prior sex act with this gorgeous man. It is as if she can already feel him penetrating deep into her glimmering black triangle and loin.

Aaron smiles at Kaybra, reflecting back to her a sigh of relief. Kaybra's smile is frozen in place just as she begins to take her first step toward him to cut him down.

Vampressa has other plans for Kaybra. She has dropped from a high altitude and quickly approaching Kaybra's rear, her eye set on the center of Kaybra's wide white back strap. She focuses to an area on it exactly between Kaybra's shoulder blades.

Kaybra winks at Aaron, he continues to smile back unto her. Momentarily a granule of time locks the expressions between the two in place.

Vampressa is now virtually on top of Kaybra. Using her soaring momentum from the aerial descent to aid her, the Harpy thrusts the spear into the center of Kaybra's back creating a loud thud sound. Having been thrust completely through her body, the large golden javelin impales Kabra. When it comes out the front of Kaybra's chest, the golden spearhead pops off the ruby clasp fastening her large cups together. The ruby plops to a stop onto the sand floor a few short steps in front of Aaron. The front of Kaybra's bra flies off and her cups recoil behind her, swinging ominously from the shaft of the spear that has the wide white back strap of the leather war bra, spiked to the center of her back.

Not unlike Fon and Nicklett, the big woman has no idea what has hit her. Still standing tall, Kaybra looks down at her battle-scarred bosom and sees the golden spearhead protruding outward from directly between her breasts. She recognizes the engraved "K" inscription and immediately understands how she just met her fate.

After impaling Kaybra, Vampressa foils the night air beneath her broad wingspan and clears the tent's top. The flying monster cackles in her sinister tone, soaring back upward and disappearing into the night sky.

Kaybra is fading quickly and stumbles toward Aaron. With both her hands, elbows extended outward, she grabs the end of the harpoon's shank just behind its large engraved golden arrowhead.

The two nymphs are still moaning as they flounder around in the bloody grit at Aaron's feet. Kaybra drops to her knees between the nymphs in front of Aaron and whispers up to him, "I wanted you one more time, Sir Warrior, to have one last moment of divine sensual pleasure with you, my close friend. This was my only desire before my departure to the south. Was it so wrong? Continue to be brave in your deeds. I know that somehow you will use your uncanny battle wisdom to escape this dilemma. Lastly, please promise me that you will avenge my death and return my soon-to-be immortal remains to my land. Sir Aaron, I promise, one day we will have our final sexual encounter when I am transformed into the form of another life. It is meant to be…"

Aaron is in no position to promise anybody anything. But as he looks down at Kaybra with tears rolling from his face, he firmly replies, "I promise you, my great white and bronze princess of war, that I will slay Vampressa in your name."

Kaybra succumbs and sprawls lifelessly onto the sand between the two wounded women.

Her eyes remain open in death, gazing directly at Aaron's erection and her look is as if she were still alive. Aaron continues to sob as he observes a small trickle of blood ease from the corner of Kaybra's mouth. He tosses his head upward and away from her half naked body and yells aloud, "Why, dear Gods above? Why after coming this far did you forsake us?"

Aaron drops his head back down at his slain comrade one more time. When he does, he finds Dilyla in her black slit skirt standing over Kaybra's body right before him. She straddles the dead woman's legs.

With her peculiar, yet alluring crossed eyes, Dilyla stares at Aaron venomously. The potion he ingested earlier still has his penis very much erect. After surveying the mayhem that has taken place within the tent, Aaron's heightened condition now catches Dilyla's undivided attention. Aaron is on the verge of ejaculating and nobody knows this better than Dilyla. She is quite familiar with the clear slow seeping excretion she observes Aaron is experiencing.

Dilyla, however is distracted when Fon and Nicklett's moans become louder. She picks up Aaron's sword from where it lies, grasps Nicklett by her hair and drags the kicking, wailing, underling nymph to the corner of the tent. She jerks back on her head by the hair, and slashes Nicklett's throat quickly.

Dilyla then marches back to Fon who has seen what just happened to Nicklett. She is trembling, and panicky from what she has just witnessed. Dilyla bends over and grasps the arrow strung through Fon's bust. She wraps two fingers under the short shaft of the arrow exposed between Fon's breasts and tugs upward, to further torment and coax Fon to her feet. Fon screams in agony as Dilyla pulls upward, lifting the nymph's large bosom up off her rib cage. The critically injured Fon is forced to rise to minimize the excruciating pain Dilyla is inflicting upon her.

Once on her feet, Dilyla pulls Fon forward. Trying to keep up, Fon stumbles behind Dilyla, screaming in horror, "Please, Dilyla. Please spare me." But, Dilyla is heartlessly cruel and she shoves Fon down on top of Nicklett's body. Fon continues to beg Dilyla, her arms and hands extended up to her, "No Dilyla, Please no! I will recover, Please help me?" Fon pulls hard on the feathered end of the arrow, adding, " My Queen of darkness, please help me remove the arrow."

Dilyla, though is merciless toward her ailing associate. Coldly, without a thought, she jabs her in the heart with Aaron's sword. In an instant Dilyla has rendered her petite foot soldier silent.

Aaron is mortified at what he has just witnessed, certain he must be experiencing a dark nightmare. In fact he is, but unfortunately he is not asleep.

Dilyla snaps her face back to Aaron from where she stands over the two dead sirens and gives him a sinister stare. She states, "They were going to die anyway. Our code is to not let a sister of the evening suffer when her condition is beyond recovery."

Dilyla knows that she does not have to meet Vampressa until the following mid-morning. It is then that she is to deliver the box containing Aaron's severed genitals. Being a little miffed with Vampressa at the moment, Dilyla begins to scheme. She jerks the sword from Fon's chest, swaggers back to Aaron and sinks the bloody point into the sand. She now gives Aaron a foxy, but malicious look and places her palm under his swollen shaft. Maintaining her questionable expression up unto the face of her victim, the Queen of the vixens rubs its underside gently.

Dilyla looks seductively into Aaron's eyes and states, "Now that your lovely, colossal woman is no more, possibly you will be more receptive to fornicate with me." She then pulls the sword from the sand and places its already-bloodied blade atop Aaron's erection, at its base. Aaron is petrified with fear and stares down into Kaybra's open eyes. A moment of silence passes. Dilyla closes her long fingers around Aaron's girth and squeezes him tightly. "Certainly Fon and Nicklett's treatment on your person did not damage you hearing!

"Describe exactly how you will, as you stated earlier, remove my skirt with your teeth." She curls the end of her fingers slowly, gradually digging her painted pointed nails into Aaron's flesh." This is your last chance big brave warrior. Speak to me now!"

Aaron is physically and emotionally exhausted, but having just witnessed Dilyla's execution of her assistants, he knows she is undoubtedly a woman of action and quickly regains his composure. He gives her a defiant, yet stud-like glare and states, "I will lay you down gently and begin by kissing your burgundy-coated lips. I will fondle and knead your round, plump breasts with my strong, calloused hands.

"Slowly I will move my mouth to the side of your neck and suck on it until you demand I stop, by ordering me to go down on you lower.' Obeying your command, I shall continue by wetting the tips of your nipples with my tongue."

Dilyla now drops Aaron's sword unto the sand, releases his penis and using both of her hands, begins to fondle her own bosom.

She impatiently interrupts Aaron's sensuous oratory with, "Go lower, down on me lower." Dilyla slides her fingers down her stomach and beneath her black skirt. She begins to twitch and gyrate like a belly dancer.

Aaron fights off the pain that radiates through his body from the strain of hanging for so long and musters up a deep breath to continue. "After your tips glisten in the moonlight from my oral juices, I will lift each of your full breasts with my face and lick your salty perspiration from their underside. When they have become refreshed I will slide my tongue down and apply a similar gesture deep into your lovely oval navel."

Dilyla now has her hands well beneath the beltline of her skirt, closes her eyes and writhing her hips about while fondling herself further. She agonizes, "Lower. I demand you go lower!"

Aaron pauses briefly, fearing Dilyla may climax from the sensual images he suggests and snap out of her erotic trance, applying some brutal act upon him. Composing himself, he realizes that either way he must give this his best performance ever, if he is to survive.

He speaks in a deeper tone now. "I will cleanse your navel until I feel your hands on my head pushing it down toward your love vessel. Then I will obey your divine Queen of darkness's every command by going to my knees between your legs spreading them apart slowly with my hands until your skirt tightens against the outer sides of your thighs. Bowing my head to you, I will then grasp your skirts taut hem strapped across your upper thighs with my teeth and biting down on it hard, I will force it upward, uncovering your hottest and most passionate place, I shall then continue where I left off, with my tongue in your lovely navel.

"Next, I will let my wet tongue continue its journey down the soft skin of your shapely waistline and slip deep into the core of your loin. I will nuzzle my unshaven face high up between your spread thighs, with my tongue fully extended to exhilarate your most erotic passions. When I hear your prolonged sighs of ecstasy, it will inspire me to extract your sweet nectars into my mouth. Then I will join you with my rod and we will be as one."

Aaron pauses, unable to think of anymore to say that will entice Dilyla into cutting him down. He looks at her, constraining his panic, as she stands before him unmoving. Her eyes are still closed and her hands still beneath her skirt. Her quivering body slowly calms down.

To Aaron it seems as if many hourglasses of time have past. Then all at once Dilyla pops her long, black-lashed eyelids open, looks at Aaron, her mystic eyes glowing gray and her nostrils steaming with passion. She demands, "I want it and I want it right now!"

She picks up Aaron's knife and struts behind him, then cuts the strap binding Aaron's ankles to the pole. He wiggles and stretches them to regain some circulation in his feet. Dilyla is breathing heavy with anticipation, but still has her wits about her. She warns Aaron, "Not so fast, my big, bad warrior. I am in complete control and for now you shall be my sex slave."

Dilyla then shifts around in front of Aaron and draws out a length of rope from the fallen netting. She reties his ankles, but leaves a comfortable measure between them so he can walk, but not enough so that he can effectively run. The wrist ropes from which Aaron has been hanging have stretched enough and so he can also place both feet on the ground.

Dilyla scurries out of the tent and returns in an instant with a large chunk of wood. She tosses it near Aaron's feet and picks up his sword. With his sword securely in hand, she kicks the wood closer to the pole at his feet and says, "Step onto the wood and lift your tied wrists up over the hook." Aaron obeys her and finally brings his arms in front of him for the first time since his capture. He then hops down off the wood.

Aaron is slightly more relaxed and feels his appendage is beginning to soften. The quick- thinking warrior attempts to place his tied hands over it, fearing that if Dilyla spots its abatement, it will jeopardize his proposition to her. It is a feeble attempt and he knows it, for his gesture will only be a temporary distraction.

Aaron sees the linen on the floor below him from which he had earlier ingested the stimulating potion and it still contains some of the yellow substance. He asks Dilayla, "May I pause for a moment, Queen of darkness, to rest my arms? It will enable me to act upon you with more vigor."

"You may, but only for a moment," she replies.

Aaron goes to his knees and retrieves the saliva-stained gag unnoticed. Trying not to draw attention to himself, he places the linen in his mouth and sucks on it.

Unknown to Aaron, Dilyla has taken this opportunity to place a tiny, white tablet under her tongue. Afterward she smiles a wide grin, then runs her fingers and pointed painted nails through her long black disheveled hair.

With her hips swaying as if they pivoted from the center of her back, Dilyla strolls to Aaron, stops, looks down at him, and then pricks him on his shoulder with the point of his sword. Aaron scorches out, "Ouch!"

He has no idea that the tablet Dilyla has placed under her tongue will transform her into a ravaging, sexual predator within moments. Her cocky smile broadens as she pricks Aaron once again and orders, "Come to your feet, your rest is finished. I want to fuck, now!" Dilyla's mind is transforming rapidly and the tablet she placed under her tongue is quickly magnifying her visions of Aaron's seductive offer.

As Aaron stands, Dilyla grabs the leather strap she has retied around his neck and pulls him back to the ground on top of her.

Aaron, still half-tied, braces his fall by jamming his fists into the sand just above Dilyla's head. He is on all fours above her and Dilyla looks down at Aaron's penis. She's not pleased with what she sees for it is apparent that Aaron's erection is softening.

Aaron begins to panic and then he looks up to find that in his new position, his head is mere inches from Kaybra's face and he is staring directly into her cold dead eyes.

Dilyla's eyes flash back up to Aaron's face with disapproval, but Aaron quickly identifies Dilyla's displeasure and attempts to regain control by kissing her burgundy lips. She responds by biting his lips and tongue and they become so intertwined and worked up that they are both starved for air. Panting in unison the couple finally takes a mutual breather.

Aaron uses this pause to glance to his side and discovers through all of this Dilyla still grasps the handle of his sword tightly. Now his sweat is dripping onto Dilyla's bare skin and he offers a suggestion, "My queen, the presence of Kaybra's corpse before me combined with the intense heat inside this tent is not allowing me to perform efficiently. Please let us complete our union out in the cool moonlight."

The pill Dilyla ingested has her aflame with sexual desire and with mere moments before the drug totally kicks in, she remains somewhat coherent and feels she can pace her ultimate sexual goal and accommodate Aaron's request, for Dilyla has never experienced such a large, strong man. Her lustful thirst for sex will not be quenched until she experiences the full extent of what she has seen Aaron has to offer, so she blurts out, "Get off of me and I will lead you to the place of my choosing."

Aaron has difficulty standing, due to his restraints. After he has reached his feet Dilyla springs up and once again grasps the strap around Aaron's neck. She also places the flat side of his sword across his abdomen and marches Aaron out the tent like a captured animal.

Not far from the tent entrance, she finds a sandstone plateau rising inches off the desert floor. It is white sandstone, free from grit, illuminated by the silver blue moon.

Dilyla steps onto the stone's edge with Aaron, who knows he must obey Dilyla's every wish. Bound as he is, he could not outrun her and would surely end up with his very own sword jabbed into his back, should he try. But all along Aaron has been concocting another very dangerous ploy to overcome Dilyla's advances.

The moment Aaron is jerked onto the stone, he feels the yellow potion is again starting to fuel his rod.

The woman stops at the middle of the flat wind-scared sandstone formation and lies on her back. She points the sword at Aaron's strengthening penis and demands, "This is your last chance. Now please me as no other man has ever done. Take the hem of my skirt in your teeth and pull it over my hips as you promised in the tent."

Aaron crouches down, his knees inside of Dilyla's legs. He proceeds to articulately perform every act upon Dilyla's person that he described and promised her that he would when they were in the tent.

Just as Dilyla demanded earlier, she again demands, "Lower! Go lower on me!" Aaron obeys her every command with precision and they have been engaged a long time, Aaron approaches the finale, he has become fully aroused. He shoves his face up between Dilyla's thighs at her love conduit and performs cunnilingus.

Up to now, Aaron has forced himself to remain mostly silent, giving out no more than a soft grunt from time-to-time to help keep Dilyla stimulated. But now Dilyla begins to sigh and groan with pleasure and

Aaron hears his sword clank down unto the rock. Within a second, Dilyla has her long, pointed fingers threaded into Aaron's mane. She grasps Aaron's locks into her fists and pulls upward, forcing his face farther up into her vagina. Her body quivers as she climaxes and cries out. Then her fingers slowly unweave from Aaron's hair as he sucks her. Her arms drop to her sides and her body goes limp. As if trying to awaken from sleep, Dilyla fumbles around the rock with her right hand until she relocates the sword and somewhat weakened, wraps her hand around its hilt. Her deep breaths subside and her eyes close.

She whispers to Aaron, "Give me more. Now I am ready for your full penetration. I want it now!" With her eyes still closed, she commands, "I say, give it to me now!"

Aaron tilts his head back and scans the moonlit clouds scattered throughout the night sky. For the first time he speaks clear and loudly, "I will obey your command and fornicate with you now, my Queen of darkness." He places the tip of his swollen rod to Dilyla's hottest spot. At his critical placement, Dilyla initially smiles and issues a soft sigh of pleasure. But when he inserts his manhood into her, Dilyla's unusual eyes pop wide open. Even indulged in her favorite sex drug of choice she is shocked by its length and girth and for the first time in her life, ponders the possibility that she may have met her match.

Aaron recognizes the shocked look that has come across Dilyla's face and chooses not to startle her more at this moment, so using the pause tactically, he moans a loud faked groan outward and upward into the sky.

Meanwhile, the leather strap that binds his wrists has once again loosened slightly and his outstretched palms lie on the rock above Dilyla's head, about eight inches apart. Aaron scans the sky and seeing nothing, decides to work on Dilyla further, so he thrusts his buttocks down harshly as he screams as loud as he can, "Fornicate with me now, my Queen of darkness." Dilyla yells out, from the exerted mass of manhood that Aaron has applied to her sensuality, "Aaaahhh! Aaaahhh!"

Her drug totally overcomes her. Dilyla's persona will never allow her to admit defeat or weakness. Refusing to be satisfied she demands, "Give me more! No mortal man can overcome my will! I want more! Now!"

Aaron joins her wailing, as he willingly obliges Dilyla's command. With this last thrust, he finally sees what he has been looking for in the sky. It is the distant profile of Vampressa darting across the moon's face.

He looks down at Dilyla, whose eyes are opened wide and filled with nervous fury toward him. Then her expression changes and she emits a peaceful grimace. She relishes the experience, but for the first time ever, admits to herself that she may be vulnerable.

Aaron peeks at Dilyla's right hand, where her grip appears to be easing on his sword's hilt. Aaron knows his timing from this point on must be impeccable. So far he has only penetrated Dilyla with about two thirds of his total length. The remainder is very wide and very hard.

Dilyla has no intention of giving Aaron any inkling that she is beginning to wane. She tightens her grip on the sword and lays its blade across Aaron's left buttocks, then closes her eyelids half way. Aaron begins to withdraw his shaft.

Dilyla thinks she has experienced Aaron's total measure. She has no idea that he has much more to offer her and just as he nearly exits her vagina, Dilyla turns the sword on edge and cuts Aaron's cheek slightly.

His tip is still in her and feeling the pain from the cut, Aaron yields to Dilyla and stops any further withdrawal. The whore raises her other hand to Aaron's thick hair and twists her fingers into it just above his ear. She then makes a fist and pulls the side of his head down to hers. When Dilyla has Aaron nose-to-nose with her, she opens her eyelids slowly.

The drug she took earlier has turned her into a delirious nymphomaniac, yet she is in too early of condition to receive Aaron's full length and girth. She tears at his hair, rotating her fist and screaming at him, "Is that it, big bad warrior! I want more!" Dilyla pulls at the sword handle, further slicing Aaron's cheek and screams, "I want it all this time, that is if you have any left, big brave warrior!"

Aaron's head is at a slight angle and he can see, from the corner of his eye, that Vampressa's black, flapping image is quickly growing larger and larger in the face of the moon. He knows she is coming toward them and his time is swiftly running out.

No longer intimidated by this deadly wench, Aaron willingly complies with Dilyla's final demand. With all of his remaining might, he pile drives the mass and length of his entire penis deep between her legs, directly into the center of her steaming vagina. His hips are now wedged tightly between Dilyla's spread thighs, her legs parted like a wishbone. Her feet flop about as if her ankles were broken as she kicks her lower legs about.

Having realized that she has badly miscalculated Aaron's size, she cries out, "Aaahhh... Aaahh... Aaahh..."

With this last heaving blow to her sensuality, Dilyla releases Aaron's hair and throws her arms outward, his sword clangs unto the rock, a few inches out of Dilyla's reach. Aaron maintains total penetration with his full weight on her as she quivers and quakes under him, groaning, "Ooohhh...Ouch...Ooohhh...Ouch..."

Dilyla is too proud to plead for Aaron to stop. She grapples for the sword with her right hand as she wails, but realizes it's just beyond her reach. Frantically, she grips Aaron around the neck and begins squeezing and tearing at him with her pointed nails. She tries to wriggle Aaron off of her. But as Dilyla thrashes away beneath Aaron, she pushes his neck and face up, which enables Aaron to lift his bound wrists off the rock.

His hands have been right above Dilyla's head throughout the copulation and the rope between his wrists remains the same short length it was. Now Aaron is able to overpower Dilyla, even as she gouges her pointed nails deep into his neck. He thrusts the weight of his broad chest and shoulders upward, then slams his hands down, his hands land on either side of Dilyla's neck. With this act it has enabled Aaron's hand binding rope to snap taut across Dilyla's throat and the rope begins to choke her. Aaron locks his fingers behind Dilyla's neck, tightening the rope further and pushes his forearms downward on top of Dilyla's shoulders as he prods his swollen shaft ever further upward between her legs.

Dilyla's crossed eyes bulge in terror as she tries to frantically pull Aaron's hands from around her neck, to no avail. Her torso is hopelessly locked between Aaron's muscular lower abdomen and his mighty forearms.

Aaron feels warm air swoosh across his back, accompanied by the familiar stench of Vampressa. He has become acquainted with Vampressa's flight patterns over the years and knows this may be his last chance to avenge Kaybra's death and bring him favor from the Queen of Patrious.

The muscle-bound warrior decides to lure the Harpy closer and excite her further. He knows the monster's favorite sinister attack occurs when the engaged couple climax in unison, so Aaron places his lips to Dilyla's and plunges his tongue into her gasping mouth. He loosens the cinch around her neck slightly and gives her a forceful boost from below, now removing his tongue from her mouth. In distress the suffering Queen of the nymphs reacts to Aaron's inflicting motion by shaking her head back and forth for air and screaming.

Aaron is so angered with Vampressa's and Dilyla's evil deeds that he cannot climax, but he pounds Dilayla again and again, praying that the Harpy will misinterpret her cries as climaxing.

But Aaron has no way of knowing Vampressa is angry, having been deceived by Dilyla earlier. Her intention now is to devour both of them this very night. He feels the air swoosh over his naked back one more time and decides it's time to act.

As he applies more pressure to Dilyla for what will turn out to be the last time, once again she wails, "Aaahhh... Aaahhh..." With her painful lusty shrieks echoing into the dessert sky, he holds her neck firmly with the rope and rolls over on to his back, careful to keep them united. Dilyla's squirming, naked body is now on top of him.

Within an instant, Vampressa, talons extended, pounces on Dilyla's bare back, hooking her razor-sharp talons into her victim's ribcage and flaps her wings for lift off.

But, Vampressa has a problem, for Aaron refuses to let go of Dilyla. He wrapped the rope that was between his ankles around Dilyla's feet, which has enabled him to hold her punctured, bleeding body by her neck and feet.

Flapping wildly, Vampressa is stymied. Her wings cannot create enough lift to take off with both Aaron and Dilyla.

Aaron sees Dilyla, although still coherent, has had her abdomen partially eviscerated by Vampressa. He looks to his sword which could be within his reach if he will release the failing nymph's neck. He looks back to her and asks, "Is it true you killed your sister whores in the tent because there was no hope for their recovery? " Dilyla's expression emits pain as she whispers, "That is our creed."

Aaron looks down to the rope wound around Dilyla's feet to make sure it is still tightly secured. He says to Dilyla, "I'm sorry you have chose evil pathways in your life. May the Gods shine on the jagged shadows of your dark soul in the life hereafter." He softly kisses her lips and releases his hands. Upon his release the rope around her neck frees the upper torso of the Queen nymph.

Vampressa immediately snatches Dilyla's body away from Aaron, but the rope binding Aaron's feet to Dilyla's goes taught. The Harpy flails about, cackling with perceived success and her great strength slowly drags Aaron across the rock on his back. The rope begins to burn his ankles and numb his feet as he is dragged.

Before Vampressa has been able to pull Aaron any significant distance, he has succeeded in snatching up his sword and the Harpy is beginning to tire from her constant fluttering motion. Intermittently, Dilyla's body flops down to Aaron due to the monster's weakening state.

Now Vampressa is no longer pulling Aaron with Dilyla. It's to the point that the monster pumps herself upward and then loses strength. While still clinging to Dilyla, the winged beast plops the nymph's body down on top of Aaron, several times.

Aaron presumes that Vampressa cannot see him entirely, for Dilyla is being held so close to the Harpy's feathery chest that her back is embedded into the monster's coarse breast down. He places the butt end of the hilt of his sword to his chest, its sharp point upward, aimed just below Dilyla's left breast. Her blood-drenched body bobs up and down only inches away from its tip.

Aaron tries to calculate Vampressa's airborne palpitations, but the red liquid from Dilyla is dripping unto his chest, face and eyes. He shakes it away and sees Dilyla looking down at him, as if understanding her fate. Holding her breath she closes her crossed eyes tightly.

Aaron has not missed his guess. Vampressa falters once more. Not wanting to relinquish her prize, the Harpy hugs Dilayla tightly to her. Being held body to body, monster and maiden plop down forcibly unto Aaron.

The minute the pointed tip of his sword punctures Dilyla's upper left chest, she gives her final cry, "Ooohhh." Now with her lips and nose touching Aaron's face, her eyes open slowly and her mystic grey pupils uncross. A split second later Vampressa's agony joins Dilyla's with a horrid screech, followed by a loud venomous, hiss. While his blade is firmly planted into the bodies of his two victims, Aaron slides his wrists up and down the knife's sharp edge until the rope parts and his hands are free.

Upon Aaron's sword passing through Dilyla's body, the Harpy received a substantial length of its blade into her chest and instantly opens her claws. Dilyla's bloody remains flop on top of Aaron.

The evil Harpy flips onto her side on the flat sandstone, scratches her claws across the rock as she flails and backstrokes about.

Aaron pushes Dilyla's lifeless corpse off him and cuts through the rope that bound him to her feet. Dripping with red sweat, he comes to his feet and observes that Vampressa has been seriously wounded. She does not appear to be able to fly and is bleeding profusely from her left wing.

As Aaron approaches her, the Harpy scoots backward, beating her right wing back and forth. Every time she beats her uninjured wing unto the rock, her feathers fly into the air as from a split pillow. With each step Aaron takes, she hisses at him, accompanied by the scratching sounds of her talons scraping across the flat rock.

Aaron has a flashback of the sight of Kaybra's spear protruding from the center of her chest and her ruby clasp tumbling to his feet. With this vision, he lunges at Vampressa and stabs his sword deep into the joint of her uninjured wing. "EEEEKKKK!" Vampressa screams, and hisses as she lay on her back on the rock tabletop, with her new wound oozing blood. "You will never slay me. You are a mere mortal. It is only I that can return your precious Uma to you. Ha, ha, ha, ha."

Infuriated, Aaron stands over Vampressa's ugly carcass and places the point of his blade at the center of her gurgling throat. The Harpy's transparent eyelids blink open and closed over her black, green and yellow pupils. Once again with her feet paddling away like a helpless baby duck on its back, the loathsome beast glares to Aaron with an abominable expression.

Aaron wants to see Vampressa sweat before he rams his blade through her windpipes. He pauses to further induce fear and suffering upon her and notes that the Harpy's breathing has become quite labored. Aaron watches her feathery chest heave in and out as the monster struggles for air.

As Aaron stares at Vampressa's down breast, he is surprised to see it's gradually turning into human flesh and soon he is looking at the unclothed body of a beautiful woman.

A familiar voice rings out, "Aaron, my love, please don't hurt me further. I can still survive." Aaron shakes his head, realizes the point of his sword now rests on the throat of his true love, Uma.

The woman sprawled out on her back on the sandstone continues, "Spare me, for I love you and miss you dearly. I forgive you for lusting with the women who have enticed you during my absence. I long for what

I see before me. You have no idea how your capture on that day, emptied my heart. If you inflict no further harm on Vampressa, she has assured me that that we will be one until the ends of eternity."

Aaron is befuddled. He tries to sort through the conundrum before him and sees tears weep from the eyes of Uma's image. He pleads to Uma, who bleeds from the same proximities, as did Vampressa, "How can I be certain that you are truly my Uma?"

Uma replies, "You must trust me. I'm certain that you will remove the point of your knife from my throat after I tell you something very dear.

"Aaron, while you held prisoner, I bore you a son and named him after you. He lives in Nemmin with his grandmother. Please accept Vampressa's kind offer so that we can return to Nemmin and raise him to be like his brave father. Please, my love, it is you who holds the key to reunite our family."

Aaron's strong constitution begins to soften after hearing Uma's words. He always wanted a son and he and Uma worked hard to produce one. He cannot conceive how Vampressa could have possibly attained this knowledge. The muscles in his arm relax but he still rests his sword on Uma's throat.

Aaron does not recall Uma's mother speaking to him about a new boy child when he visited her before the battle at Genipsus and so he queries Uma further. "My love, tell me something no one else can know but you and I. Tell me the precise location where this boy child was conceived."

More tears run down her face as she whimpers, "I cannot remember the exact place I conceived Aaron II, for we have engaged in our passions of love to one another in many different places."

Aaron is about where he wants to believe Uma, at the threshold of cutting a deal with Uma and Vampressa. He asks, "Just tell me, my love, did you conceive near the river or near the meadow where my father and I tended our stock?"

Aaron vividly recalls the many places where he and Uma made love. He wants so hard to believe her that he has inadvertently given the temptress a fifty-fifty chance at getting the answer to his question correct.

Uma responds with, "You don't love me anymore. You want to hurt me by slaying me in the same manner as your new woman, Samanda. If you doubt my answer, think of her when you sever my windpipe. How can you possibly remember with certainty where your seeds inoculated my womb?"

Aaron's arm now trembles. He begins to feel sorry for her recalling the vision of Samanda stabbing Uma in the neck. His voice yields to her as he says, "Please my love, tell me was it near the river or where I was a young shepherd. Please try to recall that one night in particular when we were certain it was to be so."

After a long pause of sniffling and rubbing one eye, Uma replies, "I could always hear the river's rippling current when we made love."

Aaron now begins to weep as he looks at her pretty face, his body trembling, "Uma, I am uncertain if you are really here or not. I am certain, however, that you and I never once made love anywhere near the river."

Uma's eyes turn black and instantly glare up at Aaron. His tears now trickle off his cheeks.

Uma opens her mouth wide and waggles out a large split serpents' tongue at him. She hisses in anger, "I am your Uma. Take me back to Nemmin and I will show you our son!"

Aaron closes his eyes and plunges his sword into Uma's windpipe. He feels the point crunch through her vertebra and into the sandstone beneath her neck. Tilting his head back and gazing unto the moon he affirms, "Kaybra, let this act allow you to rest with your ancestors in peace." Slowly Uma's body transforms back into Vampressa, who is finally very much dead. Dark green globs ooze from the plumed monster's neck and drip from the end of Aaron's sword.

Stressed and exhausted from his toils, the noble warrior sobs and collapses. He flops onto his stomach, still grasping the hilt of his sword. Within a moment, Aaron has passed into a deep void of sleep, escaping from the devastating ordeals of this horrible, horrible day...

Chapter Eight

It is now mid morning of the following day. The winds across the sands begin to pick up. As they increase, the gusts rustle the feathers of Vampressa's carcass. That slight movement is the only motion on the sandstone tabletop.

The lifeless Dilyla's blood has pooled around her body and the scarlet puddle that formed drains off the edge of the rock. As it drains it leaves ominous dark wine red trails across the flat sandstone, with its burgundy streaks dripping off of the edge of the rock.

Aaron is face down between the remains of the two dead tyrants. Dusty crystals begin to gently pelt his naked skin and soon his eyes open, but he does not move.

In the striped tent, two young nymphs have appeared and they inspect the carnage within the torn fabric walls with disbelief of what they see. They express shock as they inspect the brutalized bodies of Kaybra, Fon and Nicklett.

They exit and one of them spots the outlines of Vampressa, Aaron and Dilayla lying on the flat sandstone. She points out the downed trio to her sister and the other young nymph brings her hand to her mouth with amazed curious concern as she gazes on. The two young women are scantly clad, but clothed appropriately for the heat of the day and cautiously approach the edge of the sandstone. When they observe what is before them, they look at each other as if they are orphaned fawns.

One whispers, "They are all dead."

The other whispers back, "Now we are free from Dilyla's reign. We can do as we wish with our bodies and our lives. I wonder who will teach us the true ways of the world?"

The first nymph responds, "No more Vampressa, I cannot believe it is so."

Aaron has heard their whispers, but remains still. As they continue to talk, the girls' voices become lower, so Aaron cannot hear the youngest whisper to the other, "The man is still alive! I see him breathing."

The two women step up onto the rock and walk to Aaron. The taller girl asks Aaron, "Sir Warrior, are you alright?" Aaron senses he is not in danger after overhearing the larger content of the women's exchange. He opens his eyes and rolls over unto his back.

Looking at the young nymphs, he speaks very softly, "I will be fine."

Regaining his composure, Aaron realizes that he is still naked. He makes an embarrassing attempt to shroud his genitals with his hands. The girls bend over and each grasps one of Aaron's forearms to assist him to his feet.

Aaron's bloodied, nude body does not even remotely faze the young women. They tend to him as if they were experienced nurses and Aaron is pleasantly surprised by this considerate treatment. He asks, "Why do you assist me after you have clearly seen that I slew your mentors?"

The younger of the two girls speaks, "We are all that's left of their band and our future looked grim under their control. Our elder sisters have already deserted the cause by fleeing into small villages that are scattered across the desert, so we have no one and no home. Therefore, we hope you will help us find a new home where we can live in peace, and raise families."

Aaron and the two women form an immediate bond and he treats them as if they were his younger sisters. Soon after hand-mending his garment, Aaron is ready to move on.

In the late morning sun, the newly formed trio has buried Dilyla, Fon and Nicklett in shallow graves and Aaron has carefully removed the spear from Kaybra and wrapped her body cocoon-like in a large swath of the blue and white tent. The fabric is secured around her body with some of the same ropes that had bound Aaron the day before. He and the two girls place Kaybra's remains over the back of her horse.

Aaron finds two strong straight wooden branches of the same length and uses them to make a litter drag to transport Vampressa's carcass. He directs one girl to board his horse behind him and the other to ride Kaybra's horse and keep her body from sliding off. Then they shove off toward the western horizon and Kaybra's camp.

It's early afternoon when they arrive at the center of deceased warrior woman's temporary bivouac. The inhabitants become silent with awe as the two horses halt. The large bundle over Kaybra's horse has spoken for itself.

Many of the crowd gathers around Vampressa's stench-ridden remains. They mumble as if viewing some grotesque freak in a sideshow.

Aaron calls a meeting with Kaybra's leaders and tells them of the horror of the past day. It is decided to build a large hewn raft near the river and place Kaybra's body in its center. The raft will then be floated down the river in ceremonial fashion until it reaches their home delta village by the sea. Upon its arrival, there will be a festival in celebration of her life achievements before she is laid to rest.

Aaron also explains the dilemma of the orphaned nymphs and the elders agree to take the young women in, if they so desire.

One of the older women approaches the two young nymphs as they sit atop the horses with forlorn looks on their faces. She explains the elders' offer and the girls' faces light up with happiness.

The commanders next put the word out that they are to break camp and reassemble at the river's edge. At daybreak, they will begin their trip home with Kaybra's remains.

*   *   *

The large raft had been constructed throughout the night and early morning as Kaybra's body has been rewrapped with her island's colors and placed in the middle of the vessel. Bright gold and green battle pennants have been fastened to the four corners of the raft.

Before the vessel is set afloat, Aaron boards it and kneels next to Kaybra's body. He states, "Our spirits shall remain united for eternity, my great white and bronze mistress. Be assured that, in whatever form you may return, we shall carry out the Queen's and her sister's last command with slow, sensual pleasure." He then kisses the fabric that covers her forehead, returns to his feet and steps off the raft onto the shore.

One group of Kaybra's people crosses the river to the west. A like number remains on the eastern shoreline. Long ropes are attached to the corners of the funeral flotation and strung across the river to each escort party.

The horseback pallbearers on the western shore tighten their ropes and tug the raft off the eastern beach into the mainstream. When the float reaches the center of the river, lines are pulled taut and Kaybra's final journey begins. The funerary procession heads south with her patrician remains, as the small barge with its green and gold colors flapping in the wind, drifts down the middle of the river. The brilliant color contrasts from the green flags on Kayba's floating hearse against the pale blue river water and the golden brown sands, make it visually obvious to any bystanders that this is not a common event.

Aaron, on horseback, stands in the shallows and watches the procession disappear around a rippled bend in the winding river. After awhile in meditation, the sad warrior returns to the bank and hitches his steed to Vampressa's litter.

Aaron rides west across the river and the water's depth become such that the Harpy's body is actually afloat behind him. After he has gone a short distance toward the western horizon, the hot, desert sun begins to heat up Vampressa's corpse and from it come horrible rancid odors that are unbearable.

Aaron estimates he has a two-day ride to reach Patrious. He thinks of bedding down for the night and in the distance, he sees a small village of stone structures. As he nears the scattered clump of cobbled structures, a circle of hovering vultures escorts him to the edge of this newfound town. Aaron trudges down what was the main street of the town. The village has been long abandoned and sand has settled in the open doorways of many of the structures.

Aaron has no knowledge of this deserted town and there are no names painted or carved into any walls to identify it. He decides his best plan is to get his cargo out of the afternoon sun and out of sight from the hungry vultures.

He finds one structure with a broken opening large enough to accommodate his horse and litter. He enters, undoes his steed's harnessing and gathers broken wall blocks from the building's entrance to cover

Vampressa's body. Afterward, he exits the structure to further inspect the ruins.

After searching every street, he finds no signs of life, but he has found one building that does not possess any musty odors as most of the others. It appears to have been an inn of sorts and is still in relatively sturdy condition. There are a few individual rooms with dusty bunks hinged to the walls, strung from ornate chains.

At the center of these rooms is a great room of sorts with seats that resemble benches. Other single seats are placed around long, wooden tables, which look as if they were used for a feast of some kind.

On the far side of this great room is a wall filled with urns and bottles, in pigeonhole openings recessed into the wall. Everything in these rooms is covered with layers of dust.

Aaron finds a few oil lamps in various locations throughout the building, gathers them and places them on the far end of the largest table. From all the lamps he can only extract enough oil to fuel six. He then clears the dust off of the end of the table and arranges the lamps to his suiting. He exits to fetch his bedroll and check on his horse, as well as Vampressa's remains.

Aaron returns after a short period and places his rations on the end of the table and his blankets in one of the overnight rooms he inspected earlier.

When all is in place, he seats himself at the end of the table, lights the oil lamps and eats his rations. When he looks forward, he sees the wall of bottles and urns before him and cannot overcome his curiosity. He rises, approaches the wall and as if inspecting them for some identity, he peers into the dusty openings.

One flask catches his attention, it reminds him of the leopard skin container from which Samanda poured their drinks the night he first met her. He carefully removes it from the opening and blows the dust off it. Aaron smiles to himself when he realizes that it is in fact, the same type of wine he and Samanda drank on that first night. He returns to the table, seats himself, opens the flask and then whiffs the cork. Now there is no doubt to him that the wine is of the same fermentation as was Samanda's.

Nightfall is upon the abandoned village. Aaron sits at the table with the oil lamps flickering as he drinks and dines.

*   *   *

Back in Patrious, Samanda has just arrived. She expresses gratitude to Aaron's men for their safe return and asks that they spend the night in a barracks just outside the fortress walls. She explains that they will be fed and treated well from this point on. They thank her and agree. Two- by-two they exit the courtyard's grated gate.

Samanda looks up to the Queen's window. Although all the torches that surround the interior walls of the palace are lit, the Queen's upper room remains dark. Samanda approaches the large wooden door at the base of the Queen's tower, lifts its latch and ascends the spiral steps, which are dimly lighted by smaller torches.

Samanda reaches the point where the small staircase window is located and pauses. She can see out over the city of Patrious and into the vast, darkened desert and speculates about Aaron's location this night as she stares out into the cloud-shrouded moon. After a moment, she continues upward.

Samanda arrives at the Queen's chambers and finds it unlit and absent of her sister. She fumbles in the darkness until she locates a flint striker and crosses the circular room to two large ornate gold candelabra, which sit atop narrow, golden, twisted pedestals. She lights the candles and turns to the opulent open space of the room. She is mildly startled to find the Queen's reflection in the large oval mirror.

Samanda speaks to her sister. "So, my sister, have your messengers returned any ill tidings that I have failed to carry out your orders?"

The Queen replies, "No, but I do want to express my gratitude to you, my sister, for participating in such a dangerous task. Further, I will state, that I've heard nothing nor received any word at all. Therefore, I fear that something has gone amiss, although I know not what at this time. I would be pleased if you could give me your version of the events that have passed since your departure. Please carry on?"

With the Queen's use of the term, "amiss," Samanda begins to worry about Aaron. Attempting to put her concerns aside, she walks to the mirror and questions, "You must certainly know that we arrived at Kaybra's village without incident." As Samanda speaks the words, she struggles to keep her face expressionless. She looks into her sister's eyes with caution. Samanda recalls her act of fellatio on Aaron on the river's bank, the second night into their journey.

Samanda, remaining composed, continues, "After merging with Kaybra's forces, Aaron, Kaybra and I split off and gained valuable information from the spirits that reside in the Valley of the Phantom Pyramids. We were able to use that information to find Vampressa's nest of eggs. We destroyed all of them but two, only one of which was fertile.

"After a few days passed, Aaron met with his troops and ordered them to assemble north of Kaybra's bivouac. Once united, our joint forces forged to the east and converged on Genipsus. The battle was bloody, yet we were resoundingly victorious.

"Aaron and his men escorted me to a northern site at the river and once there, he departed to reunite with Kaybra. Aaron's remaining men accompanied me home, to where I arrived but a short time ago. I chose to come directly here, to you."

The Queen interrupts Samanda. "You said Aaron was to reunite with Kaybra. Explain to me the circumstances of the first time they became united?"

Samanda replies in a matter-of-fact, manner, "My sister, you know as well as I, that due to our blood line, there are times our thoughts are as one. Kaybra had a strong desire to fornicate with Aaron and asked our joint permission well before she seduced him. One side of me did not want this act to take place. On the other hand..." The Queen jolts back, "STOP! Samanda, are you telling me you willingly allowed Kaybra to seduce my slave? My very own personal property!"

Samanda replies, "Well, yes... Well, no... Well, what I was explaining to you was that I felt obligated to Kaybra for all her sacrifices for me... I mean, for you and our kingdom."

There is a long silence as the Queen and Samanda stare at each other with an identical expression of anger and frustration.

The Queen breaks the silence with, "So, Samanda, where do you believe my property is at this moment? Is he nestled next to Kaybra's large warm breasts as they sleep this evening?"

Samanda answers, "I do not know... I do not know... Please forgive me, your majesty. Aaron was to meet Kaybra two nights ago for their final union before Kaybra was to return to her village with her troops.

"At this very moment, Aaron should be in search of the Harpy monster, for he is determined to slay the beast. I know he was not comfortable with Kaybra's advances, so we must forgive him and be grateful Kaybra aided our cause."

"Very well, my sister. Just remember, if our new Master General returns with Vampressa's bloodied body, he is all mine and mine alone! If he does not return, he may spend the rest of his days pounding Kaybra's large shapely loin and be banished from my kingdom."

Samanda states, "Why so cruel, my Queen? Why so cruel?" The Queen replies, "You know why, Samanda. Do not be coy with me. Now, go to your tent of women and prepare Layla for my physical inspection tomorrow morning. I must determine if she is with child. If she is, that means Aaron's reproductive seeds are capable of bearing fruit. If she is with his child and Aaron brings me Vampressa before the next silver moon, your women will prepare him for my conception ceremony. Then we, and only we will be one until the end of time."

Neither Samanda nor the Queen are aware the old man with the chain and cross necklace, has been standing at the top of the staircase during their entire conversation. With what he has just heard, he thinks to himself, "Oh my word, she's getting worse with everyday that passes. I must pray for the safety of the warrior. If he fails to return, I'm certain an emotional breakdown is at hand for the Queen."

Before his presence can be detected by the occupants of the upper chamber, the old man hurriedly hobbles down the stairs.

*   *   *

At the ghost town, Aaron has finished his rations and has drunk the majority of the ruby wine from the flask. He rises from the table with a slight wobble. He's tired and now obviously somewhat intoxicated. He blows out all but one of the lamps and uses the remaining one to guide him to the room he prepared earlier. Once there, he flops on his bunk and a deep sleep immediately overcomes him.

After a passage of time, Aaron has a dream. At least he thinks it's a dream, in which a young woman appears to him, her radiating image appears as light glowing from a life-sized-like brushed glass figurine. The woman standing beside Aaron's bed begins to speak to the weary sleeping traveler, "Hello. Excuse me, sir warrior. Can you hear me? Hello, sir warrior, please lend me your ear."

Aaron tosses about in his sleep as the voice continues, "Mister warrior, please wake up. My name is Mareeja and I must speak with you. You must help me. No one else can. Please help me?"

The voice is so vivid that Aaron opens his eyes and is shocked to find the beautiful glowing crystal maiden standing by his bedside is equally as vivid as her voice.

Aaron speaks out, "What is it? What do you want with me?"

Mareeja replies, "You are in the ancient village of Oregasma. Horrible things happened here many, many years ago. My soul is lost and I cannot cross on to be with my family. I have wandered through this building for nearly a century. Every day, shortly after sunrise, I relive my fate. Every year on the anniversary of my death, my mother visits me here. Try as she may, though, she cannot bring me from this haunted place to be with her."

Aaron is certain he must be hallucinating until Mareeja leans over to him and kisses his cheek. She says, "You are the first human I have seen in decades. You must help me. Please, sir warrior, please?"

Aaron is beside himself. He wants to help the maiden but he is determined to return to Patrious with the Harpy carcass as soon as possible. He explains to Mareeja that he is on a tight schedule and must return to the Queen of Patrious by the end of tomorrow's sun. He explains in great detail what he's gone through the past several months. "If I do not return the Harpy's body to the Queen, my fate will be sealed. My life will remain in limbo into eternity."

The ghostly image states, "Then, if you do not return to complete your quest, you must remain here with me." Small teardrops drip from Mareeja's face and she looks very sad. Her image slowly fades away.

Aaron flops back down on his bed and falls back to sleep. His thoughts, however, are restless as he tosses and turns throughout the remainder of the night.

At daybreak, he awakes with an urgent, panicky feeling. He recalls his experience with Mareeja during the night and is quite uneasy. Aaron hustles about the old inn, gathers his bedroll and holds it under his arm.

As he races for the door of the ancient structure, he glances to the table where he dined the night before and decides he had better gather what is left of his rations. While doing so, he notices the flask of wine he drank from last evening is gone. Only a dusty ring remains on the table where he left it.

Aaron dismisses the peculiar circumstance and bounds out of the building, walking swiftly to the makeshift stable he created for his horse. He looks back over his shoulder at the abandoned inn with every third or fourth stride he takes.

Soon he reaches the hut and stuffs his bedroll and rations into his saddlebags and prepares the litter for Vampressa's carcass. Aaron goes to where he covered the Harpy's body and frantically throws the mud and stone bricks off Vampressa's temporary grave. As he pitches aside the last stones, he finds Vampressa's body has vanished.

*　　*　　*

In Patrious, the Queen is now at the large tent of Samanda's bevy of lovely women, where Layla has been prepared for her physical inspection.

Layla is naked on her back in the center lounge of the tent. The Queen approaches her and kneels by her side.

Layla's upper torso is scarred and contains many streaks of proud flesh that have formed over her wounds. The bulk of her injury was inflicted throughout her back, breasts and face, yet her beauty still radiates out from beneath her scars.

Expressing concern, the Queen says to Layla, "How are you feeling these days, my young beauty?" Layla replies somberly, "I feel much better as each day passes, your majesty. Thank you for your visit and I know why you are here. Over two silver moons have come and gone since my coitus. I have been without my cycle, ever since my encounter with your slave, thus I believe he will be ripe for your harvest when that time comes."

The Queen places her palm on top of Layla's slightly bulging abdomen and resumes, "I see, my young beauty. Is there any matter about Aaron's act upon you that you could tell me?"

Layla smiles at the Queen as she replies, "This man of yours is quite large and hard, his embrace is passionate. He also seems to take great pride in his ability to prolong the act. You will be pleased, my Queen. You will be very pleased."

The Queen smiles back at Layla, then bends to kiss her lightly on the lips. She states, "Thank you for your sacrifice, my sister. You can be certain that you and the child will be well taken care of." The Queen rises, turns and exits.

*　　*　　*

Aaron is not experiencing such fulfilling thoughts. He is feverishly digging around in the sand and dirt floor of the makeshift stable with his hands. He is in disbelief that he cannot find so much as a stray feather from Vampressa's body. He wonders if Mareeja has cast a spell upon him, or if he drank too much wine the night before. Or both.

Momentarily accepting defeat, he sits with his legs spread and heels dug into the dirt floor. He supports his shoulders with extended arms as his palms press into the dirt at his sides. He screams out, "GODS ABOVE, WHAT AM I TO DO NOW?"

Aaron leaps back to his feet and exits the hut. He places his hands on his hips and looks up and down the street, puzzled.

After convincing himself there are no marks on the ground that indicate Vampressa's exhuming, he meanders up and down the streets of the abandoned town.

Much of the day passes and Aaron believes he has searched every building in the village. He returns to his horse, mounts and gallops off to the perimeter of the town and after circling in and around it for hours, seeking a clue, he returns to the stable as darkness is once again nearly upon him.

As Aaron ties his horse inside the hut, he looks into the animal's eyes and says, "If only you could speak. You could surely tell me what happened last night." His horse snorts and shakes his head up and down as if to acknowledge Aaron's request. Surprisingly his charger's left eye is now open wide and focused directly on Aaron, something Aaron has never seen before from his trusty pal.

He looks deep into the horse's eye as it peers at him knowingly and sees a reflection of the window opening behind him. Concentrating his thoughts and focusing on the reflection, he sees something sitting on the window sill.

Aaron whips around to look at the window opening. He walks to the window and is surprised to see the object is the same leopard skin flask he drank from the night before.

Aaron picks it up as his horse shakes his head up and down vigorously and snorts with approval. Aaron turns back to the horse and once again his stallion shakes his head up and down approvingly.

Aaron is trying to decipher the message being sent to him and concludes that he must return the bottle to the table at the inn. He turns to his horse and states, "Now I shall name you Noble, for you are truly that."

Aaron anticipates he may be in for a long evening and retrieves his rations and bedroll, then heads toward the inn. When he enters the building, he finds a freshly-opened flask of wine sitting in the identical place as the container the previous night. Only this time, there are two ornate goblets placed at its side.

Aaron tosses his bedding into the same room where he slept the previous evening and walks to his seat at the head of the table and stares at the freshly opened leopard skin carafe. He relights the oil lamps, plops down on his chair and says aloud, "I 'm ready to speak to you, Mareeja."

All remains quiet as the reflections from the lamp's flames leap about the room and Aaron patiently waits for a sign. After a long time of silence passes, he attempts to be a little more creative and fills his goblet with the wine. He also fills the other goblet almost to the brim, then, places it on the table before the seat at his right hand side.

Again time passes and Aaron is now on his third goblet of wine. The lamps suddenly flicker brightly as Mareeja materializes in the seat to his right. Her beauty negates her ghostly form.

Aaron grins, "It seems you have placed me in a position where I am forced to hear you out. That is, if you have information pertaining to the whereabouts of my cargo."

Mareeja picks up her goblet and takes a healthy swig and within moments her crystal image transforms into a live woman.

Aaron is bewildered by what he has just witnessed.

Mareeja relates her tale, "Many years ago, our town fathers were a powerful and brutal lot. They collected a group of young women they titled, 'The Ooomzowee Tribe,' who were bred and assembled for their own sexual pleasures and perversions. As the men aged, they became wrinkled and ugly and fresh members of the Ooomzowee women denied them their predatory sexual advancements. Should any woman resist, she was bound, brought to her knees and beheaded. Afterward, her skull was presented to the man that she refused, as a trophy.

"The town fathers and their henchmen would drink until they were intoxicated, while playing games of chance. Before the evening was complete, the skulls were brought into the game room and used as tokens for the final match. Whoever won the most-prized skull, would use it to simulate an act of fellatio upon themselves in front of the group. The men laughed and carried on. This was drunken grand amusement for them as the finale for the night.

"Gradually the Ooomzowee women were depleted by attrition, since so many died as a result of the fathers' brutal actions. So, recruits from outside the original bloodline were sought and I became such an unwilling recruit.

"The men lured me at a very young age, to watch their infant children when they went away with their wives. They watched me mature and soon thereafter began stalking me and eventually captured me. The men would force me to dress in scanty outfits and then rape me. I felt I dare not thwart their perverted actions or I would surely be killed. One of their most trusted henchmen was an older centurion, called Jagg.

"Before long I was impregnated by one of the older men and lost the child by my own choice due to the fact they had a medicine man at their disposal who prepared a potion that I willingly swallowed. A vaginal intrusion followed after the potion was administered. Interestingly, being I lost the child, it seemed to enthuse all of those who had forced sex upon me.

"Knowing this procedure was effective, Jagg wanted me for his concubine even though he was already wed to a woman just three seasons my senior. He continued to force himself upon me and demanded I give him oral gratification on a regular basis. He was a sickening old man and it did not take long before I could no longer stand the sight of him.

"Late on the evening before I was murdered, Jagg came to my home and slapped me about the face and shoulders because I would not join him at his secret place alongside the river. But in my new place of labor, I had just met a young, highly-decorated warrior from a large village to the north. His name was Stanusus and we made arrangements to meet in the summer moon's light late on the evening after Jagg beat me.

"I warned the old watchman that I had a brave young warrior coming to town to protect me from his evil actions on my person and he told me if I were to invite my warrior to town, he would not only slay him, but that he would give my head to the town fathers in a box.

"I warned my new friend of his threats, but the young warrior stated that he had been victorious in many a battle and he was not going to break our meeting due to the words of some fat old curmudgeon."

Mareeja begins to break down, sobbing uncontrollably. Aaron uses a clean cloth wrapped within his rations and wipes her tears. Mareeja takes the cloth from Aaron and blots her cheeks.

Regaining her composure, she continues, "Stanusus and I met at this very inn. We laughed and shared pleasant stories while drinking a popular fermented mix of that period. The concoction was labeled Ginbus.

"Stanusus possessed tokens from his homeland, which he had been paid for doing his duty. He tried to swap them for our fermented drinks, but he innkeeper refused to honor them.

"Jagg was a good acquaintance of the innkeeper, with whom he had organized games of chance and played them regularly in a cellar room.

"Jagg entered through a rear entrance and seated himself over there by the bottle wall. My friend and I were seated at a table for two situated where the far end of this long table is now. After Jagg plopped himself down he leered at both of us with contempt, which made me uncomfortable. I begged my friend to leave.

"At first Stanusus was having none of what I urged. He just glared back at Jagg for awhile and then we finally departed.

"Shortly thereafter, we arrived at a secluded area a short distance south of this Inn, where Stanusus kissed me and I kissed him back. Then we embraced. But suddenly, from the clouded moonlight stepped Jagg. He growled with rage, which startled both of us and being caught off guard Jagg rammed his sword deep into the side of Stanusus' chest. Reeling with great pain Stanusus rose to defend himself and protect me. But Jagg again stabbed Stanusus, this time in his genitals. All total, he stabbed him five times. As Stanusus lay there with his mouth open, gurgling in death, the centurion poured torch fuel on his face, then produced a flint striker and lit his face. His head was ablaze as I shook and screamed in horror."

Aaron cannot believe the hideous, horrible nature of this act that Mareeja describes. As she speaks, he watches her with disbelief, yet concern.

Mareeja is still whimpering, but continues, "The old man then dragged me to my feet and ordered, 'Don't say I didn't warn you of this outcome.' But by this time I was in shock, trembling in fear, willing to do whatever the old town patrolman demanded.

"He bound my wrists behind my back and gagged me using a soiled linen he produced from his inner loin area. He placed me atop Stanusus' horse and then dragged the poor dead man into the weeds. After Jagg placed his body in the weeds, he pulled his loincloth down partially to make it appear that my friend had been involved in fornication with me upon his demise.

"In two short leaps, Jagg bounded back to the horse and mounted it, driving the animal a short distance south to where his secret hut was located on the river's edge.

"Once there, he pulled me from the horse and forced me into the hut. I was bound there until the rise of the next sun under the watch of a younger assistant of his whom I had gone to school with and refused to date.

"In the wee hours, the old centurion returned the horse to a hitching rail across the road from this inn. His own horse was also tethered there. He then mounted his horse and rode home.

"The next morning he returned to the rail, petted Stanusus' horse and looked about.

"A short time later a fisherman found Stanusus' body. The man rushed back to our village and reported what he found to Jagg at the hitching rail.

"The old centurion assured the fisherman that he would investigate the matter to the fullest extent and report to the town fathers. So, he sent his deputies to the scene, remounted his horse and went to the official house of the fathers. A long meeting was had between the three men and finally, they summoned their medicine man for a meeting rescheduled late in the day.

"As the shadows of darkness blanketed our village, Jagg returned to the hut and huffed around me, unfastening the ropes binding me to a chair. He put his finger in his young assistants chest, who, by-the-way, made sexual advancements on me throughout the night and ordered, 'If anyone ever questions you about what you have witnessed, you are to tell them that a pair of young brothers from a distant village are responsible!' Then he dragged me outside to his horse, flopped me across its back, quickly mounted and rode us back to this inn.

"I was brought in through a different rear entrance that passed through the innkeeper's living quarters. Upon entering this area, I was forced down through the trap door you may now observe on the floor to your right.

"I kicked and tried to scream but the inn was locked and empty of guests. While tied up in the river hut, I cursed Jagg repeatedly and he cuffed me hard across my face. Some of my bloodstains still leave a red path through the building up to the trap door.

"Once he had me in the cellar of the inn, he shoved me into the room where the men participated in their games of chance and locked the door behind us. He cursed at me and pushed down hard on my shoulders until I dropped to my knees. The room was dimly lit and after succumbing to his desires for my positioning, he turned up the lamps until their flames illuminated the entire room.

"The light revealed the innkeeper and two town fathers seated around a large round wooden, game table. One rose from his seat and came to me. He jerked the gag from my mouth while my wrists were still bound behind me. The gag dropped down around my neck like a kerchief.

"He then ripped my top garment off and fondled my naked breasts with one hand, while using his other hand to remove his loincloth and induce an erection. He cursed at me for refusing sexual encounters with him and for not adhering to the code of the Ooomzowee Tribe.

"He removed the hand from his penis that he was milking himself with and grabbed my hair. Time and time again, he tried to force his swollen shaft into my mouth, but I was able to spit him away with each attempt.

"The men were all well overcome with drink. One-by-one, each man, including the innkeeper, attempted to have me perform fellatio on them. They finally reached a point where the drink overcame their libidos and so they became flaccid, except for one, Jagg.

"He approached me, dropped his loincloth and twisted his fingers into my hair. In his other hand he held his sword, which he placed against my left breast, then scowled, 'Suck me or die, you young mother dog!'

"He struggled and cursed as he tried to part my lips with the end of his shaft, but he finally succeeded and it gagged me. I choked and gasped for air, but he held my hair so tightly it was tearing out by the roots.

"I thought my life might be spared if I complied, but then the ugly old man strained a grimaced smile as he climaxed in my mouth. He pulled my hair tighter to him, moaned again, and plunged his sword deep into my left breast.

"As I laid on the floor, dying in my own blood, I heard the first town father demand, 'Summon the medicine man. Have him sever her head and return it to me. This young unwilling slut will never refuse me again! Now I shall place my royal shaft between her jaws at any time I so desire until the end of my day...'

"I died slightly after sunrise. They dumped my headless body in high weeds beside a path my father used every day. Two days later, a young mineworker found my remains and went into town to notify the authorities, who were the town fathers. They assigned Jagg to investigate my murder as well as the murder of Stanusus.

"My funeral was the next day, but the town fathers and the medicine man made sure my body was never publicly displayed…"

Aaron has great empathy for what Mareeja had gone through, but is uncertain of what she needs from him. "Mareeja, I feel very sorry for what happened to you, but I know not what I can do to change those horrible events. They happened so long ago that I would not know where to begin to right this wrong. Surely, all those people from that time have long been deceased. There will never be justice brought upon them."

Mareeja replies, "Justice has taken its course thanks to the Gods. When my mother visits me, she assures me that all those responsible are now living in the lava-fired pits of hell. So justice is no longer an issue, but I cannot join my family in heaven until my skull has been located and returned to me. Therefore, if you find my skull and return it to me, I will tell you where your Harpy's carcass is hidden. I am sorry it comes down to this, but someone has to help me and you are the only one capable."

Aaron is confused and frustrated and begins to speak. But, Mareeja begins to fade and Aaron calls out panicky, "No, Mareeja, No! Do not leave! Speak to me, do not fade away!"

His pleas are to no avail. Within minutes Mareeja is almost gone and her last, faint image whispers "Until tomorrow night."

For many nights, he and Mareeja meet to try to determine the location of her skull and daily Aaron searches the village for clues to the location of Mareeja's skull and the location of Vampressa. But longing to feel Samanda's soft touch once again and return to the lovely Queen, Aaron also fights the thought daily, of leaving Mareeja should he locate Vampressa before finding her skull.

The frustrated warrior has learned this town is abandoned due to the policies of the old town fathers. They were afraid that any new settlers could threaten their network of scheming ruffians.

Literally, everything in the city was connected through them or by one of them individually. Government policies, land grants, monetary institutions, work places and even the secret cult religion of the day, were just a few of the things under their reign.

After the old timers passed on, what few offspring they had that were not either killed or banned from the city, eventually left for a new life free from tyranny.

Days have now turned into weeks and Aaron continues to pine each passing day for Samanda's companionship.

*   *   *

In Patrious, late one evening, the Queen summons Samanda to her tower suite and this time it is Samanda who appears in the oval mirror. The two bicker between themselves and Samanda scolds her sister, "If you would not have imposed such an impossible mission upon Aaron, my sister, he could be in your arms at this very moment. Maybe you were correct when you aired he is likely now living with Kaybra."

The Queen snarls, "No, Samanda, he is not! You are as aware as I am that the messengers told us of Kaybra's demise. Now stop such foolish thoughts."

Samanda, equally torn with the absence of Aaron, protests, "Maybe the message we received was a lie. Would you not, if you were Kaybra, emit misinformation to maintain your bed partner? I think we should give second thoughts to the courier's words."

The women scowl at each other identically and the Queen concludes their meeting with, "Aaron has three more days to return. If he does not return by the third day, my cycle will be over and a fruitful reproductive ceremony will be out of the question for several moons.

If my lineage is to survive, I must find another mate. I will choose him from the remainder of Aaron's ranks who now live amongst us. You, my sister will test this man, as did Layla when she tested Aaron. Now depart and start canvassing the remaining stock of men..."

*   *   *

In the ghost village, Aaron has come upon many ancient scrolls in a basement room of an old, long-abandoned, public building from the period when Mareeja was slain. After careful scrutiny, he deduces that the town fathers bred and raised chariot horses. They were from a long line of very successful horsemen of their day and Jagg along with his family worked the herds for the town fathers.

The scrolls read that a large bucolic tract of land on which the horses were stabled, pastured and tended was transferred to the town fathers shortly before Mareeja's death from a high-ranking official who presided over justice throughout the area. Aaron decides to visit this area on the north side of town where many dwellings have been constructed on the southern edge of this old farm's pastureland.

When Aaron and Noble crest a grassy knoll on the northern outskirts of town, Aaron spots an old farmhouse that appears to be occupied. He approaches cautiously.

Aaron ties Noble to the rail of the stately old home and proceeds to the front door. He knocks once. Twice. Finally, on the third knock the door opens slowly, its hinges creaking. A hunched-over, older man appears in the doorway. "Yes, what can I help you with, lad."

Aaron gains permission to enter and once inside, notices the home's walls are filled with artifacts. They are eclectic in nature, ranging from cookware to weaponry. One thing in particular he sees, out of the corner of his eye is an old uniform, the uniform of a centurion from the period when Mareeja was slain. Aaron remains silently polite and asks permission to sit. The hunched-over sexagenarian grants his request.

Aaron learns that his host lives alone, is a bit eccentric, but definitely articulate and a fine collector of rare and unusual objects.

The old fellow also appears to be very wealthy, even though his abode is filled with musty clutter. Aaron learns the man is no Harpy lover and tells Aaron about his ancestor's stock being ravaged by Harpy monsters many years ago. His ancestor's stock was horses. Chariot racing horses in particular.

After Aaron tells the man his Harpy story, he has developed rapport with the old codger and their conversation reaches a point where Aaron becomes comfortable enough to query the man about the ancient centurion uniform on the wall. The man struggles to stand and crosses to the uniform, goes into elaborate detail of its period and owner, with Aaron fixated on his every word.

He explains that it was the uniform of a local enforcer named, 'Jagg,' who was very close to his ancestors. As a matter of fact, a youthful Jagg trained horses raised on this farm. The old man states further, that eventually Jagg's extended family worked for his ancestors, tending to their stock of fine-bred horses.

Jagg grew up with the town fathers and schooled with them in his youth. In his late twenties, he was knighted head centurion by the local officials to protect the town from wayward travelers and undesirables, such as the people living in the shantytown on the east side of the river who were simply disposable. That is where Mareeja resided.

Aaron can no longer contain himself. He recites his entire tale to the old man, including his relationship with the Queen, Vampressa's body and finally Mareeja's missing skull.

Upon completing his story, a cold look overrides the man's face. He bolts to his feet and begins ranting and raving. "You must go! You must leave my home and never return. I am far too old now and do not have many days left to witness rising suns. I need not be reminded of those days past. Now leave immediately! You are no longer welcome in my home!"

Aaron is uncertain which part of his story has triggered the man's tirade, but he does know he went too far, too fast. He stands and asks forgiveness, but the hunchback curator pushes Aaron out the door with a broken broom handle, the door slamming behind him with a bang. Immediately all the window shutters are slammed closed and latched. Aaron, disgusted, mounts Noble and rides back toward the abandoned village.

Later that evening, Aaron sits beside the long table at the inn going through his ritual with the wine while waiting for Mareeja to appear. Shortly, she appears.

Aaron tells her what has happened this day and begs her to allow him to find Vampressa's remains and return to Patrious and the Queen. He is, of course unaware that should he not return in two days, Samanda and her sister will be actively seeking his replacement and it is at least a full day's hard ride to Patrious from the deserted village.

Mareeja will not concede to Aaron. She does, however, state that he must continue his investigation for at least three more days before she reconsiders her demands.

*   *   *

It is the evening of the next day. Aaron has returned to the old man's home on four occasions throughout the day, but could not rouse him. The museum like home is now shuttered and its front door is boarded.

In defeat, Aaron returns to the inn and goes through every ritual possible to make Mareeja appear. She does not.

*   *   *

In Patrious, Samanda is in her tent, sobbing as her harem women try to comfort her. One girl hands her a note and states, "I found this pinned to the inside wall of our foyer. The Queen must have left it for you earlier in the day when you were touring Aaron's ranks."

Samanda's hand quivers as she opens it and reads, "My sister, the time is near. I have found the man I desire you to administer the reproductive test. In that neither you or I know the location of Aaron, or Vampressa, it is my order that you come to the palace tomorrow evening.

"We shall want a sturdy roof over your head for this event so that you do not suffer the same consequences as did Layla. Bring six of your women with you to prepare the soldier for you. If you dally, I will send a unit of the eunuch guards to impound all of you." Signed, "Your loving sister, The Queen."

Samanda drops the note and falls to the floor in tears...

*   *   *

Aaron has given up any hope of communicating with Mareeja this evening and with the oil lamps flickering their amber colored dance off the wall of bottles, Aaron rests his forehead on his crossed arms and dozes off.

He begins to have a very puzzling dream in which Samanda is strapped on her back onto an altar, her nude body covered with sheer scarves. Her legs are spread, with her feet strapped into stirrups.

He sees a curtain being parted by two young women from where a nude warrior appears. Four additional female escorts guide the warrior to Samanda. He has a dark sack over his head and the women have obviously excited the man sexually before he entered the chamber.

The warrior is led between Samanda's legs and one of his guides jerks the hood off the warrior's head. Aaron immediately recognizes the warrior as his most trusted general, Demetrious.

Samanda is screaming, "No, My sister, No! Please give Aaron another day?"

Suddenly there is a loud thud on the table before Aaron and he awakes from his dream startled.

Dazed, he focuses his eyes on what sits on the dusty table in front of him. It is a square wooden box with a brass hinged-lid and latch. The lid has a woman's face etched into its top. Aaron identifies the face as Mareeja's.

Aaron looks up slowly from the two, arthritic hands atop the box. They extend from a set of loosely robed arms, which his eyes follow to a dark, hooded face above him.

A voice speaks to Aaron from the shadow of the hood, "Take the contents of this box and put eternity to rest, for you are a brave warrior. Mark this act among your many forthright deeds and continue your journey of nobility. Let us who remain, be assured that the devastation of the Harpy breed shall never return."

With that, the cloaked figure turns slowly and departs from the inn. Aaron realizes that he won over the old man after all. He stares at the image of the young woman's face engraved on the box's lid.

The size of the box indicates it would be perfect to house a human head and Aaron gazes at the latch in eerie anticipation.

Within moments of the robed figure's departure, a silver hue appears on Aaron's right side, which radiates from a translucent image of Mareeja. She entreats him, "Thank you, my determined warrior. Now only you can undo the latch to check the contents of what is before us and you must hurry if you are to keep your date with the Queen. She grows impatient for your return, fearing you have met your demise in your battle with Vampressa. Now please, open the box. I, too, am becoming impatient."

Mareeja passes a full goblet of wine to Aaron, fills the remaining goblet to its brim and drinks it down. After drinking the wine this time, Mareeja materializes into human flesh from the neck down. Her face remains sculpted crystal.

Aaron gulps down his entire goblet of wine to steady his nerves and slowly reaches for the latch, his fingers trembling until they touch the clasp. Aaron pops the latch up over the catch ring and gives Mareeja one last look before lifting the lid upward. She grins back to him pensively.

Aaron refocusing on the task at hand pulls upward on the box's lid, it sticks at first, for it has not been opened in many years and its hinges are badly corroded. So, Aaron applies more upward pressure with his thumbs and as he gives it his all, the lid pops open and flops up and over the rear of the box.

Aaron then pulls the wooden box across the dust-ridden table closer to him to peer downward into it. As it comes closer, he sees beautiful, golden, hair extending from the center of the container. He stands to see better into it and views Mareeja's beautiful beaming, face looking up to him with the same smile she had moments before.

Mareeja says, "Once again, thank you, kind sir. Will you now be kind enough to place my head back onto my body." Aaron gingerly reaches his hands down into the box, places them at the sides of Mareeja's golden locks and carefully lifts her head up. He then turns to his right and places the young beauty's radiance atop her shoulders.

Mareeja blinks her eyes several times and moves her neck to the left and to the right. She stands and steps closer to Aaron. On her tiptoes, Mareeja embraces and kisses him softly on his lips.

She announces, "The moon will not be full for three days after tomorrow's sunset. The Queen has inaccurately estimated her cycle, but you must depart on this evening to stop your warrior friend's unwanted union with Samanda.

"Should this happen, the future will drastically change for all the northern kingdoms, so time is of the essence. If your union with the Queen is voided, an evil shadow of hopelessness will prevail for generations to come. Once again, thank you from my heart. My spirit will be forever grateful for your wisdom and help. Now hurry, be on your way."

Mareeja hands Aaron what is left from his rations and the wine in a leather sack. She then ushers him hurriedly to the door.

Mareeja rises on her tiptoes once again and kisses Aaron on the cheek bidding him farewell. Aaron pauses, "Wait. Mareeja, what about my cargo? I must have Vampressa's body in order to be welcomed back into Patrious and to the Queen's fold."

Mareeja smiles knowingly and replies. "You will find Vampressa where you left her, master warrior. It was your heart that could not see her, not your eyes. Now your heart has become fulfilled with the light of goodness and may its beam shine on your destiny."

Aaron departs the inn with most of a late full moon shining. He is bewildered with Mareeja's final statement, but walks to where Noble is tied. He's been in and out of this decrepit makeshift stable for weeks and finds it hard to fathom that the Harpy monster's body has been there all along.

Upon entering the building, he sees the pile of stone and block that he had originally covered Vampressa with. Aaron admits to himself that he was somehow mystically duped by Mareeja and diligently prepares the litter for his return to Patriuous.

As Aaron and Noble plod past the inn, Mareeja is in one of the windows. She waves goodbye and then ascends from the open window into the moonlit sky. Aaron watches her disappear into a galaxy of distant stars.

After several weeks, Vampressa's body has decayed to where it has not only lost weight, but her stench has diminished as well. Aaron is pleased, as this new situation increases Noble's stride.

*   *   *

As the sun rises in Patrious, Samanda's women are hustling about their tent getting ready for the evening's ceremony. Layla also helps and now goes to where Samanda sleeps to awaken her. She tugs at her shoulder and says, "Samanda, I know this is all very confusing to all of us but, you must awake. The Queen feels your cycle is the same as hers and she has ordered that you test the new warrior's seeds when the moon goes silver this night. If you do not cooperate, we will all be punished. So please, I willingly performed my duty nearly three moons ago and you, too, will be able to share a similar happiness someday."

Samanda has been awake for some period, in thought. She longs for Aaron, but knows her sister has the first shot at his affections. She imagines she is the Queen and not the one being used as a surrogate to test a strange warrior's seeds.

Samanda bounds from her bed, dons some apparel and within moments mounted her horse, Windra, and gallops off toward the Queen's tower. Samanda's beautiful associates watch her depart the tent, in curious anticipation. One woman says, "Wait for Samanda's return before making any further preparations…"

*   *   *

Aaron has reached a point where he can spot Patrious on the very distant horizon. He is exhausted and so is Noble. Hoping nothing else goes wrong he trudges along. But then disaster strikes. One of the litter's poles bounces over a rock and snaps in half, throwing the Harpy's body onto the sand.

*   *   *

Samanda has reached her sister's tower and storms up its spiral staircase with her body veils flaring out behind her. Reaching the top, she demands of the oval mirror, "You must not make me do this, my sister. I am in love with Aaron."

The Queen snaps back, "Well so am I, but he has not returned to us, has he? Are we to risk the proliferation of our race because of Aaron's almost certain demise? Or is it that you would like to be Queen? Isn't that it, my sister?"

Samanda replies, "We've had many a split decision of our thoughts over the years, my sister. Let this not be one of them. Please wait just one more day for Aaron's return."

The Queen responds, "And if one more day passes without his return? Then, what do you suggest, my lovely little Samanda? My loins yearn for a man, so do as you were instructed! Now leave me and appear at the royal conception chamber before the moon goes silver."

"My Lady! Please, I could not help but overhear your inner turmoil," a voice interrupts, the voice is of the short round old father. "I was coming to administer the daily prayer and please forgive me for eavesdropping, but I could not help but hear. Now, my Queen, um, um, Samanda," he nods. "May I please have your full attention? I think Samanda's side of the story should be given some acknowledgement. I feel as if your inner conflicts are my fault and I especially, fully understand your dual yearnings."

The father pauses a moment as he paces the floor, assembling his speech in his head. He continues, "I am not certain the Queen's calculations of the moon and her cycle are entirely accurate, which can create some dire circumstance if not put to the proper application for successful procreation. I will leave you with those thoughts and ask you to revisit your planned actions for this evening's ceremony intruding upon your femininities in an untimely manner."

The father turns and walks to the stone stair well. He has descended half of the spiral flight of steps when he hears the familiar bellowing voice from above,

"We must act upon our calling prescribed by our forefathers to continue our race, my father!!!

*   *   *

The late afternoon sun beats down on Aaron as his thoughts scramble for a solution to his problem. It will take a little time to do it, but he thinks he has an idea for repair.

After a few hours, he's fixed Vampressa to the remaining pole, reinforced with pieces of the broken one. He now has the Harpy carcass hanging from it like a rabbit on a spit.

Aaron fastens the single pole to one side of his harnessing even though he knows this will make a lopsided ride. But it is what he has available. Once again he and Noble plod off to Patrious with Vampressa in tow.

*   *   *

Samanda is back in her tent, pouting over what will be the outcome of this evening's events. Her women are absent, gone for some time to assist the sexual preparation of the replacement warrior. Before the act begins, they will make all the necessary preparations, take measurements and weigh precaution. Then they will report their findings to the Queen prior to the union.

Samanda is quite angry and decides not to go willingly. She peers through her tent's opening at the rising moon and anticipates it will be full silver within the hour.

Samanda grabs some leather straps and rope and binds her hands and feet to the largest of the tent support pole. Soon thereafter the eunuch guard-patrol storms into the tent and the head eunuch asserts, "Miss Samanda, we are here by written order of the Queen to bring you to the royal conception chamber within the palace walls."

Upon completion of proclaiming the Queen's order to the offender, the patrol guards move to Samanda and cut her bindings and escort her forcibly from the tent. Samanda screams and claws at the guards like a crazed bobcat as they drag her to the palace.

*   *   *

Aaron is now so close to Patrious he not only hears faint voices, but thinks he hears Samanda crying out in distress. He pats Noble's neck and exhorts him, "Faster my trusted friend. Please go faster..."

*   *   *

Inside the conception chamber, Samanda has been stripped and is unwillingly being strapped to the altar. Because she is such a muscular woman, the guards must use all of their might to spread her legs and bind her feet to the stirrups. Her wrists are then tied as if she were on a crucifix. She has also been gagged to stifle her agonizing, tearful cries. Finally she is bound to the point that she can only barely wiggle.

In the warriors' preparation room, there appears to be a problem. Layla and the other girls have preformed every known procedure to arouse Aaron's comrade, Demitrious, but when the women begin to lubricate his genital area, they cannot help but notice that this man comes nowhere near measuring up to Aaron's length and girth. They panic and feel they must notify the Queen immediately.

Layla disappears through a secret passageway that leads to the base of the Queen's tower and once there, she darts up the stairs to her majesty's suite. No one is there. Layla shouts, "Your majesty, where are you? We have a problem. My Queen, where are you?"

Layla searches every nook and cranny of the circular room. She has never been allowed to enter the Queen's chambers before, but even in her concerned state, Layla notices the large ornate oval mirror. She steps before it and for the first time sees her horribly scarred face and body. She traces the scars with her fingertips and begins to weep as she backs away from the mirror in shock, then turns for the stairwell and runs down the steps.

When she arrives back to the preparation room, three of the other girls enter from an opposite doorway. They have been searching for the Queen in other areas of the palace and have had no luck either.

The women huddle together and whisper. The murmur is, "What shall we do? We are responsible for the outcome of this union."

Demitrious, with hood on, moans in ecstatic anticipation for what he has been brought to this sexual height. Layla demands, "We must proceed or the Queen will have the guards flog us in the center of the market streets." The women agree, so they walk to Demitrious and take his hand.

Two women spread the entrance curtain to the conception chamber as the others lead the naked warrior through the opening toward Samanda...

*   *   *

Aaron has reached the village but is still moving slowly. He feels a great sense of urgency to speed his pace, but knows Noble is doing all he can to expedite their arrival. Then, Aaron has a flashback to his dream about Samanda earlier at the inn. He draws his sword upward and slashes down on the ropes that bind Noble to the pole with Vampressa's body. The pole and the Harpy thud to the ground, releasing Noble from his load. Horse and horseman now race at full speed and disappear among the dwellings of the village of Patrious.

*   *   *

In the royal conception chamber, Samanda's eyes bulge in panic. She can now feel the naked body warmth of Demitrious between her legs even though her women still have the warrior by the hands and have not removed his hood. Samanda defiantly shakes her head back and forth and muffles out a disdainful cry through her gag, "No! Please no! I must await my true love!!!"

*   *   *

The old father paces back and forth on an open walkway atop the front fortress wall, deeply disturbed that the Queen did not heed his advice given earlier in the day. He stares at the moon and stars for guidance. When he looks down, he spots Aaron and Noble racing through the streets of Patrious.

The father grins ear to ear, and then his face goes blank as he looks back at the moon. It is nearly silver, but partially shrouded by a large passing cloud. He knows that the moment the cloud floats past the silver face of the moon, that Samanda will be penetrated, by Demitrious' lubricated shaft.

The father, in a quandary waddles back and forth until he mutters, "No, no, no! That will never work!" Then, as though a light went on in his head, he shouts, "I've got it!!"

The old clergyman runs across the wall toward a bell tower with many steps winding up to its belfry. As he takes the first step upward, he looks down, nearly losing his balance. But he spots Aaron only a few short blocks from the gateway into the courtyard. The father grabs the rails that ascend upward and lifts his foot to the second step, pulling his chubby body upward.

In the chamber Samanda's women are near the final act of preparation. Layla orders one assistant to go to the window and observe the color and location of the moon.

She nods to two other women who obviously know what she wants them to do. They place a wide black belt around the warriors waist with a metal loop fastened to its backside. The two women thread a rope through the loop and tie a knot at its end. A length of the rope is then played out and wrapped around an anchored post behind Demitrious.

Layla and her assistant slowly guide the hooded warrior forward to within an inch of Samanda's quivering pelvis. The rope is now taut between the warrior's back and the post.

*   *   *

The father has now made significant headway up to the belfry and a rope that activates its huge bell hangs a few short feet over his head. He sees the cloud will be past the moon any second. As he stretches upward for the next step his foot slips off the rung step and his body now dangles high above the courtyard wall, his hands grasp the ladder tightly as he kicks his feet toward the lower steps to regain his footing.

*   *   *

Noble's nostrils are flared as he and Aaron gallop around their final corner only one block from the palace's arched gate.

*   *   *

Layla looks to her assistant at the window who still gazes into the night sky. Layla then nods to the two women who secured the rope to the warrior and the post. One of them moves to a far wall of the chamber and removes a sword from a rack. She returns and stops two short paces from the side of the tightly stretched rope. She raises the sword high over the rope and awaits Layla's signal.

Layla drips warm oil onto Samanda's vagina and inner thighs. She then places the warrior's hands on Samanda's upper thighs. He grips them firmly and sighs.

Layla once again checks with her sister in the window who still gazes out at the moon. She has her arm and hand raised, ready to drop it down at the precise moment as the signal to the woman with the sword to slash the rope restraint that keeps Demitrious from penetrating Samanda.

Samanda still struggles to free herself and gargles out a muffled, "No! Please do not do this to me Demitrious!"

Ignoring Samanda's pleas, Layla jerks the hood off Demitrious's head, who becomes even more aroused at what he sees spread out before him. He thrusts his hips forward with great force, tightening the restraining rope even further.

Just as the women turn to their assistant in the window for the final time, a loud ringing double "CLANG," is heard from the bell tower. Everyone in the room knows that the bell is rung only for very special celebrations or when danger is impending.

Startled by the bell, the woman with the sword drops the huge knife and its blade bounces off of the rope, nicking its outer strands. The frayed rope begins to unravel as Demitrious pulls harder.

Samanda's women race around as the bell continues to clang away as though the danger is imminent.

Demitrious is undeterred by the ringing bell and tries to carry out his sexual act upon Samanda. Four of the women jump on the warrior and knock him backward onto the floor.

Layla immediately removes Samanda's gag. She screams out, "Thank the Gods above. Now remove my restraints. I must go do battle!" She's released and there is much confusion with everyone scurrying about the room. Samanda, still nude, quickly slips away through the secret passageway.

Aaron gallops into the courtyard in full uniform. He rides around the torch-lit walls shouting, "I have returned. I have returned with the carcass of the dead, evil monster Vampressa!"

As he rides past one of the torches he pulls it from the wall and waves it from side-to-side desperately trying to draw attention to himself. He then circles the courtyard, waving the torch, shouting of his victory.

Within moments, a large crowd gathers in the courtyard, not only from the castle, but scores of village people flood the torch lit courtyard as well.

The bell continues to ring and everyone in the crowd cheers Aaron's return.

Long moments of delight elapse, when a silence slowly creeps across the multitude. Even the old father stops ringing the huge bell.

Aaron becomes bewildered by the sudden calm until he turns to where everyone else's eyes are focused. He turns Noble around and looks up to the top of the Queen's tower.

She stands there in her red satins contrasting the darkness above the flaming torches. From within, a yellow, pulsating hue is cast outward by her oil lamps behind her. The light outlines the stern-faced woman's veiled silhouette.

Aaron approaches the base of the Queen's tower, pulls Noble to a halt and raises his torch victoriously. He announces, "I have returned to you, my Queen. Our joint conquest over man and monster is complete. I am now yours to use however you see fit."

Through her veils the Queen calls down to Aaron, "And what of the whereabouts of the monster's dead carcass my brave warrior?"

He answers proudly, "My men from the barracks guard the monster at this very moment. It is but a short distance in the desert from the edge of the city. I felt an urgency of danger for your sister, Samanda, as I neared Patrious, so I cut Vampressa loose to gain speed."

The Queen, trying desperately to cover her obvious excitement over Aaron's return, orders him, "Your first command upon your return is to cast Samanda from your thoughts! Return to me at the break of dawn with the Harpy's body and if it is so, we will plan for our future. Now disperse with the multitude you have created. If all that you state is true, tomorrow will be a day of Royal celebration."

The crowd files back into the village and Aaron and Noble accompany the people out the gate and then ride to the location of Vampressa's cadaver.

The Queen turns and crosses to the front of the oval mirror. Seeing her own reflection, she opines, "Maybe you are not as wise as you think, my sister." But then Samanda's face appears. Samanda repeats the Queen's words verbatim, "Maybe you are not as wise as you think, my sister?"

Chapter Nine

Early the next morning, just outside the barracks, Aaron and his men have held Vampressa's corpse secure. Now Aaron, alone, prepares her cadaver for the Queen in the palace courtyard.

He adjusts the straps and ropes that tie the monster to his new litter and ponders what is in store for him.

He misses Samanda a great deal and is surprised he did not see her in the courtyard the night before. Aaron tries not to dwell on the fact that the Queen desires him for her very own and casts aside thoughts that Samanda will likely become an obscure part of his life. Still his heart aches over why she had not greeted him upon his victorious return.

As Aaron and Noble proudly drag the dead Harpy through the streets in the direction of the palace gates, the crowds once again surround them. Scores of villagers are lured from their abodes by the grotesque sight and line the streets. As he passes through the crowds of bystanders most of them follow closely behind his one horse caravan.

When Aaron nears the wrought-iron gate, the eunuch guards swing its huge right and left hinged partitions open wide for him. As he passes the gatekeepers, he looks to them with some apprehension and recognizes most of them from the mines where he and his men toiled for over a year. These eunuchs were not gatekeepers when he departed for battle.

The guards quickly slam the gate closed behind Aaron to keep the following residents from entering the courtyard. Aaron immediately spots the Queen sitting on a large boulder at the footbridge over the stream. She rises and walks to him as he nears her.

Aaron halts Noble at the Queen's feet and takes a cursory glance around the courtyard. Finding no one else about, Aaron dismounts, kneels before the Queen, and then bows to her royal highness.

Aaron lifts his head slowly from his respectful stance and his face is in very close proximity to the woman before him. He cannot help but notice that under her transparent face and body veils, the Queen is completely nude. She smiles at Aaron invitingly and bids him to rise.

Aaron rises slowly, discerning her every curve as he does so. Once erect he stares into her beautiful blue eyes and offers, "I have returned to you, your majesty and fulfilled your every wish of me except one. I am your property. Do with me as you will."

The Queen remains silent as she slowly turns from Aaron and strolls around Vampressa's remains. She is quite impressed with Aaron as she views the hideous, rotting monster hanging from the traverse poles.

Aaron is surprised when he hears the Queen let out a subtle demonic toned giggle from beneath her scarf. He has never been a witness to such a gesture as this from her. The accomplished warrior dismisses it, surmising that her majesty is especially pleased with his accomplishments.

After fully circling the dead beast, the Queen once again faces Aaron and says to him, "Tonight shall be the first of three ceremonies. You are not only my property, Sir Aaron, you are as well, my new General-of-Arms. Our people must know this. They must confide in your strengths in order to achieve the perception that it is now safe to again successfully propagate without the danger of injury or death.

"The first ceremony will be a festival to celebrate this renewed sexual liberation for our people. Tonight, in full view of the residents of Patrious, we will burn Vampressa's remains in the center of our market square. This will represent a victory for our reproduction and you will be at my side during this event. Then, tomorrow, at noon, we will conduct the second ceremony, a grand spectacle with much color and fanfare. The streets will be lined and our people will cheer as we pass. At the start of the procession, we will announce our devotion to each other and anticipated union.

"The third ceremony will be one of fertility. After the parade, you will be taken to the preparation room. Soon after, you will be joined by Samanda's harem women, who will go through great lengths to administer our ancient fertility ritual on your person to assure conception. When the harem's ritual is complete, they will notify the Father and he will, in turn, notify the order of wise women. Soon thereafter, we will be united in the royal conception chamber. On this occasion, due to my cycle, we may no longer rely upon the silver moon. Fertility will only come by the hand of Zuse, the God of fire. He will determine the precise moment of conception.

"If, for whatever reason, the yellow finch does not fly upon its perch at my head when we come together, our union will not be complete. That can only mean you are not a suitable mate and most likely you will be banished from our kingdom by the wise women. With that in mind, I suggest you cooperate to the fullest with the women who prepare you for me.

"After we burn Vampressa this evening, you shall return to your tower suite and shortly after tomorrow's dawn, our Father will visit you. At that time he will prepare you spiritually for our eternal bond."

The Queen walks to the Harpy's corpse, bends over and plucks a large purple and black feather from her. She returns to Aaron and sticks the quill end of the feather into the front of his war apron. She smiles and places her palms on his cheeks, guides his face to hers, lifts the bottom of her veil slightly and busses him with a very passionate kiss. Aaron puts his arms around the Queen, embraces the lovely woman and kisses her equally as passionate.

After the two disengage, the Queen places her fingers to Aaron's lips and tells him, "Now go to your men in the barracks and have them assist you in preparing the fire for our celebration tonight. Make sure the beast is fastened to a stake high in the center of the fire ring. String her up in such a fashion that all of the village people can watch her turn to ashes."

Aaron nods, turns to cross to his horse, but before he mounts, he stops, turns and asks the Queen, "Your majesty, what of your sister Samanda? Should she not be notified of this evening's ceremony? After all, she has certainly put forth a great effort over the past several weeks toward your cause."

Aaron's inquiry appears to miff the Queen. She steps up to Aaron, pulls Vampressa's feather out of his loin wrap and using the quill end, pokes Aaron in his chiseled abdomen as she speaks, "My Master-of-Arms, why is it you have such overwhelming concern for my sister? I have heard a few sordid tales involving your relationship with Samanda while at the battlefront. Not to mention even more sordid stories about your involvement with Kaybra during the same time period. To this point I have been willing to dismiss these rumors as hearsay.

"If I were you, I'd do as just instructed and leave any communication with Samanda to me. I assure you we visit daily and she has been well apprised of all matters."

The Queen walks behind Noble and pushes Vampressa's feather back into her lifeless carcass. She then orders, "Now, be gone with you!"

Aaron knows he's been put in his place and sensing he should not respond, hops onto Noble's back and rides for the barracks.

The Queen calls out as he rides off, "I will see you on the marketplace stand at the first sight of the moon. Build the fire high, so that its flames tickle the night sky."

*   *   *

Aaron and his men erect a huge pile of wood in the town's marketplace square, with the Harpy's body bound to the top of a tall, straight timber anchored in the center of the woodpile. Evening comes upon them.

Little does Aaron know Vampressa's evil cryptic spirit is about to unleash one last devastating act that he will remember her by for quite some time.

The people of Patrious gather and surround the mound of brush and timber, holding torches that illuminate their faces and walls of buildings that line the town's square.

To allow the Queen's entourage to enter the center of the square, the crowd parts slightly.Leading is the old father who possesses a small bell that hangs from a leather tie in his hand. With each step, he rings the bell twice. He is followed by the order of wise women, who step in unison as they approach the stand. They are followed by four eunuchs supporting the Queen in an ornate sedan chair.

They stop at the center of the tiered seating that rises upward in front of the huge funeral pyre and the eunuchs lower the Queen to the ground. She steps off and walks to Aaron, takes his hand and leads him back onto the stands.Once in the royal platform, the Queen takes Aaron's wrist and raises his arm high. She turns him in all directions as the crowd cheers him on and on.

Overwhelmingly accepted by the people of Patrious, Aaron delivers a broad smile.

Horns blare from the upper stands and the crowd subsides. The horns stop and all is silent.

Aaron takes the Queen's fingertips in his hand and leads her down the steps to the front of the large log and brush fire pile.In the center of the pile, Vampressa is strapped to the upper part of a large square wooden stake, reduced to the likes of a large common garden scarecrow.

A path going up toward the Harpy has been saturated with torch oil.

Aaron and the Queen stand quietly as one of Aaron's men hands him a lit torch, which he passes to the Queen. She bends and touches the fire stick to the oil path and the flame races up the mound of stacked wood. It immediately ignites the top of the brush pile, engulfing Vampressa and soon after the revolting smell of burning feathers spreads through the town square. The crowd cheers when they see black clouds of smoke belch and billow upward into the sky from the monster's blazing body.

Aaron and the Queen kiss and just as they close their eyes in contentment, the cheers from the people turn into shrieks of horror.

Both the Queen and Aaron jolt their faces back from each other due to the crowd's exclamations and look up to the fire's center. What they see and hear is frightening. Where Vampressa was, now hangs Uma. She cries out in loud painful horror as the flames burn her naked flagellating body, "I will soon meet both of you fornicating in hell!!! Aahh, aahh, aahh. Your union will be cursed by my offspring!!! Aaron, I poisoned your seeds the night you tried to slay me on the mound and Dilayla poisoned them a second time when you fucked her on the sandstone! You will live in torment until the end of your day, you forthright bastard!!! And remember of what I speak on the night you consummate your Royal union !!! Aaahhh, aahh, ah, ah…"

She becomes, at last, silent, as her charred body incinerates. Piece by piece, phosphorescent charred chunks of her remains disintegrate and tumble into the growing pile of embers below.

Aaron and the Queen look to each other, their eyes filled with concern. They wonder if there's any fact in Uma's final flaming proclamation.

From the shadows the old Father hustles to the worried couple and pushes them aside. He holds a wooden pail filled with a gold-like dust, which he hurls high onto the pyre.

The gold dust turns into gold flakes and falls into flames at the very spot Vampressa was staked. When the magical concoction comes in contact with the flames it sparkles and twinkles, snapping and popping away. Like fireworks, this array of sparked illumination shoots high into the sky above the village square.

The Father turns to Aaron and the Queen. "Do not be worried, my children. Everything in your future will remain bright. My daughter, please continue on with the ceremony."

The old man disappears into the darkness behind the stand.

The Queen motions upward signaling to the horns. Once again the trumpets blare and the pleasant aftermath of the sparkling gold dust display reinvigorates the crowd. Aaron and the Queen return to their royal box. The people resume their gestures of pleasure.

After the mood has been restored, the Queen rises with Aaron at her left. He raises his hands, signifying to the crowd that the Queen wishes to speak.

He words project through her veil, "Thanks to our new Master-of-Arms, the days of Vampressa's oppression upon our people are over. She or her ilk will never again be able to suppress our race. We will live as a free nation of, brave, bold and courageous people.

"Much has changed since the days of my husband, your late King's, rule. Much will continue to change as new suns rise and set. I have been widowed for over two full seasons. Under these circumstances I cannot bear a royal child to carry on the rule of our reign. Therefore, our new Master-of-Arms and brave warrior, Aaron, who stands before you, has accepted my hand." The crowd roars with endorsement.

The Queen continues, "At tomorrow's high sun, there will be a royal procession that will travel through the main arteries of Patrious and reach its end in my courtyard. There, there will be a grand feast to celebrate our engagement and all people of my kingdom are invited to attend. Now, continue this evening's festivity until the coals of this fire glow grey and then return to your homes to prepare yourselves for tomorrow's celebration."

The people of Patrious celebrate into the night, but before things have completely wound down, the Queen excuses herself. She and her procession depart the square for the palace as Aaron remains to mingle with those who have not yet left the square.

After some time has passed, almost everyone but Aaron has departed and his last comrade has just left when Aaron steps up to the smoldering fire ring. With his foot, he brushes sand over some of the wood not completely burnt out.

Finally he decides to call it a night and smiles to himself, knowing his tower suite is warm and ready for him. He turns for one last view of the stands and the royal box from which the Queen made her announcements earlier. When he does, his expression becomes one of shock, for sitting in the exact spot he sat moments before, is Samanda, dressed in a long, white gown with a silver chain belt. Her tempting garment's neckline is cut so low that Samanda's breasts are mostly exposed.

Aaron immediately becomes romantically enchanted with what he sees and begins to climb the steps to the pretty woman and exclaims, "Samanda, my love, is that really you?"

Samanda replies, "Yes, Aaron, it is I." Samanda looks beautiful to Aaron and he has greatly missed her. His smile returns as he approaches where she sits. Samanda whispers aloud, "Stop, Aaron, come no further. I just wanted to let you know that I have been here all along.When I heard the palace warning bell ring out last night, I was in a very sexually vulnerable situation and somehow, I knew it was you who caused its clanging. Once again, you saved me, just as you did from the teeth of the croc. Do you recall how I repaid you on that night, by the moon-kissed water?

"Once again, I must repay you before you bond with my sister. I know you miss me and I miss you as well. Nothing or no one can put our love for each other asunder, but we have only a short time to act on our passions. I want you to return to your tower abode and after the Queen's lamps go dark, I will join you and we will have one final hourglass of time together before your union with my sister."

Aaron realizes the danger of what might happen should the Queen catch Samanda and him together in his tower suite. Attempting to reply, he grapples for words. Ultimately, Aaron willingly relents to Samanda's request. "Alright, my love, I shall do as you wish. It seems like an eternity since I have felt the soft touch of your skin. Please be quiet and careful upon your approach."

*   *   *

Aaron rests on his bunk in his tower. He faintly hears the hinges creak on the large wooden door at the tower's base and then hears the scuffing sounds of Samanda's slipper-covered feet climbing the stone staircase.

Aaron is in excited anticipation as the footsteps draw near the top, yet inside he frets over the potential outcome of this last minute tryst before he unites with the Queen. Then, as those thoughts of woe are fading, Samanda reaches Aaron's top step, pauses in the opening and smiles at Aaron. The once strong-willed warrior is hopelessly captivated by Samanda's allure.

Longing to once again touch Samanda, Aaron slowly rises from his bed as Samanda's full length white gown pulls tightly across her upper thighs with each stride, as she sweeps across the floor into Aaron's arms.

She stares straight into Aaron's eyes as she reaches down and unfastens his waistband to his apron. It drops to the floor.

With her eyes still staring into Aaron's, Samanda unbuckles her silver belt and tosses it onto the bed. She crosses her arms and grasps the waistline of her dress fabric and in one swift, rising motion, Samanda pulls the dress up over her head and carelessly pitches the gown aside.

Aaron melts as he admires her tanned, shapely, naked body and is entranced by Samanda's aggressive performance. He tries to soften the moment, but the beautiful woman remains unfazed. Using both her arms, Samanda shoves Aaron backward onto his bed and relentless in her passionate pursuit, she leaps on top of him.

Within a heartbeat, the couple's lips lock together and their limbs intertwine, as they caress each other and roll about the squeaky bed.

Aaron pulls his lips from Samanda's and whispers, "Stop, my love, stop. We will awaken your sister who sleeps only a short distance across the courtyard."

Samanda, still undeterred, whispers back, "Do not fear the Queen, my General-of-Arms, I know my sister. She has fallen into a deep sleep by this late hour. Now hush, while I arouse you further. You know we love each other beyond the ends of time, so please cooperate."

Aaron withdraws his plea and plops his head back down into his pillow. Samanda positions herself on her knees, her thighs straddle Aaron. She reaches down and grasps Aaron's shaft firmly. He is startled at first, but calms down and allows Samanda to continue her hand stimulation on him.

Aaron feels his manhood pumping up and Samanda has placed the tip of his penis so close to her golden triangle between her thighs that he can feel the heat radiating from in it. He reaches up, places his hands on her shoulders and his face emits concern as he states, "Wait, Samanda, my love. Please wait."

Samanda ignores him as if she's is deaf and continues to stroke her closed fingers up and down Aaron's throbbing shaft.

Attempting to slow down this painful pleasure, Aaron blurts out in a loud whisper, "Samanda, wait!"

This time he has her attention and Samanda stops, turns her head in the direction of Aaron's open window. She peers through it across the courtyard as if checking for a light in the Queen's tower suite. Seeing it is dark, she turns back, looks down into Aaron's face and asks, "What is it, my love? I assure you not to be concerned about my sister. Surely you cannot tell me you do not wish to join our flesh on our final night together?"

Aaron replies, "My dearest Samanda, you know I love you and that I have no desire to wed your sister. She is a lovely and magnificent woman, as are you, but I have no choice and my union with her is to restore the royal bloodline.

"I will willingly copulate with you this night and enjoy every moment of our intermingled passion for each other. But please, you must help me. There is one thing I must know before I become one with you."

Samanda has meanwhile resumed stroking his manhood. She continues to methodically work on him, says, "Go on, my Master General. What is your query?" Samanda's hand motion becomes more deliberate and firming her grasp on Aaron's penis, she steps up the beat. Elevating her voice to impede Aaron's momentary resistance, Samanda repeats herself, "Go on, my Master General!"

Aaron tilts his head forward and views Samanda's long and persistent ringed fingers squeezing him as she works her hand up and down. He has all he can do to contain himself, but Aaron forces his words through his grimacing lips. "This woman, your sister, I must know her name. If I am to be unfaithful to her on this night, uh, uh, Samanda, please pause a moment! Uh, uh! I must know her given name."

Samanda becomes enraged with Aaron's request. She can feel his veins throbbing within her tightly clinched fingers. Unable to restrain herself, she is stimulated further and there is no way the sex-starved woman is going to cast this opportunity aside.

Samanda bends forward and lifts her hips. She places the tip of Aaron's shaft touching the outer edge of her vagina and looks down to Aaron as if about to accomplish some valiant quest. She vents, "You may be the Queen's property, but tonight you are mine alone. Now stop your questions regarding my sister and enjoy what I have to offer you!"

To perfect Aaron's penetration Samanda makes one final repositioning adjustment before she thrusts her hips downward and as she achieves the desired alignment, a loud, deep voice shouts from the opening to the stone staircase, "Samanda no! What are you thinking? Guards, seize this woman and take her to the dungeons!"

Four eunuch guards converge upon Samanda, wrap her in blankets and pull her off Aaron. Aaron grabs his wrap to cover his huge erection and fastens it hastily.

Samanda kicks her feet and screams as the eunuchs cart her away, "Why? Why not me? Why is it permissible for this man to mate with Layla and Kaybra and not me! Soon he will sleep with my sister and I will have never experienced any of their pleasures."

As the guards stomp down the stairwell Samanda's whimpering shrieks can be heard echoing up its arched walls, "My sister the Queen, I hate you! I hate you!"

The old man who shouted at Samanda crosses to her clothes, grunts and picks them up. The Father drapes her white gown over his extended forearm and holds Samanda's slippers and belt in his hands.

Aaron assumes he's in a world of trouble, so he remains silent, sitting on the edge of his bunk. To Aaron's surprise, the old man speaks to him in a moderate tone as he moves to the stairs. He offers, "Please forgive Samanda, my General-of-Arms and soon to be King. Both the Queen and her sister long for you to be their mate, however in very different ways.

"It is unfortunate for Samanda, but our ancient scriptures mandate that only the Queen can participate in the Royal Conception Ceremony to produce a leader for our land. Our generations to follow must rely on the fact that we have fulfilled our scripture to the minutest detail. Soon you will understand.

"I was to arrive here in the morning's first light to speak to you. Instead, I wish you to meet me in my room inside the grand hall well before tomorrow's parade. There I will enlighten you further, but for now, you must rest. I will expect to see you no later than mid-morning. Goodnight."

The Father gives Aaron a pleasant nod and descends the stone steps.

Somewhat perplexed and definitely sexually frustrated, Aaron paces his room, knowing that what he was about to do with Samanda was wrong, but he truly loves her and not the Queen.

Aaron gains some solace knowing the Father is not upset with him, but is curious of the subject matter of his meeting next morning with the old fellow.

Aaron has never seen the Queen's unveiled face by other than a minute glimpse. Her scantily covered figure and profile are revealing though, of her beauty. But now Aaron must think about her personality. He is acutely aware that if her highness does not conceive his child, dire straits lie ahead for him. Aaron is unsettled, knowing that his wedding will be abruptly terminated if the yellow finch does not fly to its perch upon the climax of their union, yet if it does not go well, he may possibly pair up with Samanda. Then again, with visions of the old women scourging him from the village, he has his doubts.

Aaron crosses to his bed and sits, wriggles his hand between his mattress and padding beneath. After a bit he pulls out the red scarf the Queen gave him in the dungeon, closes his eyes and sniffs its pleasant perfume. He thinks back to that time and remembers the Queen telling him, "Return this to me." then turning and walking away. How was that gesture to be interpreted? He closes his fingers around the scarf and bends his head to his hands. He thinks he knows the cloth's meaning, but then his thoughts are broken. He says to himself, "I wonder if the eunuch guards took Samanda to the same dungeon where I was kept on that first night?" His thoughts become painful as he visualizes Samanda strung up to the dungeon wall and hopes the small family of mice that dwell there will keep her company through the night.

Aaron tries to purge that saddening vision from his mind and still holding the Queen's scarf, he stands, crosses to his window.

He gazes across the courtyard at the Queen's window and is not surprised to see her standing on its ledge. Although she holds a flickering oil lamp in front of her, the distance is too far for Aaron to determine her expression. The scarlet woman is once again shrouded with her satins, but is obviously looking in Aaron's direction.

The Queen brings the lamp up before her lips and Aaron can now see the light reflecting off the whites of her piercing blue eyes. Just as he squints for better view, she blows a slight puff and all goes dark.

*   *   *

It is early the next morning. Aaron is awake and alert. In excited anticipation of what is expected of him this day, he anxiously prepares for his meeting with the Father.

By early mid-morning, Aaron is standing outside the Father's door inside the grand hall and as he raises his hand to knock, the door swings wide open by the old man from the inside. Still holding the handle, he speaks to Aaron. "Ah, I'm glad you are early, my Master General. We have much to discuss before you can be properly ordained King. I have cleared my scripture table. Please be seated."

Aaron approaches the table and seats himself on a small wooden bench at the end. The robed Father peeks out the door into the grand hall, looking all around the interior of the mammoth temple as if trying to detect anyone else's presence. Seeing no one, he pulls the door closed and locks it, then crosses to Aaron's right. Showing a wry face and emitting a slight groan, he plops himself down and speaks again. "My, my, my. What trying times these past few years have been since the King's death. Curiously enough, it seems your actions have created the situation. Now, here you are, sacrificing your future to rebuild a kingdom that was once your fiercest enemy. What will be left for the Gods to bestow upon us after this amazing twist of events? My, my, my.

"Very well, we must begin somewhere. First, I will administer the sacred creed."

The old clergyman removes the cross and chain from around his neck, swings the cross back and forth in front of Aaron's face.

Aaron's eyelids begin to droop as the Father's monotone voice continues, "It is the decision of the Queen and the Devine Order of Wise Women that you become our King. You will be loyal to the Queen and fulfill her every command without hesitation. An invincible bond will form between the two of you, which shall be a divine union of your spirit to hers. It will live into eternity.

"The two of you will rule as one. Upon the Queen's conception, even the Anti-Gods will be unable to ruin this holy of holiest unions as outlined in our ancient creed.

"Your loins will bear fruits, creating endless generations of our people to come."

The Father looks over Aaron's head, at a large, gold, silver and jeweled coat-of-arms hanging on the wall behind the warrior.

He raises his cross to aim a light ray at the center of the coat of arms. He stands and uses the ray of light to trace a line of ancient hieroglyphics that are engraved onto a gold tablet there. As he does so, the man closes his eyes and chants, "Abobba lest shal vey quant dum unus tabbal. Unum maxum la ve shaleste to moor, la ve, la ve, la ve."

Upon finishing his chant, the Father places his hand on top of Aaron's head as a tremendously loud roar of thunder is heard in the distance. The floor trembles, then small pieces of mortar crumble from the wall of the Father's chamber and fall to the floor. Immediately thereafter, like a spear hurled from heaven, a bolt of lightning crashes through the sky and hits the steeple atop the grand hall.

An instant later, a spark bolts from the insignia's gold tablet and connects with the cross the old man holds. The electrical charge passes through his hand, across his chest and to the hand he has on Aaron's head. In obvious pain, the Father's body shakes as he squeezes his fingers tightly around the cross.

Aaron's eyes open wide as his body twitches from the electrical shock. Aaron has remained speechless throughout this whole ordeal, but can't help but react with a loud "Ugh!"

A moment of silence passes, then the bell tower rings out one loud, "Clang!" as the lightning bounces off the belfry back into the sky.

Meanwhile the Queen has been in her tower suite preparing for the festivities of the day. Upon hearing the bell ring, she stops, looks out her window and murmurs, "Zuse has just ordained Aaron." Smiling contentedly, she resumes her preparations. Unexplainably in an instant her mood changes and she pauses.

Samanda has also heard the bell ring and whispers her final revelation, "It has finally come to pass. Zuse has ordained Aaron and his time is quickly approaching the conception ceremony with my sister."

Because of her passion for the brave warrior, the reality is too much for her. Fraught with emotion, tears stream from her eyes and roll off her cheeks. She dabs them away with a royal pink kerchief.

In the chamber off of the grand hall, the Father tells Aaron, "My General-of-Arms, you are now ordained by Zuse, our great God of fire. Your soul has been engraved onto the charter of immortality. The offspring you and the Queen shall bear will be the great grandchildren of the mighty Zuse himself."

The Father reseats himself, looks to Aaron and states, "However, there is one other matter, my soon-to-be King of Patrious."

Aaron, still groggy states, "It is my will to serve the Queen, even though I know not her given name. Hopefully you will share that information with me before I depart your chambers."

The clergyman, undeterred by Aaron's inquiry continues, "Unfortunately, I believe the Queen's sister, Samanda, has been less than honest with you."

Hearing Samanda's name, Aaron snaps out of his trance and interrupts the Father, "Please tell me what you mean about Samanda?" He sits up straight on the bench, a concerned look on his face as he listens intently.

The Father continues, "It is true that our former King treated his wife cruelly in many ways. While he was far away and engaged with the crusades of his era, the poor woman was locked in her tower suite for days, sometimes weeks at a time.

"Her chastity belt remained on for such long periods that it caused deep sores and infections on her person. It was further ordered that she was to be given only small amounts of food and water daily in her husband's absence. Then when the King returned he would feed her abundantly acting as if he were doing some heroic deed. When he was home, the woman was constantly abused by the King, before, during and after his drunken binges.

"Then after her mother reported the King's abuse of her daughter to the Order of Wise Women, things changed drastically. A clandestine meeting was held by the Order at which I recommended we release the Queen when the King was away in battle. That was, however, under one very serious condition, that the Queen must wear an elaborate disguise when in public.

"In time, she became very proficient with her array of clever masquerades. Our highness would portray herself, to our people, as an individual from many different walks of life. She might appear as an old man or woman, or walk the streets of Patrious as a schoolgirl or even an armored warrior.

"She crafted her camouflage outfits so uniquely that on more than one occasion, she actually rode with the King's troops onto the battlefields. One evening while there, she was a silent witness to the King's indiscretions with a lust-filled desert nymph.

"Needless to say, her tribulations caused the Queen to fall into a grave state of mind. The power she originally possessed to relate to her own identity was quickly diminishing. The King's abuse, placed her in dire need of treatment, but no one could help.

"Fortunately, you slew the King before he caught on to his wife's peculiar behavior and elaborate charade. But, unfortunately, the loss of her husband only intensified our lady's disorder. A part of her became very logical and rigid, while the other side if her border-lined manic moods, often involving erotic ceremonies with other women. Her condition exists until this day. But, there is one hope-filled solution to this cruel saga.

"One day, not so long ago, our town was visited by an elderly traveling man who looked to the stars for answers to our dilemma. He was summoned to a meeting of the Devine Order and I felt worse than anyone since, the Queen's facade was my idea. But I made certain the old soothsayer attended and he went into great detail at this meeting. He produced a crystal ball that glowed and pulsated light outward into the dim shadows created by the small Grand Hall lamps.

"He predicted a man such as you would be brought to Patrious against his will. He added that the man would be a brave warrior with forthright thoughts and held out hope for the Queen if his specific orders were followed. He said that the only hope for the Queen to keep from eventually going completely insane was for her to unite with this warrior from the enemy land.

"The scraggly bearded oracle concluded the meeting with, 'This warrior of iron, must never forsake the Queen, for by the time he appears, her majesty's mind will be far too frail and her days numbered.'

"You see, Aaron, that is why you must completely eliminate Samanda from your thoughts. Due to my recent input Samanda is well aware of this condition, but cannot help herself while in your presence, therefore you have a choice. But if it is the wrong choice, Patrious will become another mound of dust before the next generation is born.

"Please reward my honesty by having no further contact with Samanda prior to your union with the Queen. And if you are able to resist her temptations, you will be rewarded beyond your wildest dreams"

Aaron is stunned with the information he has just learned and thinks that the Father and the Devine Order are trying to pawn off a crazed, high-ranking woman on him and these new doubts dangerously reinforce Aaron's feelings for Samanda.

Aaron pleads with the Father, "Please Father, at least tell me the Queen's given name. I plead with you. I must know the name of the woman to whom I am soon to be wed."

The Father stands and begins to pace the room in silent contemplation. He stops, turns to Aaron's troubled face. "Please brace yourself, my soon-to-be King. Your Queen's given name is…"

He is abruptly interrupted by a loud, banging at his door. A deep voice shouts out from outside the door, "Open the door! Be quick, we are here by order of the Queen! We must speak to Aaron immediately. There is a very grave matter at hand!"

As Aaron and the Father rush to the door, the palace bell repeatedly clangs away. Aaron unbolts the door and jerks it open to a unit of eunuch guards bunched in the doorway.

The head guard states, panicked, "Simba has returned to Patrious! The smoke from Vampressa's roasting body must have lured her to the village! The vicious, fanged cat was seen at the sight of last night's ceremonial fire. Aaron, you must assemble your men and help us!"

Aaron has never crossed Simba's path, but is well aware of the large, black leopard's thirst for blood. He pushes through the eunuchs and runs for the exit.

As he leaves the Hall, the Queen runs up to him, hugs him with all of her frantic might and opines, "Aaron, I do love you and once again you must help us. I have just been told that Simba has smelled the faint odors of Samanda's women who are in cycle and at this very moment the dreaded black cat is circling her tent."

Aaron grabs the Queen by the shoulders and pushes her away as he commands, "You must order Samanda released from the dungeons and have her assemble as many eunuchs as she can.

"Simba is the size of four horses and so I will need more than just my men to outflank her crafty movements. If you unshackle Samanda so that she may aid me, I vow to slay the giant panther in your name, my Queen."

The Queen stretches her arms to Aaron's head, pulls his face to down to hers and gives him a reassuring kiss. Pushing him away from her lips, she replies, "My sister will join you in battle shortly."

Aaron leaps across the courtyard to where Noble is tied, hops onto his steed's back and gallops out of the courtyard.

The Father, standing in the doorway, has heard the interchange between the Queen and Aaron. He rushes to the Queen's side as she strides swiftly towards her tower. Trying to stop her highness, the clergyman blurts out, "My daughter, please wait up for me." But the Queen still moves determinedly for her door. Finally, the Father runs in front of her just as the Queen reaches for the knob. He braces his back against the closed door.

Completely out of breath, the old man stammers, "My daughter, I heard Aaron's request for Samanda's assistance. Please, I beg you, do not release this female character. Our Master General is a strong willed-man, but he is just that, a man and your sister's personality has a lusty captivating effect on him. If they weaken and she entices him to succumb to her desires, all has been for naught."

The Queen gives the Father a sympathetic look, places her hands on his and says, "I have had a long, heated debate with my sister. You need not be concerned any longer. As sisters, our divided personalities have finally found peace. Nothing shall ruin my union with Aaron in the few short hours to come before we are wed. Please forgive me Father, I have much to prepare for and must be on my way." The Queen pulls her door open as the bewildered clergyman steps aside.

*   *   *

All of Aaron's men have assembled outside their barracks. The tower bell continues to clang away and they look up and down the streets in an attempt to identify the emergency.

Aaron, atop Noble, gives them his directive during a short briefing of the circumstances at hand and his troops part to hustle off to harness their horses. Aaron takes off at full gallop for Samanda's tent on the edge of town.

He slows to a canter as he exits the last street that leads onto the sand dunes that surround Samanda's tent. When he reaches the top of the largest dune, he cautiously peeks over its top and spots Simba. The huge Black Panther is slinking around the outside of the large tent and every few steps it takes, the cat pauses to sniff the bottoms of the canvas walls. It then lifts its head and hisses.

Aaron hears his men coming, turns and raises his hand in the air with a flat palm to signal them to approach quietly. They slow their horses to a walk and place one hand on their weapons to keep them from jingling.

Inside the tent, Layla has been huddled protectively in the center of the other women.They quietly move as a unit to the side of the tent opposite of where the large cat sniffs outside. They hold their breath with every hiss the beast makes.

Aaron orders his men to encircle the tent on the dunes and before they do, he tells them his planned course of action. Because he does not have enough remaining troops to complete the circle around the tent, he commands his warriors to man their assigned positions until Samanda arrives with the eunuchs to complete the loop. The troop quietly walks their steeds in the direction ordered.

So far there is no sight of Samanda or the guards. To Aaron it seems as if an eternity is passing.

The cat is growing impatient and the sound of her belly growling from hunger can be heard from atop the sand mound where Aaron is stationed. Finally, the animal moves to the front of the tents entrance foyer, where it hunches down. The cat extends one paw into the tent through the opening and paws at the women inside, who scurry to the back lounge chamber to avoid the cat's sharp claws.

Aaron hears a whisper from beside him, "What will you have us do, my Master General?" The voice is Samanda's, who has approached Aaron stealth-like with the eunuch guards. Aaron quickly relates his plan to Samanda and the guards, who softly trot to their posts, now completing the large circle around the tent. Samanda remains by Aaron's side.

The panther moved closer to the opening and stuck its nose just inside. Samanda and Aaron see the cat's body tensing, ready to pounce into the main room of the tent.

The animal moves again, crawling on its belly farther, until the cat's huge head is completely inside the entrance.

Samanda's women quiver in fear in the back room and with every sniff the cat takes, the thin fabric wall separating them flexes back and forth.

In an instant the leopard lunges farther, Aaron lifts his sword and signals to his commander atop the dune opposite him.

Only the cat's rear and tail remain exposed outside the tent and Aaron's first commander, at the tent's rear, charges down from atop his dune toward the structure as Aaron descends rapidly from his vantage point. The remaining men, guards and Samanda, raise their loaded crossbows and aim them downward at the cat.

Inside, the panther rips through the fabric wall dividing the front room from the rear and the fanged beast pops its head through the slit in the canvas with its claw, shakes it side-to-side and lets out a ferocious roar. The women shriek in horror as the cat's fangs are but a few short feet from them.

The panther's boulder-sized head is covered with ashes from the fire pit where Vampressa was incinerated. It reeks of smoke.

Aaron, on horseback, is now at the panther's rear, raises his sword and swishes it down with all his might lopping off half the cat's long, black tail.

The panther screams aloud as its mouth opens wide and it reels with pain from the wound. It becomes tangled inside the tent as it tries to see its attacker.

A sword slashes through the tent's rear wall near the women. It is the blade of Aaron's commander and he rips the torn opening even further with his hands and motions the women to exit through it. They immediately rush out and into the desert.

The predator manages to turn around inside the shredded tent and frees its head and one front leg. It swipes at Aaron with its claws extended, which produces a single gouge across his bare chest as Aaron slashes away at the cat's paw.

The minute the women are out of harm's way, the circular flank atop of the dunes trigger their crossbows and the giant puma is riddled with arrows. The large cat begins to look like a porcupine, but it is far from dead.

Managing to pull itself free from the mangled tent, the panther races around the shallow valley, looking for an exit. When it charges up one dune, it is driven back by another hail of arrows. Aaron and Noble pursue the beast as it crisscrosses from dune to dune, in its attempt to escape.

Finally, the beleaguered feline collapses at the base of the dune of which Samanda stands. Aaron rides to the wounded animal and sees its breathing is very labored. The cat lifts its head and vents one last hiss at Aaron as he plunges his sword through the beast's neck. The cat's head falls to the sand and its body goes limp. As promised, the warrior loudly proclaims, "I send you to your death in the name of our beloved Queen."

Aaron, on one knee, looks up toward Samanda. He's breathing heavily from near exhaustion and the blood from his wound trickles down his chest.

Samanda looks down at him and states, "My new King, once again you have made our kingdom impervious to danger. Now rise and come to me."

Aaron pulls his sword from the panther's neck, rises and mounts Noble who has been at his side. He gallops the short distance to the top of the mound and halts close to Samanda. He divulges to her, "The Father has apprised me of your sister's mental state and I do not know how I can live without you."

He turns and motions his men to return to the village as Samanda orders the eunuchs to retrieve Layla and the rest of the women. She orders the women be escorted to the palace fortress for accommodations.

Aaron turns Noble so that he and Samanda now face the remnants of her tent. "And to think that is where it all began, my love. Do you remember my first night with you there, when you sucked the breath from me to trick Vampressa? I had no idea that I would fall helplessly in love with you in but a few, short months and now I am about to lose you. Please ask your sister if there is any way she can bestow her blessing upon us?

"If she grants us our wish, we will return here, rebuild your tent and live happily with many fond memories. Then, in time, I will take you to the peaceful oasis we discovered with Kaybra."

Samanda understands Aaron's pain, but remains firm as she replies, "Aaron, I love you as well, but there are many things you still do not understand. If your union is successful, there will be no need for my tent to be revisited. I must think of my fellow citizens and not of only myself. You will be wed to the Queen, for this divine ceremony was just sanctioned by Zuse, our great God of fire. It is too late, Aaron, we are beyond the point of no return. Please accept your fate like the brave warrior you are.

"You must trust me, Aaron. I feel certain my sister will make you very happy. You must forget the times we had together. It is not to be, the future of our kingdom is at stake.

"Now come. We must return to the palace. The Queen will await you for the Grand procession and you are spattered with blood. We will have my women bathe you and prepare you for this second of three gala events."

Aaron hangs his head, immersed in lovesick pain. His heart is heavy laden with sorrow by Samanda's last rejecting words. The warrior knows his ride back to the palace is likely the last journey he will take with his only remaining true friend and love. The two head back to Patrious.

*   *   *

They enter the courtyard and tie their horses to the rail at the base of Aaron's tower. Samanda dismounts first and walks to Noble's side to assist Aaron to the ground and the couple walks to the door at the base of the tower.

Samanda, dressed in her battle garb, reaches for a kerchief in her belt, and uses it to gently wipe the bloody wound on Aaron's chest.

Without a wince Aaron watches Samanda's hands and face as she swabs his wound. It stops bleeding and Samanda says to him, "There, my brave soon-to-be King. Now go to your loft and I shall have my girls come to cleanse you further. Nightfall will be upon the procession soon, so we must hurry."

Samanda turns to depart and Aaron glances quickly to the Queen's window and reassuring himself of her absence, he reaches for Samanda's forearm, "Samanda, please wait."

Samanda responds as she pulls away, "Aaron, please do not make this any harder on us. You must abide by our scriptures so that our ceremonies are carried out precisely as prescribed by our ancestors. Now I must go and assign my women to you, then meet with the Father to reassure him of my frame of mind."

Aaron drops his arms to his side, heartbroken. Samanda smiles politely, turns and walks to the footbridge path leading to her women's temporary quarters. The hollow hearted warrior watches every step his former beauty takes until she disappears behind the closed door of her harem women's new residence.

A tear rolls from Aaron's eye as he concedes to reality. Beat from the cataclysmic events since his capture, he turns with a somber expression and walks to his tower door.

A short amount of time later Aaron is visited by Layla and three other women. They bring clean cloths, bowls and urns of warm water and work on him as he sits, slump-shouldered, on the edge of his bed.

Aaron finally notices Layla's slightly protruding abdomen and they discuss her condition. Aaron assures her that he will do all he can as King to care for her and the child in the days to come.

One girl says to Aaron, as she washes him, "My new King, you should be joyous. In just a short time, you will ride with the Queen in her covered chariot and the people along the streets of Patrious will cheer you as you pass."

Another girl questions, "Your highness, why are you so sad? You are about to have the hand of our beautiful Queen and everything our kingdom has to offer you. There, now you are ready to be dressed, so please stand and don your celebratory apparel."

Aaron rises and the women dote on him, dressing their General-of-Arms in a gold and red breastplate and a ceremonial outfit with a sweeping, gold and silver hemmed, cape.

As the women depart down the stone stairwell, he gently reaches for Layla's hand and asks her, "Layla, I must possess the Queen's name. Please, can you tell me her given name? I must know the name of the woman to whom I am about to be wed!"

Layla looks up to Aaron with her pretty, but severely scarred face and answers, "My new King, has no one told you? It is not only written in our scripture, but was reaffirmed by the old wizard that visited Patrious. You must have no knowledge of the Queen's given name until the precise moment of positive conception. Now come with us to the courtyard. Did you not see outside your window? Her highness awaits you in her chariot below."

Aaron turns to his window and looks down into the courtyard, sees the Queen seated in her chariot with the eunuch guards around her. Several of them steady her horse drawn carriage, with the seat next to her remaining vacant.

Aaron bolsters his courage and descends the stone steps behind the women. When he exits his doorway, the crowd that has gathered roars with approval and applauds upon Aaron's entrance. He approaches the Queen in her covered chariot, then waves and nods to them acceptingly.

As Aaron reaches for the side of the chariot to pull himself aboard, he recognizes it is the same carriage the Queen used when she intimately observed him in the prison mines a few short months before. Momentarily recalling those arduous times Aaron is greatly humbled by the status he has achieved since then.

The warrior gets aboard and seats himself beside the Queen to whom he nods and takes the reins. Aaron snaps them up and down and off they go under the arched entrance, past the iron gates and into the city of Patrious, where the streets are lined with well-wishing admirers. The couple leads a grand procession of royal infantry and musicians. Bringing up the end of the cavalcade is a large carriage occupied by the Father and Devine Order of Royal Mistresses. Samanda's harem women follow the Grand Order on foot, displaying gaily-inscribed signs of fertility, reproduction and prosperity.

On frequent occasions the Queen reaches for Aaron's hand and grasps it. When she does this Aaron looks at her admiringly, while inside he truly questions her mental state.

The horse-drawn pageant has made its way through the town and rounds the last corner onto a broad street that leads back to the palace. As they do, Aaron spots a woman in white among the crowd, who sprints away. Although he can only see her back, he feels certain that she's Samanda.

Aaron subtly snaps the horse's reins and the steed picks up its pace to where they are gaining on the woman in the white gown. But as the chariot gains on her, the woman runs faster up the crowded street in front of Aaron and the Queen.

The Queen still smiles and waves at their fans in a pleasant manner, which tells him his soon- to-be-bride has not caught on to his distraction. He signals the steed to again increase its pace and this time the motion snaps the Queen back into her seat. She looks to Aaron with a smile and asks, "Are you impatient for the third ceremony my General-of-Arms?"

Aaron realizes his actions have been detected and smiles at the Queen with a guilty grin and answers, "Yes, my love, that is it, the third ceremony." The instant Aaron turns his eyes back to the streets, he sees the woman in white has darted out of the crowd, into the street and has fallen on her face right in his path. Aaron almost blurts out, "Saman…" but catches himself.

The colorfully decorated General of Arms jerks back hard on the horse's reins and it stops just before its front hooves trod on the fallen woman's back. Aaron hops from the buggy and bolts to the woman's side, goes to one knee and grabs the distressed maiden by the shoulders to turn her over.

As Aaron tugs on the woman's shoulders to flip her over he sees the Queen's feet before him. She stares down at to the woman and screeches, "Corina, you little slut!!! You can get up by yourself!"

To Aaron's astonishment, the woman rolls over on her back, looks up and says, "I'm sorry my Queen of Queens I was in a hurry to reach the palace courtyard so that I could greet you upon your return."

During her reply to the Queen, Aaron has assisted this woman, Corina, to her feet. She is a pretty, young lady and does resemble Samanda..

Corina jumps up, hugs Aaron around the neck and plants a wet kiss on his lips. Aaron senses domestic peril and steps back abruptly pushing Corina away.

The Queen steps close to Corina's face and reprimands her, "You are never to again touch this man! He is now Royalty and you are less than a common peasant with an ill-fated past. Furthermore, you are quite unwelcome at any festivity at the palace. Now, go to your mud hut on the outskirts of town or I shall have the guards take you to the dungeon."

Corina reaches over and tickles Aaron's breastplate with her fingers and sarcastically quips back, "Well, alright your royal highness, I was just being grateful for such a considerate deed of concern for my safety. You do not have to get so huffy over such a simple matter." Corina turns and walks away, hips swaying.

She takes a few short steps when the Queen, completely out of character stoops to the street and picks up a clump of dried mud.

The Queen is so furious with Corina, that she wings the hard mud ball at the departing woman and it strikes her in the center of the back and shatters. The back of Corina's flashy white gown is now covered with dirt.Corina stops dead in her tracks and turns around slowly.

By now the Queen has ordered Aaron back into their carriage, boosts herself in and holds him close at her side.

Aaron is certain the Queen has just gone a little further around the bend mentally, but resumes their progress toward the palace. As they move Corina stands near Aaron's side and when the chariot passes the scorned woman, she pulls the top of her gown down and completely exposes her naked breasts up to Aaron. She shakes them and gyrates her body as she yells to him, "Here's your wedding present, King. You'll never see any like these sleeping with that lunatic."

The Queen, now incensed, stands up in the chariot and turns to the guards that are dutifully located directly behind her and Aaron. She commands out, "Seize that slut and take her to the dungeons immediately."The guards rush to where Corina stood, but she has disappeared into the mass of bystanders. They sort through the crowd, trying to locate her as the parade proceeds.

There is a long silence between Aaron and the Queen, but Aaron cannot constrain himself. He asks, "Your majesty, my love, what is your history with this woman that has caused such a scene between the two of you?" Aaron peers into the Queen's red veil cautiously awaiting a reply.

The Queen grips Aaron's arm tighter and while still looking straight ahead, says, "Corina is no friend of mine. She used to be one of Samanda's loyal harem women. Samanda would often visit me in my tower suite and while she was there my husband would sneak off to her tent of women. Upon my sister's return one evening she caught the King and Corina fornicating in the women's lounge and after extensive questioning, Corina admitted the affair between them had been going on for some time."

The Queen directs her satin covered face to Aaron and continues, "I think with this knowledge, you will understand my exhibition of displeasure."

Aaron suddenly feels his bride may not be the crazed tyrant he was led to believe. He kisses her lips through her veil and says, "I understand, my love. I am truly sorry about your past misfortunes and that my Queen and her sister have their lives filled with daily turmoil. I pray to the Gods that a new course will now be set."

Now Aaron and the Queen are entering the gates into the palace. As the sun settles into the horizon, the groundskeepers hustle about, lighting the scores of torches lining its interior and exterior walls. Others bustle around several long wooden tables set for the feast. The pleasant smell of food cooking on a large, open pit fire permeates the cool, evening air.

After everyone has eaten, the guests rise to toast Aaron and the Queen. The large group of celebrators clink their wine glasses and ale mugs together and sing a song whose lyrics are filled with happy salutations to the new couple.

Aaron and the Queen stand to raise their ornate chalices to the others and a movement on the far side of the courtyard at the base of his tower catches Aaron's eye. It is a woman in a white gown, but in the blink of an eye, the sweeping image disappears.

Aaron is concerned, but forces a smile toward his newfound followers. He and the Queen give a toast and then drink their wine. Aaron leans to the Queen, lifts her veil slightly and kisses her.

While the people of Patrious applaud, Aaron secretly looks toward his doorway just in time to see the door close. He's certain the person who entered was either Samanda or Corina.

Aaron does not want a dark cloud over such a grand gala event and chooses to remain silent about what he has just witnessed, for surely bringing up either Samanda's or Corina's name could have a devastating outcome to this festivity.

The bell in the tower rings once and the crowd's cheers become a murmur as the Father approaches the royal table and stands directly in front of the Queen and Aaron. He reads from his book of scriptures, "Our doctrine mandates proof of consummation between you before your union can be inscribed onto the tablets in the halls where the Gods dwell.

"Now, rise from where you are seated before the people of your kingdom and ascend the stairwell to the Queen's suite. Once there, cross to the balcony opening located above us and greet the people of Patrious as a matrimonial couple.

"Once you present yourselves, I will ask you to assert your vows and then you will be taken to separate royal preparatory chambers.

"If the yellow finch appears on its perch no later than this time tomorrow, the bell in the tower shall ring. That will signify that you, Aaron, and you, my Queen, shall have conceived a child and your names will be immediately recorded in the grand hall of the Gods." The Father closes his book, extends his hand toward the Queen's tower and bows to the royal couple.

Aaron and the Queen rise and walk to the door at the Queen's tower. Aaron opens the door for her majesty and after she is well inside, he enters, closes the door and they join hands as they ascend the spiral steps together.

With each step upward, Aaron, desperately recalls a variety of flashbacks, encompassing all that he has experienced since the day he slew the husband of the woman he is now about to wed.

As Aaron passes the small window where he saw the white dove on his first visit, his thoughts drift to the days when he and Uma were one. After a few more steps, he thinks of meeting Samanda in her tent, followed by a flashback of the evening at the river where she forced oral sex upon him. Finally, he envisions the deadly harpoon that Vampressa plunged through Kaybra's back.

Aaron shakes his head to rid himself of the horrible memory as the Queen squeezes his hand knowingly and says, "It'll be different now, my King. Have peace with your thoughts. Remember what I spoke of when I said, 'The fertile fragments of your heart.' I am now your heart and your heart is mine. By this time tomorrow evening they will beat as one inside my womb." Aaron grips the Queen's hand firmly, smiles and replies, "I honor your wisdom, my Queen." As the couple reaches the top step, they have no idea that within moments, disaster will threaten to end their bond. The townspeople in the courtyard below are becoming impatient with the absence of the royal couple at the Queen's stone balcony opening. As they begin to chant, Aaron and the Queen appear on the open threshold, hand-in-hand.

Looking up to them, while standing on one of the tabletops, the old clergyman clears his throat loudly and the crowd becomes silent. With his book spread open in his hands the Father recites, "Sir Aaron of Nemmin, as the current General-of-Arms of Patrious, do you, Aaron, take our Majesty's hand to be united as one upon her conception of the royal child?" Aaron looks into the shrouded face of the Queen and says, "I do take this woman to be my wife."

The Father clears his throat again and continues, "Do you, your Royal Highness, Queen of Patrious take Aaron's hand to be wed…"

As the Father relates the Queen's vows, an expression of horror gradually comes across Aaron's face. In the opening of his tower chambers across the courtyard from where he stands with the Queen, the female figure in white has reappeared. Aaron still does not know if it is Samanda or Corina, but does know whoever it is, has a cocked dual-arrow crossbow aimed at him and his soon-to-be-bride.

The Father's voice continues from below, "…upon conception of the Royal child?"

The Queen begins her reply, "I do take Aaron…" Aaron pulls her into his arms and turns his back to the balcony opening.

The woman in Aaron's opening triggers her cross bow and two arrows take flight. They are dead on their mark, streaking toward the Royal couple with lightening speed.

Aaron pushes the Queen to the floor just as the arrows rip through his fluttering cape. When the couple lands on the floor, still embraced, Aaron's eyes slowly close as the Queen finishes her vow, "…to be my beloved husband upon conception of the Royal child."

The crowds of attendees are in disbelief at what they have just viewed and a loud sigh of disappointment is heard throughout the courtyard jammed with well-wishers. The guards immediately try to disperse in all directions, but are obstructed by the mass of weeping women and astonished men.

The arrows passing through Aaron's flapping cape narrowly miss him and the Queen and have whistled through her Majesty's suite, shattering the large, oval mirror. The broken glass tingles to the floor, leaving the dual arrows embedded into the mirror's wooden backing. The Queen looks at the mirror and sighs in relief. Not only has Aaron saved her life, but, in addition she realizes now, Samanda can never again use the mirror as a device to communicate with her again.

It is obvious that an attempt on their lives has just been averted, so while still on her back, the Queen hugs Aaron with both arms, saying, "Once again, my brave warrior, you have saved me. How shall I ever repay you for your countless brave deeds?"

Aaron, however, is more concerned that he may have injured her on the take-down. Once she assures him that all is well, he springs to his feet and dashes onto the balcony.He sees the woman in white has left his tower opening and the guards have flooded into the tower's entrance.

Aaron focuses below to find the Father has passed out and lies flat on his back on the tabletop. Several village people surround the table, prop him up and fan him. Aaron shouts, "Father, we are unscathed. Do not fear for our safety."Gradually the old clergyman comes around.

The Queen has now come to her feet with Aaron's assistance. She tugs him in from the window's ledge, and says, "My love, remove yourself from the threat! Do not further risk your life on the eve of our divine union." Aaron concedes and turns to hug the scarlet clad woman once he is out of harm's way. The two caress each other and sway back and forth in silence for a long time until their mood is broken by footsteps ascending the spiral steps.

The couple disengages from their embrace. Aaron, with his face touching the Queen's veil, whispers, "My Queen, is there a possibility that this attempt on our lives was committed by your sister Samanda?"But, before she can reply, the Father is on the top step with most of the harem women.

Aaron asks, "My Father was the attempted assassin captured by the guards?"

Huffing and puffing to catch his breath, the Father replies, "No, my brave son, the woman in white fled the tower by way of a secret passageway before the eunuchs could size her. Our question though, is a troubling one."

Aaron urges, "And that question is?"

Aaron listens impatiently as the Father speaks guardedly looking hesitantly at him and then the Queen, "This woman across the way... Um, Um, ...the woman who made an attempt on your lives must be quite familiar with the palace. Not even Aaron knows of its secret passageways. It was, in fact, only two years before his death that the King ordered construction of this particular confidential passageway by which the woman escaped. It would be near impossible for anyone without prior knowledge to detect and until this day it is so maze-like that no one can figure out exactly where it leads."

Aaron pulls his sword from its sheath, raises it upward and declares, "I shall locate the woman and bring her before your Majesty!" He then marches across the room to the stairwell.

The harem women and the Father stand firm, choking up the opening. Aaron now commands, "Disperse! Allow me to exit so that I may find this vamp who threatens our lives!" No one in the room moves.

The Queen crosses to Aaron, takes his arm and states, "My General-of-Arms, there is no time for such a pursuit. Tomorrow is our day. Your preparation must begin tonight, so please don't violate our scripture and hinder our future before it begins."

The Father interrupts, "Excuse me your Highness. Our General should know that we have a report she was seen fleeing in the direction of Samanda's destroyed harem tent. Your men, my General, have joined the guards and are in control of the matter. There is little doubt the deadly vixen will be either slain or incarcerated in the dungeons by morning. So, at this moment you must depart to be prepared for tomorrow's Royal conception ritual. There is no other resolve." The harem women immediately approach Aaron and silently, the Queen places his hand in Layla's outreached palm. Aaron looks to the Queen as she bows her head and releases her fingers. Slowly, looking up to Aaron, she emphasizes, "I will be one with you at this exact hour after tomorrow's sunset, my love. Now please, let these trained women escort you to your preparatory chamber."

Aaron reaches for the Queen's hand as the women pull him onto the stairwell. Her majesty lifts her veil slightly, places a kiss onto her palm and then blows the kiss off of her palm to Aaron.

The Father and the Queen remain silent until they hear the large wooden door slam shut at the tower's base. Together they walk to the window opening, look down and see that the crowd has completely dispersed. The only activity observed, is the harem women escorting Aaron along the torch-lit walls. They travel quickly toward the Grand Hall, which houses joint ceremonial rooms down one of its many corridors.

Stepping back into the Queen's room, to the oval mirror, the Father asks, "My daughter, judging from where the arrows are lodged into the mirror's back, you were the prime target. Are you certain that all is well with your frame of mind and that somehow Samanda did not orchestrate this attack to upset your holy union that is about to take place?"

The Queen replies, "My Father, as I assured you during counseling earlier, I believe that, due to the certainty of the conception ritual taking place, peace has settled in the minds of our diverse personalities. When the palace bell rang and Zuse ordained Aaron to be my husband and the next King of Patrious, the inner conflicts between Samanda's personality and my personality finally found eternal resolve.

"The woman the troops must seek is surely Corina. I beg you to advise them of my opinion if you would. Now please, I must get rest. At the dawn's first light, the women of the Grand Order will arrive to give me their blessings and escort me to the chamber of the royal conception alter. Once there, my thoughts must be pure and at peace."

The Queen escorts the old man across the floor to the top of her spiral stairwell. They pause there a moment and the Queen takes the Father's hands in hers saying, "Now please, if you are to pray for me and our new King, you, too, must purge your mind of these troubling thoughts."

The Father nods, turns and descends the steps. With each hobbling stride downward, he is confronted with one troubling concern. He was advised shortly after the procession's arrival in the courtyard that Corina had been captured, removed from the streets of Patrious and locked up in one of the dungeons...

Chapter Ten

It is shortly after midnight when the harem women enter the preparation chambers with Aaron. The room is generally pleasant to the eye, square in shape about twice the size of Aaron's tower abode. A padded square bed hangs from the ceiling, suspended by a flawless arrangement of gold chains. The silk-covered pad is deep purple, which richly contrasts its gold, ornate bed-frame.

The four chains are connected to the corners of the suspended bed frame and then, angle upward to a single larger chain that is anchored into the center of the stone ceiling. The angle and contours of the chain's arrangement, resembles the outline of a pyramid.

The walls are filled with ancient hieroglyphics painted on a wide border around the top of the walls. On one wall, below the band of colorful hieroglyphics, are numerous, unusual metal and leather contraptions which appear to be harness-like. They hang from spikes driven into the mortar between the wall's stones. These devices contrast with the plush, swinging bed and the décor of the space.

The wall directly across the room from that wall is covered with thousands of small, mosaic tiles. The tiles were installed artfully and project a kaleidoscope of shapes and colors.

Protruding from the wall, flanking the tiles are life-sized sarcophagus lids standing upright. The cover of the one on the left was obviously fashioned after a mythic Queen of the territory, with the face of this lavish beauty covered by a golden mask. The mouth has three expressions, transposed one over the other, of pain, placidity and pleasure. The figure's engraved garments are stunningly articulate.

The other sarcophagus is equally as handsome as its counterpart. It, however, portrays a King who radiates the same glowing, golden splendor, as his Queen. His expression though, only emits somber authority.

In the center of the design between the sarcophagus lids is a life size mural that portrays a man and woman mating. The woman lies on her back atop an elegant waist-high altar. She is obviously of royalty, as she wears a golden half mask that exposes only her face below her nose and above her hairline. The mask resembles the face of a young virgin the Patrious scripture defines. Her highness' hair is adorned with a twinkling jeweled tiara.

The royal woman's arms and legs are spread eagled, with her wrists and ankles loosely bound to the extensions of the altar by four, short, silky-white, braided ropes. Her naked body is partially covered with a transparent, red, body veil.

The man stands facing her, positioned deep between her thighs. His head is covered by a dark hood with no openings to see from. As they copulate, the male tightly grips the majestic mistress's waist below her emerald, studded navel.

The man wears a wide, black belt with strap-like leashes extending from its rear and attractive harem women hold the end of the leashes, appearing to be regulating the couple's intercourse while reading ancient scripture tablets.

On the wall opposite the entrance door is a short hallway with a dark-burgundy colored, silk curtain draped over it's opening.

At the head of the bed are pedestals with wide, flat tureen bowls that resemble birdbaths. Incense rises from the bowls and their sweet aroma lingers throughout the glowing torch lit room.

While Aaron has been observing the chamber in awe, the women have been bustling about, removing his ceremonial attire. The soon-to-be-King is so busy taking in his surroundings that he has paid them little attention. Then Layla, with her bulging tummy peels open the back of his white tunic and undresses him. Aaron, now standing completely naked, decries, "Wait!" But once again the girls pay no attention to their General-of-Arm's order and hang his garments and weapons on the wall.

Layla says to Aaron, "Forgive us for our intrusions on your person, my commander. Our actions are an intricate part of the reproduction formula mandated by scriptures. Surely you would not defy the writings of the Queen's ancestors. Now, please sit on the bed we have prepared for you."

Aaron looks from one woman to another and they all produce identical, silent stares as they approach the corners of the suspended ornate bed. When they reach the bed, Layla nods to them and the women hold the corners of the bed to keep it in place as Layla puts her hands on Aaron's chest and pushes him backward onto it. With the women grasping the golden chains firmly, Aaron lands backside down on the bed.

Aaron is very hungry as he was intentionally deprived of his meal during the earlier feast. Aaron grabs the golden bed frame to raise himself to a sitting position just as one of Layla's aides places a plate of cooked shellfish on his lap.

Layla tells Aaron, "Go ahead and eat. This is a specially prepared meal for you this night. While you eat, I have to ask you some very important questions that must be answered clearly and honestly."

Aaron takes the eating utensils and wastes no time digging into the steaming plate of shellfish.

Layla sits beside Aaron on the bed. She looks toward another of her pretty aides and nods. The aide approaches with a small bronze ewer and when she arrives at where the two sit, she tilts the small vase and pours a dark, ruby wine on Aaron's shellfish. Aaron, unsure of what the ewer contains, pauses briefly. With a puzzled look, he says, "Thank you," to the woman. She smiles at him and departs.

Now Layla explains the procedure. "Aaron, we must determine the quality of your seeds before you retire tonight." Looking from the corners of his eyes cautiously at Layla, Aaron remains silent as he continues to eat.

Layla turns her head toward Aaron, looks straight into his eyes and asks him point blank, "Aaron, did you copulate with and impregnate Vampressa on the dune when she transformed herself into Uma?"

Aaron, startled by Layla's question, chokes on his food and coughs a mouthful of it out.

There's a long silence until Aaron turns his head to Layla and the two now stare directly into each other's eyes. Layla's expression is stern, while Aaron's is troubled. He wonders how Layla could possibly have the knowledge to ask such a question and is far too embarrassed to admit he was tricked into having sex with a big bird.

Aaron lifts his hand and wipes his mouth. He answers, "I am uncertain if I penetrated the Harpy's body. I was totally aroused, but the pain she inflicted upon me with her talons was too excruciating for me to properly perform the act." Aaron wipes his mouth again. As he returns to his meal, he finds the harem aide dribbling more red liquid onto his dish, but he is too hungry to question the fluid's origin and resumes eating.

Layla replies, "I see. We must now determine what, if any, sexual activity you have had since the night you impregnated me. To that point we are certain all was well. Now tell me how many times and on what occasions you expelled your seeds since that night?"

Aaron has now finished eating. He sets the empty dish beside him and looks around at the harem girls who surround the bed. The beautiful women smile at him as if anxious to hear his sexual exploits since the last time they were voyeurs to his and Layla's encounter.

Layla is becoming impatient and urges, "Please Aaron, it is critical you divulge the information now so that we know which ritual to perform. The hour is growing late and you must be made ready by dusk, tomorrow."

Aaron knows he's had. He must be honest or all can be lost if he does not impregnate the Queen the following evening. His answers to Layla's question are embarrassing, but he begins with, "The evening Samanda and I arrived outside Kaybra's delta village, I became partially trapped in the mud at the river's edge. Samanda had been swimming nude, to bathe and soothe herself from the heat of the day.

"As she splashed around in the water, she attracted a large, black crocodile which attacked her. I responded and went to her rescue. Afterward, we were so fatigued from fighting the beast, we passed out. Our bodies were half out of the water with our upper torsos resting belly down on the beach.

"When we awoke, we were intertwined and my beginning stage of arousal had started. I was determined to retreat from any sexual imposition Samanda applied to my person, for my determination was fueled by the certainty my Uma still awaited me and I wanted to remain true to her.

"Before I knew what happened, I was totally erect and when I tried to push myself away from Samanda my feet slipped into a deep pocket of muck. I tried to stand, but could not move from my knees down, so there was no escaping the Queen's beautiful, nude sister.

"She ultimately planted her pink lips over the end of my shaft and it seemed like an eternity as she stroked her head up and down, occasionally accommodating the majority of my length. I grabbed the sides of her head and hair and tried to push her hot, wet lips off of me to no avail. Then on my last attempt to remove her head from me, she bit down hard and her bite actually heightened my arousal. I peaked an instant later and Samanda received a full load of my seeds in her mouth. Although I could give no more, she kept sucking and sucking on my cock. The experience was utterly pleasure-filled pain. But, suddenly out of the darkness, Kaybra appeared and separated Samanda by threatening to sever my manhood with her sword."

Layla listened intently to Aaron's rendition of what took place and the blow-by-blow description of his oral encounter with Samanda has her slightly titillated. She glances at the other women, who appear to be equally enthused by Aaron's recollection of his evening on the beach with their harem mistress. One girl speaks up, "Go on, Aaron, tell us more of your escapades while in the leisure moments of battle."

Aaron looks up and around to the women, finds the majority are looking directly at his genitals and he quickly snatches the large plate from the bed beside him and places it on his lap. The women then redirect their eyes back to Aaron's face and smile admiringly. All remain quiet as they listen intently for more of his story to unfold.

Layla apologizes, "Please forgive Samanda's women. They are young and unfortunately have few personal experiences to revisit. So please continue, this information is critical and we must know everything. There may be some substance to the Harpy's last proclamation as she burned at the stake."

Aaron is beyond discomfort with the topic Layla pursues, but resumes. "A few days passed after we merged with Kaybra's forces and Samanda, Kaybra and myself traveled together at this point. We were camped in a small tropical forest on the eve of battle. It was a pleasant night and Samanda, at my side had fallen fast asleep, or so I presumed. Kaybra, on the other hand, was wide-awake.

"Throughout our travel, just before bed, Kaybra would remove her white leather top. She was a buxom woman and her bosom was shapely and large. She would tantalize me by massaging one breast intimately in an upward fashion, then let it drop back into place and do the same to the other.

"On one night, I awoke to her pleasured sighs and before I could come fully awake, the large, tanned, naked woman was on top of me. She swung her breasts back and forth bumping them across my lips.

"The large beauty then reached beneath her body and began to fondle my manhood and it did not take me long to react. I did try to resist, but as you have learned, Kaybra was a big woman filled with her own style of determination.

"She took complete control of the situation and me, by placing her long fingers around my shaft, grasping me firmly and forcing my erection deep into her place of sexual pleasure.

"She drove her hips up and down on me, wailing sensual laments. Then, I could no longer hold out, for her beautiful large shapely body working on top of me was too overwhelming. So, I willingly reciprocated by pulling her buttocks tighter down on me, and shortly thereafter, we climaxed together.

"Samanda said that later, Kaybra told her, 'Only a man of Aaron's size and girth could ever please me again.' And Samanda ordered me to have sex with Kaybra one more time before our trip ended, but then Kaybra was killed by Vampressa before the act occurred"

Layla is now becoming a little more than slightly aroused by Aaron's accounts, as are the remainder of the women. She is trying to think through his tale to determine how frequently Aaron can successfully mate. She calculates that his seeds restore themselves to a healthy harvest daily.

Some of the harem women are so entranced with Aaron's narration that they now sit on the bed near him, as Layla continues her interview. "Aaron, I must know the last time you had sex. What did Vampressa's flaming image of Uma mean when she stated that Dilyla poisoned your seeds when you fornicated with her on the flat rock? Who, or what, is Dilyla?"

Besides the circumstances of this long day, something in the food Aaron ingested, or possibly the aroma that wafts through the room, seems to have weakened him further. Fading in and out, he recalls in slow, but accurate detail all the events that occurred on the night of his encounters with Vampressa and Dilyla.

Throughout his recital of this final sexual encounter, four harem women have climbed on the bed and are rubbing scented oils about his back, neck and shoulders.

Aaron finally describes how he plunged his broadsword through Dilya's gut and deep into Vampressa's chest. As those words leave his mouth, he falls asleep sitting up on the edge of the bed and the pewter plate tumbles to the floor from his lap with a clang.

The women lay him down and raise his legs onto the plush bed, which now begins to sway on its gold chains.

Layla stands up from the bedside, walks a few steps and signals one of her female cohorts to approach. This woman's name is Tyina. She is dark-haired and as attractive as the remaining bevy of beauties.

Tyina goes to Layla's side and asks, "What is it, my sister, your expression is unsettling?" Layla replies, "This final act of Aaron's, where he describes brutally fecundating and slaying Dilyla, gives me great concern. It is possible that Uma's last flaming words can be true. His description of the act would indicate that he had long and deep penetration into the vixen and with her reputation, it is likely she could have a disease. Our problem is that time no longer assists us.

If Aaron successfully mates with the Queen and the child is tainted, we can all be in danger when the youth grows older. This is not to mention the fact, that any disease could be spread to the Queen. It is no secret that her mental state is already frail."

Tyina understands the crisis on hand, but has an idea. She asks Layla the whereabouts of the old oracle and Layla instantly catches on as to where Tyina is going with her thoughts. She orders the other women to gather around her.

Once they are huddled close to Layla and Tyina, Layla speaks, "My sisters, it appears our duty has become even more delicate. Please listen closely. We must extract a small amount of Aaron's sperm seeds to have the old soothsayer test them for the safety of the Queen and her offspring. Our stargazer dwells not far from here, but too far to send a messenger to fetch him and still return in time for tomorrow night's conception ceremony.

"Let Aaron rest throughout the remaining night, undisturbed. We must use every precaution to protect his seeds at this point. The shellfish and wine, as well as the opium incense should be acting on his reproductive organs by now. He will be consumed with the temptation to masturbate, to relieve his reproductive fluid pressure when he awakens. Scripture mandates we must bind his wrists and ankles to the four gold chains that suspend the preparation bed from the ceiling while he is unattended.

"Tyina, it is my wish that you and the others secure our General before we leave. At daybreak, we will return and feed him more of the wine and shellfish potion to even further enhance his reproduction fluids that escort his seeds upon ejaculation.

"We must induce and maintain a mildly delirious state within him early in the day. If we are able to create enough seed pressure within our General's scrotum and arouse him without touching his shaft, he will drip a clear fluid which will contain a few of his oldest seeds. I caution you though, if for whatever reason, Aaron spews all his seeds shortly before the ceremony, all hope for the yellow finch's arrival will likely be lost. We will then have a messenger ride one of the Queen's fastest steeds to where the oracle resides atop the tallest of the distant dunes. If the old man gives his approval, the messenger will light a large fire on the peak of the dune. We will place an expert eye in the palace bell tower to detect the flame and report to us his observation. Now, secure your Master General's wrists and ankels to the bed chains and then report back here at daybreak. Tyina, please make certain the doors to this chamber are heavily bolted after we depart. Please, carry on my sister."

Tyina and her assistants carry out Layla's order with great proficiency. Aaron is sound asleep and flat on his back with his limbs stretched outward to the bed's corners.

All the women leave for the night except for Tyina, who looks over her shoulder toward the door and listens carefully to the sounds of her sister's footsteps as they eventually fade down the corridor. She then returns to the bed and sits down on its edge close to Aaron. She looks back to the door one more time and seeing no one, leans close to Aaron's thighs, reaches over and begins to fondle her new General's penis. She looks at it admiringly as she recalls the stories of Aaron's sex-filled conquests.

Tyina is amazed at the size of Aaron's manhood and shakes it about playfully. Even though the brave warrior sleeps, Tyina's hands are inducing an erection.

Her eyes open wide in awe as it grows very large and stiff. She thinks, "The Conception Ceremony on the following eve must be closely regulated by the harem women so the Queen is not harmed." Suddenly Aaron groans in his sleep and a voice rings out from the open doorway, "Tyina, can you not be trusted?" The voice is Layla's, who noted Tyina's absence from the rest of the women as they exited the Grand Hall and returned to check on her sister's whereabouts.

Tyina hops off the bed and regains her composure. She smiles at Layla with a guilty expression and says, "Sorry, my sister, I am coming." Before Tyina exits, though, she gives Aaron's bed a big push. When she reaches the doorway where Layla stands, she turns around and views the bed swinging gently back and forth with Aaron's penis standing erect, like a marble pillar. She says, "Good night, my brave King."

The two women exit the chambers and close the door tightly. There is much ado on the outside of the door as Layla and Tyina go to great measures to make sure it is properly locked. Shortly thereafter all goes quiet.

Only two of the torches in the chamber remain lit and they cast a flickering orange and yellow hue, illuminating the walls of hieroglyphs, bondage devices and reproduction mural.

The majority of the evening has passed, but there is still a significant period before dawn. Aaron has rested well and is now in a light sleep that has him engulfed in slumber enough that he is unaware of a creaking sound coming from the mural.

The sarcophagus lid depicting the Kingly figure opens slowly outward from the wall. Finally it stops. Moments pass and then a haunting white-gowned figure emerges from the secret passageway opening and moves to Aaron's side. The figure is a hooded woman with a white veil over her face. She kneels by Aaron's head as he continues to sleep and whispers in his ear, "I am the woman who will conceive on this day, not the Queen."

She stands up and methodically removes her gown, but her hood and veil remain in place. As the now nude woman walks slowly around Aaron's bed, her eyes twinkle from under her hood. She is pleased to find that apparently something in Aaron's dreams have him sexually aroused.

In one short leap, the figure hops into the bed and immediately starts to work on Aaron's penis. The warrior awakes instantly, for the bed is now swinging vigorously as the unidentified female pounds her closed hands up and down on Aaron's rapidly growing shaft.

Aaron shouts, "What is this! Who are you?"

A voice comes from beneath the veil announcing, "So you wish to know who you are about to fornicate with, my big strong, General-of-Arms? Let me give you one large hint." With those words the woman removes her hood and Aaron strains to raise his head to see who it is. But, due to the veil, which still covers her face, he is unable to recognize her.

The woman continues as she removes her face scarf. With a cocky grin, she resumes stroking Aaron, looks down at him and asks, "Did you forget all about poor, little Corina already?"

Although Aaron is groggy, he cannot believe his situation. Having discovered that he has been bound to the bed chains while he slept, he is in a panic. Franticly, he struggles in a futile attempt to free himself.

Corina laughs aloud in a haughty manner as Aaron's muscles flex and contort when he tugs at his restraints. Pausing to analyze his dilemma, the warrior general stops struggling and tries to regain his breath. The moment his muscular body goes still Corina goes down on him with her mouth wide open. Aaron yells out, "Ugh, No! Ugh, Ugh, Stop in the name of the Queen!"

After Aaron's utterance, Corina stops bobbing her head up and down, but while emitting a spiteful stare up to her victim's face she holds her lips in place about half way down on Aaron's swollen shaft. Then Corina clenches her jaw open and shut slightly a few times, sinking her front teeth into the restrained warrior's filled staff. Aaron calls out in pain. "Oh." and then lifts his head. Pressing his chin onto his upper chest he looks down toward his bared abdomen and dead on right into the vixen's eyes. Corina now has his total and undivided attention.

The sex-starved female shakes her head and scowls as she slowly slides her wet lips off Aaron, then bounds out of the bed to Aaron's head. The shapely nude woman bends her face down to her quarry and roars, "Do not demand I act to please that bitch again, or next time I will bite it off!!! Do you understand me?"

Corina bends and picks up her white gown. As Aaron looks up to her, the uninhibited vamp wads her dress in her hand and shakes it in front of his face taunting, "Your love affection, little Miss Queenie, soiled my pretty white gown today! And then had me locked up in her damned, dirty, old dungeon! So now, I will repay her for her actions by ruining her wedding day. After the Devine Order expels you from the Palace for your inability to propagate, you can come and live with me in my hut just outside the village. There you will provide for me and your child!"

The entire time Aaron has been looking up at Corina's inverted face, he noticed the ceiling is filled with paintings of people participating in an orgy. The paintings are very graphic.

Aaron's has already been primed to fornicate and so the pressure has been building the entire time he slept. Even though Corina is aware of that, she could care less and desires not to take any chances. She produces a small, yellow tablet from her gown and forces it into Aaron's mouth with one hand, while covering his nose with the other. He shakes his head side-to-side, trying to thwart her actions, but Corina wins the bout.

Corina smirks, "So you like to scream out for the Queen, do you? I think I can fix that. I really do not wish to hear her Royal Highness's name mentioned again. Especially when you are fecundating me."

Corina takes her veil and gags Aaron. She then walks to a corner chain of the bed and says, "Hang on big boy, and I do mean big boy. We are going to do it how the late King and I loved to do it."

Once Corina has a firm hold on the chain, she circles around the room and with each completed lap, the center anchor chain of the suspended bed twists and tightens up tighter and tighter like a braided rope. Corina has been reciting to Aaron the entire time, emphasizing, "You're going to like what you're going to get, my big brave warrior. Just like the King used to like it, when I gave it to him. The only difference is, you will give me a child that he could not.

"Oh, yes, yes, yes, the King used to lock me in the dungeon as well. My luck was that your fiancé's guards locked me in the same dungeon as did the King, the dungeon the King had built just for poor, little Corina, the same dungeon that leads to all the secret passageways throughout the Palace... Ha, ha, ha!

"Aaron, did you know that the King and I used to fornicate in the very same bed you've slept in during your stay at the palace? Oh yes many times... At least he had the sense to lock that lily-white, simpleton wife of his in her room when he did me. Ha, ha, ha! And now here we are, all alone just you and me. And I'm about to do it to her again. Poor Queenie. Poor, poor, Queenie."

By now Corina has slowly spun the plush hanging bed around so many times that the center chain is beginning to buckle and twist upward. It is so tight that the bed cannot be wound any further. Still gripping the corner chain, Corina stops and looks anxiously at Aaron's large, swollen shaft pointing straight upward from the center of the bed. A broad grin comes across her face as she smiles to Aaron and offers, "Well, it would appear that you are now quite ready to be mounted, Kingy wingy! Did my little bedtime story excite you to this state?" Aaron shakes his head back and forth pleading out a muffled, "No, please, Corina no! I will be cast from the village if the yellow finch does not appear!"

Corina tilts her head to one side, smiles at Aaron and taunts him softly with, "I ate the yellow finch earlier today, for breakfast!" then releases the chain and springs onto the bed. She wraps her fingers around her goal post. Holding on to it with all her strength, she then uses it to pull herself onto Aaron. The instant Corina's feet left the floor the bed began its counter spin and Aaron fights the motion by closing his eyes tightly, but it doesn't work and each time he opens them he observes the paintings twirling above him on the ceiling. His accelerated spinning motion makes the painted figures appear as though they are moving and have come to life.

Aaron feels Corina thrust her hilt down on him as she cries out in pleasure, "Ah, Ah, Ah!" When he looks to Corina he sees that the bed spins so fast that her long hair flies outward and away from her head due to the centrifugal force.

Then the bed completely unwinds and counter jerks harshly. So does Corina. She has accomplished her mission. Each time the bed jerks one way and then, back the other, trying to right itself, Corina continues to cry out, "Oh ah… Ah! Ah! Ah!" Even though Aaron has desperately tried to contain himself he has injected the vamp's vagina with an abundance of his reproductive serum.

Finally the bed settles back to the original position that it was in before Corina started winding it up.

The clever whore is now as exhausted as Aaron. Corina's hair is strewn about her head and completely covers her face. She throws her head back and the action flings her hair about, uncovering her face. While still quite out of breath, she tells Aaron, "You are delightfully huge! And I shall hunt you down after the Queen discards you and we shall fuck again."

The crazed woman lifts her hips up and off Aaron. When she steps on to the floor, she is unsteady on her feet, and still trying to catch her breath wobbles around the room, picking up her garments from the floor. She gets dressed and staggers toward the sarcophagus cover's opening to the secret passageway.

Aaron sees this and shakes his head back and forth, crying out a muffled, "Corina, Corina!"

She stops, turns, runs her fingers through her straggly blonde hair and grins, "You are right, big man, I guess we best not leave my scarf in your mouth for the Queen to surmise my actions on you."

She returns to Aaron and removes the gag. Gasping for air, he looks up to the vixen and pleads, "Corina, I must know, was it you who fired the crossbow at the Queen last night? Please, you now possess what you wanted from me. Admit to me, was it you in my tower window with the crossbow?"

Corina appears as if she's in a half-drunken stupor. She weaves around, glancing about the room irrationally, then walks silently to the passageway opening and enters. The coffin's lid begins to close as slowly as it opened earlier. While still ajar, Corina pops her head back out and says, "If you must know who shot at the Queen, the next time you see your good friend, Samanda, ask her who fired the arrows. That is if you ever do see her…"

Corina gives Aaron a coy pursed frown as she pulls the sarcophagus lid closed. Once again, all appears as it was, prior to her arrival.

Aaron lies stretched out thinking about what has just happened to him, sensing he has likely impregnated Corina. As the warrior looks down toward his manhood, he finds he is still very much erect and fraught with uncertainty, he ponders the pending day as he slowly drifts back to sleep.

Aaron feels like he has only had a brief nap when the harem women return at sunrise. Now he tries to convince himself that his encounter with Corina was just a bad dream.

Layla and Tyina greet Aaron with a pleasant, "Good morning General." Aaron cracks a faint smile and nods to the women. Tyina titters, "Look, Layla!" The women see Aaron's sexual condition appears excited. The two, motion the other girls to join them and Layla whispers to her assistants as she points to Aaron's erection.

The women separate and two move the opium urns across the floor to Aaron's head. They light the incense and fan its smoke at the warrior. Three other women approach the wall where the body harnesses are hung.

Layla brings Aaron a goblet filled with the wine potion. When she reaches the bed, she lifts Aaron's head and directs him to drink. After

Aaron has consumed a considerable amount of the aphrodisiac, Layla kneels and speaks softly into his ear. "Aaron, I want your union with the Queen to be successful, for if you are banned from our kingdom, you will have no influence over your child that I carry.

"We have nearly a full day to prepare you for a successful union, but because of your sexual encounter with Dilyla, we must extract a sample of your seeds. A courier will take the sample to the old oracle and after he has determined your health through his examination, we will be notified of his answer by the light of a distant fire. It is true, that our great God of fire, Zuse, will choose the exact moment of fertilization and hopefully, we will find the flame in the horizon from afar before he makes his judgment.

"What we must do to obtain the sample may not be pleasant, but it is imperative we receive only the sample. So, if you weaken and ejaculate completely, the Queen will be robbed of the critically timed moment she has been patiently awaiting.

Layla stands and addresses two women who, as lookouts, have remained in the doorway awaiting her direction, "Ladies, it is time. Go to the Queen's suite, take her from the elders and escort her to the conception chamber. I will meet you there after we finish Aaron's next phase of preparation."

The two women dart from the doorway as Tyina and four other women approach Aaron's bed. Layla cautions them, "Remember, you must not touch his shaft."

Aaron is becoming mildly delirious from the potion and from the fumes created by the burning opium.

Two women move to the bed and begin to massage Aaron's body. They use warm oils on their hands and once he has been oiled from head to toe, the women remove their clothing and rub their naked bodies on their subject, seductively.

The maiden who works on his lower torso cups his scrotum with her oily hand and tugs it gently. Aaron rolls his head from side-to-side as she does this, moaning softly. Layla, who still stands by his head, states, "Aaron, this act is per our scripture, please be strong."

Tyina steps in close to Layla and whispers, "I think we should have the other assistants act soon." Layla nods to her sisters working on Aaron and when her two assistants see Layla's direction, they leave the bed. The berth swings slightly from the energy of the women's departure from it.

Standing beside the bed, two other assistants have been waiting for their direction. These each hold a long, wide, leather strap and Layla nods, saying, "Not too hard, just make it sting slightly. When his penis becomes limp from this distraction, you may cease."

The two women begin to whip Aaron about his legs, arms and upper torso with their straps as an attempt to distract their subject's attention from anything sensual or sexual. Aaron seems to understand and bracing himself, he winces, gritting his teeth with every lash the women inflict upon him. Soon his carnal visions are shattered by the pain he experiencing. Thoughts of the attractive, naked women who had worked him up with their oily naked bodies dissipate.

When the process achieves its goal, Layla orders her assistants to stop and Tyina produces a small, white, linen kerchief. She walks to the far side of the bed and sits at Aaron's waist. Tyina then takes the cloth and dabs it on the end of Aaron's now relaxed rod, but she has no way of knowing Aaron is faintly seeping fluid from his encounter with Corina. The dutiful harem aide looks to Layla smiles proudly. "I have the sample."

Layla dashes around the bed to Tyina and says, "Be quick, my sister, hand me the specimen." She examines the cloth briefly, then folds it neatly and places it in a small, bronze box, which she hands to Zelina. She races from the chamber, down the corridor and out the Grand Hall to the horseback courier.

It is now mid morning and the Queen has arrived at the Royal conception chamber, adjacent to where Aaron has been sexually stabilized and kept throughout the night. Her Majesty is still accompanied by the two women who notified her that the time has come.

Layla and Tyina hear the Queen speaking to their sisters through the burgundy curtain that covers the opening at the end of the hall connecting Aaron's room to the conception chamber.

Layla directs Tyina to unbind Aaron and feed him more shellfish. Then she walks down the hall, parts the curtain and enters the royal mating chamber.

The Queen sits on an elegant throne sculpted with coiled, golden cobras at the center of the far wall. Her seat is on a dais, three steps above the floor and back-dropped by a plush, shimmering gold and silver, woven tapestry. All the other walls of the chamber are covered with elaborate inscriptions, paintings and hieroglyphs. The images portray all imaginable situations that one's soul could experience from birth to death. They include war, harvests, royal family gatherings and children being tended by their elders.

The walls cast off the light from lit torches that are anchored securely to them in brass fixtures.

In the center of the elaborate chamber is the altar, cushioned and covered with a deep, ruby-red fabric. It is about waist high, with padded extensions for its occupant's legs and arms. The narrow extensions make it appear as if a large "X" crisscrosses it. Off the corners of the altar's "X" extensions are gold pillars rising from the floor. Each ornate post has a metal ring affixed to its side nearest to the altar. All sit under a large canopy draped with satins and silks in a variety of colors. Hanging from the canopy, on two slender chains, is a small bird's perch. It's a short distance above where the Queen's head will rest during the ceremony.

The stepped riser that the Queen's throne sets on is a few short feet from the head of the conception alter and canopy. The short hallway with the burgundy curtain, which leads to Aaron's chamber, is directly across from the throne wall and in close proximity to the foot of the conception altar.

As Layla approaches the Queen, she sidesteps the altar and canopy, while giving it a reassuring glance. Her two assistants sit on the lower step at the Queen's feet, slowly waving large palm leaf fronds at the Queen to comfort her from the heat of the afternoon sun.

Layla addresses her majesty. "Good day your highness. We have several hours until the ceremony begins. As you can see, we've already prepared the royal altar. Moreover, it would be advisable for you, according to our scriptures, to rest at this time. We will leave you here to meditate until the first indication of the day's sunset. Do you have any further need of our services until that time?"

The Queen asks Layla, "Tell me, for what reason did the messenger race from the courtyard after your women approached his horse earlier?"

Layla is unaware that the Queen observed the messenger when he departed for the oracle's abode. She does not want to concern her Majesty as the ceremony nears, but she fears telling her a falsehood can later come back on her negatively. After all, she does have a child to rear in the years ahead and will likely need assistance.

After a brief pause, Layla answers. "I took it upon myself to send a lock of Aaron's hair to the wise old stargazer who visited us some time ago. The hair was placed into one of your treasured white kerchiefs and my message to him was to examine the hair and the kerchief, then return a hand-written, special occasion scroll to you, as a wedding gift. The scroll will contain all of the good tidings you and our new King will experience in your future as one."

A loving smile comes from below the Queen's veil. She extends her hand to Layla and says, "You are truly a sister of the Queen's court. I will anxiously await the contents of the scroll."

Layla kisses her majesty's hand then motions her two assistants at the Queen's feet, to return with her into Aaron's chambers. They lay their palm fans down beside the throne and rise. All three women join hands, turn and walk toward the drape hung over the entrance to the hallway connecting the adjoining room.

By now Aaron has finished his last portion of shellfish and as Zelina takes the plate from him, Layla and her assistants enter. Layla orders, "Zelina, have Tyina and the other women assist you in binding Aaron once more to the bed chains. However leave them loose so he does not experience any distress. He must rest comfortably until dusk, when we return for the final preparation."

With Aaron reluctantly cooperating, the women do as instructed and finish securing the wide metal cuffs around Aaron's wrists and ankles, which are attached to the corner bed chains. The ropes binding the warrior have been left loose enough so he can rest, but not so loose that he can touch himself. The women leave the room and bolt the door, just as the evening before.

The Queen, still seated on her throne in the adjacent chamber gazes through the canopy that covers the altar before her. She can also see the curtain that covers the entrance to Aaron's chamber. She is in high anticipation of the coming event this evening, but knows that for now she must rest. In a few short hours the women will reappear and prepare her for the conception ceremony.

*   *   *

The hourglass has drained and has been reset seven times, for now it is dusk. Both Aaron and the Queen have rested peaceably in their rooms for hours by the time Layla, Tyina, Zelina and their sisters return.

There are eight women in all and Layla selects three from the group to exit Aaron's chamber through the hallway to where the Queen awaits filled with nervous anticipation.

While Aaron and the Queen rested through the afternoon, Layla instructed Tyina on what must take place. Tyina learned all the necessary techniques that must be employed to prepare Aaron for his union with the Queen. She has also been warned not to vary from what is outlined in Patrious doctrine.

Tyina snaps her fingers. Her assistants, who have also been trained on what is to take place, now bound to duty. As they did earlier, two of them disrobe and approach Aaron with the vials of scented oils. They slink into his bed and massage his muscles with the oils. Tyina lifts Aaron's head as the remaining maiden tips the wine goblet to his lips for his final dose. Then after Aaron has consumed the potion, Tyina relights the opium incense in the large urns affixed to the pedestals.

Tyina nods to her helpers and the women move to opposite corners of the suspended bed. In nearly identical fashion as Corina, the two slowly wind the bed by grasping its chains and walking in a circle. The women massaging Aaron become a bit more exotic and suggestive with their hands as the bed is wound.

In the adjacent room, the Queen steps down from her throne and disrobes as the women approach. She dons only her scarlet face veil. Layla and her aides assist the Queen from her throne and place her on her back on the cushioned altar. When her majesty's arms and legs are spread and secured with soft ropes to the extensions of the altar, all four women anoint the Queen's body with the same scented oils being used on Aaron. After some time passes, the Queen succumbs to the women's relaxing gestures and her naked body goes limp as she releases her many stressful thoughts from the passing months.

With fond visions of finally being impregnated after such a long wait, she rests with her eyes closed as the women slide two pedestal urns near her head, one on each side. The dishes are mounded with what looks like charcoal. They are also in line with the supporting corner posts of the ceiling canopy above the Queen's alter.

Layla asks her assistants to turn away from the Queen and face the wall, then steps back up to the throne's platform, then on to the seat and reaches above its back to a brilliant, feminine, golden half-face mask which hangs on the wall.

It glows with radiance and exudes a rich golden hue. There are larger than needed oval openings molded into it for the bearer's eyes to see out of. The forehead, brow and eye expression fashioned into the mask emits soothing placidity.

Layla carefully lifts the precious item from where it hangs, then turns and descends to where the Queen lies on the altar.

After she reaches her Majesty, she pauses to check that her assistants are not peeking and seeing they are still as they were, Layla slowly removes the Queen's satin veil and replaces it with the one of gold. As she places it on her Majesty's face, she awakens. Her beautiful eyes and lashes now fill the eye openings of the golden metal veil and she trustingly smiles to Layla, who now instructs Zelina and the other women to cover the Queen with her sheer body scarf.

In Aaron's chamber, the bed has been twisted and unwound four times. Tyina and her women by now have the soon-to-be, Queen's mate totally aroused. The combinations of three oily, naked women squirming and rubbing their curvaceous bodies against Aaron, as well as the aphrodisiac potions, have brought him to a state of sexual frenzy. The warrior pulls and tugs at his restraints as he sighs with heightened anticipation of what is yet to come.

Tyina knows it's time for the next step in Aaron's preparation and so she strides to the utility wall and removes a wide, black leather belt with a metal loop in its backside. She crosses back to the bed and hands it to the women. The three boost Aaron's midsection up which allows them to cinch the leather cummerbund snugly around his waist.

Tyina returns to the utility wall a second time and returns with a black silk hood bearing a drawstring. She leans over and places the hood over Aaron's head.

Aaron questions Tyina's actions from beneath the hood. "Why the facial cloak? For what reason, my maiden?"

Tyina answers, "My General, It is written that you must not see your naked wife to be, until your bodies touch." Tyina then orders her aides, "Leave the bed and unbind our new King."

The women carry out Tyina's command promptly. As they assist Aaron to sit up, Layla appears in the opening to the Queen's chamber and recognizes that Aaron's condition is ripe for the ceremony to begin. She crosses to the wall and removes a length of heavy rope, then orders Aaron's attendants, "Tie one end of this rope to the loop in back of the ceremonial belt. Two of you use the remaining length of rope to tether our soon-to-be King as he is escorted down the hall, through the curtains and into the Queen's chamber. Tyina, you and our remaining sister go to Aaron's side, place his hands in yours and guide him to this side of the drape from where the Queen awaits in the adjoining room. But allow me a moment to have some last words with her Majesty before the ritual. Then enter at the sound of the gong."

Layla turns and wisps herself back down the short hall and through the curtain at its end.

As the four women carry out Layla's instructions, Aaron asks them to pause. "Wait, maidens, please fetch the red ribbon scarf from my parade garments." Tyina walks over to where Aaron's uniform was hung the evening before and sees the scarf of ribbon Aaron seeks. It is neatly folded and tucked into an opening in his breastplate.

She removes the ribbon and returns to where the hooded general stands with his escorts. Tyina places the ribbon in Aaron's left hand. Wanting to make certain that this is the same ribbon the Queen gave him when they first met, he brings his cupped hands to his nose and takes deep whiff through the silk hood. He identifies the Queen's specially scented perfume on the ribbon, smiles to himself and carefully places the folded cloth under the wide shackle on his left wrist, then states to his escorts. "Continue as you will." With Tyina holding his left hand and her assistant his right, they walk Aaron down the hall to the curtain at its end.

When they arrive at the burgundy drape, Tyina says, "Stop. We must wait here for the gong." The two women halt.

Tyina looks at Aaron's penis and nods to her sister at Aaron's other side. Together they gently fondle their General's erection with their free hand.

Aaron sighs and takes deep breaths as his attendants squeeze his oily shank and snug up the rope restraining him. The women holding the tether rope gradually release about a foot of slack as the escorts at his side step him forward to take it up. The women then position their subject at the curtain with only Aarron's erection exposed outward between the closed curtains.

Layla, at the Queen's side, sees Aaron's huge twitching penis protruding through the burgundy drapes, taps her Majesty on the shoulder and points to the curtain.

The Queen strains and lifts her head to get a view, at what Layla is pointing. She is shocked at the length and width of what she sees and starts to breathe faster in heightened nervous anticipation of what she soon will experience. She glances pensively from side to side tugging at her restraints, realizing there is no way of escape as a last minute option and confirming to her the inevitable is soon to come.

The sound of the gong crescendos out from the other side of the curtain and Tyina and her counterpart nod to each other, spread the curtain apart and slowly enter into the Royal conception chamber with Aaron.

Tyina and the other attendants walk their naked subject to the foot of the altar and pose her Majesty's broad-shouldered stud so that his hips are between the Queen's raised ankles.

Once Aaron has been positioned, Layla, Zelina and their two assistants produce a thick gold rope, which they meticulously thread through the metal loops on the canopy support pillars.

To the right and left of the Queen, where the urn dishes have been placed, the women are careful to make sure the rope is strung only inches above the unlit charcoal.

When the rope has been threaded through all four eyelets it is pulled tight and tied securely to one corner pole, colorfully enclosing Aaron, the Queen, and her altar. Tyina and her assistant stand just outside the Queen's spread legs and hold Aaron in place between them.

The Queen watches the women work and realizing the hourglass drains swiftly she becomes even more excited. Her eyes bounce side-to-side in the openings of her golden mask as she sees the girls thread the rope near her sides.

Aaron has heard the subtle commotion but can't see his exact proximity to his soon to be mate.

Zelina crosses to her sisters who grasp the end of Aaron's tether, now outside the ornate rope that fences in the altar. Zelina takes the rope from her two sisters and loops the end around the golden rope a few feet behind Aaron's bare buttocks.

After that, Tyina and her sister slowly guide the warrior-general closer between the Queen's legs up to where Aaron's pulsating shaft is dangerously close to the opening of the Queen's fertile basket.

Tyina turns her head to Zelina and says, "Move quickly, Zelina and knot the two ropes together. Zelina promptly secures the tether rope to the surrounding golden rope at the foot end of the canopy. Now the tether rope is taut between Aaron's belt and the rope that has been threaded through the canopy pillar eyelets.

Layla pours a moderate amount of lamp oil on to the coals in the urns and strikes a hand flint to ignite the coals on the left, then scurries to the other side of her Majesty and ignites the coals in that urn.

Layla passes quickly back to the opposite urn to make sure that it is burning and smiles as she sees its flames slightly tickle the underside of the golden rope that ultimately keeps Aaron restrained.

Tyina and the other women in the room have watched Layla light the coals, which now smolder. They crackle and spit as they slowly roast the taut, gold rope strung above them. Observing this, the occupants turn their faces upward and chant in unison, "To our great God, Zuse. We have carried out your orders and now the creation of the royal child is in your hands. Let it be our great God of fire, who dictates the climax of this interlude as our King and our Queen now become united as one."

Tyina and her attendant now place Aaron's large, callused hands on top of the Queen's upper thighs. The instant he feels her warm, uncovered thighs in his hands, he lunges forward, but is restrained from advancing further. However, the Queen flinches and quakes upon his unexpected touch.

Aaron is well aware of where the tip of his shaft is, so close to the deep breathing, twitching beauty on her back before him.

Because of all the prolonged erotic teasing and aphrodisiac potions Aaron has ingested over the hours, combined with the image of what he might view before him if not for the hood over his head, the strapping warrior's manhood pulsates and grows larger than ever before.

The harem women are shocked at their General's size and girth. The two alarmed women at Aaron's side each receive a small vial from the maidens outside of the ceremonial rope. The vials contain a thick, clear perfumed lotion, which Tyina shakes onto her extended fingertips and then anoints the Queen's most passionate place. Her Majesty sighs softly and heaves her tummy upward as the warm oil is applied.

While Tyina has been oiling the Queen, her assistant has used the clear lotion to lubricate the bulging head of Aaron's imposing rod. The thick clear substance has been warmed to make it easily applicable, which makes it slightly uncomfortable to Aaron. Recoiling, he squeezes the Queen's thighs tightly and sighs as it is applied.

To finalize this last preparatory procedure, Tyina reaches up atop Aaron's head, grabs the black hood and jerks it off him.Tyina then yanks the scant body veil over her highness from her. She faces to Aaron and says, "My new king, in the name of Zuse, our God of fire, we present you with your new bride, the Queen of Patrious."

Tyina and her attendant kneel and whisper out a brief, inaudible prayer. When they rise, they duck under the ceremonial rope and stand with the other women gathered there. Now only the Queen and Aaron remain under the canopy.

The chamber wall torches cast an amber hue into the room and across the sheik canopy of assorted colored scarves. Shadows from the flickering lights dance across the naked couples bodies.

Aaron looks at his beautiful wife-to-be and his eyes capture her every curve as they glide across her oily soft skin. He can also feel her radiating warmth below as now they barely touch. Aaron completes his visual tour of the alluring, naked woman on her back before him, locks his eyes with hers and thrusts himself forward against his restraint like a determined bull. Sweat trickles down his face from his heated forceful exertions.

The Queen's expression from her forehead to the end of her nose is frozen without gesture by her golden mask. But her highness's lips smile up to her soon-to-be-mate. Her beautiful blue eyes twinkle through the oval openings in her metal veil.

Aaron pauses briefly, lifts his right hand from the Queen's thigh and reaches under the metal cuff on his other wrist. He pulls out the folded red cloth the Queen gave him the first time they met. He flicks his hand and the ribbon opens.

With his eyes focused to hers, Aaron leans forward, pulling his tether taut. Still, he can stretch his arms forward enough to place the scarlet fabric around the Queen's neck and even ties a small bow in it at the side. Aaron says, "My Queen, as you requested the day we first met, I return this scarlet keepsake to you. My love for you shall never falter." The Queen replies, "And neither shall mine for you, my brave King."

As the last syllable exits her majesty's mouth the glowing embers in the urns have now burnt through the first braid of the ceremonial rope. It smolders and unravels slightly. This creates an appreciable amount of slack that is immediately pulled taut from Aaron's body straining into the Queens loin. The slack, however, allows sudden and unanticipated penetration.

At the instant of Aaron's partial entry, the Queen's eyelids pop open wide and her lovely long lashes actually bounce off the rims of the oval openings of the mask. The whites of her eyes radiate outward almost filling the openings. She screams out loud, "Oh, ouch! Ah..."

Aaron becomes more sexually excited as he now feels the Queen's very hot, wet warmth covering the head of his shaft. Afraid he may have caused some discomfort for her, Aaron slightly withdraws, but the Queen calls out, "No, my love! This act is sacred. Please do not upset our divine ritual. It is meant to be as Zuse has ordained."

Aaron halts his retreat, removes his hands from the Queen's neck and gradually stands. He lovingly caresses his mate's breasts and then slides his hands down to her outer hips. The muscular warrior's large thumbs point inward nearly touching her Majesty's jeweled navel.

The iron man of battle tilts his head down, his sight lowering from the ruby to the spot where the couple is now connected. Squeezing his hands into his mate's puritan skin, he proceeds to further indulge in what the Queen has just prescribed. She sighs out, time and time again, "Oohh, Oohh, Oohh," as Aaron thrusts. She quivers and squirms, as her wrists and ankles tug at her ornate rope restraints. The Queen spreads all ten fingers apart like a fan and her many jeweled rings glimmer in the light cast from the torches.

The harem women are huddled in a far corner of the chamber with Layla at the center. She expresses her concern to the others that they have not been notified of any fire signal from the distant dunes where the oracle resides.

Tyina agrees to check with the lookout in the bell tower. Then after Tyina leaves, she instructs Zelina to lead the remaining women in a musical event.

Zelina crosses to a large trunk beside the Queen's throne. She opens the lid of the trunk and removes flutes, bells and metal rings. After she passes out the instruments, the girls begin their musical extravaganza by circling the altar. The tunes they play are identical to those they frequently performed in Samanda's tent.

As the music and dance heighten, Aaron and the Queen are in rhythm with each other. They are attempting to physically satisfy their passions, when another braid to the rope burns through. The rope pops and unravels further, leaving only three remaining strands of narrow braid.

Aaron penetrates the Queen now with more than half his total length and she moans again aloud pleasure filled, "Eue, ah, ah!" The potions the women administered to Aaron have totally kicked in and he struggles to penetrate deeper, but the tether rope will not allow him to advance more. After an appreciable period passes, the pounding warrior is coming to a full boil rapidly, well aware that the heat of the moment is also beginning to overcome him.

Trying to pace himself, Aaron again begins to withdraw and her Majesty pleads with him, "No, Aaron, No! You must not withdraw! Please continue to make love to me."

Hearing the Queen's exhortations, Layla's concern increases, for she knows that if Dilyla did poison Aaron's seeds, disaster is just moments away and if the Queen conceives, the Royal child may possess demon-like attributes, or even worse, the Queen could be infected and develop a horrible and painful bleeding rash ultimately leading to her death.

Layla crosses to the door to the main corridor and looks anxiously up and down the hallway in both directions, hoping to find Tyina has returned with word from the lookout.

Meanwhile, Aaron musters his will power and thrusts himself back into the Queen, obeying her pleading commands. She responds by expounding more accolades of sensual pleasure, "Yes, Aaron, yes, yes, yes! I want your entire length in me now! Pull against your restraint with all of your might! I must possess you seeds immediately. Yes, Aaron, yes, I'm about to come!"

The strong-willed warrior can feel his eruption about to come and grasps his mate's hips firmly in his hands and thrusts his muscular abdomen forward. He pulls so hard that his leather belt cuts into his skin as he feels the first slug of his seeds flood into the base of his pulsating shaft. The

Queen's eyes fidget back and forth, from side-to-side in the openings of her mask as she tries desperately to view the condition of the remaining strands of the rope that smolders over the flaming urns at her sides. She exclaims, " Now, Aaron! Now Aaron! Now! Please harder, harder!

The harem women, sensing the time has come, play their music louder and louder, banging their bells and metal hoops on their bodies to compete with the Queen's wails.

Aaron pants, struggles with all of his might as her Majesty tries to entice the rock-hard stud to pull harder by wiggling her torso about like a belly dancer.

Aaron stares down at his woman's jeweled navel and contorted belly movements in hopelessness, but in that instant, the rope burns through to its last remaining braid, which due to the warrior's determination and strength snaps apart like a dry twig.

Suddenly lunging forward, Aaron bellows, "Oh, Ough, Ough, Oh my God!" as he plunges the entire length of his huge swollen shaft deep into the Queen's vagina.

He's in her as far as he can go and she screams, "Aahhhh! Oh my God!!! Ah…Ah…Ah!!! Oh my God!!! Ah…Ah! The Queen paces herself down from the sensual pleasure with each pump of Aaron's robust spurts of semen, injected into her steaming fertile basket. At the feel of each intermittent warm squirt coating the walls of her inner sanctuary, she whispers, "Yes, yes yes," into Aaron's ear.

While still engaged, Aaron lifts his torso from on top of her Majesty's body and even though he cannot feel her face under the golden, ceremonial mask, he hugs her cheek-to-cheek. The frantic music and dance by the women winds down and the excited female voyeurs calm down. The Queen whispers into Aaron's ear, "I love you, Sir Aaron."

Aaron, trying to remember the last time he was dubbed, "Sir Aaron," whispers to her Highness, "And I love you as well, my Queen."

Layla still stands in the doorway, wringing her hands together with uncertain despair and an ominous calm suddenly fills the royal chamber with dead silence. All heads in the room turn to the empty wooden perch above Aaron's head and in front of the Queen's face. Curious about the silence, Aaron lifts his head and looks at the Queen whose eyes are fixed on the perch as well. Aaron then pushes himself up and back slightly, so he, too, can view what everyone sees-the empty perch. He remembers its purpose and it seems like eternity waiting, yet no one takes their eyes from the perch.

The fear in the room is escalating when suddenly a small, yellow finch glides across the room and lands on the perch.

The perch swings back and forth and the colorful little bird cocks its head from side to side. With one tiny black eye at a time, the finch stares at Aaron and then the Queen. Seconds later the bell in the tower clangs away.

Her Majesty calls out, "Conception has taken place! Please, my sisters, allow my husband and I a private moment."

Just as if a gleeful party has just wound down, the women return their instruments to the trunk and depart the room in single file.

Layla still stands in the doorway, looking down at her protruding belly and thinks, "Maybe I can somehow swap my infant child with the Queen's, should her Highness's child be born tainted.

Still embracing her new husband, the Queen states, "Layla, I still feel your presence. Please depart from my chamber." Layla exits and fastens the latch so that the newlyweds can have privacy.

The Queen is still naked, except for the scarlet choker that Aaron placed around her neck. She smiles at her new King. "Thank you for returning my scarf to me at such a poignant moment. So, my husband, it seems we have a fresh start to a joyous life. Would you agree?"

Aaron replies, "I will serve and care for you with all my heart, my Queen. That I am sure you already know, but my transition from slave to General-of-Arms and then to your husband and King would be much easier if only I possess knowledge of just one thing."

Smiling brightly, the Queen replies, "You are correct, my King, the time has come. You wish to know the name of your wife and bride, am I not correct?"

Aaron, while still very much connected with the Queen, nods his head.

She asks, "Please untie the wristbands that restrain my arms?"

Aaron willingly obliges and removes the ornate restraints. She massages her wrists briefly, and then places her fingers into the locks of her golden brown hair. She removes a fall of false hair and the hair this exposes is pure blonde, curiously familiar to Aaron.

Her Highness then places her fingertips at the edges of her mask and lifts it ever so slowly stating, "My name is Queen...." The instant the mask uncovers her face she finishes with, "....Samanda!!! And I have loved you dearly for a very long time, my new King."

Seeing his wife for the first time without a veil, scarf or mask, Aaron can plainly tell that the woman he has just made love to does look identical to his wonderful friend, Samanda. To be certain, Aaron looks down at her left leg, hoping to find the slender scar on the outside of Samanda's calf.

Upon seeing the wound, Aaron is overcome with joy. He caresses his bride and kisses her passionately. After the moment of enamored lust passes, the faithful warrior, looks into Samanda's eyes and states "and I, have loved you for quite some time, my new wife and Queen."

Samanda asks Aaron to unbind her ankles and obliging, Aaron assists her to her feet. Once again they embrace. Samanda pushes Aaron back slightly and takes his hands to hers, confiding, "The bed in your preparatory room has been made ready by the women for us to spend the remaining night. Lead me there and make love to me until dawn's first ray is cast onto the walls of our palace."

Aaron smiles, puts his arm around her and they walk through the curtain to Aaron's previous quarters.

The couple finds the bed remade with red, silk sheets and fluffy-white, down-stuffed pillows. An array of gifts, have also been set out throughout the room.

Aaron starts in the direction of the largest display of gifts, but his bride stops him gently by pulling on his hand and redirects him to the swinging bed.

The two climb on the bed and slide under the satin covers. Samanda nestles her head into her pillow and snuggles to Aaron and like a hopeful little girl, she asks him, "For our celebration trip, will you take me to the oasis where Kaybra, you and I rested on our journey between battles?"

Aaron replies with a smile, "I will be honored to escort my Queen to that utopian oasis of unblemished pools, sandy beaches and waving palm trees."

Aaron is about to kiss Samanda, but before he can, she interrupts him in the same little-girl voice, "And may we go by way of Kaybra's village, so we may thank her people for all they have sacrificed?"

Once again Aaron smiles to his wife and replies, "I think that gesture will be fitting, my love." Aaron attempts to kiss Samanda again, but once more she interrupts. "And may we travel to…." Before Samanda can speak more, Aaron places his fingers to her lips and conveys, "If it is my Queen's desire, I shall escort her to the ends of the earth on a moment's notice."

Samanda's eyes light up with their familiar twinkle and she smiles. Seeing she's paused, Aaron removes his fingers and steals the kiss he was pursuing.

Samanda responds passionately. The two cannot keep their hands off of each other and continue to make love throughout the night.

The dancing flames of the torches glow on the couple's intertwined bodies and cast a bigger- than-life shadow on to the mosaic wall depicting the fertility ceremony.

The shadows cast unto the wall along with the arrangement of the bed chains, make it appear the shadows of the couple's lovemaking session is taking place within a pyramid.

Samanda and Aaron are so engrossed with each other that they do not notice the lid to the pharaoh's sarcophagus is slowly, silently opening. Just as the newlyweds fall asleep Corina peeks out from behind the lid and stares at the sleeping couple with a venomous scowl.

*   *   *

Dawn is breaking on the eastern horizon and as the sun rises, its warm rays are absorbed into the palace's green courtyard. King Aaron and Queen Samanda are loading their royal carriage with clothing and supplies for their honeymoon.

To bring closure to their close relationship with Kaybra and to celebrate the couple's new matrimonial bond, this is a meaningful quest for the two. Samanda is also looking forward to spending a quiet, romantic time with Aaron at the oasis, under the palm trees. Meanwhile, Aaron has received word that a large monument tomb has been constructed to immortalize Kaybra's legacy. He keeps that news to himself to surprise Samanda upon their arrival.

Once the carriage has been loaded and the two in their seats, Aaron snaps the reins and off they go through the large arched gateway into the streets where well-wishers from the Queen's court and townspeople wave and bid them a happy trip and safe return.

The couple figures that they should arrive at Kaybra's island by dusk.

A few hours have passed and their horse has run at a hearty gallop most of the time. They finally reach the place where they rested, nearly three months ago, on the first night of their trip to meet Kaybra.

Aaron slows the charger to a walk as the couple eye the spot at the river where they made camp not so long ago. Samanda points to the tree, where Vampressa roosted while they slept. The two look at each other with a relieved expression, then Aaron snaps the reins once again to drive south along the riverbank, toward the mouth of the river.

It is early afternoon when the newlyweds approach the sandstone rock columns where Samanda staged her disappearance for Aaron's attention that fateful day.

When they pass the rock formation where Aaron found Samanda wedged between the two boulders, Samanda throws Aaron a sheepish smile and a forgiving grin comes across his face.

The royal couple's conversation now focuses on their memories of Kaybra. "Samanda, my love, how shall we document our first meeting with Kaybra for our generations to come?"

Samanda replies, "Well, my husband, I believe it would be best if we kept the very first encounter with her between the two of us."

Aaron nods and vividly recalls the edge of Kaybra's sword nearly touching his manhood that night and briefly envisions Samanda's lips on him. Recalling the events of that night, he becomes mildly aroused and turns to Samanda. Just as his eyes catch the sight of her pretty lips, she, too, turns to him and smiles seductively, as if she has read his mind.

Aaron tells his new bride, "After what you did to me that night, I could not dissuade my passion for you, my love." Samanda replies with, "I know. I had to get you to notice me in a way that you would not soon forget." Aaron leans over and kisses the very lips his thoughts had been dwelling on for the past several moments.

Samanda thinks she may be able to recreate a similar romp if they reach that same spot before nightfall. She jiggles the horse's reins, which Aaron still holds, up and down, saying, "Make him go faster, my King, we must be on our way!" Aaron wastes no time fulfilling his wife's request and the carriage exits the rock formation, in a trail of dust as it gains speed.

Samanda has certainly perfected getting her way over the years and she figures this day shall be no different. Just as the sun sets, the newlyweds arrive at their old campsite across the river from Kaybra's village.

The residents of the island are just lighting their fires for the evening and Kaybra's hallowed island grounds become aglow, like embers in the night.

Samanda and Aaron waste no time preparing their own fire, then retrieve their bedrolls and tend to their horse.

They unroll their blankets on the sand between the fire and the river's edge and the flaming wood lights up the beach with a rich, amber hue.

Aaron lies thinking they're settled in for the evening, but Samanda feels like a late-night dip. She stands on the blanket and disrobes. However, this time she neatly folds her travel gown and drops it on Aaron's face. He plucks the gown from his face, leaps to his feet, disrobes and chases Samanda into the dark glimmering waters.

The couple splash and frolic in the waist-deep water for a short time. Then Aaron grabs Samanda's hand and pulls her to him. He embraces her and kisses her hotly.

Samanda reciprocates briefly, then pushes him back from her and takes his hands in hers. The orange firelight glows off the side of her face, highlighting her high cheekbones, petite nose and ruby lips.Queen Samanda inflicts one of her eye-piercing locked stares deep into her mates blue gray pupils, flares her nostrils and regally orders, "Make love to me now, my slave!!! Carry me to the blanket and fulfill my fantasy, now that I own you. You shall perform on me as I direct."

Aaron doesn't have to hear more. He swoops his wife up in his arms, splashes out of the river and lays her on the blanket.

The King obeys the Queen's every command with precision and the two make love as the hourglasses drain across the sands.

Aaron drifts off to sleep and Samanda covers both of them with their blankets and cuddles up close to her husband. She lies there, contented, looking at her sleeping husband's face. The fire has about died when Samanda hears something not far from where the couple lays.

Straining to see what it is, Samanda peers toward a shadowy boulder in time to see what appears to be a large, nude woman dash from behind it and run into the darkness. Samanda is concerned but calms herself, knowing her infallible defender is at her side. After the lengthy discussions she and Aaron had for the past day about Kaybra, Samanda decides it was imagined and puts it out of her mind. Soon she is fast asleep by her husband's side…

*   *   *

The new day's sun crests the walls of the courtyard in Patrious and the horseback courier who was dispatched to the oracle with Aaron's specimen sample arrives in the courtyard at a full gallop. He shouts, "I summon thee, Layla! I summons thee, mistresses of the Divine Order!!!"

Within seconds, all the harem women, with Layla in the lead, rush out of their quarters and sprint across the courtyard to the messenger. The courier hands a scroll to Layla, stating, "You must read this immediately. The words of the old stargazer are distressing at best."

Layla takes the scroll and opens it. As she reads the oracle's writings, her scarred face grows silently cold. Tyina and Zelina plead, "What is it, Layla? Please do not keep us in suspense. Tell us the content of the writing."

Layla rolls the papyrus up and looks outward with a blank face. She exclaims, "It is no wonder we did not find the light of fire in the distance on the night of the Queen's conception. Tyina, Zelina, quickly disperse through the city and summon all the women of the Divine Order of Mistresses. Tell them to meet us in the Grand Hall at once!"

*   *   *

At the river, Samanda and Aaron have broken camp and proceed across the shallows of the river to Kaybra's island. Once again they smile to each other and hold hands as the wheels of their vehicle divide the shallow ripples of the sandy riverbed.

As the early morning mist lifts from the river, Aaron and Samanda are awed by what they see towering upward on the island's shoreline before them. It is a large, three-sided pyramid that stands at the point of the triangular shaped island.

Aaron, gazing up at the monument, directs their horse closer. They come onto the beach at the base of the edifice.

Aaron halts the horse and the couple gets down. They walk closer to the monument and spellbound by its grandeur, they join hands and walk around the structure's base.

The side that faces south, toward the village, is boldly engraved. "Kaybra-Warrior Princess-Queen of Warriors."

The Royal couple continues around the monument and find another inscription on the side that faces the distant kingdom of Patrious. It reads, "Samanda-Warrior Princess-Queen of Patrious."

Reaching the last side of the pyramid that faces Aaron's hometown of Nemmin are the words, "Sir Aaron-Conqueror of Strife-King of all Warriors."

Aaron and Samanda are deeply moved as they examine the monument further. But suddenly, an extra-ordinary image appears on the large masonry. Before them is a huge, imposing shadow of a towering warrior woman. The dark silhouette is cast by someone standing directly behind the couple. The shadow dwarfs both Aaron and Samanda.

Aaron and Samanda squeeze hands and very slowly turn around and find the source of the silhouette. The Royal couple's mouths drop open at the sight of a large, beautiful, warrior-woman who is identical to their old comrade in dress, stature and face.

The tanned, buxom beauty looks at them, smiles and explains, "No, I am not your warrior comrade, Kaybra. I am her twin sister, Saybra and have been waiting to meet with the two of you for some time…"

*　　*　　*

Back in Patrious, the wise women of the Divine Order have gathered at Layla's request at the long table in the Grand Hall. Layla stands at the head of the table with the oracle's unrolled scroll on the table before her. She begins, "Wise mothers and grandmothers of our kingdom, first of all I want to thank all of you, as well as our Father for keeping the city of Patrious safe and orderly while Queen Samanda was away at battle with Aaron and Kaybra, but I fear we now have grave tidings. Our messenger has just returned from the old stargazer and I shall read from the parchment he has sent us; 'Please forgive the delay, but it took me two nights of communication with the celestial bodies above before I could obtain answers to the questions the women of your kingdom seek. My heavenly servants make the following predictions: The first woman your new King impregnates after having intercourse with the evil slut, Dilyla, shall be plagued with dire circumstances.

'This woman shall fall ill and her child shall be marked by the demons which have contaminated that particular batch of the warrior's seeds. Shortly after this union takes place, the warrior's mind shall become poisoned by potions, this will drive him to successfully mate again. The child from the second union will be healthy and normal, to carry on the noble, brave and forthright traditions on which your kingdom was founded.

'The child from the first pregnancy, however, will seek out its father and attempt to end his life. In time, the minds of both the mother and offspring shall become frail and their only goal in life will be to slay the father of the demented child.

'I regret these tidings are grave in content. I however, remain your kingdom's most trusted confidant. Your friend in the quadrants of time travel, Osage the oracle.'"

After Layla finishes reading the oracle's message, she removes her hands from the scroll and the moment she does so, the scroll rolls itself up in a snap and disintegrates into dust. A dead silence permeates the Grand Hall and fear comes across the faces of the members of the Divine Order.

Layla and her sisters look at each other in dismay. They have no knowledge that Corina snuck into Aaron's preparatory chamber and robbed him of his initial batch of reproductive fluids. The women are fearfully convinced it is the Queen who will suffer from the oracle's prediction.

But, Layla has a plan and she gathers her sisters after the women of the Divine Order depart. She tells them that she plans to switch the Queen's baby with her own and then slay the other baby, to prevent an attempt on the King's life ...

*   *   *

On Kaybra's island, Aaron and Samanda have visited throughout the night with Saybra and now, on this morning, the trio has finished a feast at the very table where Samanda and Aaron sat with Kaybra and her field generals a few months ago. They find Saybra to be equally as courageous and accommodating as her sister was.

Aaron and his bride finally depart the village in peace. Aaron signals the horse to splash across the shallow broad waterway to the far banks of the river. Samanda closes her hands around Aaron's forearm, smiles at him and says, "Thank you, my King, this journey has brought great contentment to my heart. Please proceed to the oasis. Once there, we may continue to share this time together, before we must return to rule."

After an extended ride, Aaron halts the royal conveyance at the spot they recognize to be where Aaron, Samanda and Kaybra camped the evening before discovery of the Valley of the Phantom Pyramids.

The two smile to each other again, with fond memories of their towering female friend. After Aaron urges the horse to continue their journey, Samanda says, "Isn't it true, my husband, that we can save a great deal of time in our journey to the oasis by not detouring through the Valley of the Pyramids?"

Aaron replies, "You certainly have a keen perception of our location, having only traveled this area once before, my Queen." Samanda does not reply. She just tilts her head and rests it on Aaron's shoulder as they bounce along...

*   *   *

Back in the dungeon at the palace, the oracle's predictions are starting to unfold. Even though she has complete knowledge of the secret passageways that run through the fortress, Corina is getting restless and on this particular late afternoon, she is particularly distressed. The disturbed wench has discovered a dark red rash on the inside of her thighs. The once dominant vixen has her gown pulled up and runs her fingertips across the painful rash. Corina raises her fingers close before her eyes and sees they are covered with her blood. Corina curses aloud, "Aaron, you bastard! What have you done to me! I must escape and avenge this condition you have infected me with. I vow that somehow I will also infect your new bride!!!

*   *   *

By now the King and Queen have found their oasis and break the perimeter of palm trees that surround the oasis. Aaron smiles at an already jubilant Samanda and snaps the horses to enter the depths of the tropical haven.

Moments later, Aaron halts a few feet short of the clear pool. The couple lifts their eyes, scanning the panorama of broad palms, coconuts and placid ponds bordered by sandy beaches. They find all is as they remembered.

Evening is soon upon the royal couple and they have prepared their places for the night. On this evening, however, the three-quarter moon is uninhibited by clouds that normally shroud its silver hue and because of the warmth that still rises from the sands, from the day's pounding sun, the newlyweds decide not to build a fire and place their bedrolls snugly together near the water's edge.

Samanda drops her gown, kneels and opens the blankets invitingly. She looks up to Aaron and motions him to lie beside her.

Aaron disrobes and willingly obliges his wife's command. The two intertwine as Samanda whispers into Aaron's ear, "I shall love and cherish you until the end of my day, my King of warriors."

Aaron responds, " I shall love and cherish you my Queen until the end of my day."

Later the Royal newlyweds snuggle together under their lightweight blankets and Samanda is fast asleep. Aaron, still awake, looks up into the sky and finds one unusual cloud that appears to possess Mareeja's sweet face. Her smiling lips and twinkling eyes look down upon Aaron and as the cloud slowly breaks up, Aaron smiles and whispers, "Goodnight, Mareeja." He closes his eyes in slumber.

The three quarter-moon reflects off the calm pond near the shoreline where they sleep. All is quiet and the sleeping faces of Samanda and Aaron hold expressions of lasting contentment...

*   *   *

A peaceful calm has also fallen over Kaybra's island. All its inhabitants are fast asleep, except for one, Saybra. She sits on a sculptured stone bench at the base of her sister's monument and stares across the shimmering, moonlit river toward the honeymooners' distant oasis.

An instant later a thin, white bolt of lightning leaps from the heavens and strikes the tip of the monument. The charge shoots down the side of Kaybra's tomb and jolts Saybra. For an instant, her body glows in the darkness and her brown eyes emit two amber beams in the direction she is focused on.

An unexplainable feeling comes over Saybra, who feels transformed and confused. Then she realizes what her confusion is about - she's taken by the handsome new King of Petrious. As she tries to interpret her feelings, the large beauty plans how she can make her future relationship with the charming Royal couple more intimate.

*   *   *

Back in Patrious, Corina has escaped the dungeon easily and like a thief-in-the-night, she has swept off into the darkness, undetected. As Corina's thighs rub together with each painful stride she takes, she plots to avenge her infliction.

*   *   *

In the Valley of the Phantom Pyramids, a new conflict has begun. As is, on every evening about this time, the Golden Pharaoh and the hideous beast battle to determine the outcome of the following day.

*   *   *

Back in Aaron's hometown of Nemmin, Uma's mother tucks a small boy-child into his bed. She kisses him on the cheek, saying, "Some day your father will return and I shall tell him the truth. Please forgive me, my grandson. Your mother's death was enough for the brave warrior. I could not burden him further during his brief return here and so I had to hide you when he visited your mother's grave. He needed all of his emotional strength for battle, to save our village."

*   *   *

At Vampressa's volcano nest, the boulder still remains tightly lodged in the troll's cave entrance and the once-divided waterfall still gushes its one torrid stream, pounding onto the rock that has entombed the fat smelly troglodyte.

*   *   *

The only real menacing closure for this would-be silent night is Vampressa's last remaining fertile egg. In the steaming nest atop the volcano, this Harpy egg still incubates and in the deafening silence under the silver hue of the moon, tiny cracks in the shell of the large, glowing egg grow larger and longer. Then one large piece of shell pops off to the floor of the volcanic nest and the quiet of the moonlight is broken by a soft, shrill, "Eeek, eeek... Eeek, eeek, eeek..."

Epilogue

...having narrated the hieroglyphics throughout most of the night, the attractive female in khakis and safari hat can interpret no more.

The etched writings have disappeared into the depths of the earth where she kneels.

Inspired by reading of the women's determination depicted by the hieroglyphs branded in stone, she vows to return.

As the wind picks up, the silicone crystals begin to twirl. The woman stands tall, turns to the early-rising sun and removes her hat. With her long brown hair blowing in the morning breeze, she states defiantly, "I must know the ending to this story of love and tragedy carved in stone ages ago. In the days to come, I alone, will unearth this monument from "The Shifting Sands..."

The End

Printed in the United States
62166LVS00003B/232-315